PRAISE FOR FREYA BARKER

Freya Barker writes a mean romance, I tell you! A REAL romance, with real characters and real conflict.

~Author M. Lynne Cunning

I've said it before and I'll say it again and again, Freya Barker is one of the BEST storytellers out there.

~Turning Pages At MidnightBook Blog

God, Freya Barker gets me every time I read one of her books. She's a master at creating a beautiful story that you lose yourself in the moment you start reading.

~Britt Red Hatter Book Blog

Freya Barker has woven a delicate balance of honest emotions and well-formed characters into a tale that is as unique as it is gripping.

~Ginger Scott, bestselling young and new adult author and Goodreads Choice Awards finalist

Such a truly beautiful story! The writing is gorgeous, the scenery is beautiful...

~Author Tia Louise

From Dust by Freya Barker is one of those special books. One of those whose plotline and characters remain with you for days after you finished it.

~Jeri's Book Attic

No amount of words could describe how this story made me feel, I think this is one I will remember forever, absolutely freaking awesome is not even close to how I felt about it.

~Lilian's Book Blog

Still Air was insightful, eye-opening, and I paused numerous times to think about my relationships with my own children. Anytime a book can evoke a myriad of emotions while teaching life lessons you'll continue to carry with you, it's a 5-star read.

~ Bestselling Author CP Smith

In my opinion, there is nothing better than a Freya Barker book. With her final installment in her Portland, ME series, Still Air, she does not disappoint. From start to finish I was completely captivated by Pam, Dino, and the entire Portland family.

~ Author RB Hilliard

The one thing you can always be sure of with Freya's writing is that it will pull on ALL of your emotions; it's expressive, meaningful, sarcastic, so very true to life, real, hard-hitting and heartbreaking at times and, as is the case with this series especially, the story is at points raw, painful and occasionally fugly BUT it is also sweet, hopeful, uplifting, humorous and heart-warming.

~ Book Loving Pixies

ALSO BY FREYA BARKER

Cedar Tree Series:

Slim To None
Hundred To One
Against Me
Clean Lines
Upper Hand
Like Arrows
Head Start

Portland, Me, Novels:

From Dust
Cruel Water
Through Fire
Still Air

Snapshot Series:

Shutter Speed
Freeze Frame
Ideal Image
Picture Perfect (Coming Soon!)

Northern Lights Collection:

A Change Of Tide
A Change Of View
A Change Of Pace (Coming Soon!)

La Plata County FBI
ROCK POINT SERIES 1

FEDERAL

FBI

BUREAU of INVESTIG

KEEPING 6

FREYA BARKER

Cover Design: RE&D - Margreet Asselbergs

Editing: Karen Hrdlicka

Proofing: Joanne Thompson

Interior Design: CP Smith

ISBN: 978-1-988733-10-4

AUTHOR'S NOTE

I would like to apologize to those of you whom I've kept waiting for the release of this first book in the Rock Point Series. Life sometimes happens when you've made other plans.

As some of you know, this last year has been a tumultuous one, and my schedule for releases and public appearances was impacted.

Both my parents passed away in short succession. My father had been ill for quite some time and his passing was not entirely unexpected. My mother, however, was still a vital and strong woman who was the core of our family when she suddenly fell ill.

I had the honor and privilege to stand by my mother through her last months and as she transitioned from this life into the next. A heart-breaking, but also beautiful experience as my mother passed on; in her own living room, warmed by the late afternoon sun through the window, and surrounded and held by her children.

She was a most remarkable woman; a multi-talented, warm-hearted, generous and wise matriarch. A woman who will leave a void not only in the lives of her family, but far beyond.

My mother was a shining star.

DEDICATION

To every single one of my readers who hoped for more books from the GFI crew in Cedar Tree. Thank you for loving those small-town Colorado characters that started my passion for writing.

This story and the ones to follow in the Rock Point series, are for you...and who knows, you might bump into an occasional familiar face.

You all inspire me with your love for my stories, and continuously encourage my apparent bottomless imagination.

I'm so very grateful for you all!

KEEPING 6

PROLOGUE

KERRY

Two years ago…

DAMN!

I swear, these days any time I even look at a cup of coffee, I need to pee. It was probably not a good idea to snag that latte at the Starbucks on my way to the airport, since they're about to start boarding and my bladder is making itself known.

Again.

One of the many, many pitfalls of entering my middle years. Gravity is another such annoyance, and one that, despite the promises that yoga is supposed to keep me high and tight, has my tits and ass plummeting to earth. I could add to that the abject horror I felt when I found a few strands of gray hair last month, but I promised myself I would eradicate them from memory as I carefully plucked them, root and all, from my scalp.

Bliss! The bathroom is empty and I shuffle into the accessible stall with my carry-on. I'll only be gone for a weekend, but since it's Vegas, my checked bag wouldn't have been enough. I swear I packed my entire closet, wanting to be prepared for any occasion. I don't think I've ever been anywhere by myself since Greg and I got married, and I'm giddy at the prospect. I've certainly not been anywhere of *my* choosing. I've been looking forward to Las Vegas with Kimeo and the girls.

Poor Kim has been stressed to the gills and really needs this break. Her quiet life had been turned upside down when her boss was killed right under her nose. Murder, shady land deals, mineral rights, and a very handsome, dark, and dangerous investigator, who has caught my girl's eye, make for more excitement than she could've imagined.

I flush as I vaguely hear someone come in and take a stall on the opposite end, just as a barely distinguishable voice garbles from a speaker somewhere, announcing what I think is a final boarding call for flight 5620 to Las Vegas. I hurry to wash my hands at the sink, and barely have time to register the figure coming up behind me before I feel a crushing blow to my head and the world fades away.

I'm not sure where I am.

My hands and feet are hogtied and I'm on a concrete floor in a dark, damp space.

Thankfully, I'm alone. The man who was looming over me the first time I opened my eyes is not here. It's hard to think when your head is throbbing from the knock it sustained, but from what I could glean from his questions, he's looking for Kim. I safely assumed he's not intending to send her flowers.

No way in hell I was going to point him to her. I didn't hesitate to inform him of that fact, but I didn't quite expect the first, swift kick that knocked the wind right out of me. By the time his fist connected with my jaw, and turned out my lights once again, I welcomed the dark. I'd been questioned, kicked, and pounded on for what felt like hours but was likely minutes, however, as I sank into oblivion, I did so with the smug satisfaction that I kept my silence. More brawn than brains I'm afraid, since I'm not sure how much more of these beatings I can withstand.

It may have been hours, or days. I'm not quite sure. At some point, I must have relieved myself because the strong smell of urine burns in my nostrils. After a futile struggle against the bindings around my wrists and ankles, I close my eyes, exhausted and hurting.

I wonder if anyone's missing me.

The hard slide of a metal latch has my eyes fly wide. The door swings open, almost blinding me with the bright light from beyond. All I see is a massive dark shadow standing in the doorway, starkly contrasted against the glow.

He's back.

It had taken us too long to track the maroon Ford Edge. All fucking night this guy has had his hands on the woman, and I have serious doubts we'll find her alive.

The building is quiet when we make our approach, but the car is parked around the back. A witness reported the man carrying a woman he called his wife in his arms to the dark red car, yesterday. They should still be inside. Durango PD is standing back, reluctantly agreeing for my team to head in first to get the lay of the land. They'll provide backup if needed.

The creaking of the rusty door, beside the loading dock, echoes into the empty space beyond as one of my team pushes his way through. Surely we've been made; the sound is loud enough to wake the dead. A hallway on the far side, underneath a storage loft above, is illuminated. Without the need for words, my team makes its way over, hugging the walls as we go. One of my guys darts across the lit doorway to the other side, giving us a better bead on what might be waiting for us.

The hallway is empty, but a door at the end is slightly ajar. I only see darkness beyond, but can hear movement: a rustling of clothes and a small gasp. Hard to tell for sure, but it sounds like the noise a woman might make. When we get to the door, I manage to catch a glimpse through the crack by the hinges. A woman is visible in the light from the doorway; her body drooped awkwardly, as the barely visible man beyond holds her up with an arm around her waist and a large hunting knife to her throat. With hand signals, I relay the suspect and victim's whereabouts to my team, and indicate for one of them to wait for my sign.

"FBI! Come out with your hands raised," I yell through the crack, and as I'd hoped, the suspect turns toward the sound, keeping the woman in front of him. The quarter turn is enough to expose more of his body to one of my guys, who is ducked low and crouches around the open edge of the door. I give a small nod and almost instantly the sharp sound of a gunshot pierces the air.

The suspect goes down instantly, but so does the victim, and I shove open the door and rush to their sides. A knife lies useless in the open palm of the man we've been looking for, and I remove it, before turning my eyes to the woman.

Long, blonde, tangled hair is draped over her face, turning pink where it drags through a small puddle of blood collecting underneath her. Her gasp is a welcome sound when I turn her body over.

Wide gray eyes, the color of morning mist, stare up into mine. Just for a moment I find myself sinking in those clear pools, the promise of passion at their depths, but when I see the trickle of blood running down the side of her neck, I shake myself free. The suspect's knife left a sizable gash. Her face is bruised and swollen, and from the tight way she holds her body, I suspect the rest of her is as well.

"Kerry?" I prompt her, earning me a small nod. "I'm Special Agent Damian Gomez. Hang tight, we've got an ambulance on the way."

I'd sent an agent to pick up Kerry's husband, Greg Belfour, from Cortez, and he had been less than complimentary about the victim's husband. Said he was a dick.

I get my first clue when I walked into the victim's hospital room and caught him complaining to his wife that he was missing an important meeting. Like her ending up in the hospital was an inconvenience to him. Miserable bastard. Fine fucking husband he makes. He's done nothing but complain since, treating his wife with misogynistic disdain when he discovered they would both need to stay in an FBI safe house until our investigation is finalized. He should count his lucky stars; underneath the bumps and discolorations, and despite her slightly haggard appearance, Kerry Belfour is a beautiful, and apparently, quite resilient woman.

"Would you stop blaming yourself? You have no responsibility in this," Kerry tells her friend, Kim, who apparently hasn't stopped apologizing since getting on the phone. Normally we don't allow contact with the outside world when we have witnesses in protective custody, but I made an exception this time, giving Kerry my cell phone. A small favor since I happen to know Kim's boyfriend, with whom I've had a few professional encounters. The owner of the security company he works for and I go way back.

I'm fast regretting it; Greg appears unable to keep his mouth shut in the background, as the women try to maintain some normalcy in their lives by making plans around Kerry's bookstore. Some shit about missing his bowling league night or something. Selfish prick. I have no idea what a woman like that sees in a guy like him. But then I generally have no idea around women. It doesn't matter that I've been surrounded by women, one way or another, all my life. They're still a complete mystery to me.

"Don't worry about him. He's just pissed he's missing his weekly bowling league. He'll have to get over it," she says, dismissing her husband with a wave of her hand, which only seems to fire him up.

"That's enough," I interject, holding out my hand for my phone.

"My *handler* tells me I have to hang up."

I lift my eyebrow at her snide tone as she signs off and returns my cell.

"Mostly I wanted your husband to shut up." I ignore the loud protest from the man in question as I keep my eyes on Kerry's expressive face. Right now she has a small smile teasing her lips, hinting at her amusement, but in the next second her face smoothes out into a blank mask as she turns to face Greg. He takes that as an invitation to go into a long dissatisfied ramble about shit I don't want to hear about, but apparently Kerry does, because she stands there taking the trash he spouts without blinking. She's proven herself strong and unyielding during her captivity, and again during my interview with her, but seems pliant and submissive with that tool.

I'll never understand women.

Without even bothering to say goodbye, I lift my chin at the agent in charge of their safety, and leave the couple to their fucked-up marriage.

Good fucking luck to them.

CHAPTER 1

DAMIAN

"YOU?"

My head whips around at the sound of a woman's voice.

It's been a long-ass morning already with meetings I would've loved to have avoided. Since being put in charge of the Durango field office, it seems I spend more time in meetings than working in the field. I swear each week there are new task forces put together, and I can barely keep up. I stepped out of the office for a much-needed break to find that the coffee shop around the corner had a sign plastered on the door stating they were closed due to a family emergency. Desperate for my caffeine fix, I kept walking and bumped into Kerry's Korner: Books & Brew. Something about the name is familiar. I push the door, which opens with the ring of a bell, when I hear her voice.

She's pretty. The woman behind the counter looks like a seventies flower child, with wild, dirty blonde hair, some kind of flowy top leaving her collarbones and a goodly amount of cleavage exposed, and a pixie face. Something about her is familiar, and it appears she knows me, too. Fuck if I can't place her.

"Got me at a disadvantage, sweets," I tell her with a shrug.

"You're FBI," she says, propping her hands on her nicely rounded hips. "I remember you."

I look at her a little closer. Not a hardship, there's a lot to check out. Those pale gray eyes trigger a memory. "You're Kimeo's girl," I say, remembering the case a few years ago when I first saw her for the briefest of moments. A case long since put to rest, but not before this woman was snatched and roughed up before we got to her. We'd been called in by Gus Flemming, a friend of mine who owns an investigation and security company in Cedar Tree. Kimeo, the wife of one of Gus's guys, found herself in the middle of shady land deals and this woman, her best friend, had been kidnapped to ensure her silence. I may not have remembered her name until I saw her standing behind the counter of Kerry's Korner, but I sure as hell remember her. I also remember the wedding ring on her finger, which is why I didn't bother looking twice at the time.

The hands resting on her hips no longer sport that wedding ring, just a large knuckle ring on the middle finger of her left hand as a sort of *fuck you* to the world. I bet she flips that bird easily, judging by the attitude she throws off. I like it.

"Kerry," she says, almost as a challenge.

"Right. You look better now," I tell her, making her snort loudly.

"No shit. I'd just been used as a punching bag when you found me and shoved me into the back of a van without a word." Yup, most definitely a challenge. She doesn't like me much, I deduct from the slightly distasteful look on her face.

"Was a little preoccupied with my investigation. Sorry if I didn't take the time to make nice." Fuck me, I sound like a dick. Something about her attitude grates on me, especially when she rolls her eyes dramatically before placing her hands on the counter in front of her and leaning over.

"Damian. Right?" She doesn't wait for my confirmation before she continues, "Well, *Damian*, what brings you to my bookstore?"

"Coffee. Straight up," I tell her without blinking. She turns her back without a word and starts fiddling with the expensive-looking machine on the sideboard, and I take the opportunity to check out her backside. "Double shot?" she asks over her shoulder, catching me ogling.

"Good guess." I smile at her, which only earns me another eye roll. Attitude in spades, this one. As much as it irritates me, it somehow turns me on, too.

She's late thirties, maybe forty, if I had to venture

a guess from the lines around her eyes. She obviously laughs a lot—something I wouldn't mind hearing. I have a feeling with that slightly raspy voice of hers, her laugh will sound even sexier. She's not wearing a stitch of makeup from what I can tell and seems totally at ease in her skin. Not usually the kind of woman I find myself drawn to, but this one has an appeal all her own. Most women I end up with are well put together: stacked, sweet, and sultry. Just the way I like them. This one, though? This one is like the fucking girl next door. Fresh-faced, with a hippy vibe, barely enough tit to fill my hands, but an ass that should be framed, it's that lush. Always considered myself a boob man, until I just got an eyeful of her backside.

While she doctors the elaborate coffee machine, I take the time to check out her shop. An older building, it has an old-fashioned facade with shallow bay windows, displaying an assortment of books, framing the door. Old wood floors that have been left bare to the wear and tear of foot traffic, resulting in a well-worn look more suited to an old saloon. Rows of rugged bookcases, jutting out from the back wall, with chalkboard display signs indicating the different genres. The counter is on one side in front of the window and on the opposite side, in front of the second bay window, is a small seating arrangement with an old, brown leather couch and two club chairs around a small, round coffee table. On the counter is a large, round, glass cake stand with pastries.

"Here you go. Anything else with that? A pastry to sweeten you up a bit or perhaps a book on appropriate social behavior? I have both." I can't stop the smirk tugging at my mouth. This one's a handful, for sure. Too much of one. I pull out my wallet and slap a couple of dollar bills on the counter.

"Nah," I drawl. "Not the kind of sweet I'm looking for, and as for the book, I'll just wait until you get done with it. You're probably due for a reread." I snag my coffee off the counter, and with a wink, I saunter out the door, leaving her standing with her mouth hanging open and fire shooting from those pretty gray eyes.

KERRY

Asshole.

I'm still fuming from that brief encounter a few hours ago. First time I met him, he virtually dragged me from a seedy motel room to a waiting black van with dark tinted windows. If not for the shirt sporting the letters FBI that were stretched across his chest, I wouldn't have known the cavalry had arrived. He didn't say a damn word, just shoved me rather unceremoniously in the back of the van and shut the doors on me. Later, I was told that their first priority had been to get me to safety before my kidnapper returned, but at the time, I was hurt, scared, and incredibly pissed off. I learned later who he was from the two agents assigned to stay with me in the safe house until they dealt with the threat. Somehow I'd never been able to shake the dark, smoldering look or their slight squint when he first clapped eyes on my sorry self. Heat, anger, danger all came rolling off him in thick waves. My eyes blurry from the almost twenty-four-hour ordeal I'd just been through, I'd never been able to take in all of him. But I did today.

The good six feet of bulky muscle encased in navy cargo pants, a navy shirt, and a thin windbreaker, combined with the sharp edges of his lightly graying goatee and his thick wavy hair, were familiar enough. But then he lifted his eyes, and there was no mistaking those brown, almost black, eyes staring back at me. I was barely able to hide the shiver that ran from the top of my head down to the tips of my toes.

Apparently he'd made more of an impression on me than I had on him at the time. It took a bit for him to place me and that made me inexplicably irritated. I guess I deserved his little jab, since I poked him first, but the overall arrogance that he exuded just rubbed me the wrong way. Or maybe it was just that he affected me at all.

I've been able to keep my eyes and legs firmly closed to the opposite sex since finally filing for divorce a year and a half ago. My ex, Greg, had fought tooth and nail, which only ended up delaying what was inevitable for the better part of a year. I'd married Greg straight out of college. He'd been my first serious boyfriend after I'd spent my earlier college days playing the field. I most certainly had not been a virginal bride, but Greg had a reputation of his own. When we graduated, he was eager to settle down, and at the time, so was I. Or so I thought. Right after graduation, Greg was offered a job in Cortez and we moved into a rental place. He preferred me to stay home, and stupidly in love at the time, I complied. We tried for kids right away, as per Greg's wishes, but we didn't get pregnant and after a year of that, I was sick of playing housewife like he wanted.

I'd always dreamed of having my own little bookstore, but Greg had been adamantly against it, claiming it would take too much of my time. He kept a tight rein on our finances, so I ended up getting a job as a proofreader for the local newspaper, and I tucked the money away in a separate bank account. Five years later, still childless, I had enough saved up for six months of rent on an old, small storefront in Cortez and some secondhand inventory. Greg ridiculed and belittled my business, but despite his lack of faith, I ended up not doing all that bad. After my first six months, I was able to sustain my business, doing a little bit better each month, solely by word of mouth. It was around that time I met Kimeo, and we became fast friends over books.

The mountains called to me though, and I really wanted to go back to Durango, but my ex wouldn't hear of it. I suspect it had less to do with Durango itself than it did with my plans to expand my business. That was the final straw for me. I need someone who can stand beside me in support, not someone who expects it but doesn't reciprocate.

"Can I have a cappuccino?"

For the second time today, a tall, dark individual is standing at my counter. This one is dressed to the nines: suit, crisp white shirt, and a tie. But his eyes are all but heated, they are cold—dead—unlike the almost smarmy smile on his face. Also for the second time today, shivers run down my spine, but these are in recoil.

I drop the books I was sorting back into the box and notice him watching my every move. "Sure thing," I say, more chipper than I feel as I move behind the counter and grab a fresh filter.

"Nice place you have here. Do you sell books in all genres?" he asks, the creepy smile still plastered on his face.

"Thanks. Yes, all genres and both fiction and non-fiction," I answer as pleasantly as I can.

"Fabulous," he responds, and only now do I notice a British accent. "So do you only sell new books or secondhand as well?"

"Both, actually." I scrape the top of the filter before clicking it in place. "To go?" I ask him, holding up a paper cup hopefully.

"No, I think I'll have a look around if you don't mind. A regular cup is fine." I swear he noticed my shoulders sag, because he ever so slightly raises one eyebrow.

"I don't mind," I lie bold-faced. Because I mind. I mind a lot. I would much prefer he take his coffee and go. He makes me genuinely uncomfortable, and I wish Marya, my part-time employee who comes in the afternoons, would show.

The coffee finishes brewing, and I busy myself steaming the milk while keeping half an eye on the stranger roaming my shelves. I don't know why I'm getting such a bad vibe from him. He looks like a clean-cut, very handsome man. Maybe that's why— Durango is not known for clean-cut. Most men here are of a hardier breed, mountain men. This one just doesn't fit in. "Are you from around here?" flies out of my mouth before I can check it. His head comes up from my select shelving where all of my finds, my first editions and signed copies, are stored behind glass. The smirk on his face is almost triumphant as he makes his way back to the counter just as I top his coffee with foamed milk.

"Actually, I just arrived in town. I'm trying to decide whether to stick around for a bit. Looking at some business interests in the area in the next little while. Why?" he asks, his head tilted to one side as he blatantly checks me out. Yuck.

"I noticed an accent, that's all. British?" I don't expect the raspy chuckle, but he seems to find my conclusion amusing.

"You are sharp, aren't you? I thought I had it well-covered, but you caught me. Yes, I'm from the UK," he says, as he takes the cup from my hands and takes a sip. In what can only be described as a lecherous move, he keeps his eyes on my face as he licks the foamed milk off his lips. Double yuck. "Since I'm new to town…" I know what's coming, and I curse myself for having opened my big mouth in the first place. "…Would you perhaps be interested in joining me for dinner? Maybe give me some insight from a local business owner's perspective?"

I almost snort. Almost, but not quite. What a load of crap. I decide to call him on it. "Are you looking to open up a bookstore slash coffee shop? Because that's about the only thing I might have some knowledge on."

Too late I see the satisfied glint in his eyes. "You caught me," he says magnanimously. "I'm a collector of rare books and have an interest in first edition English language literature. Of course, it hasn't escaped my notice that you are a very bright and lovely young woman, and sharing interests over a good meal would in no way be a hardship."

Oh, gag. Young woman. As if. He can't be much older than early to mid-thirties, which makes me as much as a decade older. Did I mention I detest smooth operators? Greg was one until he had a ring on my finger, and then his true colors came out. Yeah, I have a solid aversion to slick talkers. Give me brutal honesty every day.

I briefly think back to the slightly scathing jab from Mr. FBI earlier, which I have to admit, was preferable to this charmer. "I'm sorry," I say, but I'm not at all.

"I'm afraid that won't be possible." I smile friendly but still notice his eyes go hard, and his responding smile is anything but warm.

"I will wait for a better opportunity then. But perhaps you can tell me if you have any more first editions?" He quickly changes tracks. "I noticed a lovely J.K. Rowling behind glass there, but I already own a few," he says, indicating my select shelves. "I'm thinking more along the lines of Ernest Hemingway, James Joyce, perhaps even J.R.R. Tolkien or Mark Twain?"

I shake my head. I don't mention the box of books I bought at an online auction a month ago. The box is supposedly filled with first editions of all kinds, a bit of a mishmash of mostly North American books. I took a chance when I put an offer in, but the seller was one well-known for the high quality of merchandise, so it seemed worth the five thousand dollars I shelled out. I have a customer in town, a gentleman with expensive hobbies, and one of them is collecting first editions, specifically by North American authors. It's possible there is something to this guy's liking in that box, but I'm not about to invite him back for any reason. Not even a good sale. He just gives me the creeps.

"I'm sorry," I tell him. "What you see there is all I have." Even though I've been known to suck at lying, this doesn't really qualify as a lie since I haven't received the box with the first editions yet. I'm still waiting for them.

The man's cold eyes squint at me before he speaks.

"Very well. I shall leave you with my card," he says with a determined edge. "I would greatly appreciate a phone call when you receive new inventory. I will be around for a while." With that, he turns on his heels and walks out of the store, just as Marya walks in, leaving his cold and only half-empty cappuccino sitting on the counter.

"Who was that?" Marya asks with a smug smile and a wagging of eyebrows as she picks up and studies the card he tossed on the counter. I shrug my shoulders, emptying his cup in the sink.

"Someone to steer clear of," I warn her. "He gives off a totally creepy vibe."

The single mom of three looks at me with one eyebrow raised. "Are you sure? He's not bad to look at." For emphasis, she fans her hand in front of her face.

"Behave." I give her a little shove as I pass her on the way to the abandoned box of cookbooks I was working on.

"Killjoy," she smarts back, sticking out her tongue in the process.

CHAPTER 2

DAMIAN

I'M NOT SURE WHAT brings me back the next day, but I find myself pushing open the door to Kerry's Korner once again. I tell myself it's because my favorite coffee place is still closed today, but I really just want to see her again. Unfortunately, today there is a different woman manning the coffee counter.

"Can I help you?" she asks with a friendly smile, looking me up and down thoroughly.

"Please. Double shot of espresso," I reply, tamping down my disappointment. "Kerry here today?" I look around the store, but other than an older lady roaming the shelves, I don't see anyone.

The short brunette tilts her head to one side, squinting her eyes at me. "Are you a friend of hers?"

"More like an old acquaintance," I tell her.

"Ah. Well then, Kerry is just running some errands,

but she'll be back in half an hour, tops. Feel free to wait around." The last is said with a wink before she turns and busies herself with my coffee, but I can still hear her mumble, "Lucky bitch, second hot guy in two days." I chose to pretend I don't hear, but I can't help wonder who the other guy is. A boyfriend? "Are you staying or taking out?" she asks, interrupting my thoughts.

"Take out," I tell her. I don't even know what I'm doing here, and when the woman hands me my coffee, I quickly pay and head for the door. I reach for the handle when it suddenly swings open, knocking the hot coffee all over me. "Fucking hell!" The piping hot beverage is burning my hand and soaking the front of my dress shirt.

"Oh no! I'm so sorry." A familiar, sexy voice has me raising my eyes to find Kerry looking at me with a worried frown. "Come with me," she says, grabbing my wrist. "Marya? Get another coffee ready. Double shot." I'm surprised she remembers and allow her to drag me to the back of the store and through a door marked private.

It appears to be a storage area with metal shelving filled with more books, boxes, and packing materials. A long table is butted up against the far wall with two stools tucked underneath. I can just see a door open to my left, showing a closet-sized space with a desk and computer, as Kerry is pulling me into a bathroom on the other side.

"Sit," she orders, closing the lid on the toilet and

shoving me down. She turns on the tap on the small sink beside it and yanks my hand under the cold stream. I keep my lips firmly pressed together, fighting off the smile that wants to break out. I take the opportunity to check her out. Today she's wearing another of those boho tunics, paired with a long necklace, dangly earrings and chunky bracelets on both wrists. The fuck-you ring is firmly in place on her middle finger, but this time instead of jeans, she's wearing leggings that show off her solid but shapely legs. The contrast between her carefree attire and her bossy demeanor is damn cute. When her tongue pokes out as she twists my hand this way and that, I almost groan out loud.

"What?" she asks, having caught me focused on her lips. I lift my eyes to hers and just shrug my shoulders to which she rolls her eyes—something she seems to do quite a bit. She turns off the tap and studies my hand. I'm just enjoying the feel of her fingers on my skin. "I think your hand will live," she says before focusing her attention on my shirt, the one I wore for my meetings this afternoon that is now pretty much ruined. Not that I care, except I don't have anything but a few spare tees in my locker to change into. "Let me see what I can do," she offers with a pained expression on her face. I let her rub a wet towel over my chest, knowing full well the exercise is futile, but selfishly enjoying her hands on my body.

The buzzing from my pocket interrupts the moment, and I lightly grab onto her wrist while pulling out my phone with the other hand. I can feel her rapid heartbeat under my fingers and hang on to her as I answer the call, looking her squarely in the eye. "Gomez."

"Hey, lover. Haven't heard from you in a while." The high-pitched, slightly nasal voice is loud. Too loud. I see Kerry's pretty gray eyes narrow before she twists her wrist free and turns away, dropping the wet towel in the sink before walking out. Fuck me.

"Been busy," I tell Cora, a woman I've occasionally hooked up with. She's a nurse I met last year when I was in the hospital interviewing a witness. Big boobs, sultry lips, and come-hither eyes, she made it clear she'd be up for anything. Just the kind of diversion I could use to break the stress of the job. I don't have time or inclination for any kind of relationship, and Cora understood that. I thought. Until she started calling me a few months ago, making it clear she saw us as something more than just an occasional relief. It's my mistake that she is still calling, because I caved a few times against my better judgment, only encouraging her pursuit.

"Too busy for me?" she purrs, and where before it might have stirred a different reaction, now it only gets on my nerves. Especially as I watch Kerry's back disappear into the store.

"Cora, look," I start, but she quickly cuts me off.

"No worries. I know your job is important and all. I just missed you," she says a bit breathlessly.

"Don't," I grunt. "You know that's not what this was."

"Was? Really, Damian? You're a bastard." With that I hear the line go dead. This is exactly why I always avoided any long-term arrangements. Not only is my job demanding and unpredictable, making anything more permanent complicated, but I'm also well aware of the risks it brings with it, and I don't want to expose anyone else to that. It's a decision I made a long time ago when the wife of my partner was killed in retaliation by a Mexican drug lord we were investigating. The guy ended up getting killed in a shootout, but my partner never got over it. Ended up eating the barrel of his service gun the week after the shootout. No. The risk is too high.

I'm still sitting on the toilet with my phone in my hand. What the hell am I doing here then? A soft ping alerts me to an incoming text from one of my team.

Jasper: *Where are you? Everyone is already here.*

Fuck.

According to the time on my phone, I'm already five minutes late for the task force meeting at the office.

Me: *Stall. Be there in five.*

I get up and check myself out in the small mirror above the sink and flinch at the dark stain covering my shirt before taking one last look at my slightly red hand. It'll have to do. With determined strides, I walk back into the store, aiming for the door. I shouldn't have come.

"Don't forget your coffee!" The brunette rounds the counter with a fresh paper cup and hands it to me. My eyes shoot over her shoulder to Kerry, who seems busy moving books around on a shelf, her back turned.

"Thanks," I mumble at the smiling woman in front of me, and without a word to Kerry, I leave the store. Coward.

"The fuck happened to you?"

Jasper, the IT specialist on our team, is standing by the door when I walk into the office.

"Coffee mishap. Give me a minute to put on a clean shirt. I'll be right there." Without waiting for an answer, I slip into the locker room and shrug out of my suit jacket, holster, and the offensive shirt and quickly change into a T-shirt. A few eyebrows are raised when I walk into the boardroom in my casual attire, but I ignore them and sit down. "Sorry I'm late," I offer without any additional explanation.

I look around the table at the group assembled. Durango PD Operations Commander, Keith Blackfoot, lead investigator Boris Parnak from the La Plata County Criminal Investigations Unit, along with James Aiken of the FBI International Operations Division, and Ella Friesen, an art trafficking Interpol specialist seem to be waiting for me expectantly. Luna Roosberg, one of my agents, is passing around folders.

"I apologize again for keeping you waiting," I start. "Ella? Since you and James called this meeting on short notice, why don't you bring us up to speed?"

"Very well," she says with only a hint of her Dutch accent. "In the last year and a half, we've noticed an increase in the theft of rare manuscripts and print work from libraries, museums, and private collectors. The apparent trend started in the UK with the burglary of some of its finest libraries and quickly expanded to the rest of Europe. The MO suggested an organized effort by more than one individual. Almost a year ago, several rare works were stolen from a private collection in Switzerland for a collective value of twenty-six million dollars. One item alone, a copy of *The Birds of America*, by John James Audubon, was last valued at twelve million dollars in 2010. Six months ago, we finally got a lead when one of the stolen manuscripts, a copy of *Don Quixote* by Miguel de Cervantes, appeared in the collection of a wealthy Texas enthusiast here in the U.S. The collector was a rich cattleman with no real knowledge and was clearly duped. The man was easily cleared but was able to provide us with some information on the auction house." She indicates the files Luna distributed. "As you can see, the auction house appears to be U.S. based, and we've been able to monitor some of their online activities. Two weeks ago, we picked up on a communication to a British gentleman named Troy Sinclair. He's a rare-books specialist, who used to work for the University of Cambridge. He was terminated two years ago by the University when an early Shakespeare sonnet he was working on went missing from the library, only to be discovered in his possession. He claimed he was behind on his work and had simply taken his work home. The University terminated him since removing any of the rare documents from the library is immediate cause for dismissal. However, there wasn't evidence at the time of intended foul play. Still, his name went on our persons of interest list. You'll find a copy on page three."

I flip through the file and find the message.

Pkg en route DRO

DRO stands for Durango-La Plata County Airport.

KERRY

"What's with you and these fine male specimens?"

Marya stands beside me as we watch the FBI agent's broad back disappear down the street. Yes, I gawked. The moment I heard the door shut, I hustled to the window to get a good look at his enticing backside.

"Don't know what you're talking about," I tell her, turning back to this morning's haul from the post office; a box of recent romance releases. Most of my customers are female and the romance genre is one of the more popular ones, so I try to stay up to date with my selection.

"Whatever," I hear Marya mumble before she says a little louder, "If you're not interested, you won't mind me having a go at this one, right?" It's a challenge and I know it. Still, I just shrug my shoulders, keeping my back turned and my focus on the stack of books in my hand. Normally, I love the smell of books above all else, but right now I can't smell anything but the lingering scent of Damian Gomez. Damn him.

"You know it wouldn't hurt for you to have some fun from time to time," she says under her breath.

"By the way," I ask in an attempt to distract her, and myself. "Did you get any calls or deliveries while I was gone?" I'm still waiting on that box of first editions. I figure maybe they would've sent it by courier instead of USPS, but Marya shakes her head.

"No deliveries, no calls," she confirms.

"Well, dammit. Those books should've been here already. I've dealt with these guys before, and they've always delivered on time. Never had a problem."

It's just before six, closing time, when the store phone rings.

"Kerry's Korner. Kerry speaking, how can I help you?"

"Hi, girl." I hear my bestie, Kim. on the other end. She's run my original store in Cortez since I opened up in Durango.

"Hey, sweetie. Everything okay there?" I ask. Kim has struggled finding decent help since the birth of her son, Asher.

"Yes," she says enthusiastically. "This new girl is really working out. I'm so relieved. But that's not why I'm calling. With everything going on, I forgot to mention that last week I received a box in a shipment I think was meant for Durango. It was addressed to the Durango address, but just like my boxes, had Kerry's Korner in big print. They probably failed to check the actual address when they were sorting and simply shipped the whole thing here."

"Thank God," I exclaim, relieved. "I've been wondering where it was. Okay," I tell Kim. "I was planning to head into Cortez at some point to see my favorite little man anyway. Maybe sometime next week?"

"Sounds good," Kim chuckles. She knows I adore my godson. He's such a sweet little baby, and I rarely go longer than a couple of weeks before I need my snuggle fix. "If you come a week from Wednesday, Mal will be out of town so maybe you can spend the night? We'll have a chance to catch up with a bottle of wine." Kim's husband is a security specialist and sometimes has to go out of town for a few days for work. It's been ages since Kim and I have had a girls' night, so I'm immediately on board.

"Let me check to see if Marya can open next Thursday." I turn to Marya, who is cleaning the coffee counter. She's already waving her hand in the air.

"No problem," she says, having obviously listened in on the conversation.

"You're the best, Marya." I give her a big grin when she throws a smile over her shoulder. "Looks like it's a plan," I tell Kim, who squeals on the other end. After promising her I'll be there after seven and will bring the wine, we end the call.

Ten minutes later, I lock the store and wave goodbye to Marya, who is climbing in her car, when an unexpected hand on my shoulder has me swinging around.

"I guess I got here a bit too late," the guy with the British accent says with a smile. Dick.

"You scared the crap out of me," I tell him, pissed he thought he could just put his hands on me. The offensive hands come up defensively and he smiles apologetically. The most unconvincing smile I've ever witnessed.

"I apologize. I simply came to see if I could convince you to change your mind and have dinner with me."

Seriously? My mouth falls open at the gall of this guy. He appears to be a tad slow on the uptake. Yesterday I stayed polite, not wanting to piss off a potential customer, but it's obvious this guy's interests go beyond my store and I need to cut him off at the pass. Trying to calm my heart, still pounding a hole in my chest, I take a deep breath before responding. "I guess I wasn't clear enough yesterday, so let me be blunt; I am not interested. Does that help?" I can't help adding a layer of sarcasm. He apparently doesn't take too well to that since his eyes narrow to slits. Something he tries to conceal with a toothy smile that once again has my hair stand on end.

"It's clear," he grinds through his teeth. "I'm sorry to have bothered you." With one last glare, he turns on his heels and walks in the direction of town. It strikes me as weird he apparently is walking. My store is on the outskirts of town in a small plaza off the highway, and there is no sidewalk. For a minute, I keep my eye on him as he simply marches along on the side of the road, looking ridiculous in his suit and tie.

He never once turns around though, and when he disappears around the corner, I let out a relieved breath. That guy really creeps me out, and I'm glad it's still light out with quite a bit of traffic on the road. I walk at a stiff clip to my Subaru, parked around the corner. I'm eager to get home and get some dinner going. Luckily, I don't have to stop in town for groceries; I filled my fridge earlier this week. I hate to admit I'm a little shaky and am glad my little rental is only minutes from the store, just up the mountain. I managed to get a one-year lease on the small bungalow. A little remote, but nice and quiet, just west of town. When I pull into the driveway, I take one last look at the road behind me.

CHAPTER 3

DAMIAN

"ANYTHING NEW ON that trafficking case?" I ask Luna when she walks in.

It's been a week since I'd last heard from Ella. The meeting was just to put us on alert, but without more intel, there is very little for us to do. Not complaining though, as we're having a hard enough time keeping up with other cases. Interpol is working the information garnered from the Texas collector, trying to get a bead on this Troy Sinclair. James Aiken is following up on the U.S.-based auction house. For now, we have nothing concrete to work with, except for that intercepted message.

"Actually," she answers. "I do." Sitting down across from my desk, she hands me a printout. "That's a list of local individuals and businesses known to deal or collect rare books. I cross-referenced with the list James sent us and marked those."

I look at the two-page printout and right away my eyes zoom in on a name I've tried, and failed, to forget this past week. Kerry's Korner. Well, fuck. A bright red mark sits beside the name. When I scan down, there are two more red marks. One is White Rabbit Books, a store around the corner from Main Street in the center of town. The other is an individual—Bruce Willoughs—a name I am familiar with. An exorbitantly wealthy retired oilman from Texas, who built a massive mansion in the mountains outside Durango. I know him because, over the years, he has been involved in just about every charitable function in the region. I can't say I particularly like the guy, having run into him a handful of times, but that doesn't mean I can see him involved in anything like this. Still, the fact he's possibly had dealings with the same auction house is enough reason to go have a talk with the man. As for Kerry's business, it would be a perfect front to fence stolen rare manuscripts and books. From what I can recall, she has a locked, glass shelving unit against the far wall that appeared to hold some older print works. I probably should have a closer look.

"Two stores and Mr. Willoughs. You want to take a run up the mountain?" I ask Luna. Since Bruce and I are far from friendly, I figure she'll likely do better with him. He has a penchant for younger women, which is one of the reasons he rubs me the wrong way.

"You sure you don't want to take him on?" Luna

says with a smirk. She knows. The last run-in I had with him was very public, when my youngest sister, Bella, was visiting from Farmington. The bastard had followed her to the bathrooms, when I'd taken her out for dinner at Seasons, and accosted her in the hallway outside. Bella had come back to the table with a face like thunder. After I finally got out of her that he'd put his hands on her uninvited, I headed over to his table and set him straight, loud enough for the other diners to hear. All he gave me was an arrogantly dismissive wave of his hand, and if not for Bella's intervention when she grabbed me from behind, I would have had him by the throat. Despite his name as a local philanthropist, Bruce Willoughs is a self-righteous bastard.

"Har-har," I tell Luna. "You head up. I'd be surprised if he were stupid enough to try and put his hands on you. After all, you carry a mean weapon. That damn gun is almost bigger 'n you are."

Luna snickers and pats her hip holster. "That's what she said," she says with a wink in an uncharacteristic display of humor, before turning serious. "I'll head up there after lunch. Want me to pick you something up?"

"No, thanks. I'll grab something in town. I'll go check out the bookstores."

I start at White Rabbit Books, telling myself it makes more sense to start at the one furthest from the office. I'm told the owner isn't around, but the elderly woman manning the store is able to tell me, after consulting the computer in the small office in the back, that the only time they'd received a shipment from this online auction house had been about a year ago. No other orders are pending from what she can see, but she assures me she will check with the owner and have him contact me. I leave her my card with my cell phone number written on the back.

I stand outside by my Expedition, taking in the warm June sun and looking around for a place to grab some lunch before I head to Kerry's Korner. I'm delaying and I know it. Nothing really strikes my fancy since I suddenly seem to have worked up an appetite for sweets. Giving in, I climb behind the wheel and turn the car in the direction of the small strip mall just west of town.

It only takes me about five minutes to pull into the parking lot in front of the store, and through the window I can see Kerry moving between two rows of shelves, a stack of books in her hands. Just like last week, her messy hair hangs free and loose, a flowing top hides curves I'd like to explore. Goddammit. I'd just managed to scrape off Cora—although she might not have received the message since I've ignored several texts and at least five calls this past week—and for damn sure don't want to start anything else. Especially not since this particular woman, at the very least, appears to be a potential person of interest in this new case. I don't color outside the lines. Not ever. Rules are there for a reason.

My resolve firmly in place, I push open the door

and head in. The little bell alerts Kerry as she comes out from between the shelves and stops in her tracks when she spots me. The hint of alarm on her face, as her eyes meet mine, is quickly replaced with irritation. One hand comes to rest on her cocked hip and her pose screams attitude. Instantly my resolve melts because, as it turns out, I like attitude—a fuck of a lot. "Double shot?" she asks, caving first when I don't say a word and simply stare back at her. Those pale gray eyes turn away first, and her body starts moving toward the counter.

"Please," I say politely, although the thoughts going through my head are anything but polite. Coffee is a good way to break the ice, and I'm glad to see she's fully stocked on pastries. "And a cinnamon roll, if you have one." I receive a curt nod in reply before she reaches for a paper cup. "For here," I add and watch her hand freeze midair.

"Here?" The high-pitched squeak is almost comical and telling of how much I rattle her. Good. She rattles me, too. "Here?" she repeats, this time at a more natural tone. I just smile and nod, pointing at the couch in front of the window. A few local newspapers are strewn across the coffee table, and I pick one up. The *Dove Creek Press*, a small newspaper from a town by the same name. The guy who writes the articles has a quirky, direct style I enjoy. I do my best to focus on a piece about their upcoming Pick 'n Hoe festival but am too distracted by Kerry's movements behind the counter. The soft tinkle of the copious bracelets around her wrists makes her impossible to ignore. A gypsy—that's what she looks like, despite her blonde hair. She carries the appearance of being footloose and carefree, but something about her seems tightly wrapped up. It's hard to believe this woman would have anything to do with an international trafficking ring, but you never know.

I watch as she walks over, almost stumbling over her own feet when she sees me looking. Immediately, a dark blush spreads over her face and her teeth bite down on her lower lip. Christ—even that is sexy. I put the newspaper down on my lap to hide my insistent physical response.

"Sit with me a minute," I quickly say, as she puts down my coffee and a plate with the biggest cinnamon roll I've ever laid eyes on and threatens to walk away.

"I have something—" she starts but I interrupt.

"Just a minute. Please?" Her eyes soften a little at my plea, and she sits down in one of the club chairs, perched right on the edge, with her back ramrod straight. She looks decidedly uncomfortable, and I'm about to make it worse. "How long have you had this store?" I ask, to try and get her talking without showing my hand right off the bat.

"This one? Not that long. A couple of years. Why?" she wants to know.

"Just curious. I know Kim is managing your place in Cortez. I'm simply wondering how the expansion is working out for you." She lightly shrugs her shoulders, relaxing back a little in her chair.

"I'm doing okay," she says, trying unsuccessfully to hide a little, smug smile. "Having Kim on board really opened up a lot of possibilities I wouldn't have been able to explore without her. Opening this place and starting the online bookstore—it's all fallen into place." I can see by the way her face glows she's proud of what she's accomplished. Good. That's good. I just hope to God she did not get herself involved with this band of thieves.

"Your online business, is that the same as the stores'? New or secondhand books?" I ask, easing into the area I want to question her about.

"Online is mostly pre-owned. People who are looking for certain books that are no longer in print or sometimes they want something special, like a first edition of their favorites. I have a decent network of dealers and sellers who specialize in special prints or rare editions." Kerry is completely animated talking about her business, using her whole body to speak. If what she was saying wasn't so important to my case, I'd be happy to watch her talk about anything. But this is the information I'm after, so I go in for the kill.

"Have you ever had any dealings with The Gilded Feather Auction House?" My question is followed by dead silence, as Kerry's hands still and her mouth falls open.

KERRY

The bastard!

It's my own damn fault for getting carried away, thinking I may have misjudged this man when he starts asking me how my business is doing. Enjoying the fact that a man is actually interested in what I do—appreciates what I've built. Should've known better.

The asshole is looking into me. That's the only reason he's been in here in the first place. Not for me. Don't I feel like an idiot.

"You're not an idiot," he says, making it clear that I said that out loud.

I push up from the chair and walk to the counter where I mindlessly start wiping down the coffee machine—just to give my hands something to do. Otherwise I might actually throw something, I'm so pissed.

"Kerry—look at me." He's walked up right behind me, and the sound of his voice so close startles me.

"Agent Gomez, why don't you just spit it out? Tell me what the hell you really want to know, since it's clear you've come with an agenda and not for my pastries," I snap, swinging around to face him. He's standing a little closer than I'd anticipated, and I have to tilt my head back to look him in the eyes. Deep, dark pools of chocolate, rimmed with ridiculously long lashes for a man, that trace my face with curiosity. I fight to hang onto my anger, seeing as the intensity in his eyes makes me a little weak in the knees. Damn him.

"Very well," he says slowly, after a very pregnant

and slightly uncomfortable pause. "I believe you might be able to help out with a case I'm working on." He stops to gauge my reaction, and I'm determined not to give him one.

"Go on," I urge him, none too kindly.

"The Gilded Feather Auction House," he repeats the name of the online company I've dealt with a couple of times now. "I understand you've had some dealings with them?"

I've done nothing wrong so I don't hesitate telling him. "I have. I've bid on some unique books and won my bid twice. Why?"

He ignores my question and asks one of his own. "What did you buy from them?"

"Like I said, some unique books. First editions, out of prints, and a few author signed copies," I tell him honestly.

"Is there a market here for those things?" he wants to know.

"Not huge here in Durango but for my online store there is. I mentioned I get requests for specific editions, and when I see them come up on the auction block, I take a chance and put in a bid. Sometimes there are more books in the lot and I end up with extra stock, but I often find takers for those as well." I watch Damian nod pensively.

"So let me get this: the lot you buy gets shipped here and you send the requested edition to the customer and hang on to the rest?"

"That's usually how it works," I tell him with a

shrug, turning to the door when the bell rings in a customer. "Give me a second." I hold up my finger and greet Jeannie Brooks, a frequent customer since I opened the store. "Hey, Jeannie. Anything specific today or are you just browsing?" I like the middle-aged woman. She lives in the mountains just north of town. Despite her rough appearance—she generally looks like a lumberjack, always wearing plaid flannel and a ball cap—Jeannie is highly intelligent and quite sweet-natured. Almost shy. I'm not surprised she gives Damian a thorough once-over before answering softly.

"Anything new?" she asks.

"Yep. Go check the mystery and suspense section. I received a load of new releases I've added to the shelves." I point her in that direction. "Want a coffee while you browse?" On her nod, I turn to brew her a fresh one, finding Damian leaning with a hip against the counter, staring at me.

"What?" I snap.

"I see you're busy, so I'll cut it short," he says, tilting his head in Jeannie's direction. "Two things: First I'd love to have a look at any paperwork you might have on those bids you placed and would appreciate a detailed list of the shipments. I'll come back for it later." I can sense him take a step closer, feeling the heat of him in my back. "Secondly," he whispers, his breath brushing my ear. "I may have come with an ulterior motive, but make no mistake, Gypsy—I volunteered for the job for a reason."

Without waiting for my response, he moves away. My hands are gripping the edge of the counter so hard, my knuckles turn white. Only when I hear the bell on the door announce his departure do I move.

"Phew," I hear Jeannie say. "I could feel the heat over here."

I turn to see her standing by the window, watching Damian stalk to his car, before she turns to me. "Don't know about you," she says, a smile tugging at her mouth. "But that man gives brooding alpha a whole new meaning."

Yes. Yes, he does.

That afternoon, after Jeannie leaves with three new paperbacks in her bag and Marya arrives for her shift, I dive into my office. Booting up my computer, it doesn't take me long to print out the information Damian requested. Two invoices and a list of books I received in the first shipment. I don't know exactly what is in the second shipment, since it had only been identified as a collection of first edition prints. I grab the phone to give Kim a call.

"It's Kerry," I say, when she answers. "I have a quick question. Do you have that box close by? I need to know what's inside."

"Crap. I brought it home already, right after we last spoke, so it would be there when you come over. Didn't want to run the risk of forgetting," Kim explains. "I can open it tonight when I get home."

"No worries. Whenever you have a chance," I assure her. I don't tell her what I need it for and she doesn't ask.

"I'll give you a call tomorrow," she says. "And by the way, I'm emailing an order. Running low on some of the newer releases."

The rest of the conversation revolves around normal day-to-day business, and by the time I hang up, it's already closing in on five o'clock. I have to hurry if I want to get my errands done today.

I rush out the door with a final wave to Marya, who is closing tonight. I've got to hurry if I want to get to the DMV office before they shut the doors.

By the time I finally roll into bed, I've managed to get my license renewed in the nick of time and hauled a week's worth of groceries up the mountain. I'd grabbed dinner on the fly in town so I could skip cooking. That's one of the things I still can't quite get used to; cooking for one. Don't get me wrong, I love puttering in the kitchen, and baking for the store is one of my favorite things to do in my spare time. Cooking a meal, though? It's only fun when there's someone to enjoy it with. Still, a lot of the time I force myself and end up cooking for an orphanage, giving me individual portions to freeze for a few days.

It's just after nine when I snuggle in bed with my Kindle. I love the smell and feel of books, but when it comes to reading, I really like the convenience of my e-reader. It fits in my purse and I lug it everywhere. My eyes are gritty, and I can't seem to keep my focus on what I'm reading. Instead my mind insists on replaying the conversation with Damian. I probably should worry about his line of questioning, but every time I think of his voice, the feel of his proximity, the barely-there touch of his breath on my skin, I break out in goosebumps.

I finally give up, put my Kindle down, and turn off the bedside lamp.

The persistent ringing of my phone wakes me up a few hours later, and I reach over to my nightstand.

"Hello?" I answer it, my eyes still closed, without checking the caller first.

"Ms. Emerson? This is Superior Security. The alarm just went off at Kerry's Korner," the woman's voice on the other end of the line calmly states.

"What?" I shoot up straight in bed and flick on the bedside lamp to look at my clock. Three-twenty, it's the middle of the damn night.

"I guess it's not you then," the woman concludes. "Our security is already en route, but I am putting a call into police right now. Please stay on the line."

With my phone tucked between my ear and my shoulder, I try to get dressed as best I can. In sweatpants, my sleep shirt, and my purse, I'm already on my way out the door when the woman comes back on.

"Police are on the way. Please don't approach or enter the premises without police escort," she cautions. As if I would.

"Thank you. I won't," I answer anyway, ending the call and jumping in my car.

I'm surprised to see a dark SUV pull into the

parking lot at the same time I do. There is already a Superior Alarm Services car and two patrol cars parked out front. My surprise is even bigger when I see Damian step out of the SUV and stalk over to my car, his eyes piercing through the windshield.

CHAPTER 4

DAMIAN

"ARE WE GOOD HERE?" Luna asks when the suspect is lead off in handcuffs to the back of a waiting Durango PD vehicle. The guy was wanted in relation to a child porn investigation in Ohio and had been hiding out in a rental apartment here in Durango. Police got wind of him a few days ago and kept him under surveillance while getting the appropriate warrants issued. Tonight was supposed to be an easy pick up, but the guy turned out to be armed and highly agitated. Our office was called in for backup and by the time we got on scene, a full standoff was in place. Luna is a good negotiator and easily took over talks with the unpredictable suspect, managing to talk him into giving himself up.

By now it's after three in the morning, and we've been out here all night. "Yeah, we're good. Head on home. I'm not gonna bother, will grab some shut-eye in the office." It's too late for me to head home. Living thirty-five minutes away, north of Hermosa, can be a pain in the ass sometimes, but there's no way I'm going to give up my house by the river.

Luna gets in her car and lifts a hand as she turns onto the street. I'm about to get in my own car when Keith Blackfoot walks up.

"You off?" he asks, hanging on to my door.

"That's the plan."

"Thanks for your help. That girl's pretty good," he says, watching Luna's taillights disappear in the distance.

"Agent Roosberg has a knack," I tell him with a bit of an edge. I like the guy, but he'd better show some respect to my agents. Luna would likely knee him in the gonads if she heard him refer to her as girl.

"That she does," he mutters before turning his eyes to me. "Worked with her for long?" he asks, and I roll my eyes, making him chuckle.

"Ask me straight. You want to know if she's got a man?" I'm not fucking Cupid, and I have no desire to stand here playing a game of twenty questions. I have a conference call scheduled for eight thirty tomorrow morning, and as it is, I'll be lucky to catch a couple of hours sleep.

"Just wondering," he says, shrugging his shoulders. "She colors me impressed. On quite a few levels," he adds, grinning.

"Shit. I don't wanna know it," I grunt, flinching

at the thought. Luna is a colleague and has become a friend over the past few years. She's more like a sister than anything else, and I just can't look at her any other way.

"I don't have the same hang-ups you do, Gomez. I don't have a problem grabbing an opportunity when it presents itself," he says with a smirk. He was there not too long ago when I had to kindly but firmly tell the police department's pretty PR liaison I don't ever mix business with pleasure. This after she'd propositioned me for the fourth or fifth time. It had been embarrassing for her, for me, and I thought for Keith as well, but he'd apparently found it amusing. So much so, that he likes poking at me from time to time. *Asswipe.*

Keith is about to say something else when his radio goes off. "*Burglary in progress. 21619 US-160. Superior Alarms en route, called for backup.*" My ears perk up the moment I hear the address.

With just a "later" to me, Keith calls out to one of his officers and tells him to follow. I'm right behind them, keeping six and careful not to get in their way, but right fucking behind them.

As luck would have it, I notice a car, a wagon, pulling into the parking lot from the other side. Doesn't take a genius to figure out who it is. I'm out of the car and walking straight toward the Subaru, never losing sight of the woman behind the wheel.

"The fuck are you doing here?" I bite off as I wrench open her door and lean in. I'm tired, I'm hungry, and I'm fucking cranky. Seeing this woman potentially put herself in harm's way, in the middle of the goddamn night, pisses me off to no end. Still, I regret the words as soon as they leave my mouth, and I see the flash of fear in her eyes. Smooth, Gomez—real smooth.

"It's my store," she snaps back, no longer fearful but now obviously angry. "Maybe I should ask what the fuck *you're* doing here." She throws my words right back at me. The fire in her eyes such a damn turn on, it makes me lose my focus. Again. As if scripted, her teeth start gnawing on her bottom lip, a now familiar sign she's not quite as feisty as her words.

Against better judgment, I reach out my hand and with the pad of my thumb, I pull the plump lip free from her teeth. The moment I withdraw my hand, her tongue sweeps out to trace where my thumb just was. Fuck me. Now I just want to kiss the damn woman.

"Gypsy," I say softly, watching as her eyes widen at the name. "I was out on a call with these guys when it came through on the radio. I'm just keeping their six, and yours."

"What does that even mean?"

"Means I'm keeping an eye out for them. And for you," I add.

"Right," she says, turning her face away to stare at the building through her windshield. "Because of the case." No. Not because of the case, but I'm not about to get into that with Keith walking with long strides in this direction.

"Ms. Emerson?"

"That's me," Kerry says. I step to the side so she can get out of the car. Only now do I notice she's wearing some kind of shirt with paw prints, a pair of sweats, and flip-flops on her feet. Her hair is all tangled around her head, and I'm pretty damn sure she's not wearing a fucking bra. Her nipples are poking through the material in the cool night air. Immediately my eyes shoot to Keith, who seems to be enjoying the view, and I can't hold back the growl. The bastard smirks when he drags his gaze to me. Way too damn slow for my liking. He hears me. He fucking knows.

Kerry looks between us a bit confused by the silent communication and the now thick tension. It takes everything not to wrap my arm around the woman and shield her. Or claim her. "I'm sorry?" she says.

"Yes. Ms. Emerson, I'm Detective Keith Blackfoot with the Durango PD. I'd appreciate it if you would come with me for a minute. Looks like someone disabled your exterior alarm and forced entry at the back door. Luckily you have the secondary motion alarm on a different circuit. It only went off once he was inside. He must've noticed the red light blinking, because whoever was there, was gone by the time the security company got here."

"Was anything taken?" Kerry asks, worry creasing her face. "I mean I have insurance, I probably should call them." She immediately starts rummaging through her purse, presumably in search of her phone. I put a steadying hand on her shoulder.

"First let's have a look, shall we?" I tell her calmly. She looks up at me, and for a moment, her eyes are unguarded. She's scared. Then she nods.

"Okay," she says. "Let's have a look." She immediately starts following Keith to the store. I fall in step beside her and put my hand on the small of her back. I tell myself it's for moral support, but really I just want a chance to touch.

KERRY

"What is it?" Damian asks, leaning against the doorway of my small office.

"My computer..." I mutter, frantically looking around the mess that was left behind by whomever was in here, trying hard not to touch anything as instructed.

"Desktop?"

"Yeah. I have a laptop at home, but I just use it for personal stuff. I had this one set up for the business," I dejectedly tell him.

"Fuck." He says it under his breath, but I hear him anyway. My computer with the entire business administration has disappeared. Panic crawls up my throat. I can't wrap my head around the fact I have no idea how I'm supposed to run my store, and especially my web store, without it. I'm scouring my brain to try and remember the last time I did a Dropbox backup.

Too fucking long, that's for damn sure.

I haven't even gone into the store yet, too afraid to, but now I want to see. I need to know.

I try to move past Damian, but he puts his hands on my shoulders to hold me back. "Where are you going?"

"Store—I have to see the store." I twist myself from his hold and storm past him, only to find the police officer, Keith something, from earlier, blocking my way.

"Ms. Emerson, you can go in, but please remember not to touch anything," he reminds me. I simply nod as I step around him as well.

The store looks the same as I left it earlier. Untouched. That is until I feel glass crunch under my feet and turn to find the locked display smashed. The shelves are empty. My carefully collected treasures are gone.

I must be in shock, because I don't even resist when Damian puts his arm around my shoulders and guides me to the couch. "Sit down before you fall," he growls, pulling a fistful of tissues from the box I always have on the coffee table. I hadn't even noticed I was crying, but here I am, tears streaming down my face and Mr. FBI wiping at my cheeks. "Need some water?" he asks gruffly.

I shake my head. I feel like an idiot, breaking down in front of a bunch of cops and this man, but dammit, this store represents my independence. It's my life. It's what held me together during my miserable marriage and what has kept me sane since my divorce.

"Need anything more from her?" Damian directs to someone behind me. "Good, then I'm taking her home." My head snaps up.

"You don't need to take me home," I protest. "I'm quite capable of driving myself."

Damian squints his eyes and is about to say something when the detective beats him to it. "Ma'am, I'd advise against driving in this condition." His slightly condescending tone instantly dries my tears and has me straighten up in my seat.

"And what condition would that be, Detective Blackfoot? The fact that I'm upset about the break-in or the fact I don't pee standing up? I'm curious to know." If not for Damian's restraining hand on my leg, I would've stood up to my full height, all five foot six of me, to give my words more emphasis. As it is, I'm still sitting, and the detective is crouching down beside the couch so his eyes are level with mine.

"Neither," he calmly states. "But if not Agent Gomez, be assured I would send someone else home with you to make sure your house is secure. I would've said the same to anyone else, man or woman." With that he rises tall, leaving me to feel effectively small and put in my place. "Agent Gomez will text me the address, and I'll have one of my officers drop off your car. I'll be in touch tomorrow," he says before correcting himself after a glance at his watch. "I mean later today."

I just nod. There's so much more to worry about,

so much to sort out, I don't want to waste any more time. So when Damian stands up and holds out his hand, I quietly take it and let him lead me through the store and out to his SUV, mouthing thanks to the detective when we pass him.

"Where to?" Damian asks, as he buckles himself in after making sure I've done the same. I direct him west on US-160 and up County Road 206. Passing some of the more affluent houses up this way, I tell him to turn left onto my driveway. My little house is only a hundred yards or so back from the main road, surrounded by trees. I can't see my neighbors from here, but I know they're within walking distance. One of the reasons I finally decided on this rental; I like being away from the hustle of town, while still having the security of people close by.

By the time Damian pulls up in front of the small porch, I've already unbuckled and have my hand on the door. "Thanks for dropping me off," I mumble, still a bit embarrassed over the breakdown he witnessed, and get out of the truck without waiting for a response. I should've known he wasn't going to leave it at that and am not surprised to hear his truck door slam and footsteps following me up the steps.

"Hold on," he says behind me when I fit my key in the lock, his arm coming around me and his hand covering mine. "Let me check first." With sure movements, he sets me aside and pushes through the door first. "Wait here," he says over his shoulder, as he unclips a gun from the small of his back and enters my home.

I stay put as I'm told, wondering why his protective behavior has my heart pounding. I'm not a pushover, I have a loaded shotgun beside my bed and insist on locking my doors. Still, his take-charge attitude makes me feel oddly comforted. The break-in must've rattled me more than I thought.

"All clear," Damian calls from inside. It didn't take him long with only an open concept living room and kitchen, plus one bedroom, a bathroom, and a small mudroom slash laundry room in the back. I step inside and close the door behind me. Damian's turned on a few lights, and I watch him put his gun down on the counter in the kitchen. I'm not sure what I was expecting but it wasn't this big, bulky agent opening my fridge door and ducking in. "Thank God," I hear him say when he straightens up, a beer in his hand. "You want one?" He waves the bottle in my direction. I don't know whether to laugh or get pissed. Instead I just nod, walk over to the comfy sectional couch and plop down, tucking my feet underneath me.

"Are you hungry?" he asks, handing me a bottle, which I immediately put to my lips. The taste of the cold beer perks me right up.

"God, that's good," I sigh, holding the cold bottle against my cheek. Damian is still standing over me, amusement on his face but with heat in his eyes. Yikes. "This is good for now," I tell him, watching as he sits down beside me and unceremoniously props his feet on my coffee table.

My eyes are drawn to his throat when he takes a deep swallow from his beer and then lays his head back on the couch, his eyes closed.

"Tired?"

"Mmmm," he mumbles, turning his head in my direction while slowly opening his eyes on me. "Long night."

DAMIAN

I could fall asleep right here on her couch, but I have a feeling there won't be much sleep for me. A quick glance at my watch tells me the sun will be up shortly.

"I have to call the insurance company," Kerry says, digging through her purse. I reach out to stop her movements.

"Gypsy—Grab some sleep. It'll wait for office hours." She pulls her hand from under mine, and I watch as she restlessly picks at the label on the bottle while looking at me from under her eyelashes. I've done my best to ignore the fact she's still just wearing a sleep shirt so thin, it barely conceals her breasts. Especially when, like right now, her nipples poke out to play.

I don't know if it's my lack of sleep and therefore judgment, to stop her from fidgeting, or whether it's those hard little nubs taunting me, but any restraint I may have had flies out the window. I take her bottle and put it on the table with mine before grabbing her under her arms and pulling her on my lap, her mouth falling open in shock. I don't hesitate and make use of the opportunity, taking her mouth with a hungry growl. Fuck yes—the beer left her tongue cool against mine, and the taste of hops and Kerry is a potent combination. Her body goes solid on my lap, but a few deep strokes with my tongue along hers draws out a tiny whimper. Like hitting an ignition button, she comes alive and burrows her fingers in my hair, while her other hand clings to my shoulder. Her ass wiggles in my lap, and if I hadn't been hard as a rock already, this would've surely done the trick. Christ, she feels good. Hungry and fierce as she kisses me back and my hand, perched on her hip, slides up her ribs to cup her breast through her threadbare shirt. A nice handful. My thumb flicks her taut nipple, and the woman in my arms groans deeply, a sound that travels down my body.

With a twist of my torso, I take her down on her back, my body covering hers. My eyes open and I'm looking right into her shiny gray ones. The emotions I see reflected there bring me to a grinding halt. Confusion, heat, insecurity, need—they're all visible behind the veil of her lashes and work like a cold shower.

"I'm sorry," I mumble, pushing myself up right away. I need to get my head on straight. This woman spells danger, tempting me to break the strict rules I've abided by most of my adult life. From the corner of my eye, I see her scrambling to sit up and pull down that ridiculous shirt with doggie prints. She doesn't even have a dog, although that might not be such a bad idea, up here on the mountain.

"This was a mistake," she says heatedly, but not quite able to hide the hurt in her voice. "We'll blame it on the beer." With her chin tilted up, she gets up from the couch, picks up the bottles from the table, and walks to the kitchen where she empties them in the sink. "You can let yourself out," she says, setting the empties on the counter before making her way to the bedroom door, not once looking back to me.

Probably best since she would surely have seen regret advertised all over my face.

CHAPTER 5

KERRY

MY HAND REACHES over to shut off my annoying alarm. I've hit the snooze button three times already, not ready for this day to start, but I can't keep avoiding the inevitable. I peel one gritty eye open to find it's already past eight. Well past time to face the music; the first order is to call Marya and tell her not to come in. She's understandably upset about the break-in and offers to help clean up. I thank her and tell her I'll call as soon as I have an update from the police.

Next is my insurance company, but I don't have the number saved, which means I have to get up to find it, dammit. Between the cracks of my curtains, I can see the sun is already bright today. Going to be a hot one. I take care of business in the bathroom, but instead of taking a shower first thing, I saunter into the kitchen to start a pot of coffee. The sight of two beer bottles sitting beside the sink stops me in my tracks. The only alcohol I have in the house is beer and a bottle of wine, and I only drink when I have company. Living with not only an alcoholic father, but a husband who knew how to hit the bottle as well, cured me from any excess drinking. So unfortunately, I couldn't blame what happened on the booze. Whether on purpose or unconsciously, I'd not thought once about what happened on the couch last night. Not until now.

Damian's mouth and hands on me had set me aflame, and any resolve I may have had to avoid any entanglements were instantly vaporized. It'd been so long since I'd been that turned on. His mouth was gentle but commanding nonetheless, and his rough, calloused hands on my skin felt so very good. Even now, thinking about it, my traitorous body responds. But then he whispered that damned apology, and everything that was lit up inside dulled instantly. I managed to keep my composure until I made it to my bed, where I buried my face in a pillow and cried out my hurt at being rejected, my anger at myself for letting it get out of hand, and my physical frustration. I'd fallen asleep without even taking off my sweats or getting under the covers. No wonder my eyes feel like they're full of sand.

I grab the bottles from the counter and drop them in the crate of empties in the mudroom before making quick work of my coffee. I like brewing my own, using freshly ground beans I store in the freezer and a heaping teaspoon of cinnamon—a trick my mother taught me. It makes the coffee taste richer. Fuller.

By the time the pot is brewed, I have found my insurance policy and a telephone number. Thank God I had the foresight to keep a copy at my house, as well. I wish I'd had such foresight with everything else on my computer, but that's a worry for later. First things first.

I grab the phone from my purse and notice a text.

Damian: *We've got to talk.*

Right. Like that'll happen.

I may have made a mistake letting the guy get close early this morning, but I sure as hell am not going to volunteer to be humiliated again. I resolutely ignore the text but before I can dial my insurance agent, there's a knock at my door. No one's ever come to my door, except one of my neighbors when I first moved in. A bit cautious, I first peek through the window to see my car and a Durango PD patrol car sitting in my drive. I hadn't even heard them come up.

Opening the door a crack, I find the detective from last night standing on the small porch. "Morning," he says, his eyes scanning me top to toe. I'm suddenly painfully aware I'm wearing the same clothes he saw me in last night, except this time the bird's nest on my head is even more tangled. *Lovely.* I inconspicuously try to wipe the corners of my mouth, in case I have drool caked to my face, but I'm sure he notices. The man is imposing. Not quite as bulky as Damian but a little taller and just as dark and dangerous, however, the detective seems to be less broody. Too late for me to dart into the bedroom to make myself presentable, I square my shoulders and open the door all the way.

"Morning, Detective," I respond, waving him in. "I see you brought my car back. Thanks for that." He throws a look over his shoulder before turning back to me.

"No worries. Officer James did the driving, I just followed behind," he says with a shrug of his shoulders. "Is this a good time to ask you a few questions?"

"Sure. Please invite the officer in, as well, and help yourself to some coffee. I just need one minute." I point in the direction of the kitchen before I disappear into the bedroom to put some decent clothes on. I'm feeling a little uneasy with my girls on display once again. Funny enough, that didn't seem to bother me with Damian. I quickly whip off my nightshirt and sweats and put on some underwear, yoga pants and my favorite tunic. Horrified, I yank a brush through my tangled mane and splash some water on my face. A far cry from presentable but it'll have to do.

"Good," I tell him when I find the detective sitting at the counter with a mug in his hands. Alone. "You found everything, but where is your colleague?"

"In the patrol car. Don't worry, this won't take long."

I quickly top up my own coffee before pulling a stool around to my side. "Do you have any news before you ask your questions, Detective?" I ask him when I sit down.

"Keith," he says. "The name is Keith Blackfoot. Not Detective." His tone is firm, in contrast with the broad smile on his face. If I'm not mistaken, the man is flirting with me. Normally I'd be flattered, but for some reason it feels wrong.

"Very well...Keith, can you tell me anything more?"

"We're keeping the store off-limits while the team is still working on collecting evidence. They should be done sometime this morning, and then I'd be grateful if you could get me a detailed list of missing items. For now, as far as we can tell, the only items gone are the ones you kept under lock and key and your computer, but there could be things we miss. My guess is the burglar hit your office first, hauled out the computer and got spooked when he came back for more and spotted the red light blinking on the motion detector. He smashed the glass display and took off with the special editions."

"He must know something about books then if he took those," I volunteer, but Keith shakes his head.

"Not necessarily. The fact these were the only books behind lock and key, anyone with an ounce of common sense would guess that's where you keep the valuable ones. We managed to lift some fingerprints from the broken glass, and they're being looked at as we speak but not everything has been dusted yet.

We'll need yours and those of any employees or anyone else who might have touched the display so we can rule them out."

"Do you need me to come into the station?" I want to know. "I have one part-time employee, Marya Berger. I'll see if she can come in with me."

"That would be helpful. The sooner the better," he says. "Perhaps between the two of you, we can come up with a list of other people whose fingerprints we'll need to check. The other thing I will need is a list of the books that were taken from the display case. Do you think that's possible on such short notice?" The detective is very kind, but serious and professional. A bit different from the way this conversation started. This I can handle.

I offer to give Marya a call right away to see if she's available this afternoon. Unfortunately, she has to take her youngest to a dentist appointment, so with Keith's agreement, we make it for tomorrow morning at nine. That gives Marya time to drop her kids off at school, and it gives me a chance to get that list of books together.

I purposely don't offer a refill on his coffee, and he seems to get the hint when he gets up shortly after. At the door, he stops and turns back to me with a card in his hand. "Anything you need, any questions you have, give me a call. Day or night," he adds with a wink. Cocky bastard. I bet you he charms women out of their clothes like that all the time. Not for me.

"For sure," I nevertheless tell him as he pulls open the door, revealing the hulking figure of Damian Gomez with a dark scowl on his face.

DAMIAN

I hated leaving like that this morning. Her obvious hurt had stuck in my throat all the way back to the office, where I went after she'd stomped off to her bedroom. I hadn't even bothered trying to sleep and instead had made a pot of coffee and grabbed a quick shower in the locker room, which barely made a dent in the bone-deep fatigue. Still, with a clean set of clothes and a few cups of coffee, I'd at least started feeling human again.

In an effort to get the look on Kerry's face out of my head, I checked email to see if there were any developments for the conference call scheduled for eight thirty this morning. Luna had sent a copy of the report on her meeting with Willoughs and attached a note that simply said: Thanks, he's yours next time. That gets a chuckle out of me—burly Bruce Willoughs facing off with Luna. Sure, he got the surprise of his life when he thought the little woman would be easy pickings. She may be short, but she doesn't pull any punches. I should know, I made the mistake of taking her onto the mat when she was first assigned to my office to gauge her abilities. Small, but fast and damn lethal. It had taken her all of five minutes to have me flat on my back.

It appears Willoughs had little information other than that he's dealt with The Gilded Feather before, both privately and through brokers. He also readily volunteered that he'd had dealings with just about every book dealer in the Four Corners area. Luna passed on a tour of his collections, making a note in the report that the offer sounded too much like an invitation to see his etchings. She did note an impression at the bottom of the report, that Willoughs seemed too slick, his responses a little too practiced and clean. I trust Luna's gut. Despite her sometimes slightly awkward social interactions, she's proven to have a keen insight. I'll check in with Bruce Willoughs myself sometime soon.

I'm about to call in to the conference line when Jasper sticks his head around the corner. "Morning, boss. Change in plans. Blackfoot just called in, conference call is rescheduled for the same time tomorrow morning. Ella has some information she wants to confirm beforehand. And Blackfoot said to tell you he's about to interview a witness this morning?" There's no love lost between the detective—or operations commander, his official title—and Jasper Greene. Jasper's a straight shooter and doesn't enjoy Blackfoot's sick brand of humor. I do, which is why I'm up and out of my seat like a flash. Keith is off to see Kerry, I know he is. I saw the interest in his eyes when he got his first glimpse. I thought I'd done enough to warn him off, but apparently he enjoys dicking with me, because he's on his way there now. And he wants me to know. Cocksucker.

His ride and Kerry's piece of shit Subaru are parked outside her little house, and I'm surprised to see an officer sitting in the patrol car. He's in there alone with her and wanted me to know. The door opens just as I step up on the small porch. That douchebag is stepping out of the doorway, a satisfied smirk on his face, with Kerry right behind him, confusion on hers. At least she was dressed and not still wearing that nightshirt that hid nothing.

"What brings you here?" Keith says, feigning surprise. I hear the challenge, though. Ignoring Kerry's sharp intake of breath, I step right into his space. I need him to know he's pushing my buttons.

"Could ask you the same thing, Blackfoot."

The bastard doesn't even flinch, even though we both know I could take him down if it came to that. "Just dropping off the lady's ride. Asking a few questions—that's all." I can tell he's enjoying this. The glint in his eyes is unmistakable.

Shy of planting my fist in his face, there's only one way to get my message across. With a few steps, I round him and put my arm around Kerry, tucking her to my side. The move leaves Keith standing outside and me on the doorstep with a shocked Kerry rigid against me. His eyebrows shoot up in his hairline before he lets out a chuckle and shakes his head.

"I got what I came for," he says with a fucking

wink at Kerry. "We'll be in touch." With a chin lift to me, he steps off the porch and gets in the patrol car.

The moment he is out of sight, Kerry shoves me hard and disappears into the house. I close the door behind me and follow her into the kitchen, where she busies herself at the sink. Her back may be to me, but anger still radiates from her body. When I pull out a stool, the sound startles her and she whips around, dish brush in hand flinging suds everywhere.

"What the hell was that?" she snarls, her eyes squinted into thin lines.

"He's messing with me," I tell her, watching disbelief wash over her face. "He's got a sick sense of humor and is trying to get a rise out of me by getting in your space."

"What the fuck?" Kerry tosses the dish brush in the sink, causing water to splash up. She takes a few steps and puts her hands on the other side of the counter. "I'm not some kind of chew toy for your joint amusement."

"I'm not amused," I tell her calmly. "I'm pissed right the hell off."

"I don't get it." She shakes her head. "Just a couple of hours ago you had your tongue down my throat and then practically sprinted for the door. Now you're back and…I don't even know what you're doing. Why are you here? What reason do you have to be pissed off? From what I can tell, you and he are no different. Bunch of overgrown egos with more testosterone than sense. Go have a pissing contest over someone else, but leave me the hell alone!"

That went well. Not exactly according to plan, though.

Once again Kerry stalks to her bedroom, but this time I follow. No way I'm going let her walk out with the last word again. She swings around when I push open the door to her bedroom, and her eyes get big when I don't stop there but keep moving until she is backed into the closed bathroom door. Planting a hand on either side of her head, I lean my face close enough for our breaths to mingle. I press my body against hers.

"I'm not playing," I grit out between my teeth, knowing she can feel I mean it. "I don't get involved with people I work with, let alone people linked to active investigations."

"Fine," Kerry sputters, trying to push my body away but I don't move.

"Hush. This time you're going to let me explain and quit jumping to conclusions at everything I say." The little spitfire snorts and rolls her eyes at that, but I'm not letting that stop me. "I want you. Fuck, woman, I wanted you the first time I saw you, but you belonged to someone else. Besides, I was working on a case you were involved with. Just like you're involved in this case. I can't seem to fucking catch a break with you." I blame lack of sleep, anger at Keith for yanking my chain, and frustration with the situation for my lack of finesse.

"Me?" she spits out. "I did this? You are delusional,

Damian Gomez! I didn't ask for any of this. Not a damn thing. Not even that panty-melting kiss you planted on me earlier. You planted on me...I did nothing!" Probably not a good time, but her words put a smile on my face.

"Panty-melting kiss?" I throw back at her, and with an exasperated sigh, she leans her head back against the door and closes her eyes. The move leaves her perfect mouth slightly open in an invitation I'm not man enough to resist.

Knowing I am digging a deeper hole for myself, I drop my mouth to hers, sliding my tongue over those luscious lips.

CHAPTER 6

KERRY

"ARE YOU GOING to listen now?" he says, pulling his lips from mine.

I don't know if I can, my head is empty after all coherent thought was sucked up by that mouth. Good grief, he took me from boiling angry to whimpering with need. He takes advantage of my inability to formulate words and places one hand on the side of my neck, his thumb lazily stroking my jaw.

"Speak," I finally manage.

With his forehead leaning against mine and the rasp of his thumb against my skin, I get lost in the dark chocolate pools of his eyes. I suddenly feel very vulnerable. This is intimate. More so than the punishing kiss we just shared. I squirm a bit under his intense gaze, but for all the butterflies having a party in my stomach, I can't seem to drag my eyes away.

"I have rules," he says softly, the deep timbre of his voice sending a little shiver over my skin. "And you make me want to break just about every one of them."

"I don't understand." My voice sounds breathless. "Rules?"

"I meant what I said earlier, I adhere to clear boundaries between work and play."

"But..." Damian's thumb presses down on my lips, effectively cutting me off.

"When I walked into your shop the first time, I wasn't expecting you. Took a bit for me to place you but I knew I'd seen those beautiful eyes before. You were memorable, even then, married and all. Now— fuck me—you're unforgettable." His words wash over my ruffled feathers and smooth them out. Without thinking, my hands come up to his chest and clutch his shirt. "I know I should walk away because of the case, but the truth is, I really don't want to. Didn't even have a shot the first time we crossed paths, and I'm not about to let this opportunity go. There may not be a third chance."

"But," I start again. "You have a girlfriend."

For a moment, he looks utterly confused before realization sets in. "Cora," he says with a shake of his head, his eyes closed. "It's nothing."

Okay. That rubs me the wrong way. I push off against his chest, but with my back still against the door and his size, I'm not getting anywhere. "It sure sounded like something. I have rules, too," I announce, pushing myself up on my toes to get in his face. "I don't mess with attached men. Not ever."

A dark shadow rolls over his face and, for a moment, I wonder if I should be worried, but his hand still cupping my jaw stays gentle.

"Cora and I had an understanding for a while, until she changed her mind and wanted more. I was never on board and made that clear. She just chooses not to listen. Whatever it was has been over for a couple of months." He leans back in and runs his nose along mine. "Like I said, it's nothing." His full lips skim delicately over mine, and I hum softly at the gentle tease. At the first touch of his tongue along my bottom lip, I open to let him in. This time I'm prepared and ready, rubbing my tongue along his and taking in his taste. My hands flatten on his chest and slide over his pecs, up to his shoulders, and around his neck, tangling in his lush hair. His knee presses between mine, and I find myself rubbing against his thigh, hungry for the friction.

"Fuck," he swears as he abruptly pulls back. Again. "I'm on the clock."

Exasperated, I drop my arms and knock my head against the door behind me. Turned on, frustrated, and not just a little pissed at the rejection. I feel him take my face in his hands. "Open your eyes, Gypsy." Reluctantly I look at him through slits and see him struggle to keep a smile off his face. Good thing, because I'm about ready to knee him in the gonads. "I'd like nothing more than to make use of that girly bed of yours," he says, indicating my comfy nest with layers of colorful quilts and a gazillion pillows in assorted colors and patterns. "Get a good taste of you naked, but I'd need to take my time. And time is not something I have right now."

"You're not helping," I grumble, even more aroused at the thought of getting naked on my bed with this frustrating but extremely enticing man. I can feel him chuckle as he presses my face against his shoulder with one hand in my neck, the other wrapping around my waist and holding me close. "Besides, I don't do casual sex," I bring up a tad defensively. "Not my style."

"Who said anything about casual?" he mumbles in my hair.

I don't know what to say to that. My feelings are all over the place right now. So when he finally steps back and gives me the room to escape, that's exactly what I do, clear out the door. I stop in the kitchen, at the sink again with my back turned. I'm not sure I'm ready for what his words suggest. True, the attraction I feel for him is explosive, I can't deny that, but I've just started finding my own feet again. I don't know if getting involved with anyone is a good idea. No matter how much that idea appeals to me. All I know about him is that he's FBI and is friends with friends of mine. Hardly enough to start anything on.

I hear him walking up behind me, but I don't turn around. I shiver slightly when I feel his fingers pull my hair away from my neck, pressing an open-mouthed kiss there.

"Have dinner with me." His breath strokes the shell of my ear, and for a minute, I forget my own name.

"Can't. I have work to do. The store to clean and lists to make." With considerable effort, I manage to distance myself enough to formulate words. I'm avoiding and I know it, but I need a bit of time to get my head straight.

Damian puts his hands on my shoulders and eases me around to face him. "We'll see, I'll check in with you later. See how you're doing. And don't go alone," he insists, getting my hackles up again, but before I have a chance to protest, he leans down and gives me a hard kiss. By the time I have my wits about me again, he's already by the door. "Gotta go—and Gypsy? Not alone," he repeats over his shoulder, then he's gone.

Bossy. If he thinks I'm just going to follow his orders, he's got another thing coming.

DAMIAN

"Hey, Bro!"

I've barely left Kerry's driveway when my sister calls. "Bella, what's up?"

"Not a whole lot, except I have a job interview at the hospital in Durango the day after tomorrow!" Her excited squeal makes me smile. My sister has had a hard time since her douchewad ex-boyfriend bailed, leaving Bella with a giant mess on her hands. I never liked the guy. A doctor at the same hospital in Farmington, where my sister was an EMT, Philip Presley had apparently slept his way through the bulk of the female staff behind her back in the seven years they'd been together. When one of the residents he'd been trying to pull into a hall closet against her will went to her boss to make a claim for sexual harassment, a slew of other women came forward. Poor Bella had to find out from hushed conversations in the halls of the hospital. Philip was suspended and disappeared that same day, taking as many of his belongings as he could from their joint apartment. The wagging tongues, pitying eyes, and constant questioning as to his whereabouts by the administration and law enforcement had finally worn Bella down. She had a nervous breakdown and moved back in with my parents, while taking a leave of absence. That was six months ago.

I knew she had an eye on a position in Durango. She and I have always been close growing up, and when she showed up for a visit a couple of months ago, she'd mentioned she might look for a job here.

"That's great." I'm smiling at her excitement. "When are you coming up?"

"I was thinking of driving up tomorrow, spend some time with you. Do you have a bed for me?"

"Always. You know that, but you'll still be at least a twenty-minute drive north of town. That gonna be okay? I mean, I can get you a hotel room in town, if that works better?" I offer, but it's met with silence on the other side. "Bella?"

"I just want to spend some time with you," she says quietly, but I know my sister, there is more going on that she's not telling me. That's fine, I'll get it out of her when she gets here.

"Of course. Do you want to swing by the office when you get into town? I'll bring you a key. Give you some time to settle in." I'll have to remember to grab a spare from the kitchen drawer tonight.

"Damian?" Bella interrupts my thoughts. "Thanks," she says, a little hitch in her voice, but before I can find out what is going on with my sister, she has hung up the phone.

The office is busy when I walk in. I'm surprised to find James Aiken waiting for me. "Hey—I thought you'd be back at Quantico?"

"I came back," he states dryly. "My leads keep pointing here."

I sit down at my desk and give James my full attention. "Durango specifically?"

"Colorado specifically, but Durango has come up a couple of times now. The message was first, and early this morning word came in on another intercepted communication." He hands me a sheet of paper.

DRO package not secure

"Then," he continues. "I find out through the pipeline one of the bookstores you have on your list was broken into last night." He looks at me with an eyebrow raised.

"True," I admit. "We were out on an arrest with the Durango PD last night when the call came through to them. They're investigating, but I'm keeping track of it."

"What do you know about this place? Could this be a distribution point for them? And what about the owner?" He shoots off a barrage of questions that ruffle my feathers.

"A simple bookstore slash coffee shop. New and secondhand books of all kinds and a handful of signed or first edition fiction books. Those were taken, by the way, along with the computer. A secondary alarm appears to have scared off the burglar, and other than a busted glass cabinet and a ransacked office, there wasn't much more immediately apparent." My tone is clipped, something that doesn't go unnoticed by James. The eyebrow goes up again.

"And the owner?"

"Kerry Emerson, I actually just spoke with her. She's waiting for the all clear from the detective in charge before going in to take a good look around to see what's missing."

"Okay," he calmly says. "But what about Ms. Emerson's background. Any flags?"

"None," I answer far too quickly. "She owns a store in Cortez and opened this one, as well as an online store, just a year or so ago. She's had dealings on two occasions with the auction house and is preparing detailed lists for me of the shipments. I have no reason to believe she is in any way involved. She's been forthcoming and helpful." I snap my mouth shut before I say more than I should. Still, James Aiken didn't get where he is today because he's a stupid man.

"You know her." It's not so much a question as it is a statement.

"Friend of a friend," I offer. "She also was involved in a case I was working on a few years back."

"I see," James mumbles. "So this woman has been involved with the law before?"

I'm on my feet with my hands firmly grasping the edge of my desk in an effort not to haul out. "As a victim of kidnapping." I can't quite keep the volume down on my response. James just quietly stares at me until I finally let go of the desk and sit back down.

"Tell me about it," he says, and I do. I spend the next twenty minutes outlining the circumstances of Kerry's involvement in that old case and her connection to Gus Flemming's investigative unit. James knows Gus well since his company occasionally is hired on by the FBI, either independently or as part of a taskforce.

"Very well. Stay on the local PD for some answers and see if you can get a copy of those fingerprints they've lifted. Won't hurt to run some comparisons beyond what AFIS stores. And as for the girl…" He leans forward in his chair. "…Make sure you don't let your sharp eye be clouded by a pretty face."

I barely manage to keep myself in my chair. "Do

you have any reason to believe I would?" I grit out between clenched teeth. Never have I, or my work ethic, been questioned like that before. Then again, I've never felt quite this protective before of anyone related to a case. Maybe I should've stuck to keeping those boundaries straight—already the impact of crossing them stares me in the face.

"Calm down," James says as he pushes up from his chair. "Of course I don't. All I'm saying is you make sure the waters are clear before you dive in. That's all." He tucks away his binder into his briefcase and moves to the door. "By the way—I'm at the Hilton Homewood Suites. Call me when you have something." With that he pulls the door shut behind him.

With a deep sigh, I drop my head in my hands. Doing well so far, already two of my colleagues can read me like a book. Dammit. The sound of the door has me lifting my head.

"Rough morning, boss?" Luna smiles as she sets a take-out coffee in front of me and drops a report next to it. "Don't get excited about the coffee delivery; Jasper went and got a tray. I just volunteered to deliver it since I wanted a word anyway."

I gratefully take a sip of the hot brew. "Thanks." I give her a curt nod and pick up the report. "What's this?"

"Jasper looked into Willoughs for me. I told you that other than making my skin crawl with his obvious come-ons, something about him seemed forced, uneasy. That's Jasper's report on his findings." She indicates the single piece of paper.

I look up at her with my eyebrows raised. "There's hardly anything here. It reads like a resume instead of a background."

"Exactly," Luna answers. "Family history, work history, straightforward financial records, property titles: It's all clean as a whistle. The man doesn't even have a traffic violation to his name, it's just not natural for a fifty-two-year-old millionaire to be spotless."

"I agree. So what are you suggesting?" I want to know.

"I'm thinking a perfunctory background check is not enough."

"Is Jasper busy?" I ask.

"He's in a telephone conference."

"I want him to dig deeper as soon as he has a chance. I want telephone records, credit card accounts, anything and everything Jas can get his hands on. Once we get a clearer picture, I'll go visit the man," I instruct Luna.

"Sure you don't want to check him out first?" she asks.

"No. I trust you, I trust your instincts and if you say something is off, then it is." Luna lowers her head to hide the smile. She's a great agent but occasionally suffers from insecurity. Needlessly.

"Thanks, boss," she says as she walks out.

I turn around and push through the door leading to the small balcony off my office. The view is stunning. Our office is set on a cliff at the end of Rock Point Drive, in a small industrial park, on the edge of Durango. From my vantage point, I overlook the valley with the Animas River flowing almost right below me and beyond it the historic downtown. Standing here feels a little like being on top of the world. I was born in Farmington, where my family still lives. I desperately wanted to leave when I was young and headed to Boston, where I joined the police department after I finished the academy. I'd been hungry, but I could never settle in the big city. When an opportunity to join the FBI came along, I jumped at it. I had fifteen years in the field when I was offered the La Plata County field office, and with my roots in the Four Corners area, I didn't hesitate. As far as I'd been running from my home, I suddenly felt a strong need to be closer. I never expected the weight and diversity of the case load this office would carry. Ironically, now that I've reached this point in my career, I find myself losing focus. The distraction being a fiery blonde, beautiful bookstore owner.

The buzz of my phone on my hip pulls me away from the view. "Gomez," I answer and hear a familiar voice.

"Damian?"

KERRY

Refreshed from my shower after an already eventful morning and a call from Detective Blackfoot giving the store the all clear, I head out to do some damage control. A quick conversation with my insurance company ensures me that a local appraiser will be by the store at noon to assess damages. I want to get there before he shows, so I can have a look around, even though they told me to leave everything as is.

The police tape is still up when I pull into my parking spot. One of my neighbors, Bill Franklin, is standing outside the door of his hardware store.

"I see you had some excitement?" the friendly older man asks with his hands on his hips. "Should've called me, missy. There's a reason I gave you my number." I had totally forgotten he made sure I entered his contact information in my cell phone shortly after I opened the store. Not that I would've contacted him in the middle of the night. He has enough on his plate taking care of his sweet wife, suffering from advanced COPD, and managing his store all by himself. He doesn't need me to interrupt his much-needed rest.

"Must've been young kids," I tell him as I walk up, trying to minimize the concern clear on his face. "Took a couple of books and my computer and took off before security and the cops got here."

"Scared the bejesus out of me this morning, girl."

I feel instantly guilty to have given him a scare, something that could've been prevented if I'd thought to give him a head's up. "I'm sorry, Bill. I wasn't thinking clearly, I should've given you warning," I apologize.

"It's all good," he rumbles kindly. "Some detective left a short while ago and ensured me you were all right. He also gave me your keys."

I hadn't even thought of the spare keys I left with police. I take them from Bill, put my other hand on his arm, and give him a squeeze. "Still—I'm sorry it gave you a scare." He just shrugs.

"Annie made a banana loaf last night. Gave me the leftovers to bring in. I've also got a fresh pot on," he offers, tilting his head to his store.

"I'd love a cup while I wait for the insurance guys. I just want to have a quick look around and write an exact list of what's missing and damaged," I tell him. "I'll be over shortly." With a little wave, I duck under the yellow tape to unlock the door.

The first thing that hits me is the thin layer of dust on every surface. They'd evidently been thorough taking fingerprints. With a bit of luck, the appraiser won't take long, and I'll have the afternoon to get the place cleaned and ready for business tomorrow. Hopefully.

I head straight for my office to find the lists I'd made for Damian, detailing the shipments from the auction house. My inventory is on the computer that is missing, but those lists will give me a good start on the books that were in the display case.

Half an hour later, I realize what I'm looking for is no longer here. Odd. Maybe I'd already given him the information? I can't remember. Only one way to make sure.

CHAPTER 7

KERRY

"MS. EMERSON?"

I'm on my knees next to a shelving unit, trying to wipe off the sticky, black dust left behind by the investigators, when a man's voice from the back door startles me. It's been silent here since I got off the phone with Damian. He pissed me off with his one-syllable responses. He confirmed I hadn't, in fact, already given him the lists and sounded almost angry I couldn't find them. The only time he used a full sentence was when he instructed me to stay put until he could get here.

Whatever. The man runs hot and cold, and I don't have time for that. At least that's what I continue to tell myself. Truth is, even before he planted a wet one on me, the ridiculously handsome, dark, brooding man intrigued the hell out of me. Against better knowledge.

I've been there before, at least the brooding part, and that didn't turn out so well for me.

"Yes," I call out, groaning as I scramble to my feet to greet who I assume is the insurance adjuster. "I'm in the store."

Before I manage to drop my sponge in the bucket and wipe my hands dry on my ratty old jeans, a kind-faced older gentleman comes through the door.

"Ah, there you are. Ms. Emerson? My name is Michael McCoy with Liberty Mutual. I believe you've been expecting me?" I stick out my partially dried hand to shake the portly man's proffered one.

My smile is forced. "Yes, Mr. McCoy, pleased to meet you," I respond by rote, causing him to chuckle.

"Pleased is not an emotion I generally invoke, but let's see if I can make this as fast and painless as possible for you," he jokes with a wink.

"That would be wonderful." This time my smile for him is genuine.

I wait while he pulls a clipboard and pen from his briefcase. With a slight nod he indicates he's ready, and I proceed to show him the damage to the back door, the office, and the store. I managed to jot down most of the books I could remember being in the display case and quickly ran off a copy on my surprisingly unharmed 4-in-1 printer.

"Would you happen to have a copy of the police report handy?" McCoy asks me.

"I don't, but I am supposed to meet with the detective tomorrow morning. I can perhaps send you a copy after?"

"Not to worry. I can pop by the police station and pick one up. Who should I ask for?"

"Detective Blackfoot."

The insurance adjuster leaves, ensuring me this appears to be a straightforward claim, and I can go ahead and get at least a locksmith in to fix the door. He says he will call me later, and I turn back to my dirty shelves.

I'm not sure how long I've been scrubbing, but when I finally come up for air, the bookcases are clean, the books dusted off, and the floor is free of glass. My creaking body reminds me that I've been slacking off on my yoga. Something I did religiously to exercise and stay limber, despite my advancing age. When I was still living in Cortez, Kim and I would join forces every Saturday morning for yoga and coffee. Since moving here and having to go it alone, it hasn't been half as pleasurable and too many weeks—or is it months—have passed since the last time I worked up a good sweat. The lingering stiffness is a good motivator to get back into the routine.

I also placed a call for a locksmith who promised to be here before five tonight. I'll be a lot more at ease when every lock in the place is changed.

Picking up my bucket, I head to the bathroom in the back to dump out the dirty water. I'm just flushing the toilet when I hear a noise from the storage room, spooking me a little. What if the burglar came back? Maybe I should've listened to Damian when he instructed me not to come alone.

Slightly panicked, my eyes scan the small, confined space for anything I could use as a weapon. The best defense is offense...or something like that. With my foot, I kick open the door, which slams against the wall, startling poor Bill into dropping a cup he was holding. It falls to the floor into pieces with a loud crash. Next thing I know, the back door is flung open and Damian storms in, a gun at the ready in his hand.

"Freeze!" he yells at my neighbor, who meekly raises his hands. Then his intensely dark glare comes to me. His eyebrows rise and a twitch starts tugging at the corner of his mouth.

"That's my neighbor, Bill Franklin," I say stupidly.

"I know who he is," Damian rumbles, putting the safety back on his weapon and tucking it in a holster under his arm. "Bill?" he addresses him. "Sorry if I startled you. I heard a crash and..."

"Not to worry," Bill interrupts, his hands still slightly shaking as he runs them over his balding head. "Was just checking on our girl here." He waves his hand in my direction and suddenly both men are eyeing me, amusement clear on their faces.

Damian slowly approaches me reaching out his hand. "Give that to me," he says, barely containing a smirk. "Wouldn't want you to hurt yourself." He touches my right hand, where I am still clutching the toilet brush I was brandishing as my weapon of choice.

DAMIAN

Fuck, but she's cute.

I have to admit when the crash sounded from the other side of the door, my senses—already primed since Kerry called me earlier about the list—jumped to high alert. The news those lists were gone confirmed my suspicions this had not been a simple break and enter. They wouldn't mean a damn thing to the average perp. But what was even more disturbing, if not outright infuriating, was finding out Kerry had gone against my instructions and was at the store alone. Then I'd had to deal with Jasper coming in with an update on an unrelated case just as I was heading out, so by the time I got in the Expedition, I'd already been wired.

So wired that I pulled my weapon on a man I've come to know over the last few years. My frequent visits to his hardware store for supplies I needed to fix up my house had put us in the friends category. But that tense moment is quickly forgotten when I see Kerry standing, her legs slightly spread and bent, her upper body leaning forward and ready to charge, wielding a toilet brush over her head.

As Bill's chuckle grows louder behind me, I can't hold back anymore and burst out laughing as I pull the ineffective weapon from Kerry's hand. Luckily, she sees the humor of the situation and doesn't even try to hide the grin on her face.

"And here I thought I'd do something nice, bringing you a fresh cup and Annie's banana bread." Bill tries to look remorseful at Kerry and she quickly rushes to his side, apologizing profusely. I bend down to pick up the shards of the coffee cup Bill dropped and the piece of banana bread safely wrapped in foil.

"Here." I shove the foil package at Kerry. "It looks mostly intact." She turns her smiling face to me, and her fingers brush mine as she accepts the salvaged treat. A burst of air blows from my lips at the sudden surge of electricity. I reluctantly let go of the package and therefore Kerry's touch.

Bill breaks the silence by announcing he'd better head back next door and to come get a fresh cup if either of us want one. Kerry mumbles her thanks, but her eyes never leave mine, all humor now gone from her face with only mild curiosity remaining. I don't say a word, barely registering the door closing behind him.

"You came alone," is the first thing that comes out of my mouth, eager to break the trance I find myself in. Smooth. Just how smooth is obvious when a fire lights in those gray orbs.

"I did. And I was fine until you burst through the door," she snaps defensively.

"Because it was Bill," I retort, forcing my point across. "A toilet brush is hardly an effective weapon against a real intruder," I add.

"I was fine," she tries to convince me. "I'm a big

girl. I managed to clean the store, deal with insurance, and have scheduled someone to come in to fix and change the locks this afternoon. I'm not helpless."

The tone of her voice makes it clear this is a sore spot. One I'd love to poke at a little in hopes of learning more about her, but now is not the time.

"Tell me about those papers," I prompt her instead. "Where did you last see them? Are you sure you didn't take them home?"

"On my desk and yes, I'm sure. I left them here on purpose, planning to give you a call today." Some of the edginess is still in her voice, but behind it I can hear a hint of fear. "What's going on, Damian?" she wants to know, too smart for her own good.

I contemplate lying about my concerns, but although they're only suspicions, I'd feel better if Kerry were at least aware. "Honestly, I'm not sure. I suspect the break-in may have had something to do with our investigation. Is there any chance you have the information on the auction house stored somewhere else?"

Her forehead creases in thought before she suddenly pulls her cell from her purse and starts scrolling down the screen. "Here," she says, holding up a finger. "I think I may have saved the profile name and password for their site on my phone. I should be able to access the information under my account on any computer if I have those."

I hold my tongue while she mutters under her breath and searches through her phone. My hand casually tucked in my pocket but with my fingers tightly crossed. Whoever had been in Kerry's office must've recognized the importance of the information on those papers. Why else would they have taken them? My only concern now is that if they alert The Gilded Feather, the records might already be gone from Kerry's account.

"Got it!" she triumphantly yells. "All I need to do is get to my laptop and I can print the stuff off from there."

"Use the browser on your phone," I urge her. She looks at me, puzzled. "Do it now. You can take screenshots," I clarify, trying to convey my sense of urgency. She doesn't say anything to indicate she understands the need for expedience but starts tapping furiously on her phone.

She doesn't even flinch when I close in behind her, peeking over her shoulder. I try to keep a little distance since the smell of her shampoo crawling up my nose is affecting hard-to-hide parts of my body. No need to distract her with my rebellious dick prodding her backside.

The phone in her hand starts making those faux camera sounds, and I hold my breath until she turns around, her chest almost touching mine, and looks up with a pleased grin on her face. "Got it," she repeats, almost breathlessly.

"Good," I whisper back, my mouth already descending to hers.

Too much. Her flushed face, the herb and citrus

infused smell wafting up from her disheveled hair and the excited sparkle in her eyes are just impossible to resist. I almost lose control when her mouth opens under mine and her taste forever spoils my senses.

Almost...

My hand is up under her shirt, skimming the bottom curve of her breast, and the responding sounds from the back of her throat are driving me wild when the loud clearing of a throat cuts through my lustful haze. Kerry blinks, disoriented, when I lift my head, her lips still pursed. I look over my shoulder to find a young guy standing in the doorway, a beat-up old toolbox in his hand. "Yes?" I bite off, surreptitiously removing my hand from under Kerry's shirt where it was still exploring her warm, soft skin.

"I'm sorry to interrupt," the kid says, a ruddy blush covering his face, while his eyes work hard to look anywhere but at the curve of Kerry's breast I had just been stroking. He's only moderately successful, and I can only be grateful I hadn't had a chance yet to rip off her T-shirt. I might've had to resort to murder then. As it is, I spear the kid with a deadly glare and a growl, causing him to opt for staring at the toes of his boots. Good fucking choice.

"I'm supposed to install some new locks?" the little punk asks carefully.

My eyes return to Kerry, who has recovered enough to start pulling down her shirt and smoothing it out. Unfortunately, it only serves to pull her V-neck down to a dangerous level, her breasts about to tumble out the top. Something that doesn't seem to go unnoticed by the kid in the doorway, judging by the deep gulp of air coming from his direction. Instead of turning around and permanently blinding him, I instead grab hold of Kerry's fiddling hands to still her movements, while I use my bulk to shield her.

"You called for locks?" I softly ask her, to which she blinks a few times before giving me a quick nod yes. Trusting she has her jittery hands under control now, I turn back to the guy. "Why don't you start on the front door," I instruct him, needing a minute alone with her.

He obediently backs out of the office but not before risking one last look at Kerry. When I clear my throat, his eyes fly guiltily my way before he hurries out the door. Smart kid. Regrettably, when I focus my attention back on Kerry, it is clear she is once again firmly rooted in the present. The effects of that mind-altering kiss have been rudely shoved aside by her bristly attitude.

KERRY

"What the fuck was that?" I snarl at him, irritated at the ease with which Damian can make me forget to even breathe, while he manages to keep a clear head. Seriously. I don't like feeling out of control, and I'm pretty sure his touch is detrimental to my hard-earned independence. Hence my temper flare.

Still, I'm like the proverbial moth drawn to the flame, and my traitorous eyes zoom in on those lush lips he is lazily licking with the tip of his tongue. Damn that man. I can't even hang on to a good snit.

A deep chuckle shakes me out of my fascination with his mouth and my gaze shoots up to meet his eyes, bright with mirth.

"If I have to explain it, I obviously didn't do a good job. Maybe I should try again," he threatens, stepping back into my body.

In a last attempt at self-preservation before his lips once again suck out every last ounce of common sense, I plant both hands firmly on his chest and shove him back. At least I try to. Unfortunately, he's like a tree; solid and unmovable. Before I have a chance to pull back, his hands are covering mine, pressing them to his chest, effectively imprisoning me.

"Let me go." It's meant as an order but sounds more like a desperate plea. I'm afraid I'm losing the battle when his head bends low. But instead of my mouth, his lips press gently against my forehead.

"Relax," he instructs. "I'm not going to maul you. I'll take you out for dinner first and soften you up. I prefer my women willing," the bastard says on a cocky smile. But I'm not smiling. Those words may work on some, but to me they're like a red flag to a bull. I've been there before, softened up and rendered willing. That didn't turn out so well for me.

He must've sensed my bristles going up because

he rolls his eyes dramatically and sighs. "Kerry—I'm joking. Admittedly, not about you needing to relax or dinner but the rest was just kidding around. Let it go. Please?"

It's the sweet plea combined with the warm look in his eyes that convince me. I'm projecting my own hang-ups on him and that's not fair. Guys say goofy stuff like that all the time and don't mean anything by it.

"Dinner," I say in response, figuring it will get the message across. By the way one corner of his mouth tilts up and his eyes crinkle up, I'd say it worked. "Now...where do I send these screenshots?"

I have to stick around the store for the locksmith to finish up after Damian heads back to his office. A few times I have to apologize for being closed to a couple of customers who wander in, curiously looking around. I guess word of the break-in has gotten around town. Something that is confirmed when the phone rings just as the kid starts packing up his toolkit, his cheeks still flushed every time his eyes skip over me.

"Seriously?" Kim's voice sounds on the other side. "I have to find out from Mrs. Fredericks you had the police over there? The damn woman showed up this afternoon, panting like a racehorse and pissed as hell. Said it was an emergency, she was all out of books and you were closed because of some break-in, so she had to drive in to Cortez to get her fix. She seemed personally affronted, and I didn't dare poke the witch by asking what happened. But I'm asking you: What the hell happened?"

It takes me ten minutes to give her the sequence of events, calming her down. Not quite sure why I choose to keep any mention of Damian from my report. I leave out the FBI investigation altogether. No need to get Kim all worried. Or maybe I'm just not ready to deal with any potential questions until I figure out the answers for myself. And those questions would come. I know Kim well enough, and more importantly, she knows me. She'd surely pick up on something. Her intuition has only enhanced since becoming a mother. It's eerie.

"Damn, girl," Kim mutters sympathetically. "You've had quite the couple of days. I'm guessing you aren't still coming tomorrow?"

"I don't think so. I have to go into the police station tomorrow morning, and I don't know how long I'll be. I'll give you a call after?"

"Sure thing," she easily says. "Let me know what happens."

Just then the blushing kid walks up to the counter and lays down two sets of keys.

"I've gotta go, honey. The locksmith is just leaving."

"No worries. I'll talk to you tomorrow," she quickly replies.

"Tomorrow," I promise before I hang up and turn toward the young man, forgetting all about the box in Kim's possession. Or its contents, still very much a mystery.

CHAPTER 8

"I'M GETTING IMPATIENT, Mr. Sinclair."

The slightly nasal twang of his client is grating on his nerves. Bad enough to have to do business with the uncivilized man, but even worse to have to answer to the buffoon.

"I assure you, sir, that we are in the process of recovering your shipment," he tries diplomatically. Not exactly his strong suit.

"Bullshit. That's what you said last time, but you almost got caught with your hand in the cookie jar. I have a mind to make my own arrangements for retrieving my property."

He winces at the crude profanity and shivers at the thought of his client taking matters into his own hands. He'd most certainly be like the proverbial bull in the china shop with the inevitable all-encompassing fallout that would follow. It would mean the end of their more than lucrative network. No, this situation was still salvageable, it simply required a delicate touch.

"I appreciate your concern, sir, but alternative plans have already been put in action to collect your wares. I implore you to be patient." The plea tastes like cardboard in his mouth and he holds his breath, waiting for a response. It comes seconds later.

"Because the damn Feds are breathing down my fucking neck, I'm giving you one more shot, but this is your last chance. You fuck this up, I'm not pussyfooting around anymore. Seven point three million goddamn dollars you've managed to lose, buddy. And it may not make a huge dent in my bank account, but I didn't get this rich by pissing it away! You've got two weeks."

A click announces his client has hung up. Two weeks. He'd have to speed up his efforts, but that shouldn't be a problem.

He immediately dials a by now familiar number.

"Hey…" Her sultry greeting makes him smile.

So easy—like taking candy from a child.

CHAPTER 9

DAMIAN

"SURE. THAT'LL BE FINE."

Kerry's words are understanding, but I can hear disappointment in her voice. It's both good to hear she may have been looking forward to our dinner, as well as frustrating I can't capitalize on it. I was about to shut down my computer and call to let her know I'd pick her up at seven when another case landed on my desk, requiring my immediate attention. Unfortunately, that meant I had to cancel our dinner plans. Not something I wanted to do given Kerry's reluctance to accept in the first place. Her rather bland answer when I suggest another night sounds too much like she's gearing up for a polite brush-off.

Sometimes I hate my job.

The next twelve hours are spent meeting with local law enforcement officers, digging through piles of case information, and hanging over the opened chest of a body in advanced stages of decomposition at the county morgue. Not exactly the way I imagined my night would be spent.

It isn't until sometime early the next morning that I head home to my place, just north of Hermosa, about twenty or so minutes from my office. After being elbow deep in the underbelly of society all night, I need the peace and tranquility of my house on the edge of the Animas River. Just driving up the narrow, tree-lined road to my place is enough to drain the tension from my neck and shoulders.

I push open the door and find myself listening for the telltale clicking of nails on my wood floors. A welcome homecoming I still haven't gotten used to missing since my dog was killed by a mountain lion last year. I would've gotten a new dog, but with my increasing workload, and more frequent nights spent on a cot at the office, it would hardly be fair to the animal.

Walking through the quiet house, I head straight for the bathroom. I need a quick shower to wash off the stench of death clinging to me. Five minutes later, I'm face-first in my bed, the towel still wrapped around my waist. With my last thought focusing on the blonde gypsy, who seems to have found a permanent place in my head, I finally give in to exhaustion and fall into a deep sleep.

KERRY

"What happened to you?"

The question erupts from my mouth when I look at Marya standing in her doorway. The blush on her face deepens as she is trying hard to keep from smiling. Something sure as hell happened. Marya is always chipper, but as a single mom of three rug rats, she usually looks worn out. It doesn't really surprise me; three young boys, aged six to eleven, would be the absolute death of me. This morning she looks absolutely radiant. The little smirk persistently tugging at her mouth suddenly hits me like a lightning bolt.

"You got laid!" I blurt out, much too loud. Marya erupts in unfamiliar giggles as she slaps her hands over the ears of her youngest, who managed to slip out between her and the doorpost. At the same time, I slap my own hands over my mouth, in a desperate effort to contain any other unfiltered commentary itching to escape.

"Sorry," I repentantly mumble from behind my fingers, but she just throws me a wink, shaking her head. I can't believe it. She never mentioned a thing about seeing someone. "You've been keeping secrets," I scold her, my finger now wagging in front of her face. "And as soon as I get you in my car, you better fess up."

We're supposed to be at the Durango PD offices in less than ten minutes to get our fingers printed, and it's already doubtful we'll make it on time.

I blame it on Damian. After he called to cancel

dinner, which by the way, I'd still had reservations about, I spent the entire night restlessly puttering around my house. My mind twisted in so many different directions, I was giving myself whiplash. Why the cancelled dinner plans left me feeling rejected, when I'd only reluctantly agreed to them, I still can't quite figure. All I know is that the mental game of ping-pong between 'I shouldn't want him' and 'let me at him' was the direct cause of my decision to strip the ugly wallpaper in the bathroom at one o'clock in the morning to shut up the voices. Did I mention it's really ugly? Pink and gold vertical stripes with a border of roses in the same pink as the stripes and muddy-colored leaves.

It'd been an eyesore since I moved in, I just never got around to doing anything to it. Not that it was my decision to make since the place is a rental, but that little bit of wisdom only occurred to me this morning when I stormed into the bathroom in a panic at eight fifteen, only to find myself knee-deep in wallpaper strips.

So yeah—it's all Damian's fault.

In the meantime, Marya has hustled her youngest safely back inside in the hands of the babysitter and follows me to the car. Once buckled up and on the road, I turn to her. "So? Are you gonna tell me anything?"

"Too soon to tell," she evades. "I don't want to get my hopes up. We'll see where it goes, if it goes at all."

"Fair enough," I concede, focusing my eyes back

on the road. That is something I understand, not wanting to share. When you say things out loud, it feels like you're tempting fate to piss in your Cheerios. It doesn't mean I'm not still curious as all get-out, but I'll try to restrain myself. After all, I'm not exactly forthcoming either and have no intention of giving Marya a blow-by-blow of the twists a certain FBI agent has my stomach in.

The rest of the drive to the police station passes in relative quiet, although the ruckus in my head more than makes up for it. By the time I park the car, I'm sick of hearing myself think. I'm frustrated, which despite the thick layer of self-protection I built up, that man managed to scale my walls and burrow under my skin with alarming ease.

"Detective Blackfoot please? We're a little late for a nine o'clock appointment," I tell the stern-looking female officer behind the desk.

"One moment please," she responds friendly enough as she picks up the phone.

A few minutes later, the familiar form of Keith Blackfoot comes around the corner. After holding my hand in greeting a little too long for comfort, I quickly introduce the detective to Marya, who is looking at me bemused with an eyebrow slightly raised. When Blackfoot turns to lead us down the hallway, I give her a sharp shake of my head. It unfortunately doesn't stop her from commenting. "Where do all these beautiful men suddenly come from? If I'd known a little B&E would drum up all the hotties in Durango,

I'd have orchestrated one myself long ago," she stage-whispers.

The detective pushes open a door at the end of the hallway and ushers us inside of what looks to be a boardroom but not before turning to me with a barely contained grin and a wink. Apparently Marya's voice carries.

I've never had my fingerprints taken before, and I'd been kind of looking forward to rolling my ink-covered digits over a pristine white card, like you see in the movies. The scanner Blackfoot leads us to is a bit of a disappointment. The image of my fingerprints is digitally stored so I can't even see them. Marya seems equally bummed. The whole thing is rather anti-climactic.

I tug my purse back over my shoulder and make for the door, thinking I'd have time to indulge in a Starbucks coffee and scone before I open the store, when the detective steps in my path. "We still have your statement to go over," he reminds me.

"I have to open the store," I protest half-heartedly, already knowing there really is no way out of this.

"I'll do it. I just need the new keys," Marya, the traitor, chirps with a smile. She pointedly ignores my glare as she sticks out her hand, palm up.

"You don't have a car," I throw out in a last ditch attempt, which is immediately foiled by the large, smirking man in the doorway.

"One of my officers will give her a ride," he says, as he motions at someone down the hall.

Blackfoot shuts the door behind my smiling assistant being escorted down the hall by a policeman, who looks young enough to be one of her kids. The detective pulls out a chair in a silent invitation for me to sit down at the long table. I spend the next hour and a half going over the events of two nights ago and hand my phone to the detective with the screenshots I'd taken yesterday. He patiently adds them to the list of items and only raised his eyebrow when I mention I'd already printed out that information once, prior to the break-in, but that those printouts where missing along with the computer.

I pass on the offer of the suspicious black, tarry, liquid substance doubling as coffee, and by the time I put my John Hancock on the updated statement, my brain has been stretched to its limits without the benefit of caffeine. It's almost noon and I need a fix, stat.

"If anything else comes to mind," the detective says, his hand in the small of my back as he leads me out of the door, "don't hesitate to call me right away."

"Just that I didn't have that last shipment of books yet. The second order from The Gilded Feather? You probably shouldn't include it as missing," I point out.

"I'll make a note," he says. "Just give me a call when it arrives?"

My mind is fuzzy from lack of nourishment, and I simply nod. I'd rushed out the door without breakfast, and I am in dire need of coffee and sustenance, in that order. My head is drooping, so I don't register the broad, looming shape leaning against the front desk at first. But Keith Blackfoot does, as evident from the arm draped over my shoulder without warning. When my eyes flick up at the sudden move, they collide with a set of dark, smoldering ones in an all-too-familiar face. If eyes could kill, the look Damian throws the detective would surely have him torn limb from limb, but the look he points at me is pure heat.

"I guess I didn't make myself sufficiently clear," Damian grinds out at the man, who still has a firm grip on my shoulder. His lips don't even move. Feeling like a prized chew toy between two rabid dogs, I attempt to sidestep Blackfoot's hold.

"I'd best be off," I mutter, hoping to avoid bloodshed as I move toward the exit. "Things to do." I wave my hand in a feeble goodbye and rush through the door.

I get as far as opening my car door and am getting in when I hear footsteps rushing up.

"Gypsy."

I drop my forehead to the steering wheel. Escape foiled. When I look up, Damian's holding open my door and leaning in. His face is only inches from mine. "Why are you running?"

"I'm starving," is my weak response. I don't want to tell him the tension got so thick in there I could barely breathe. The instant his hand closes on my upper arm and starts tugging me out of my car, I realize my mistake. Not sure whether he took my words as a veiled invitation, or whether his caveman instincts to protect and provide kicked in, but before I know it, he has me strapped into the passenger seat of the black Expedition parked next to my car and is driving off.

"Hey," I protest, twisting my body in the seat. "Where are you taking me?"

He barely looks at me before his eyes lock back on the road. "You're hungry. I'm getting you food."

Definitely going with the caveman instincts on this one.

Opting to ignore the fact I've been manhandled and virtually kidnapped, I change directions. "What were you doing at the police station anyway?"

DAMIAN

I've had only a few hours of sleep when my phone rings.

"Gomez," I mumble, rubbing the sleep from my eyes.

"Hey," my sister replies. "I wake you up? Sorry. Just wanted to let you know I'm hitting the road but I'm heading straight for the hospital. They left a message my interview was bumped to eleven so I'll pick up the key after."

I'm already out of bed and moving toward the bathroom. "Okay. If I'm not there, I'll leave it at the front desk. See you soon."

A glance at my phone shows me it's only ten, and when I look up in the mirror, the measly three or so hours of sleep are evident on my face. A nice long shower makes me feel half-human again, and with the first sip of my coffee, my brain kicks in.

Dammit. I just popped a bagel in the toaster when I remember Kerry mentioning something about the police station at nine. Instead of sitting down to breakfast, I end up rushing to get dressed. I don't trust Blackfoot alone with her for one second, let alone the entire morning.

By the time I'm dressed and getting in behind the wheel, it's already eleven, my long-forgotten coffee getting cold on the kitchen counter and my growling stomach a worry for later. I call into the office as I pull out of my driveway to check in with Luna, who assures me all is under control.

Given how late it has gotten by the time I finally hit Durango, I figure I should probably hit the office first to drop off the key for Bella. But when I pass by the bookstore on the way, I notice the 'Open' sign on the door and swing my wheel around into the parking lot. Looks like Kerry's back.

"You're the FBI agent," the short brunette I saw once before points out when I push open the door.

"Damian Gomez," I introduce myself. "And you're Marya. Kerry's told me about you. Is she in?" I ask as I scan the shelves for a sign of her.

"Actually, no. She's holed up with that hunk of a detective at the police station. Something about going over her statement?" The woman doesn't even notice I'm already moving toward the exit until the little bell at the top of the door alerts her when I pull it open. "Feel free to wait here," she calls out. "I'm sure she won't be too much longer. It's been hours already."

Ignoring her invitation, I lift my hand in goodbye and jump behind the wheel, urgency settling like a stone at the bottom of my stomach. Until I spot her coming down the hall of the police station with that bastard's arm tucked cozily around her shoulders. Then the urgency is replaced with an involuntary and barely controlled rage. I'm sick and tired of Keith Blackfoot pushing my buttons every turn I make, and I don't trust him not to take it too far with her. I've been accused of being too straitlaced, too unflappable, and stirring me up seems to be high on the man's agenda these days. Asshole.

I'm so focused on cutting Blackfoot to size with my death glare, I only notice Kerry has vacated the scene when I hear the exit door slam shut behind me. "Don't fucking move," I grind out at the smugly grinning son of a bitch I once considered a friend, before tearing off after her.

Still seething inside, I barely hear her question as I speed through historic Durango, ignoring every stop sign on my way to CJ's Diner: Durango's best place for all-day breakfast. "What was that?" I ask her distractedly, swerving around another typical tourist driver taking in the sights through the windshield of his Toyota Camry.

"Why were you at the police station?" she repeats as I pull into the diner's parking lot.

"Dropping off some information," I lie. I'm not about to confess the thought of her in the claws of Blackfoot had me racing over there. I don't wait for a response and am out my door, round the front, and open hers before she has a chance to react.

"I don't like eggs," she says when a waitress shows us to a table for two and leaves behind a couple of menus.

"Say what?"

"I don't eat eggs," she repeats. "Not in their natural form."

I must've looked confused because she goes on to clarify, "I like omelets, though. And pancakes. They have pancakes, right?"

"Omelets are eggs. And pancakes have eggs in them, too," I point out. The waitress comes back with two coffees and patiently waits for our order. "I'm afraid we might be a while," I apologize to her, ignoring Kerry's eye roll.

"Yes, they do," Kerry confirms. "But then they're mixed with other things that I do like. Mushrooms, cheese, ham…"

I cut off her explanation and turn to the waitress. "I'll have three eggs over easy, bacon, hash browns and white toast. She'll have a mushroom, cheese and ham omelet. Thank you." I grab the menu from Kerry's hand and give both of them back to the girl. My stomach is growling at the smells from the grill and needs quieting.

"Rude," Kerry finally says after throwing angry daggers with her eyes.

"Hungry," is my retort. "I'd really like them to get a start on our food before we waste away. You were about to launch into a detailed description of all the food items you enjoy, and I made a judgment call."

"Well, what if I wanted pancakes?" she huffs indignantly.

"I'll cook you pancakes for breakfast."

Her eyes pop open at the implication I leave hanging thickly in the air. The first grin of the day works its way onto my face at the sight. She's cute. Sure, she's ornery, contrary, stubborn, and has peculiar tastes, however she's also sharp, refreshing, beautiful, and unique. Still, mostly she's cute.

I'm about to tell her that when my phone buzzes in my pocket. A quick glance tells me it's the office calling, so I lift a finger in apology before answering the call.

"Where are you?" my sister's voice whines.

"Shit," I spit out, having completely forgotten about the spare house key still in my pocket. "Sorry, Bella. I got held up, honey." I look at Kerry to find her head slightly tilted and one eyebrow raised in question. The tight line of her mouth a clear indication she is not happy. I cover the mouthpiece with my hand. "I won't be a minute," I promise Kerry as I get up and head to the men's room for some quiet.

By the time I've convinced my sister to grab some

lunch while I 'finish up what I'm doing' and exit the bathroom, our table is empty. Kerry's gone.

"She said something urgent came up and took her omelet to go," the waitress says from behind me. I turn to find her handing me my food and the bill. "She told me to keep yours warm and you'd pay." The girl shrugs her shoulders apologetically as I take the plate and the receipt and sit down dejectedly.

I can't seem to catch a break.

CHAPTER 10

KERRY

IT'S BEEN ALMOST A week since I hightailed it out of CJ's Diner which, by the way, serves the best omelet around. My desperate stomach wouldn't allow me to leave the food behind, so I had them pack it up and I speed walked, Styrofoam container in hand, back to the downtown core to snatch a cab. By the time I'd picked up my car at the police station and made my way to the bookstore, the food had been cold, but still it was the best-tasting damn omelet I've had.

Since then, nothing but silence. Good thing, too, because Special Agent Gomez is far too irresistible and resist I must.

I work hard at convincing myself I'm lucky I dodged the bullet. I'm not about to become another notch on his clearly crowded bedpost. So why is it then that the fact he hasn't even tried to contact me is bugging me so much? It only confirms he wasn't worth my time in the first place. Sure, he's hot and his touch on my skin is like striking a match, but I refuse to let my judgment be clouded by that. Even though thinking about his lips on mine, remembering the feel of his hands skimming my body, has me in a perpetual state of craving. Damn him.

And damn Marya, too. She's not making it easier, walking around the shop every day with that damn healthy blush on her cheeks and a smile that threatens to split her face. It doesn't take a genius to see she's getting some, and getting it regularly these days, even though she insists she's taking things slow. Other than that his name is Trevor, she hasn't shared much. Says she doesn't want to get ahead of herself, in case things go south. She may be onto something, because what self-respecting man goes through life calling himself Trevor? It may be because I knew a Trevor once. It was in high school and the guy was a pretentious twat. Every time I hear that name, I'm reminded of the creepy kid who hung around the girls' locker room to catch a glimpse and then went and told his buddies. A rich kid with questionable morals, that's what that name sounds like to me.

Argh! I'm being snarky. And immature.

I slam the mug I'm holding down on the counter, sloshing hot coffee all over my hand.

"Fucking hell!" I can't help the curse flying from my lips.

"What is wrong with you?" Marya comes flying from the back of the store, where she was helping a customer. Said customer hesitantly follows behind but lingers between the shelves, looking worriedly in my direction. "Are you PMSing or something? Go home. Have a nap. Do something instead of moping around here, glaring at customers. At the rate you're scaring off customers, we'll be out of business by next month."

I'm in shock. Both that my usually good-natured employee and friend just tore a strip off me and that my current bout of self-pity has reached the crying point. For cripes' sake, I have fat tears spilling over my cheeks and I swear my bottom lip is quivering. I'm a pathetic disaster.

Not sure whether it was Marya's outburst or my emotional breakdown, but from the corner of my eye, I can see the customer sidling stealthily toward the exit. Another one run off.

"I'm sorry," Marya sounds contrite as she steps close and pulls me into a hug. "I shouldn't have said that."

"Don't be. You're ri-ight," I hiccup through my tears. "I've been a drag. Maybe it's hormonal, although I hope to God I'm not one of those women who hits early menopause way before their time. That would seriously suck."

"I doubt that," she says, patting me on the back. "It's just been a chaotic week, scrambling to recover all the information that disappeared, along with the damn computer, and trying to set up the new one. Maybe you just need a day off. An entire day to decompress. Get a haircut or go hiking; do something fun. Go out for a nice meal or have a few drinks at a bar. Take a break—it's obvious you need one."

She's right. I give myself a mental shake and straighten my shoulders. "Maybe I'll head to Cortez tomorrow. Pick up that box from Kim and get some cuddle time in with her boy, Asher," I muse out loud, the prospect of a visit with my best friend taking shape in my head. I have to remember to call Detective Blackfoot as promised when I have the box.

"Good plan," Marya concedes. "Mom's got my kids tonight anyway. I'm sure she won't mind keeping them for the day tomorrow."

"Are you sure?"

"Positive," she confirms. "Go. Get out of here. I don't want to see or hear from you until the day after tomorrow." With a gentle push, she shoves me toward the door.

I'm not sure how long it's been since I've taken a bath. I'm usually on the fly and resort to quick showers, but I have to admit; lounging in the tub, surrounded with bubbles, goes a long way to easing the tension from my body.

Dressed for comfort in my favorite pair of ratty jeans and a loose-fitting peasant blouse, I finish drying my hair and slip on a pair of old flip-flops. The perfect attire for a balmy June evening.

In a much better mood, I drive down the mountain

and head into town, looking for a place to grab a quick bite. I already spoke with Kim earlier, and she's as excited about my visit tomorrow as I am. I pull into a vacant parking spot across from the Strater Hotel on Main Street and spot the sign for the Diamond Belle Saloon on the corner. The Strater has two restaurants on the main floor, but I've only eaten once at the Mahogany Grille. The Diamond Belle always seemed so cheesy to me, with the waitresses in corsets and feathers, reminiscent of a different era. It had always struck me as a typical tourist place and like any self-respecting Durangoan, I'd avoided it. Until now. For some reason, the honky-tonk piano sounds drifting onto the customarily busy sidewalk draws me in.

The pretty girl in the emerald green strapless dress doesn't even blink at my ultra casual attire and with a smile leads me to a table for two next to a small stage. On it stands an old upright piano with an arguably even older gentleman behind it, pounding the keys in a honky-tonk rendition of Billy Joel's "Piano Man" with great enthusiasm. When I sit down, he glances over and winks. I smile back, glad I decided to wander in. The atmosphere in the place is light and fun, with a huge variety of diners; from a group of lilac-haired seniors to a pair of leather-covered bikers and just about everything in between.

The waitress returns with a glass of ice water and a menu, and it doesn't take me long to make my selection. I order the pot roast, craving something wholesome, and as a splurge, I add a Patrón margarita, which is on special. I'm already halfway through my yummy drink when a huge plate, piled high with fluffy mashed potatoes and slices of succulent beef, is slid in front of me. With big eyes, I look up at the waitress.

"That's enough for a family of four!" I blurt out, and she giggles.

"I know," she says before leaning in and whispering conspiratorially, "but it makes for great leftovers."

With a feeling of well-being—a result of the relaxed vibe and the help of my delicious cocktail—I dig into dinner, barely able to contain the appreciative moans that want to escape. It takes everything in me to stop shoveling the delicious food down my gullet. My stomach's already full to bursting, and I quickly wave over my server.

"Could you box this up before I eat myself sick? And I'll take the check, too."

"Sure thing," she replies. "Just give me a minute."

As promised, she returns with the white Styrofoam container and my bill promptly. I leave her a generous tip and pull out my chair. The pianist launches into the familiar chords of Scott Joplin's "The Entertainer" just as I tuck a bill into his tip glass, when movement on the other side of the small stage catches my eye. A familiar broad back is turned toward me, and I feel the hair on my arms stand up as I watch Damian with a voluptuous dark-haired beauty. He's moving toward the exit to the hotel lobby, tucks the woman under his arm and smiles at her as if she hung the moon. The gorgeous meal I just enjoyed is turning sour in my stomach as I hear him laugh with her.

I don't realize I've been staring until the waitress touches my arm, and I swivel around. "Are you okay?" she asks concerned. Swallowing hard, I attempt a smile and simply nod. I turn and with my head down, I weave through the tables to the door. When I risk a quick peek behind me, it's clear Damian has spotted me. His dark eyes zoomed in on me, he eats up the distance with his long strides. Determined to avoid any kind of confrontation, I rush through the door, and without looking properly, I cross Main Street.

Next thing I know, I hear my name called, car horns are honking, and I'm suddenly airborne.

DAMIAN

"Are you okay?"

It's not the first time my sister asks. I haven't been able to shake my foul mood since she got here last week. It doesn't have anything to do with her. At least not all of it.

After her excitement over the successful interview at the Mercy Regional Medical Center last week had worn off, she mentioned Philip Presley, her asswipe ex, had resurfaced and came knocking on her door a few days prior. Apparently one of his sexual harassment victims had decided to charge him with sexual assault. He sought out Bella—after disappearing six months ago without a word—in hopes she might be willing to provide him with an alibi. For old times' sake, he'd said. Bella slammed the door in his face, but he wasn't letting up, and she needed a break. Of course, I was ready to jump in my truck, drive to Farmington, and deal with the slimy weasel, but she held me back.

She's been staying with me since, even though I've hardly had time to hang out with her. A couple of investigations simmering on the back burner heated up simultaneously and have kept me tied up at the office most of the week. The stress is getting to me.

The bulk of my miserable attitude, however, has everything to do with Kerry. I was almost going to chase after her when she up and left the diner without a word, but I didn't. It seemed, at the time, perhaps the universe was trying to let me know this relationship business was not for me after all. Something I'd been quite sure of until the first time I walked into her bookstore. So I tried to tell myself it was for the best, but that didn't last more than the time it took me to drive to my office and meet up with Bella. By that time, I already regretted letting her go so easily. I didn't want to call, though, I figured clearing the air with her would be better done in person. There just hasn't been time—at least not enough. That's what's been eating at me mostly, and the more time passes, the more difficult it becomes.

"No," I tell Bella honestly, which clearly surprises her since I've been lying all week. I finally managed to get home early tonight, and we were just figuring out what to do for dinner when she asks me. "I'm not fine. I'm angry at that son of a bitch ex of yours, I'm stressed with my workload taking up all my time, and I'm frustrated I haven't had a chance to fix a mistake I made."

Bella's eyebrow shoots up. "Mistake?" she echoes, but I just look at her. After a brief pause during which she regards me through slitted eyes, her face finally clears with understanding. "Gotta be a woman," she astutely observes. "What did she do?" I chuckle at her automatic assumption the fault was Kerry's and not mine. Bella and I have always been close and very protective of each other. I have three other sisters, but they are all married and have families. Bella and I have always been the odd ones out, although Bella came close to breaking ranks with that douchebag, Philip. She was actually living with him. I've never been tempted to take it even that far with a woman. Not yet.

"She didn't do anything but draw the wrong conclusions. Something I could have easily rectified but didn't." Knowing she'd drag the full story out of me eventually anyway, I saved us some time and told her about Kerry. How we met the first time a couple of years ago when she was still married. That I was pumped when I bumped into her again in her bookstore and discovered she was now single. Bella doesn't say much, she just listens as I describe the course of events over the last couple of weeks, up until my phone ringing at the diner.

"You did what?" she finally interjects when I mention accepting her phone call and looking for some privacy. "Are you nuts? How would you like it if she got a call in the middle of a date, said 'Hi, Fabio, honey!' before disappearing into the ladies' room so she could talk in private?"

"Fabio?" I chuckle.

"Christ, Damian—for a reportedly intelligent man, you sure can be teenage-boy stupid sometimes." Bella props her hands on her hips and glares at me.

She's right. I'd probably have ripped the phone from her ear and demanded to know who the fuck he was, talking to my woman. Idiot. I should've gone after her and set this straight right away. Yes, she's the one who ran without giving me a chance to explain, but given her week to that point, and her earlier witness to my phone call with Cora, I can't really blame her. "I'm thinking I may have fucked things up before we ever even started," I admit to my sister.

"Nah," she says, her face softening. "Just be yourself: in your face, brutally direct, painfully honest, and..." she pauses for effect, "...irresistibly handsome. You should go see her now." I hook her around the neck and give her a noogie with the knuckles of my other hand.

"Thanks for the vote of confidence, brat, but I'm tired, hungry enough to eat a horse, and eager to spend some time with my favorite sister. Tomorrow, when I've had some decent sleep and am not crotchety like an old bear, I'll see what I can do."

I grab my car keys from the counter, grab Bella's hand, and drag her to the door. "Come on, sis. Let me show you the Durango bustling nightlife."

One of my guilty pleasures since moving to Durango permanently is listening to old Clive play the piano. The man is at least eighty years old and his body is twisted with arthritis, but his gnarly fingers still manage to draw the sweetest jazz and ragtime notes from the old piano at the Diamond Belle Saloon. Not exactly my youngest sister's style, who is more into contemporary pop, but I figure it won't hurt to try to convert her to the more ear-friendly classic melodies Clive masters.

"Seriously?" Bella skeptically eyes the dated interior before looking at me. "It looks like Durango's senior citizens have all come out to play," she hisses under her breath. "Do they cart them in by the truckload?"

I elbow her playfully in the ribs to shut her up when one of the scantily dressed servers greets us just inside the door. "Is the booth on the far side of the stage available?" I ask her. It's my favorite spot in the restaurant; a corner booth, out of the way, giving me the privacy to observe the entire place while still close to the music.

As luck would have it, nobody's snatched it up yet, despite the fact they have a decent crowd here tonight. Clive spots me and gives me a wave, and when I have Bella seated in the booth, I excuse myself to go have a brief chat.

"Tell me she's your sister," he stage-whispers when I walk up. "I might have to fight you for her otherwise, but I'm not liking my chances."

I throw my head back and laugh heartily. The old charmer never passes up an opportunity to flirt with any and every female that walks into the joint. "Rest easy, Clive. That actually is my sister. My baby sister needs to be shown the light, she is rather narrow-minded when it comes to her pop music, and I come to you in hopes you can guide her way."

This time it's Clive cackling his dry chuckle. "Sure thing, my friend. I've worked on a few alternative arrangements for some recent hits. I'll bring them all out in full force tonight. Let's see if we can't convert that delicious creature." He leans back so he can look around me and throws Bella a suggestive wink. I just shake my head and move back to the table where Bella is staring at me, her mouth open in disbelief.

"Did that old relic just flirt with me?"

"Don't let it get to your head. He flirts with everyone sporting the right equipment. Ignore him and concentrate on what you want for dinner."

It doesn't take long for the food to get here once we order. I'm getting a kick out of watching Bella's reaction when she recognizes some of the songs Clive plays while we eat.

"He's really good," she mumbles around a bite of her San Juan burger.

"Told ya," I smugly fire back, ignoring the stink eye she's shooting my way. I love the easy ribbing we get into. Bella makes me forget the weight of responsibilities resting on my shoulders.

We talk a little about the options she has for housing, and I promise her I'll help her cart her stuff from Farmington when she finds a place. In the meantime, I assure her she's welcome to stay with me as long as she likes.

I'm about to show Bella the historic Strater Hotel lobby and we head in that direction, when the first notes of "The Entertainer" hit my ears. I turn my head around to smile at Clive, who knows that's my favorite piece, and resume moving toward the lobby, throwing my arm around Bella.

"Fine," she concedes with a scowl. "I'll admit I enjoyed that." I burst out laughing at her reluctant admission.

I'm not sure what causes me to turn around, but my eyes zoom in on a flurry of movement toward the front door. I'm shocked to recognize Kerry's unmistakable shape darting around a table, and I automatically start moving in her direction, leaving Bella standing there. Kerry throws a look over her shoulder when she gets to the door, and I know she sees me coming when her eyes widen, but it doesn't stop her. Pulling the door open, she slips through before I can catch her.

She's just stepping into the street when I make it outside. I break into a run while calling her name. That's when I hear loud honking and the squeal of tires, and without thinking I launch myself forward, make a grab for Kerry, and roll with her in my arms out of the way of an oncoming car.

"Jesus, woman!" I bark in frustration, my back sore from the impact with the asphalt. I feel her body start to shake and I sit up, taking her with me and pulling her on my lap so I can check her out. "Are you okay?"

Kerry is blinking furiously at the tears filling her eyes, but her chin lifts up stubbornly. "I'm fine," she says, struggling to get up off my lap. I try to hold her down, but when the driver runs up from where his car is pulled off to the side to check on us, I reluctantly let her go.

"God, you gave me a scare. Everyone all right? Anyone hurt?" The poor guy looks worried.

"I'm fine," Kerry repeats to him as she straightens up. "I'm sorry, I…"

"We're good," I cut her off while getting to my feet, directing my words to the man who is nervously wringing his hands. "Sorry for giving you such a scare, and thanks for checking on us."

"Well, if you're sure," he asks, looking at his car and then back to us, making it clear he wants the hell out of here.

"Positive," I confirm, adding a smile and a firm nod.

I'm aware of Kerry brushing off her clothes as the guy scurries back to his car, and am about to confront her, when I hear my name called from the other side of the street.

"Damian!"

Bella manages to cross the street without incident and immediately walks up, buries her head in my chest, and wraps her arms tightly around my waist.

"We're fine, Bella," I tell my sister, pressing a kiss to her head. "Kerry, this is…" I turn my eyes to her and watch as she forces a pained smile on her face.

"I've got to go," she mutters, already reaching behind her for the car door. "Sorry for the…for this."

Bella pinches my waist, which spurs me into action. "Wait." She's already slipping behind the wheel when I catch the top of the door and keep her from shutting it on me. "Gypsy," I growl, leaning into the car. "Fucking stop running from me."

The stubborn minx keeps her eyes fixed straight ahead, staring at nothing through the windshield, but I can see her chin wobble.

"What I was saying before you tried to escape, I'd like you to meet my baby sister, Bella." I throw a quick look over my shoulder to find Bella right behind me, an understanding smile on her face.

"Hi, Kerry," she says to the woman looking up at her with eyes as big as saucers. "Damian's told me all about you."

The chin wobble on her face grows more pronounced, and Kerry's resorted to chewing her bottom lip. Without hesitation, I shove my sister out of the way and duck back inside the car, running the back of my fingers over Kerry's soft cheek.

"Don't cry," I say gently, and as if turning on a tap, her eyes immediately fill and spill over.

"I'm not," she snaps, wiping agitatedly at her eyes. "I'm just a little shaken up."

"Maybe you shouldn't drive then," is my rather curt response. She glares at me from the corner of her eyes, and I raise my hands defensively, softening my tone. "What I'm trying to say is let me take you home. It'd make me feel better, and besides, I think we need to have a talk."

"I'm okay," she insists. "I can drive myself home. I just want to crawl into bed."

The mention of her in bed does unspeakable things to my body. Unspeakable in the presence of my baby sister, that is. I'd almost forgotten about her. "Okay," I concede, knowing better than to force the issue when she obviously feels a bit brittle. "But I'm coming over tomorrow, and we're gonna clear the air."

She flicks her eyes at me, and the hint of a smile tugs at the corner of her mouth. "Can't," she declines. "I'll be in Cortez tomorrow. Likely won't be home until late."

"Doesn't matter. Give me a call when you get in. I don't care what time." Leaning in, I shock her by giving her an innocent peck on the cheek. "Drive safe," I caution her before I back up and close the door.

Bella steps up beside me as we watch Kerry pull away from the curb.

"Oh yeah…" she smiles, never taking her eyes off the disappearing taillights. "You're so gone for that one."

I don't bother arguing.

CHAPTER 11

KERRY

"NO, YOU CAN'T TAKE him with you!"

I chuckle at Kim's disgruntled protests when I get in the car, still holding the warm squirmy little body of Asher, who has been safely snuggled in my arms all afternoon. I love that little boy.

I once wanted children of my own, but after a few years of trying early on in my marriage, I resigned myself to the fact motherhood was not in my future. Until the waning days of my marriage, when in a blowout shouting match with Greg, he let it slip that he'd had a vasectomy before we even got married. After years of trying to get him to consider fertility treatments, or change his rigid views on adoption, that had been the ultimate betrayal.

Any maternal instincts I might have are momentarily satisfied each time I get my hands on this little boy. I take what I can get. Which is why I nuzzle Asher's little neck, and breathe in his baby scent for a last fix, before reluctantly handing him over to his mother.

"Sorry, Asher," I mumble with my lips against the palm of his pudgy little hand. "Your momma is a greedy bitch."

"Kerry! Don't swear in front of the baby," Kim scolds me through the open window, pressing Asher's ear against her chest, her hand covering the other. I roll my eyes as I plug my phone into the hands-free system—it's not like the little guy understands what I'm saying.

The afternoon was a good one. Kim had taken the day off and was waiting with a fabulous lunch that included muffins from my favorite coffee shop in town. By the time Asher woke up from his nap, we were ready to walk off the copious amounts of food we'd just scarfed down. So with Asher strapped in a carrier on her back, Kim and I headed out for a hike on the mesa; Kim's gigantic dog, Boo, turning circles around our legs. We walked for miles through the sage grass and down the canyon; we ended up at the edge of a creek, where Asher played under our watchful eyes and we had time to catch up on all the goings-on in our respective lives. By the time we got back home, it was late afternoon and the baby was ready for his dinner. Kim's husband, Mal, called to say he was held up with work, so she and I resorted to finishing this afternoon's leftovers, neither of us very hungry. I wanted to try and get back to Durango before dark and was already in the driveway when Kim remembered the box. She handed me Asher while she ran back in to get her keys. While I was contemplating taking the gurgling little boy and running, she transferred the box from her car to mine, apologizing profusely for the fact she kept forgetting to open it. Something I'll do the moment I get home.

"Love you," I yell as I back my car out of her driveway. I watch her in my rearview mirror, holding Asher's little hand and waving as I drive away.

After filling up and grabbing a coffee to keep me awake at a gas station, I head back to Durango. With my visor flipped down to block the low-hanging evening sun, I belt along with Peter Gabriel's "In Your Eyes." I love this drive. Love how the sparse but stunning landscape of the mesas and canyons morph into the lush, majestic swells of the Rockies. I wouldn't want to live anywhere else.

The sun has slowly set behind the mountains, and I keep my eyes peeled against the waning light for any wildlife along the side of the road. This time of night often sees deer or elk coming up from the valleys to dart across the highway. I've had one or two close encounters on this stretch before. Just as I'm coming up to the cutoff to Hesperus, the interior of my car brightens with the glare of headlights right behind me. I can't see much in my rearview mirror other than a grill and headlights. I'm guessing it's either a truck or SUV, something that is clearly higher up than my

Subaru. Almost everyone here drives big vehicles, so that's not a shock. What is, though, is the fact the damn thing is way too close to my tail for comfort. Almost on top of me.

In an attempt to get out of his way, I let up on the gas and inch my way toward a widened section of the shoulder, keeping a close eye on the far edge, where the road gives way to a sharp drop to the valley below. A quick glance in my rearview mirror shows the damn truck still riding my ass. In fact, it appears to be following me to the side of the road. Suddenly, my irritation is replaced with fear. It's almost dark, traffic is sparse, and I don't know what the hell this guy wants. My hand automatically reaches for my phone as I slow to a stop, the truck still behind me. I keep my eye on him in the rearview mirror as I hit 911 on the phone.

"Nine-one-one. What's your emergency?"

"Yes, hi," I respond sheepishly when the dispatcher picks up my call. "My name is Kerry Emerson, and I'm sitting on the side of Highway 160 to Durango, just west of the cut off to Hesperus. There's a truck that was riding my tail and pulled up right behind me when I pulled off to let him pass. I'm getting scared."

"Ma'am. Are your doors locked?"

"Yes," I confirm with a shaky voice.

"I'm dispatching State Patrol on the other line as we speak, hon. Stay calm. Can you give a description of the truck?"

I watch as suddenly the vehicle behind me starts

backing up, and I let out a sigh of relief.

"Ma'am? Are you there?"

"Yes. Sorry, he just backed up."

No sooner have the words left my mouth when the squeal of tires on gravel has my head snap around. It only takes a nanosecond for me to recognize the truck barreling toward me.

"Ma'am? Ma'am...?"

I barely hear the voice of the dispatcher while I watch in horror as the truck tries to swerve around me at the last second. The rest plays in slow motion. I hear the loud honking of a transport truck coming up from behind. I see the smaller truck swerve to avoid a collision. And I can feel the impact as it sideswipes the front end of my car, sending the Subaru spinning toward the edge of the road. I think I'm screaming as my car moves out of control, and I see flashes of the deep drop into the valley.

When the car finally stills, I can hear the woman on the phone still calling out.

"I think I'm okay," I manage to squeak out. I'm hyperventilating and my heart is going a mile a minute. "I think I'm okay," I repeat, as if I can make it so just by saying it again. The front of my car is pointing perpendicular to the road. I watch through the windshield as the driver of the big transport truck parked a little down the road comes walking around his rig and stops in his tracks. He suddenly starts running in this direction as the dispatcher starts talking.

"Don't move," she instructs me. "State Patrol will be there soon."

I just manage to answer her with, "Okay," when a metal groaning sound shudders through the frame of the car.

"Not okay!" I scream when the approaching driver suddenly disappears from view and instead I find myself staring at the stars.

DAMIAN

I hear it on the scanner.

I don't why I know it's her, but I do.

"—10-54, Highway 160 west of the 140 exit in easterly direction. Requesting 10-52. Watch for suspect or suspects last seen heading west in a black or dark green newer model extended cab—"

That's all I hear when I walk into my office. But it's enough.

I've been struggling with an unexplained feeling of impending doom ever since I watched Kerry run blindly across Main Street last night. My heart pounding in my throat, I snatch my phone from my desk where I left it. I notice my hand shaking as I scroll through my contact list to find her number. My jaw locks with tension as I mindlessly count the number of rings. Finally, after seven, her voicemail kicks in.

"Hi. You've reached Kerry. Leave me a message and I'll get back to you." The recording is simple, no nonsense and to the point, just like the woman herself. As I tuck the phone in my pocket without leaving a message, I pause a moment, wondering if it is the last time I will hear her voice.

With a sharp shake of my head to dislodge the fatalistic thoughts that paralyze me, I finally get my feet to move out the door. I ignore Jasper's call behind me as I storm out of the office and head for my Expedition. In the distance, I can hear the sound of the ambulance sirens on their way out of town and guessing their destination, I climb behind the wheel, slap my portable siren on the roof, and speed off to catch up.

Against the darkening night, the flashing blue lights of emergency vehicles are a clear beacon. The road is closed by two State Patrol cars, but the ambulance in front of me easily swerves around. I follow suit and stick my hand holding my badge out the window for the officer standing guard to see. He waves me through, too.

All I can see is a large semi parked on the side of the road and beyond it a fire truck and more patrol cars. Three State Patrol and one Durango PD. The ambulance moves around the tractor trailer, and I pull my vehicle in on this side of the big rig. I'm already half out the door by the time it rolls to a stop. I take off on a run, rounding the trailer, my eyes already scanning the scene for Kerry's Subaru. It's not there.

With the ambulance blocking part of my view, I move to the edge of the shoulder so I can look behind it, seeing only a group of officers and a big burly man in a baseball cap standing on the edge of the drop. One of them is shining a flashlight down the mountain.

My breath catches in my throat when I follow the path of the beam and catch the shimmer of metal. There, nearly thirty feet below, crumpled against an outcropping of rocks, are the mangled remains of Kerry's car. A trickle of smoke curls up from under the distorted hood, but that is the only movement I can see.

"Gomez!"

My head snaps up at the sound of my name, and I see a familiar figure trotting my way.

"How did you...?"

"Scanner." I answer his half-finished question, surprised I'm even able to utter that single word. My eyes wander back to the wreckage below.

"Hey, man," Keith Blackfoot says, clapping his hand on my shoulder. "It could've been worse."

Anger, hot and instant, burns under my skin as I swing around, my fist already flying at his face. His big hand is lightning fast and catches my wrist in midair.

"What the fuck, Damian? The hell is the matter with you? I thought you'd like to know she only has some scrapes and bruises," he snarls. Confusion must've been clear on my face because he adds in a gentler voice, "The EMTs are checking her out, brother. She's fine."

I look over his shoulder and see two EMTs leading a small figure, wrapped in a blanket, from the back of a patrol car to the doors of the waiting ambulance. I quickly glance back at Keith, whose expression has gone from pissed off to bemused. "Sorry…I…"

"Go," he chuckles. "Make her go to the hospital. She's got a stubborn streak a mile long."

With just a nod in response, I start jogging in the direction of the ambulance.

"Yo, Gomez!" I stop and turn when I hear Keith calling from behind me. "Keys!" he yells. Pulling the keys from my pocket, I toss them in his direction and he easily catches them in his fist, holding them up. "Keeping your six, brother."

I start moving to the open doors of the ambulance, knowing Keith will make sure my ride will be taken care of. The man is a serious pain in my ass and more than once have I wanted to deck him, but in the end, he always has my back.

"Why can't you just slap a few Band-Aids on so I can go home? Aren't there any real patients for you to worry about?"

I can hear Kerry's voice before I even round the emergency vehicle. The woman is pissed and not afraid to let it be known, but I can hear a slight wobble in her voice, indicating the temper is more likely a coping mechanism than actual rage. My first visual of her confirms it: sitting on the stretcher with her hands clenching the blanket around her, those luminous gray eyes look wild, and her teeth are furiously chewing her bottom lip.

"Sir?" One of the EMTs stops me as I'm about to climb into the rig. "You can't come in here."

I pull my badge free and wave it in his face. "Where she goes, I go," I growl, watching Kerry's head spin around when she hears my voice.

"Damian?" My name comes out on a sob and with a last dirty look at the young EMT, daring him to hold me back, I climb in and sit down on the stretcher beside her.

"You know you don't have to keep throwing yourself in front of cars to get me to come running," I joke, watching her eyes go even wider as I lift my fingers to brush the stray hairs from her face. "A simple phone call will do the trick." I pull her bottom lip from between her teeth. It's bleeding and looks like it's been mauled by a pack of rabid dogs. I gently rub it with my thumb to soothe the swelling, and she lets out a shuddering breath.

"I can't," she says, tears pooling in her eyes when I look at her, my eyebrow raised in question. "My phone is at the bottom of the mountain," she sobs, falling forward and planting her face in the middle of my chest.

And that's where she stays as the EMT quietly goes about inspecting her injuries. Then he carefully informs her the cut on the side of her head will not only need stitches but a scan to make sure she didn't sustain more damage than can be seen on the outside.

Kerry's head shoots up, almost hitting me in the chin, and her first instinct is to refuse. This time I'm putting my foot down, though. I tell her it's one thing for a woman to be strong enough to take care of herself, but it's another thing to ignore medical advice just to prove a point. When she starts pulling away, I tighten my hold on her and tuck her head back to my chest.

"Gypsy, strength is knowing when the time is right to let someone else take care of you," I whisper with my face pressed in her hair. Then I add, "Let me."

I feel her resistance slowly draining from her body, and I help her lie back, kiss her forehead, and move to sit on the fold-out seat by her head, while the young paramedic straps her securely to the stretcher. When the doors are closed and the ambulance starts moving, she turns her head to me. "Are you coming?" she asks surprised.

"Yes, I am."

"Why?" She seems genuinely confused, and it strikes me as funny and sad at the same time. I lean forward and reach for her hand, giving it a little squeeze.

"Because I'm taking care of you."

CHAPTER 12

KERRY

"I'M COMING."

I drop my head back to the pillow and stare up at the ceiling tiles.

I'm exhausted after a sleepless night of scans, probing and prodding, not to mention the midnight visit from Keith Blackfoot, who painstakingly questioned me on anything I might remember about the incident.

He insists I go over every detail of my day leading up to the accident, but when I mention Kim loading the box of books in the back of the car, the energy in the room instantly turns thick.

"Box?" Damian repeats. "How come I don't know about this?"

A little confused, I turn from him to the detective.

"But I told you about that last order last week—The one I didn't have yet?" I don't miss the sharp look exchanged between the two men. I'm guessing this information was not shared.

"I assumed it was in the mail," Blackfoot says curtly. *"I didn't know your friend was holding it for you."* The implication hangs thick in the air. I glare from him to Damian and back.

"Look here," I start, but Damian doesn't give me a chance.

"How did Kim end up with your shipment?" he asks, his eyes steady on mine as he covers my hand with his, sliding his fingers between mine.

"Not sure," I say honestly. *"It was supposed to be shipped to the Durango store. I was waiting for it when Kim mentioned she'd received a box for me. It's happened once or twice before that a shipping label had the wrong zip code on it or had part of the address torn off, and it ended up at the other address."*

"We need that box," Blackfoot directs at Damian.

It's Damian who insisted I give Kim a call before she finds out I got hurt from someone else. He correctly assumed she'd probably be pissed if I didn't tell her myself. As it is, she's pissed anyway. Angry and maybe even a little hurt I didn't contact her last night. Damian offered, but I didn't want to get her all worked up over some scrapes, bruises, and a concussion right before bed. Running a store with a baby at home is stressful enough, and I know sleep is at a premium.

But I knew he was right when he pushed the brand new phone he'd left me on the bedside table in my hand, and simply raised an eyebrow.

"Kim," I say with as much patience as I can muster up. "Honey, I haven't slept all night and I'm exhausted. The doc is about to release me, and then I'm going home to crash. I promise you if I need anything, you're the first one I'll be calling." I feel bad playing the pity card on her, but I really do want to go home, dive into bed, and not surface until tomorrow.

"You won't call," she huffs, sounding a little insulted. "You'll just do what you always do; handle things on your own."

"Kim…" I feel guilt sticking in my throat. It wasn't too long ago I had been hurt because Kim had kept some things from me. It had felt like betrayal. I'm about to change my mind when she gives in.

"I know, I know. Okay, fine. But I'm telling you, I don't like the thought of you going to an empty house with no one to look after you. And please tell me you're not driving yourself. Get a cab, or at least let me call Marya to pick you up."

Shit. The store. That's another phone call I have to make soon.

"Damian will drive me," I tell her, my eyes locking with his. He's been beside the bed all night. Even when they wheeled me from one test to another, he'd been sitting calmly in that chair when I got back to the room. After ignoring my insistence for him to head home, more than a few times, I'd given up trying. Sometime over the course of the night, I found myself expecting him to be there. A huge concession on my part but one that slipped in almost naturally overnight. And I hate admitting to myself that knowing someone has your back feels pretty damn good. Damn him.

"Damian is there?"

Shit.

"He showed up at the scene and forced his way into the ambulance." I watch little lines appearing around Damian's eyes as his mouth curves into a smile. Or maybe it's a smirk. Either way, he looks more than a little amused. Irritating man.

"He stayed with you?" Disbelief is dripping from her voice.

"He wouldn't leave." I enforce, now full-on annoyed as I watch his smile get bigger.

"Let me talk to him," Kim demands, throwing me for a loop.

"Why do you need to talk to him? I'm fi… Hey!" I throw daggers at the man in question when he snatches the phone from my hand, gets up to walk to the window, and puts it to his ear.

"Kim? Hey. I'll look after her. I'll give you a call later with an update. What? No, I'm not planning to. I know. Yes, I know."

I can only hear his side of the conversation, and as soon as he turns and puts the phone down, I pounce. "What did she want? Planning to do what?"

"Relax," he says with a smile as he sits back down.

"She's only looking out for you."

"I know that," I bite off ungraciously, not comfortable being the subject of discussion when I'm not participating in it. Talking to Kim reminded me to mention the box of books in the back of my car. I paid five thousand bucks for those babies, I didn't want them to get lost.

I don't have a chance to pursue it any further when the door pushes open and the attending with one of the nurses walks in.

"Ms. Emerson, it looks like you were lucky. Other than being a bit banged and bruised, eight stitches to close that cut on your head, and a mild concussion, you managed to escape without serious injury. You are free to go home."

I barely let the man finish before folding back the sheet and swinging my legs off the edge of the mattress. "Told you I was fine," I mumble stubbornly at no one in particular, before a wave of dizziness has me grab onto the side of the bed.

"Whoa—easy does it, babe," Damian shoots out of the chair and stabilizes me with his hands on my shoulders.

"As I was about to explain," the doctor continues rather sardonically, "you received a hard knock to the head, and even though there doesn't seem to be any permanent damage as a result, you'll likely experience some headaches and occasional bouts of unsteadiness. You may want to take it easy for a few days. I'd recommend having someone check in on you regularly."

"Taken care of," Damian's deep baritone sounds over my head, and I slump my shoulders in resignation. For now.

Leaving a sheet with instructions and a prescription for painkillers, the doctor exits the room.

"Sir," the nurse who'd been silent up to that point directs at Damian. "If you'd give us some privacy, I'll help getting Ms. Emerson dressed."

"I think I can manage," I sputter, having reached my limit of being talked about. "Been pretty proficient at it for at least forty years now." I'm being facetious, but I'm tired and cranky, and my head is starting to pound like a son of a bitch.

The older woman shrugs her shoulders and points at a closet door over her shoulder. "As you wish. Your clothes are in there and feel free to call for help when you need it." I'm not imagining the sarcastic tone of her voice but I shrug it off. Seems I'm not making anyone happy today. I'm glad to see the back of her when she leaves the room and pulls the door shut, a hint more firmly than is necessary.

"Nice to see you're making friends." Damian's calm observation ruffles my remaining feathers but mostly because his remark cuts. He's right, I'm being an outright bitch. "I'm gonna help you into the bathroom and quickly grab your clothes. Sit your ass down on the toilet if you get woozy. I'll be right outside the door."

I'm grateful when he does as he says, hands me

my clothes and shuts the door, closing me into the bathroom. If he'd insisted on helping, I might've just let him and that has nothing to do with the fact his hands on me make me feel warm all over. Nothing at all.

DAMIAN

"How's she doing?"

It's the first thing Bella asks. I spoke to her briefly last night when Kerry was taken for a scan, wanting to warn her not to wait up for me. She's immediately concerned when she picks up the phone.

"She'll be fine," I answer truthfully, even though I'm not just talking about the injuries she's sustained. The entire picture is one that begs me to recognize these are not isolated incidents: the break-in at her store, the missing computer and list, and now a hit-and-run accident. My gut tells me this is all connected.

Thank God for the presence of mind of the truck driver last night. He not only managed to give police a decent description of the vehicle, but also part of the license plate number. On top of that, he'd reacted quickly when he saw Kerry's Subaru teetering on the edge of the drop off and was able to drag her from the vehicle just seconds before it crashed down the mountain. Saving Kerry from being crumpled on the rocks, along with her car, thirty feet below.

Despite the recent steady flow of new investigations, which had taken precedence over the Interpol investigation, the case involving the stolen books and manuscripts just found its way back to the very top of my priority list.

I meant what I said. Kerry will be fine—I will personally make sure of that.

"Do you need me to do anything?" my sister wants to know.

"Actually," I consider. "It would be great if you could grab me a change of clothes. She just went down for a nap, and I don't think I should leave her. I'll have Luna drop off my files and work from here for a bit. I'll text you directions."

In the pregnant silence that follows I can hear the wheels turning.

"Can I just say I'm thrilled right now?" she finally says, a smile evident in her voice. "Mama and the girls are gonna be over the moon."

"Bella..." I groan, definitely not looking forward to fielding phone calls from all the women in my family. "I'm just keeping an eye out. She doesn't have any family close by." It's not the only reason and I'm sure Bella sees right through it, but still I'm relieved when she concedes.

"Fine. I'll let you off the hook for now, even though you and I both know what a load of crap that is."

"Thanks, sweetie." My sister makes me smile. One of the reasons we get along so well is her ability to call a spade a spade. Unlike my mom and my other sisters, who twist themselves into pretzels in attempts to be tactful and sensitive—something that grates on my nerves—Bella just gives it to you straight. In between the eyes with a two-by-four.

I quickly shoot her directions when I hang up the phone and proceed to dial the office. Jasper answers, apparently Luna is in the field, so I quickly tell him what I need.

I hang up the phone just as I hear a toilet flush. It's barely been thirty minutes since she went down, so I'm a bit surprised to hear the soft slap of bare feet on the floor coming down the hall.

"You're still here." Her voice sounds groggy and no less tired than it did earlier.

I don't respond, I just watch as she pads over to the couch, plops down and pulls up her knees, holding her head in her hands. Even with her hair looking more like a bird's nest, the dark bags under her eyes, and wearing ratty old men's pajamas, she still manages to stir me. Body and soul. I abandon my perch on the kitchen stool and go to sit beside her, putting my hand on her knee.

"Head hurts?"

"Hmmm…neck is killing me."

"I bet it does," I sympathize, shifting sideways with one leg propped on the couch and pull her toward me. "Turn your back to me, Kerry." For a moment, I think she's going to refuse, but then she shrugs her shoulders and does as I ask. I'm tempted to pull her even closer into me, but given the current state of my body, she's probably better off where she is.

"Oh my God," she groans, the moment my fingers dig into the muscles between her shoulder blades.

Using firm steady pressure, I slowly work the tight knots out of the muscles in her shoulders and neck. The little pleasure moans and groans coming from her are sheer torture, and I finally resort to pulling a throw pillow in my lap. When I feel her shoulders start to slump, I encourage her to scoot down and put her head on the pillow. I curse myself for even suggesting it, but she seems to relax under my hands and she needs her rest.

"Stop moving, babe. You're killing me," I whisper when she shifts around, trying to get comfortable. Her movements stop immediately as she glances up at my face. The tension is largely gone from hers and replaced with a hint of humor in the tilt of her lips at my current predicament. She slips down a little further, relieving a bit of the pressure, and chuckles when I blow out a sigh of relief.

I slip my hands palms up under her, cupping one at the base of her skull and with the fingers on the other, I gently stretch the muscles in her neck, alternating occasionally. Her eyes are locked on mine, completely open and unguarded, giving me full access to her emotions. We don't talk, and other than my hands on her neck and head, we don't touch—Still, I swear it's the most intimate experience I've ever had.

A few minutes in, I see her eyes flutter shut as her breathing deepens, and she finally falls asleep.

I don't know how long I've been sitting here—maybe an hour or so—just running my hands over her skin and hair while watching her sleep, when a sharp knock at the door snaps my head up. Kerry moves restlessly at the sound but quickly settles back down, allowing me to slip my hands and leg from under her.

My damn leg is numb from being folded under for so long, and I nearly do a face-plant in the little front hall. Jasper is outside, holding a box that has my laptop, a stack of files, and my portable scanner. I take the box from him and set it on the hall table, checking to see if he remembered my Rolodex, when he steps around me into the house.

"Hey," I hiss after him, but he's already moved into the living room and is standing over a sleeping Kerry by the time I catch up with him.

"Pretty," he mumbles, and before I can yank him away, Kerry is already blinking her eyes at the intrusion.

"Dammit, Greene. Get your ass out of here," I bark, no longer concerned about waking her since she's already scrambling to sit up.

Jasper ignores me and sticks his hand in her face. "I don't believe we've ever had the pleasure. Jasper Greene." His fucking smile is so bright, Kerry has to blink a few times against the glare before she shakes his hand.

"Kerry Emerson."

"Greene," I growl, as I watch Kerry trying to pull back her hand when he doesn't let go. I aim a hard punch for his shoulder, which has him release his hold on Kerry and grab onto his arm.

"Damn," he turns his big grin on me. "You still have some power left in that old body of yours, boss."

Fuck. I know I'm letting him get to me. I open my mouth to let him have it when another voice joins in.

"Suggest you don't poke the bear or you'll find out exactly how much power my brother is packing."

Bella stands in the doorway, all five foot and change of her, with her hands on her hips and her eyes throwing flames at Jasper, who looks—for once—lost for words. She must've walked right in the front door we'd left open. Kerry is just sitting on the couch, cross-legged in her threadbare, ugly-ass pajamas, watching the interaction with great interest.

"Now I know I haven't had this pleasure. Jasper Greene, at your service." The idiot has his hand out again, this time approaching my sister, who looks at him like something she just scraped off the sole of her shoe. He really has no idea the kind of danger he's putting himself in right now. My sister can be like a rabid Chihuahua, especially with men. It's that I'm her brother, or her current hatred for all God's creatures cursed with a Y-chromosome would have me shredded to strips with her sharp little canines.

I decide to intervene before blood flows. "That's my baby sister Bella, Greene. Isabella, Jasper is one of my agents." I emphasize the word baby on purpose, and Jasper reacts as I hoped, by immediately tucking his proffered hand in his pocket. Smart man.

A soft chuckle reaches my ears, and I turn to find Kerry's smiling eyes on mine. In my peripheral vision, I see Jasper backing away from my sister and cautiously rounding her on his way to the front door.

"Yes, well...I should get back to the office," he mutters. "Nice to meet you all."

"You too, Jasper," Kerry calls out to him, dissolving in a fit of giggles when Bella makes a growling sound by way of response.

The moment he pulls the door shut behind him, Bella turns to Kerry, her face morphed into one of sweet concern. "Nice to see you again, Kerry. How are you feeling?"

"Better. I..."

"Should be sleeping," I finish for her with a stern look for my sister, who seems less than impressed.

"Don't put that on me. Take it out on your cocky, self-absorbed pretty boy, who obviously thinks he's God's gift to women." I smile at the description. Jas is all that with his long, lanky frame and California good looks. He looks more like a happy-on-life poster boy for Calvin Klein, with his sun-bleached hair and disarming smile, instead of a highly respected FBI agent with an IQ at genius level topped with some serious ninja skills. He knows how to use his looks to his advantage, but they've been more of a hindrance than a benefit in getting where he is today. I'm not about to tell my sister that, though. Let her think he's a player. I don't need her getting any ideas.

"I actually do feel a little better. I wouldn't mind

some coffee. Anyone else up for a cup?" Kerry stands up and gingerly moves toward the kitchen.

"I'd love one," Bella pipes up and makes herself comfortable on the couch, ignoring my glare.

I follow Kerry into the kitchen, where she's already scooping grinds into a filter. "I can send her home, you know?" I walk up behind her, boxing her in with my hands resting on either side of her on the counter. "She's just dropping off my gear."

"Gear?" she asks, continuing to prep the coffeemaker as if she can't feel the heat radiating off my body only a few inches away from hers.

"Need a shower and some clean clothes. I figured you'd be out for a while, so I had Jasper drop off some work and Bella grabbed my stuff."

Now she turns in my arms, her shoulder lightly brushing my chest. "You realize that may not have been the smartest idea, don't you?" She smiles, placing a casual hand on my arm.

"I do," I admit. "Now."

Kerry flaps her hand in front of her face. "Those were some serious fireworks," she says, rolling her eyes dramatically.

"Don't even go there, Gypsy," I warn her, bending my head closer to steal a kiss. "I don't want to know about those fireworks," I mumble with my lips caressing hers. "Not with a nuclear fusion going on here."

CHAPTER 13

"WHERE IS IT, MR. SINCLAIR?"

He'd been expecting the phone call.

"It's under control. I'll have it to you before the deadline."

"I don't care about the deadline. I care about you kicking up more dust with your ineffective ploys to reclaim the goods. Your idea of control is disturbing, Mr. Sinclair, given that my property is in the trunk of a wreck, currently being towed to the police lab. How do you propose getting it out of there before it is found?"

He jumped on an opportunity last night and fucked it up. When he found out the woman was picking up the box in Cortez, he managed to catch up with her as she was closing in on Durango. He just hadn't thought it through much further than that and realized the error of his ways when he pulled up behind her. The split-second decision to intercept her caused him to be ill-prepared, with only a gun and no way to avoid her recognition. The recovery was supposed to remain covert, it was the only way his associate could exert any control over the current investigation. His only option was to make it look like an accident. Then, once he removed the box from the wreckage, no one would be any the wiser. When he backed up his truck and prepared to shove her off the edge of the road, he noticed the headlights of a big rig coming up the mountain right behind them. Already in motion, he jerked hard to swerve around her car, but when he had to adjust the wheel to avoid a collision with the truck that had come up faster than he anticipated, his truck nicked her front end.

Nothing to do from there but damage control. In his rearview mirror, he saw the big rig pulling to a stop on the side of the road, and he knew the only option left for now was to get the hell out of there and update his partner.

"Because no one will have a chance to touch the car before we can retrieve it."

The silence on the other end is thick as his client starts computing the information just handed to him.

"Son of a bitch." The client bursts out laughing. "You have an inside man."

CHAPTER 14

KERRY

I DIDN'T KNOW WHETHER it was relief or frustration I felt when an urgent phone call interrupted the impromptu make-out session in the kitchen. That man's hand was already down the back of my pajamas, clasping my butt cheek, and I wasn't doing a damn thing to stop him. I don't get it. These days I'm a pretty determined and goal-focused person, but Damian talks to me or touches me—hell, even if he just breathes in the same room—it seems to render me meek. Dammit.

Worst part is, for the past four hours since he's been gone, my mind constantly drifts to the way he can make me feel.

"I'd really like to know what's been going through that mind of yours, but since I have a sneaky suspicion it involves my brother in some way, I think I'll have to pass."

When Damian had to run out, Bella offered to stay. We've been getting to know each other—moreover, I've been learning lots about Damian—and chatting like old friends.

I've learned Damian is stuck in the middle of five sisters, something I find weirdly hilarious, given his über manliness. Some of the childhood torture the sisters put him through was pretty hardcore. And that's just the stuff Bella, being eight years younger than Damian's forty-four, could remember. Yes, I finagled his age from her, as well. I'd been curious. He is a hard man to date with his timeless, masculine good looks. He'll age well—damn him.

"I don't know what you mean," I lie, but Bella just laughs in my face.

"Right. We'll just leave it at that and pretend you two weren't chewing each other's faces off in the kitchen this morning. But just so you know, I've never seen my brother this way." She shrugs her shoulders. "Not that he was a eunuch all these years, he's far too passionate for that, but as far as I can recall, he's never cared enough to jump in the fray for a woman the way he did for you. Hell, he even took me on."

I don't quite know what to say to the picture she paints of a caring, protective, and passionate man. It doesn't exactly jive with the calculated, controlling man I see. Huh. I have to admit, the childhood antics Bella describes show him in a somewhat more personable light.

"Are you hungry?" I change the subject swiftly, a little unsettled with these new discoveries. Bella rolls her eyes, obviously not falling for my attempt at distraction but letting it go anyway.

"I could eat. Do you have any take-out menus here?" I direct her to a drawer in the kitchen, and she fishes out the menu for one of my newfound favorite restaurants, Rice Monkeys. "This looks good. I love Asian food," she says, already scanning the menu.

"I recommend their squid salad and vermicelli bowls. They're out of this world. But we have to pick it up, they don't deliver," I point out.

"Don't worry," Bella says cheerfully, pulling her phone from her purse. "We'll just call my brother."

Before I can protest, she's already on the phone. "When are you gonna be done?" She dives right in without saying hello. "… Because we're hungry and want to order some food from Rice Monkeys. Kerry says the food is amazing…Yeah, we'll hold off half an hour before ordering. I'll survive." She hangs up and triumphantly drops her phone back in her purse.

"Is he always that accommodating?" I can't help asking.

"For me he isn't, but I had a hunch he would be for you." She winks and her smile is infectious, and I burst out laughing at her shameless manipulations.

"You're a handful," I tell her. "But I think I like your style." Now it's her turn to laugh heartily.

We manage to kill some time watching an old episode of *Seinfeld*, and I find myself nodding off a few times. The lack of sleep and the remaining low-grade headache are catching up with me.

"I've already put in our order, and Damian's on his way to pick it up," I hear Bella say as I peel open my eyelids.

"Thanks," I manage to say, my mouth feeling like it's filled with glue. Yuck. "I fell asleep."

"That was obvious," she snorts but continues a bit more contrite. "I'm sorry if I kept you up. I talk a lot. I know I'm one of those annoying oversharers."

I simply wave her off as I try to straighten up. "Not at all."

"Anyway, I thought you might wanna freshen up a bit before he gets here. You kinda have some slobber gathering at the corner of your mouth." She very helpfully points to where I can feel drool hardening on my face. Fabulous.

Mortified, and suddenly in a hurry, I push up off the couch and find myself swaying on my feet.

"Whoa, steady does it."

I notice Bella says almost the same exact thing Damian did only this morning. Fuck me. He's probably already on his way. With a grateful smile, I carefully step out of her hold and make my way to the bedroom, noticing for the first time I never changed out of my pajamas all day long. I didn't call the store either, to find out how things went for Marya today. Something else I'll rectify, just as soon as I put some decent clothes on and wash my face.

A glance at my alarm clock as I come out of the

bathroom tells me it's only five o'clock. Feeling a bit refreshed, I grab my phone, which had been lying on my nightstand all day, and notice a number of missed calls. Ignoring them for now, I first call Marya, who picks up on the second ring.

"Hey. How are you feeling?" she answers the phone. It takes me a second to remember the store has call display.

"Better. A lot better," I admit. "How were things today?"

"Fine. Not a lot of book traffic, but the coffee sure is taking off."

"Oh really? Well, I guess it doesn't really matter what brings them in, as long as they come in."

"I also took down a few messages. Most of the calls I could handle, but there are a few here you'll eventually have to do something with." I can hear her shuffling through message slips.

"Give them to me now. I'll handle them right away," I suggest.

"They can wait," Marya says firmly. "You're going to take care of you first. Oh, that reminds me; I've got the next few days organized for the kids, as well. Since it's school break, and Mom was planning to take them with her to visit her sister's place in Silverado anyway, she just took them up there this afternoon. They're staying until at least after the weekend, so don't worry about rushing back."

I'm torn between feeling guilty and feeling relieved. "I owe you big, girlfriend. Thanks so much for doing that, and thank your mom, too, when you talk to her. I'll make sure to thank both of you properly soon." I know Marya struggles a bit financially and whatever she has always goes to her kids, but I'm sure I can think of something to spoil her. Her mom is easy; the woman is one of my staunchest customers, and I will make sure she'll never run out of books to read.

"Don't even," Marya says, but then I hear her mumble to someone with her. She must've covered the phone with her hand. "Sorry about that," she apologizes in a voice about an octave higher, and I wonder if it's her new friend who walked into the store. The same one who had her glowing from top to bottom a few days ago.

"I'm guessing you have a...customer?" I tease her, a smile in my voice. This time I hear a man's voice in the background. It sounds almost familiar.

"Yes!" Marya finally responds breathlessly. "We'll talk tomorrow. I'd better go."

Before I even have a chance to say goodbye, she's already hung up. A bit puzzled by her sudden hurry to get off the phone, I toss my phone on the bed and make my way to the kitchen, where I can hear voices.

Bella's and another. One that makes butterflies convulse in my stomach.

DAMIAN

This goddamn day has completely gotten away from me and by the time Bella phones me, I'm ready to call it.

I'm beat. Other than this morning on the couch, I don't think I've blinked, let alone closed my eyes. Just my luck this damn case seems to be gaining some traction now, when I need a good six or eight hours of shut-eye to tide me over. But before I can even contemplate getting out of here, I have to update Luna, who just walked into the office. She's been helping the Durango PD tie off a few loose ends on a case we closed recently.

"Did he talk?"

"With your buddy Blackfoot in the room? Hell yes, he talked. Took a while though, but as usual Keith was able to convey the importance of coming clean." She chuckles at the look of distaste on my face. "I know you don't approve of his methods, boss, but you've got to admit, the man's got a near-perfect track record when it comes to getting confessions."

I know he does, but I also know he disregards every rule book ever written on the proper protocol of interrogation. Not that there is ever a mark on the suspect—his methods run more along the lines of intimidation. I have to give it to him, though, he only pulls out the big guns when the case is pretty much ironclad.

It's one of the reasons I started insisting me, or one of my agents, always be present during his interviews on cases we'd been called in to assist. I want this office to be able to testify to the fact that nothing untoward happened.

"Sit down, Roosberg." I wave her to the chair on the other side of my desk, and she sits without argument. "James Aiken called this morning. Told me the Interpol specialist called him en route to the airport, demanding he 'call off his dogs.' That is us, this field office and the PD," I clarify when Luna looks confused. "Apparently she called the police station this morning to check some information. Ended up talking to Blackfoot, who told her about last night's accident. She asked him if he thought there could be a connection to the trafficking investigation, and he told her it was a possibility. Still, when she told him to wait for her to fly in, he said he wasn't gonna wait around on his hit-and-run investigation. He laughed at her and said he was planning on stripping Kerry's car for evidence, with or without her, and then hung up. Did Blackfoot say anything to you?"

Luna shakes her head. "No. He said lots, but nothing about that investigation. We were in the interview room from eleven this morning on. We never even took a break, just ate a sandwich in front of the suspect. I came here right after. Blackfoot disappeared into his office."

I run my fingers through my hair and lean my head back. Fuck. The son of a bitch had been out of reach all day and hadn't returned any of my messages. Last call I made was ten minutes ago, right before Bella called, and the dispatcher said he'd just left the office.

He's avoiding me.

"What's going on?" Luna wants to know.

"Blackfoot's doing his maverick routine again. Last night we found out from Kerry that her last order from The Gilded Feather was in the back of her car when she was run off the road. Something she'd mentioned to Keith last week already, but he misinterpreted and failed to mention it to us." Luna rolls her eyes at that, but I can't quite catch what she mutters under her breath. It sounds like *typical*. Ignoring it, I continue, "It's clear he didn't mention anything to Ella about the box. She ended up contacting James after the bastard hung up on her. Made it very clear she wants to be there before they start messing with Kerry's car. Wants to make sure proper protocol is followed in gathering any evidence. She has a point, too," I admit.

"You think this is the package referred to in the messages?" Luna points out what has been on my mind.

"It's possible. In any event, it makes it all the more important to make sure we dot the i's and cross the t's. These kinds of cases can stand or fall on the most minute detail. Dealing with a task force, working within overlapping jurisdictions, it can cloud the waters. I'm afraid I don't know what bug crawled up Blackfoot's ass, but I can guess he's gonna claim there is no evidence to support anything other than the hit-and-run at this point in time." I slam my fist on the table in frustration. "Killer is, he's got a point, too." I push myself up and pick up my phone. The food order at Rice Monkeys should be ready. "Heading out. I've gotta pick up some dinner and check on Kerry. I haven't had sleep since two nights ago, I'm beat."

"What can I do?" Luna asks, standing up as well.

"Well, this case just made it to the top of the priority list, and I've got Jasper going back over the financials, phone records, and credit card bills of everyone potentially involved: Kerry, White Rabbit Books, and Bruce Willoughs. I want him to look for anything that might be connected. Whatever he can find floating around the Internet. He's gonna have to be creative. I'd like for you to head over to the forensics lab and see if Blackfoot is there with the Crime Investigations Unit. If he is, stick close to him. I at least want our asses covered."

Luna's lips tighten in a straight line. "You're gonna owe me big, boss. First you stick me in a room with that man for almost an entire day, and when I can finally get away from him, you shove me right back at him."

For some reason, Luna's never been able to stand Blackfoot. Not from the very first time they met. Of course, Keith had been his usual cocky self, instantly alienating my agent with his taunts about her small size. It's just what he does—tease. Luna's just not very good at being the subject. I tried telling him once to lay off, but that only seemed to encourage him.

I have to admit, he's starting to really get on my nerves, too.

"Don't worry." She stops me with her hand up

when I open my mouth. "You get some sleep. I'll get on it." I snap my mouth shut and nod in affirmation.

As much as I feel like an ass for putting her in his line of fire again, I've got to get some food and some sleep. In that order.

Armed with two bags of food, I take the cutoff up to Kerry's place, pulling the Expedition up beside Bella's car.

"You're here. Finally," Bella says, waiting in the front door.

"Miss me?" I tease, walking up to her.

"More like starving. I heard you pull up," she explains, as she takes the bags from my hands and leads the way inside, my tired ass is dragging behind.

Kerry is nowhere to be seen, but I hear the faint sound of her voice coming from the back of the house. "Who's with her?" I ask, as I start moving in the direction of her voice.

"Jesus, chill, Damian," Bella warns, grabbing my arm and pulling me into the small kitchen. "You look like you're about to storm into her bedroom and make yourself look like an idiot. No one's with her—she's on the damn phone."

I let out a deep sigh, releasing the tension in my muscles. Long fucking forty-eight hours. I sit my ass down on a kitchen stool and watch Bella pull down plates and take out silverware. "Thanks for hanging around with her, sweetie." Bella throws me a little smile.

"Wasn't a hardship. She's a nice girl, but you may

wanna tone down the whole caveman spiel, brother. This is not some insipid, helpless female. She ditched the last guy who tried to put a tight leash on her. Pulled herself up by the bootstraps and built herself a good business, a good life."

"I know she did, Bella," I bite off irritated. "I also know in the past two days she almost got run over once and not twenty-four hours later got run off the road. The difference is I wasn't there to protect her the second time, and look what happened." With my elbows on the counter, I drop my head and press the heels of my hands into my eyes. What I would give for some sleep.

"I just don't want her hurt," Bella says in a soothing voice, her hand ruffling my hair.

I let out a dry chuckle. "Believe me—I don't either." I lift my head and look at my sister. "Not by me..." I confirm before adding, "...and not by anyone else."

I can hear Kerry's soft, padding footsteps coming down the hall and am on my feet when she walks into the kitchen. No pajamas this time, but stretchy black pants and an oversized shirt with a wide neck that slipped off her shoulder.

"Hey." Her voice is soft as she steps up to me, putting a hand on my chest and tilting her head back a little to look me in the eye. "You look tired."

"I am," I admit, holding her hand firmly to my chest when she tries to pull it away. "Nothing a little food and a few hours with my eyes closed won't cure." *And you tucked safely in my arms*, I add in my head. "Did you get any sleep?"

She shrugs her shoulders, causing her shirt to slip down a little farther, showing more skin and confirming my suspicion she is not wearing a bra. Despite my fatigue, my body instantly snaps alert, and I want badly to put my hands on her. The clearing of a throat behind us reminds me my sister is in the room. So instead of wrapping Kerry close—like I want to—I lift her hand off my chest and press a kiss in her palm. The soft tilt of her lips, and the touch of heat shimmering in her eyes when my mouth touches her, prompts me to sneak a little taste of her skin with the tip of my tongue. I almost forget about Bella again as I watch those silvery gray eyes flare and turn dark.

"Come and get it, guys."

Reluctantly, I let Kerry go as she pulls away and turns to my sister, who's already got a head start on dinner.

Oddly enough, after dinner and the dishes are cleared, Kerry doesn't object when Bella heads back to my place, and I stay right where I am. Doesn't even question it.

"Why don't you go lie down," she says with a hesitant smile. "You look like you're about to fall over. Take my bed. I'll make myself comfortable here." She waves her hand at the couch.

Like hell.

"I'm not gonna spend time arguing with you, Gypsy, but the only way I'm taking your bed is if you're in it with me. I'm grabbing a quick shower." I don't wait for an answer. I simply grab my bag from the hallway, where Bella dropped it earlier, and head to the bathroom.

I make the shower really quick, grabbing a towel from the shelf and pulling on a clean pair of boxer briefs, *thank you, Bella,* and a shirt. I stuff the rest of my things back in the bag and tote it into the bedroom, where I stop in my tracks at the sight of Kerry standing beside the bed, back in her ratty old pajamas.

"Thank Christ," slips out of my mouth, and I watch the corner of her mouth twitch. "Get in, Kerry," I tell her, moving to the other side of the bed and she does as instructed—but with an eyebrow raised in protest.

She rolls on her side facing the edge of the mattress, and I curve myself around her from behind, wrapping one arm around her middle and slipping the other under her head. I don't miss the deep sigh she blows out as she relaxes against me.

"I can't believe I'm saying this," I mumble with my face buried in her messy hair. "But despite what my body tells you..." I slightly press my erection in her backside. "...I just need to keep you close so I can sleep."

Kerry's hands come up to cover my arm, pulling it tighter against her. "That's okay," she mumbles, fading fast. "I need you close so I can feel safe."

CHAPTER 15

KERRY

I'M NOT SURE WHAT time it is when I wake up and find myself alone in bed. Judging by the bright light coming in, I'd say a fair guess would be sometime after eight. I lift my head to glance at my alarm clock but find it facedown on my nightstand. Instinctively, I reach out to set it straight, but my hand stills somewhere midair, only to retreat back under the covers with the rest of me. I quickly dismiss the nagging pang of guilt and snuggle deeper in the warmth and scent Damian's body left behind.

I'm slowly sinking back to sleep when angry voices shoot me wide-awake again. Two men's voices. Throwing my covers back, I quickly swing my legs out of bed, only to catch myself with a hand on the nightstand before I fall face-first on the floor. Dizzy. I take a few deep breaths to clear my head and this time proceed to move through the room a little more cautiously. By the sound of it, things are quickly escalating as I pad down the hallway.

"Fuck you, Gomez. Don't you talk to me about not following protocol. You're standing half-naked in the house of a damn suspect in this investigation. At the very least a witness. Get off your high horse." I recognize the voice of Detective Blackfoot, and the moment I round the corner, I see him; toe-to-toe with indeed a half-naked Damian. *Gee gawds...* somewhere along the line, he donned his jeans but lost his shirt. I'm not sure which view I enjoy more, the muscular legs and high, tight rear end or the broad, solid-looking back. Mesmerized by the sight of a tattoo curving along his spine before spreading wide to span his shoulders, I slowly walk up behind him.

"Nothing's going on here, man." I watch as Damian runs his hand through his hair, still sounding tired. Obviously not buying into it, Blackfoot rolls his eyes, catching sight of me standing behind Damian. But before he can say anything, Damian speaks again, "I'm just looking after her. As a friend."

I'm not sure what the heck is going on, or why he is saying that, but I can't hold back the incredulous snort at his blatant lie. I mean, a friend doesn't play tonsil hockey with his tongue down your throat or rub his cock against your ass as he cuddles in bed with you, right? Blackfoot sports a smirk as he lowers his eyes, but Damian looks downright miserable as he slowly turns to find me behind him.

I choose to ignore him and focus on the detective instead. "I'm a suspect? When the hell did that happen? When someone drove *me* off the road?" Blackfoot's guilty eyes flit to Damian before meeting mine.

"For what it's worth, I happen to think you're an innocent bystander, but until we have evidence to clear you—"

"Isn't it supposed to be the other way around?" I cut him off sharply. "Innocent until proven guilty? Seems to me you're doing the opposite."

"In a court of law that stands," Blackfoot explains patiently, only serving to piss me off more. "But in an investigation, it works the other way around."

I wave his explanations away. "Whatever—I've done nothing wrong. Investigate away."

"That's what I'm here for."

"Cut the crap, Keith," Damian pipes up for the first time. "You're full of shit. First of all, you're pissed because I sent Luna to keep an eye on you, and secondly, you came here to try and draw her into playing your game. Play all you want, but leave her out of it."

"Hold on a minute. First of all, as my *friend...*" I emphasize the word with air quotation marks as I throw a dirty look Damian's way, "...you have absolutely no right to speak for me. What game?" I demand to know. Blackfoot quickly looks to Damian—who glares back with a barely perceptible shake of his head—before apologetically shrugging his shoulders.

"Talk to the man," Keith says, before backing out of the door. "I'm sure he'll explain."

"So explain." I turn to Damian, who is shutting the door, my hands planted on my hips. His face, when he looks at me, is lined with worry and fatigue. Without saying a word, he walks past me to the kitchen. When I follow him in, he's pouring coffee in two mugs, handing one to me and taking a sip from the other.

"The box is gone," he finally says, taking me completely by surprise. I had obviously mentioned the box Kim had put in my trunk when Keith Blackfoot came to the hospital to get my statement. Now it was gone? "As soon as Keith left the hospital, he radioed the officer left at the scene to stay put until the flatbed truck arrived. Apparently, it took them half the night to haul the wreckage up and tow it off to the lab for the forensics team to go over. He got hung up on another case, and by the time he managed to get to your car last night, the box was missing."

"Maybe someone took it after they towed it there?" I offer, wondering what might've happened.

"Not likely," Damian answers immediately. "Twenty-four-hour camera surveillance, guard dogs, and a twelve-foot-high electric security fence make that doubtful. He thinks it fell out of the wreck. The back end is crumpled and the rear hatch was folded open."

"So why didn't they go look?" I point out, finding it rather obvious, but once again he counters me.

"It's a fifty foot, or thereabouts, drop in total from

the road to the valley below. Your car got hung up on an outcrop about thirty feet down, which means there's at least another twenty below. It's steep, you can't just send a guy down there on a rope. It'll take some preparation. I'm sure they'll start searching at some point today. But that brings me to the next part," he says, cupping my shoulders with his large hands. A shiver runs down my arms and back at his touch. "Keith wants you to act as if the box is recovered and back in your possession. He wants to have you bring in a dummy box and place it in your storage room."

"He wants me to be bait. Or at least my store," I recognize accurately, gathering from Damian's nod.

"Exactly, which is why I told him to go to hell. His reasoning is that if somehow, whoever ran you off the road recovered the box, they would have no interest in the decoy in your storage room. But if they haven't, they would more than likely make an attempt to reclaim it. That might put you and your girl, Marya, in danger...again," he adds adamantly.

I see his point, I really do, but part of me just wants this mess to be over. Cowering in the shadows until these guys are caught is not sitting right with me. It's not my style anymore. I'd rather actively make things happen.

"I guess we'll have to hope the police find the box soon then," I conclude. "It would save me from making a decision."

Damian's nostrils flare when I use the word *me* as

the decision maker, but I want to get my point across. "Yes, we will."

DAMIAN

I'm counting on them finding the damn box. I don't buy into the possibility the guy came back, slid his ass down the cliff in one piece, only to climb back up, a heavy box under one arm, and all that under the watchful eye of a police officer. And I don't want to even consider Kerry putting herself out there, so I'm just pleased with the prospect of a slowly progressing search due to an interdepartmental tug-of-war. I don't bother telling her about the political and jurisdictional positioning that only serves to slow down the investigation at this point. I prefer to give myself some time to deter her from letting Keith set her up as bait.

"Look," I softly implore and wait for her to look at me before I continue. "I didn't mean that." What I say and what I do are usually well thought through and calculated, but this woman is getting me all twisted up. The knowledge I probably hurt her makes me feel bad. *Guilty.*

"Didn't mean what?" Her look of feigned confusion is in stark contrast to the stiffening of her shoulders under my touch.

"What you heard me say to Keith. That you're

nothing more than a friend. It was a knee-jerk reaction and it's not true. You know it's not true." I don't stop her when she turns out of my grip and walks over to the sink, sets her cup down, and turns back to me.

"Truthfully?" she says, her chin lifted up and a deep blush high on her cheeks. "I believe you didn't mean it, but it confused me. Just like everything else in my life is confusing right now. So if you don't mind," she drops her gaze and prepares to move past me, "I'm just going to have a shower and sort out my head."

As she passes, I manage to grab her hand and pull her toward me, locking her in my arms. I ignore her stiff body and bend my head down to her shoulder, turning my face into her hair. "I'm sorry," I mumble. "I'm confused myself. At odds. Between trying to get to the bottom of this investigation with my eyes wide-open and not able to think about anything but losing myself in you...Fuck, yeah, I feel completely conflicted."

Kerry reacts by softening in my arms and slipping hers around my waist. "I understand," I feel more than hear her say; her breath stroking the skin on my chest.

I understand.

I had no idea how powerful two simple words could be. And the kicker is, I believe she does. Emotions... feelings...they've always come second to me. Easily pushed aside by the job: logic, duty, and protocol. This is new territory—uncharted. The inability to control these feelings, to set them aside, is a completely alien experience.

And already I'm fucking up. I should have been at the office an hour ago, yet I'm standing here not wanting to let go of her. I'm about to tell her I have to go, when she steps back and I reluctantly let go, but she hangs onto my hand. "I'm going to have a shower," she says again, slipping her fingers between mine. "Join me?"

My feet are already moving, picking up speed. Her soft giggle follows behind me as any thoughts about the office, about the case—about anything not related to getting my hands on a wet, naked Kerry— are washed out by the deafening, *Hell yes!* in my head. I don't slow down until I pull her into the small bathroom, close the door, and have the water running. Only then do I release her hand and turn to face her.

The first thing I notice is the hint of panic in her eyes. Fuck me, if she changes her mind now, it's going to kill me. Still, I have to ask. "Not too late to call a halt." In the harsh light of the bathroom, the bruises and red swelling around her stitches stand out in stark contrast. Knowing what she narrowly walked away from two nights ago, I wouldn't be surprised to find more of the same on different parts of her body. She drops her head down, and I reach over to lift her chin. "Hey, I mean it. You want me out of here, I'm walking." I try to ignore my raging hard-on pressing against the fly of my jeans. "I might be walking funny for a while, but I—" My words are cut short when I suddenly see her shoulders start shaking, and when she lifts her eyes, they're dancing with humor. With a firm, steady hand, she cups my painfully hard package, drawing a sharp hiss from me. "Christ, woman."

"Thought about it," she teases. "But only for a minute. It's been a while...I thought..." She shakes her head. "Never mind. The truth is, I want it. I want this. Even if I may have forgotten what to do with it." The small, self-deprecating smile on her mouth gets to me.

"Gypsy," I assure her, my voice coarse with need. "From where I'm standing, your memory is right on the money."

She chuckles at that, and with her mouth still smiling, I tag her behind the neck and pull those luscious lips to mine. My tongue slips between to taste her deep, and my hands find their way to the edge of her top. She groans when I pull back to whip the ratty old thing off her before slamming my mouth back on hers. In seconds, I have her divested of the matching ugly pajama pants and slide my hands over all that glorious skin I now have full access to.

My eyes catch our reflection over her shoulder, in the bathroom mirror, and my breath hitches in my throat. The curve of her back to the spectacular swell of her ass is beautiful. With skin much paler than mine and the soft padding all over, she is the epitome of femininity.

Gently, I push her back by the shoulders. "Let me see all of you," I mumble against her lips. She opens her eyes and despite a slight hesitation, there is determination in the way she looks at me. Slowly, she takes a single step back and rests her hands behind her on the counter. The pose both highly seductive and oddly innocent.

I take in all of her: her long neck and strong shoulders, her chest with prominent collarbones, and a light sprinkling of freckles, my fingers tracing the path my eyes take. My hands curve the weight of her full, sloping breasts, richly veined, and my thumbs brush over nipples colored a pale pink. The soft, round curve of her belly feels like silk under my touch, and the silvery stretch marks seem to lead down to the patch of tight, dark blonde curls at the apex of her thighs.

I can hear her shallow breaths and smell her arousal as my fingers play in those damp curls.

"Damn, Kerry. Just...damn," I moan, suddenly ravenous. Moving both hands to her waist, I lift her on the edge of the sink and immediately drop to my knees, hoisting her legs up over my shoulders.

The first taste of her sears itself into my brain permanently.

Groaning deeply, I close my mouth over her core, trying to still the instant craving. She whimpers and clenches the muscles in her thighs against my head. With long strokes of my tongue and deep suction of my lips, I feed my hunger for her, digesting every quiver of her muscles and sound she expels. Somewhere along the line, her hands have found their way to my head, tangling and tugging at the strands. I glance up to see her eyes staring down at me, her mouth slack and her nostrils flaring. Holding her gaze, I graze my teeth lightly over her clit, and with a low, shuddering keen, she finds her climax, holding me trapped between her legs. *Jesus, she's magnificent.*

"Perfect," I whisper with my mouth pressed against the sensitive skin of her inner thigh, as I allow her to come down gently from her high.

"Perfect," she echoes, finally releasing her hold on me.

I get up from the floor, cup her flushed face in my hands, and lower my mouth to hers, letting her taste herself on me. Her hands start up where they left off earlier, picking at the buttons on my fly. Mine quickly reach down to cover hers. "Get in the shower, babe," I instruct her, afraid that her ministrations so close to my cock will have me go off like a short-fused fireworks display on the Fourth of July.

I help her down from the counter and move aside the shower curtain so she can step in. I fish a condom from my wallet, drop my jeans and boxers, and quickly step in behind her, my dick happily snuggling in the crease of her butt as I set the foil packet on the little shelf. When she tries to turn in my arms, I stop her.

"Stay like this."

"But you…" she starts, then I latch my lips onto a spot on her neck, just below her ear, and stop her protest. Arching her neck to give me better access, she moans as I slide one hand between her breasts and rest it at her throat. My other hand slips down to cup her between the legs.

"Can't wait to sink into you," I mutter against her skin. "I loved having you come in my mouth—I can only imagine what it'll be like having you come on my cock." My fingers test her folds, finding her soft and pliable and oh so ready for me. In a few swift moves, I have my dick sheathed and ready. With gentle pressure on her back, she leans forward, bracing her hands on the wall, and tilts her luscious ass up in invitation.

"Fuck me, Damian," she says so softly, I can only just hear her.

With a sharp tug on her hips, I pull her back, line myself up, and slide forward, feeling the tight glove of her pussy taking in all of me. "Fu-uck...you feel so good," I manage, desperately trying to control the urge to buck my hips against her ass. I won't last long.

I slide a hand up over her slick skin to find that spot at her throat again, so I can feel her heartbeat under my touch, and with the other I keep her hips in place, as I slowly ease back out before I slam back home. Control becomes an illusion as my hips take on a frantic cadence, powering them as I continue to pound inside her, groaning in rhythm. As I feel my balls pull up at the ready, and a current spin up from the base of my spine, I find her swollen clit with the pads of my fingers and press down.

"Oh my God!" she screams, her body convulsing as she comes. With one more surge, I follow right behind her, grunting out my own release, with my face buried in her neck and my hips bucking wildly.

It's when I'm catching my breath, Kerry caged in my arms in front of me, her head resting back against my shoulder, that I hear the buzzing coming from my jeans puddled on the bathroom floor. The call to duty. Before I even have a chance to make a grab for it, the sound stops.

"I'm guessing that's the office wondering where I am," I suggest carefully, feeling her back straightening against me. "But they can wait another few minutes. I'm not quite ready to take my hands off you yet."

I use my time to familiarize myself with her body, carefully washing her hair, avoiding her injury as best I can, and using my hands to soap her skin from top to bottom. While she rinses off, I manage to accomplish the same for myself, in record time. All too soon, I step right behind her out of the tub, accepting the towel she holds out.

"Listen," I say while I quickly rub myself dry. "I'll probably have to go in, but I'd really like to have someone keep an eye on you while I'm gone."

"I'll be fine," she dismisses me, wrapping the towel around her body as she pads into her bedroom. "I feel a lot better, as I'm sure you can tell."

I smile at the coy reference, but I wasn't talking about her health. Walking up behind her, as she runs a brush through her hair in front of her closet mirror, I slip my hands around her waist, resting them lightly on her stomach. "Yes, I discovered as much," I admit with a smile at her reflection in the mirror. "But I would feel a lot better about leaving you if I knew you were safe."

The cold, harsh reality of what my words imply settle over her features.

"You're not talking about my head, are you?"

CHAPTER 16

DAMIAN

"TALK TO ME." I SIT down across from Keith, who's waiting for me at CJ's Diner.

The call that had come in that morning, while I was in the shower with Kerry, had been from Jasper. He needed to talk to me about how deep I wanted him to dig into Willoughs. He'd discovered the man rented a post office box in town. I gave him free rein, dig as deep and dirty as he wanted. To question the postmaster and get back to me with anything he finds out. Luna was keeping an eye on Kerry, and I used the rest of the day to follow up on some of my other cases.

Last night we ate a late dinner after I relieved Luna, and both of us fell asleep in front of the late-night news. I ended up carrying Kerry to bed and crawling in behind her.

This morning I had hopes of repeating yesterday's shower activities, but the damn phone rang before I'd gotten out of bed.

This time it was Blackfoot. He said he had something important to discuss with me, which he insisted had to be face-to-face.

It was already closing on nine o'clock, a little later than planned, but I couldn't leave Kerry without having a little taste. Besides, I had to wait for Luna to get there.

Keith waits until the waitress is gone before responding. "I have a bad feeling about this one," he drops, and it takes me only a second to realize he's talking about the trafficking investigation.

"How so?"

"I found a tracker on Kerry's car. I would've missed it if my sleeve hadn't got caught on the side mirror on the passenger side. Looked like someone tagged the back of it with a micro satellite transmitter, no bigger than a dime. This is not open-market stuff, Damian." He leans back as the server slides mugs of coffee on the table in front of us.

I wait until she's gone before I lean in. "Government-issue?" I keep my voice down.

"I suspect," he confirms, taking a sip of his coffee. "The tech who was with me had a look at it. He couldn't find any marking you'd normally see on open-market electronic equipment. He took it back to the lab."

"Do you trust him?" I have to ask.

"Yeah. Browns is a good guy, a solid guy. I trust him. I'd like him to have a look at the bookstore and Kerry's house, as well, check her phone. I'd be surprised if they weren't bugged also."

I sit back in my chair and try to digest the information. Aside from the confirmation that Kerry seems to be targeted, the use of such highly specialized monitoring equipment is very concerning. I'm glad I put Roosberg on Kerry. She's a good agent.

"That's why you want to keep the missing box under wraps. Shit. You think you can flush whoever it is out in the open," I confirm with Keith. My mind is going a mile a minute as we spend the next twenty or so strategizing and discussing options, only interrupted when the waitress serves our food.

When we step outside, Keith holds me up with a hand on my arm. "If you need help covering her, let me know."

"Right. Like that's gonna happen," I scoffingly reply.

"I'm serious," he says earnestly. "Dammit, Damian, you know me better. I like to tease and poke, but when it gets down to it, you know you can trust me. I wouldn't move on your girl, but I care enough not to want anything to happen to her, either."

I stare him down, seeing nothing but honesty in his eyes. He's right, I do know him. I know he's a rogue with little regard for the rules, but he's a man of honor. "I'll call," I simply say with a sharp nod. "I'll get Jasper to do a quick scan of the store and her place. He finds anything, I'll make sure he leaves it where it is until you get there with your guy." We agreed that rather than having to explain to Kerry why the cops are going through her house and place of business, it would be an easier sell to have Jasper do it. That way we can blame it on my overprotective nature. I balked when Keith first suggested it but had to admit he made a good point.

"Fair enough. Later, Gomez," he says as he turns to his car.

"Later, Blackfoot."

Kerry

"I've got to get to the store!"

I try to push by Luna, who is blocking the door.

She hasn't said much since she walked in earlier, once again with her laptop under her arm. Like yesterday, she just sat down at the kitchen counter, politely accepted the coffee I offered, and focused on her computer. I felt pretty good today; my head hardly hurt at all, and I felt more stable on my feet then yesterday, so I'd started on some housework that had been left for too long. I put a few loads in the laundry, tidied the kitchen, and gave the bathtub a good cleaning, letting my thoughts wander to the naked make-out session this morning. At least Damian had been naked, I had on panties...not that that stopped him from giving me an orgasm with his fingers. I was just wiping the bathroom mirror, a smile firmly plastered on my face, when the phone rang.

"Hello?"

"Hi, Kerry. It's Bella. Listen, I was out this morning running a few errands, and I decided to stop by your store to pick up something to read. I'm bored out of my brain at Damian's and needed something to keep me occupied while I'm waiting to start my job. I was thinking of trying that series you told me about? The one with the motorcycle club that was really a cover for a covert group of law enforcement agents? I can't remember the name now, *All Out* or something? Anyway," Bella gabbed on and part of me tuned out. But then she said something that jerked me from my thoughts.

"What did you say?" I interrupted her.

"The door. It was closed. Well, not just closed but locked. Lights off and everything. I was surprised because you mentioned the other day you had someone looking after it, so when—"

I cut her off mid-ramble. "Honey, I've gotta go," I explained urgently. "Thanks so much for letting me know, but I have to give Marya a call and find out what happened. I'll talk to you later, okay?"

"Of course—of course."

I barely allowed Bella to finish before I hit end and dialed Marya's number.

"Hello. You've reached—"

I cut off the call without listening to the whole

message and proceeded to try the store, hoping she got delayed for some reason and had just been late. I hung up when my own voice sounded back to me.

Something is not right.

"Kerry," Luna tries to calm me down. "Before you go racing out of here half-cocked, we should call the boss, let him know what's going on."

"It's just that she's been acting a little off lately, and her kids are away on a trip with her mom. If something happened to her..." I let the thought drift off. I know I'm panicking, but I can't seem to stop it. My life's been spinning out of control, and I don't know what to expect anymore.

"I'll call him," Luna says, already dialing. After she explains the situation to him, she hands the phone to me. "He wants to talk to you."

"Damian?"

"Babe, I need you sit tight there with Luna. I'll go check out the store, make sure everything is okay there. Does Bill Franklin have a spare key?" he asks.

"No. Not to the new locks."

"Doesn't matter. One of us will pick yours up. It'll be either Jasper or me."

"Isn't it easier if we meet you there?" I suggest.

"Easier, yes—safer, no. Give us a chance to check it out first. I just left Blackfoot, but I'll get in touch with him and ask him to drive by Marya's place. Do you have an address for her?"

"Hang on," I tell him and fish my new phone from my pocket. With shaking fingers, I try to navigate the contact list I thankfully managed to salvage from the cloud. "I have it," I finally tell him.

"Good. Send it as a text. I'll make sure Keith gets it. And stay put."

I open my mouth to tell him I will, but he's already gone. I give Luna her phone back and quickly send Marya's info to Damian from mine.

With that done, I take a deep breath and take a firm hold of my jitters. It'll be fine. Maybe she slept in or forgot about an appointment and didn't want to bother me. Not that I really buy into that, but just the process of thinking up possible scenarios seems good enough to give me back some semblance of control.

Five minutes later, Jasper is at the door to pick up the key. I watch his car disappear down the driveway through the front window and stay standing there long after he's gone from my view. As soon as I know Marya's okay, I'm going to crawl into bed and hide there until this all goes away.

DAMIAN

"Do you have your kit?"

He lifts the bag in his hand in response and tosses me the keys. We're by the back door, trying to avoid drawing attention. Just as I push open the door and let Jasper pass inside, Kerry's neighbor, Bill Franklin, steps out with a garbage bag in his hand.

"Everything all right?" he asks, dropping his trash bag in the dumpster and walking my way.

Not knowing what's inside, I hold up my hand. "I'll come talk to you after," I just say and step inside, closing the door behind me. The door did not look forced, and the front was still locked tight when we checked it in passing. Nevertheless, we have no idea what, if anything, is going on inside. Jasper is checking the small bathroom and Kerry's office, so I slip past him into the store.

The rows of bookshelves cast off long, dark shadows without the benefit of the overhead lights. Still, I prefer to go in without flipping the switch. I press my back against the farthest shelf from the front and ease my way along to the other side, my gun drawn. From the corner of my eye, I can see Jasper's caught up with me and is slipping into the next aisle over. We methodically clear each of the aisles before we meet up at the counter.

"Nothing," Jasper states the obvious.

"Get your kit. Let's check this place while we're here."

While Jasper pulls out his gear and starts sweeping Kerry's office, I put a quick call in to Keith.

"Nothing here," he says. "Her car's in the driveway, but it doesn't look like anyone's home."

"Nothing here, either. Have you been inside?" I want to know, but the pregnant silence tells me enough. It is Blackfoot, after all. "Signs of struggle?"

"None," is the curt answer.

"Thank God for that. Dammit, Blackfoot—you know we can't just go barging in without—"

"I know," he bites off. "I also know that by the time a missing persons report is properly filed, we could be up to a day or more later. In the meantime, she could've been hurt in there."

I clasp the back of my neck with a hand and lift my face to the ceiling. "Let's just stick with that," I concede. "As soon as you're done there, get over to Kerry's store. Jasper started a sweep."

"Fifteen minutes," he's quick to answer before he adds, "and you be ready for a full-on task force briefing in my office for four this afternoon. I just got a text now." Just as he hangs up the phone, the same information buzzes on my phone. *Wonderful*.

Jasper comes out of the back office, holding his phone up. "Did you see that?"

"Yup, I did. You done back there?"

"I am," he says without elaborating. "You gonna tell me what's going on?" For a moment, I'm undecided and by the raise of Jasper's eyebrow, I can tell he notices.

"Probably," I answer ambiguously, "but first I want to know what you found out from the postmaster and what turned up back there that has you playing word games with me." The fact he didn't immediately say *clear* when I asked about the office didn't pass me by.

Jasper's face settles in a lazy grin. "You're far too smart for your own good, boss."

"As are you, my friend. Now spill."

"Took a bit of convincing, the guy considers himself knowledgeable on the dos and don'ts of law enforcement, probably watches too much TV, but I managed to make him see the light."

"I bet you did." I play along, not quite able to hide a smile.

"Mostly boxes, the occasional padded envelope. No real pattern to it and not from any single source that he's noticed. He doesn't really make note of the sender but says most of the boxes arrive through UPS. He records the UPS tracking number and the weight. Apparently the last box he received weighed just shy of ten pounds and was collected almost a month ago."

"Does he have someone picking up for him?" I want to know.

"Nope. Always him. Always first thing in the morning."

"Did you take down the tracking number?" He doesn't answer, but his expression says enough. "Fine then. First chance you get, see what you can find out. Now," I shift gears. "What did you find?"

"What? No tit for tat?" he says with a smirk.

"I want both your tits before you get anything."

"Boss!" Jasper burst out laughing. "You joke? Man, I wish Luna was here to witness it. She'll never believe it." My growl is enough to get him back on track.

"Two bugs. One on the top ledge of the doorframe and one in the phone. Micro-sized, unfamiliar markings," he informs me, his face now devoid of any humor. The grinding in my gut just got cranked up a notch.

"Save them for Blackfoot. He's on his way. Start with the phone in here."

KERRY

It's been two hours since Jasper picked up the key, and I haven't heard a thing. That's good, right? I figure it means they're still looking and they haven't found anything...worrisome.

I haven't moved from the window, although Luna urged me to have some lunch with her. She finally gave up and brought me a sandwich, which is still sitting on the side table, untouched. I can't eat. The events of the past weeks have been swirling through my head, and aside from the major ones, I can't seem to shake the feeling something was up with Marya. Almost the entire time. Then that weird rushed end to our last telephone conversation, almost as if she wanted off the phone instantly. It was right after I'd noticed the voice in the background and called her on it. It had sounded familiar. I've been racking my brain to place it. Maybe I should tell Damian about it.

I'm still contemplating if I should mention anything when his familiar dark SUV comes up the driveway. I'm not even aware I'm running for the front door until I hear Luna yell at me to stop. By that time, I'm already swinging the door open. A hand on my arm stops me from tearing out of the house when Luna catches up. As Damian steps out of his SUV, a second car, a patrol car, comes pulling in right behind it.

"Get inside, Kerry," Damian orders as he walks up in long strides. I try to read the answers to my questions on his face, but his professional mask is firmly in place. When he reaches me and I haven't moved yet, he puts his hands on my shoulders. "Babe—Inside." This time his face gentles as he turns me around, wraps his arm around my waist, and walks me straight to the couch.

I just now notice Keith Blackfoot coming in behind us, closing the door. This can't be good.

"We haven't found Marya." Damian doesn't pussyfoot around. "She's not at the store, and Keith checked her house, she's not there, either. Honey? Is there anywhere else she could be?"

"Oh…I…I'm not sure," I stammer. "Normally I'd say her mom's, but she's taken Marya's boys with her to visit her sisters. Silverado I think, Marya said."

"Don't worry," Keith speaks up. "I'll find her contact information. Maybe she decided last minute to go up with them," he offers lamely.

"That makes no sense," I counter. "She'd never do that without letting me know. I just talked to her yesterday, and she never said anything. In fact, she told me she'd talk to me today."

"Can you think of anything else? Someone she could be with? A friend she might seek out if she ended up sick?" Damian is gentle with his questions, but I can sense the urgency behind them. He's worried, too. That's when I start talking. I start with her uncharacteristic behavior, the insistence to keep her new man's identity a secret for now. And I finish with yesterday's telephone call.

"Where could you've heard it before?" Blackfoot asks, referring to the male voice in the background.

"Trust me, I've tried hard to think of it, but I just can't place it. It could've been a customer or a store clerk or maybe someone at the bank. I have no idea." Damian and the detective share a look. One that has the hair on my arms stand on end. "What?"

Both sets of eyes turn to me, but this time it's Damian who speaks. "Jasper is on his way. As soon as he gets here, he and Keith are going to search your house."

"My house? But I—" I almost shoot up from my seat, but Damian's large hand on my shoulder keeps me firmly in place.

"I need you to go pack a bag. You're coming with me."

My stomach drops. It's like I've landed in a parallel universe. This morning I had this man's mouth on me and his fingers in me. Now he's going to take me in? I don't understand.

"But why are you taking me in?" I manage, my voice wobbly.

"Taking you in? What are you talking about?" He tightens his grip on my shoulders and pierces me with his eyes.

"Oh, for God's sake," Luna blurts out. The first I've heard her say since the men got here. "Your bedside manner sucks, boss. You haven't explained one damn thing to her. Why don't you try that first before you scare the crap out of her?"

I keep my eyes on Damian, who is glaring at Luna, but then turns to me with a remorseful smile as Blackfoot starts to chuckle behind me. "Sorry, Gypsy. Force of habit. Keith and Jasper are going to check your house for bugs. Listening devices or cameras," he explains when my face twists in distaste at the mention of bugs. He's talking about another kind of bug.

"There were two in your office and another three in the store. Each of your phones were bugged. There's a possibility whoever managed to get into the store, managed to get into your house, as well."

CHAPTER 17

DAMIAN

"AT LEAST IT MAKES a bit more sense now."

I turn to look at Kerry, who received the news someone was keeping some serious tabs on her rather quietly. Once Jasper went to work, she reacted with only a flinch the first time his handheld gadget gave off the high-pitched whine, indicating the presence of one of those little suckers in her kitchen phone. Only when Jasper followed us into her bedroom and started running the detector over the clothes she had stacked on the bed to pack did she gasp, as a full body shiver ran through her.

I think it hit her at that time how vulnerable she is. When you discover someone's been in not only your car, but your business and your house, it tends to put things into perspective. And it's scary as hell when a wireless camera the size of a pinhead is found in your living room.

"What does?" I ask her. We're on our way to my house, and I'm taking the long way, making sure I don't have any tails. It wouldn't be too far-fetched to think they are keeping an eye on her, as well. Not many people know where I live, it's not something I advertise, and I believe it's the safest place for her to be until we get this sorted out. Once again, Kerry's Korner is closed for business because of this investigation, and there's no way I'd let Kerry stay at her place under the circumstances.

"I'd been racking my brain to figure out how they'd know I would have the box in my car, but they probably heard me mention it when I talked to Kim. Only thing I'm still a bit confused about is if the box is gone from the car, does that mean they have it? And if that's so, they wouldn't have reason to be interested in me anymore, right?"

"Maybe," I start carefully. "But we can't know that for sure. In fact, we know very little for sure at this point. I'm guessing, though, that you received the wrong shipment. Two boxes, two locations. Except, whoever was waiting on the shipment of stolen goods received your order and sounded the alarm with the auction house. They likely discovered the two shipments left at around the same time and concluded you must have received the other one. The attempt to retrieve it was obviously unsuccessful, because by some weird twist of fate, you never had the books there. They were sitting in Cortez." I glance at her and see she's mulling this over. I release one hand from the steering wheel and put it on her leg. Without even looking, she puts her hand over mine and laces our fingers.

"I hate feeling this out of control," she admits softly while still staring out the window.

"I'm getting that."

"Do you think Marya's disappearance has to do with this?" she asks, and this time I feel her eyes on me. I give her hand a quick squeeze before I answer.

"I think true coincidences are rare, but I promise we'll do everything in our power to find her."

"She has little boys, Damian. And her mom. She wouldn't just take off." The wobble in her voice almost has me pull over, but my cutoff is coming up. Best just to get her to safety first.

"I know, babe."

The moment we round the bend at the top of the hill, the Animas River spreads out in front of us, and from the corner of my eye, I see Kerry leaning forward to take it all in.

"Oh my God. This is gorgeous!"

I smile at the instant change in mood. It's what coming home does to me after long days of poking around in humanity's underbelly. It's the reason I bought this place. My house is a two-story log home with a porch that wraps around the front and halfway down the sides. In the back, I built a large deck that overlooks the Animas River. My sanctuary. A place only my family visits occasionally.

Bella's car is parked on the circular drive, and as I park behind her, she steps through the front door. Any surprise she might have displayed at seeing Kerry in the passenger seat is gone as quickly as it appeared.

"I was just about to get your bed made up," Bella says to Kerry as we walk up the steps. A nice attempt at a save, but I get the feeling it doesn't escape Kerry. Still, there's a world of acceptance in that simple statement, and I'm grateful my sister is trying to make this as easy as possible for her.

With a smile and a soft spoken, "Thanks," Kerry follows Bella inside where she is immediately dragged through to the kitchen in the back, leaving me to deal with the bags.

I briefly toy with the idea of moving Kerry into the master bedroom but quickly change my mind. I don't know how long she'll be here, and given that she just told me she hates feeling out of control, I figure it would be wiser to let her have her own space. I have a feeling the harder I push her, the stronger her resistance will be.

Bella is staying in the room on the opposite side of the hallway, so that leaves the spare room on the other side of the master bath. Close enough for her to come find me if and when she wants.

Downstairs in the kitchen, I find Kerry sitting on a stool at the island and Bella pouring a healthy glass of wine for her.

"You want something to drink?" Bella asks.

"I can't. I've got to get back to the office. I should

be back for dinner but will give you a call later."

James Aiken called a meeting. I'm guessing to clear the air between Blackfoot and Ella. She must've been pissed when she got here and found out he'd ignored her instructions to wait for her. I'm going to take the lead from Keith on this one. I know he's suspicious and I understand why. And I'm not about to divulge I've got Kerry staying at my place. Jasper and Luna know, and so does Blackfoot, but I have no intention of volunteering that information. Not with so many questions up in the air.

Ignoring my sister, I turn Kerry's stool so that she's facing me and tilt her chin up. "You're safe here. I have a top-of-the-line alarm system, and in case of an emergency, Bella knows where I keep my guns. Just so you know, other than Blackfoot and my family, no one knows about this place. Have you handled a gun before?" I ask her.

"It's been a while, but yes."

"Good. And Bella is a pretty decent shot." I ignore the huff coming from my sister. "Just in case," I reinforce. "I hope to be just a couple of hours, but if it gets much later, I'll call."

Without waiting for an answer, I cover her mouth with mine, kissing her thoroughly. When I come up for air, my sister is dramatically fanning herself with a potholder, donning a big smile. "Behave, brat," I shoot in her direction.

"Whatever," she fires back, completely unimpressed.

"Bella..." I growl, and she rolls her eyes, sighing deeply.

"Fine, oh Lord and Master," she concedes with a curtsy.

I lean in for another quick taste of Kerry's mouth, who is watching our sibling interaction with a smile, and then I round the island to give Bella a peck on the cheek on my way out the door.

KERRY

Damian's house is stunning. Surprisingly light inside, due to the full-height, two-story windows that go up almost clear to the cathedral ceilings at the back of the house. Both the kitchen and a family room are bright and open, and from wherever you are, you can see the gorgeous river valley. I have no problem seeing myself staying here for a few days, despite the somewhat awkward realization I'll be housing with Damian *and* his sister.

Taken in by the charm of the house, I almost forget why I'm here when the realization hits like a cold bucket of water and I wince.

"Want to tell me what happened?" Bella asks, her head tilted to one side. We'd been sipping wine and Bella talked about her new job coming up but never questioned why I was here. "My brother left before I could grill him, and I didn't want to pry," she adds, making me smile, because I have no doubt she could drag out his best-kept secrets. It's obviously clear how much these two care about each other.

"We can't find Marya. She's the one who was supposed to open the store today. I talked to her yesterday, and she encouraged me to stay home another day. Said she'd take care of the store. Her boys—she's got three young boys—are off with her mother to visit relatives." A lump gets stuck in my throat at the thought of those kids.

"Is it possible she would've taken off on her own for a bit?"

"And leave the store unattended? Not a chance. Especially not after she was the one to push me to stay home."

"I guess...does her mom have any ideas?"

"Keith Blackfoot was going to try to get hold of her. I just can't believe she'd take off like this, and your brother and Blackfoot seem to feel the same way. There's too much going on to have it be coincidental."

The thought something may have happened to Marya because of the situation I've landed myself in is eating at me. Bella, who appears to be as perceptive as her older brother, seems to pick up on my somber mood and quickly changes topics. I'm quietly grateful as she begins to list our options for dinner, and the next hour or so, we work surprisingly well side by side in the kitchen to put together a meal. Worry about Marya is never far from my mind, though. Despite our companionable chitchat about places to rent—I give

Bella the name of my real estate agent—and things to see and do. Even though I am cautious enough not to think too much about any kind of future with Damian at this time, I can't help get excited with the prospect of Bella moving here. I really like her, and it would be nice to have a real friend near. I miss Kim.

With the salad and dressing made, the asparagus as well as the goat cheese and spinach-stuffed chicken breasts roasting in the oven, we take our wine glasses out to the deck. The view is breathtaking, especially in the early evening sunlight. You can only hear the sound of rushing water from the river and an occasional animal cry. Nothing else.

Bella tells me a little about the break up with her boyfriend, who sounds like a grade A asshat. Engrossed in her story and with the din of the river in the background, I don't notice Damian coming home until I feel his hands on my shoulders. Odd that I seem to recognize him immediately by his touch only. I tilt my head back to look up at him, standing behind my chair. He looks exhausted, stress clearly lining his face. Still he manages to smile down at me.

"Something smells amazing," he says, as he leans in and kisses me upside down. His goatee tickles my nose and a shiver runs down my spine.

"All right, you lovebirds," Bella teases as she jumps up. "I'll get dinner sorted so you two can... catch up." She winks as she disappears inside. Damian moves around me and sits down in her chair, his elbows resting on his knees, his hands wringing in between, and his head hanging low. He is the picture of someone who carries the weight and responsibility of the world. When I tentatively reach out and cover his hands with my own, he turns one palm up and laces his fingers with mine.

"I don't have any news on Marya," he says solemnly, knowing that would be my first question.

DAMIAN

I hate seeing disappointment on her face.

I spent the past three hours going over all the details of the case with the full task force. Even Boris Parnak, with the La Plata County Criminal Investigations Unit, had been pulled away from his busy workload. With everyone present, it dawned on me it was entirely possible that one of these people might not be there with the best of intentions. It made me sick to my stomach to think that one of our own might be involved. I guess James picked up on my scrutiny at some point since he threw me a questioning glance, which I pointedly ignored.

First point on the agenda had been Kerry's car. Keith was grilled by both Ella and James. He managed to dodge Ella's vocal displeasure, at his failure to wait for her, by explaining he felt speed was of the essence since it would appear someone was playing fast and loose with Kerry's safety. I could tell Ella wanted to argue, but given that Keith's first responsibility is to the public, she quickly drew in her claws.

Ella had some news, too. Apparently Interpol had just discovered that Troy Sinclair had made his way to France and boarded a plane from Paris' de Gaulle Airport to Denver about three weeks ago. He'd been in Colorado the entire time and immediately became prime suspect for running Kerry off the road.

The disappearance of the shipment of books from Kerry's car seemed to raise concerns. Boris had brought in fingerprint reports from the break-in at the store, and at that point there was no question the cases were related. Boris confirmed one partial print, found on a shard of glass from the display case, was identified as Troy Sinclair's.

James, who had focused on the U.S. component— the auction house—reported that he is close to shutting down their online operations. His team may have pinned down a physical location, and they were moving with caution, for fear they'll alert whoever is behind it.

When Keith brought up Marya's untimely disappearance, he barely had a chance to get into specifics before the meeting broke up. I was relieved. I didn't want to get into too many details to begin with. Inevitably Kerry's name would've come up, and I wasn't about to tell them she's safely at my place.

Keith lingered when everyone else left, never having mentioned the listening devices and cameras we discovered. I didn't volunteer that information either, but it sat like rancid butter in my stomach, and he quickly updated me on the search for Marya. He'd spoken to her mother, who told him she hadn't heard from her since the night before. She'd called to wish the boys goodnight and mentioned she was going out on a date. She also confirmed her daughter would not just up and leave on her own accord. Keith apparently had to stop her from heading back to town immediately. Used her grandsons to force it home by telling her the best she could do for her daughter was to make sure her sons were shielded and looked after. She reluctantly gave in, but only after he'd promised to stay in close contact with her.

"Are you okay?" Kerry's voice breaks through my thoughts, and I capture the hand she reaches out in mine.

"Yes," I answer, giving her hand a squeeze. "Frustrated I can't give you some good news, that's all."

I give her a short, modified version of the meeting, sticking only with the results of the fingerprint analysis and Blackfoot's phone call with Marya's mother.

"I'm afraid for her..."

"I know you are, but we'll find her," I promise, not quite able to vow for her well-being when or if we do.

"Dinner's on the table," Bella calls out, and I pull Kerry up from her chair.

"I am so full," Bella says, leaning back in her chair with her hands over her stomach.

Dinner was great. I'm getting used to these

homemade meals waiting for me, and that's a dangerous thing. I can fry an egg, maybe toss together an omelet, and of course, I grill a mean steak, but that's about all you'll get out of me. Mostly I pull something quick from the freezer when I get home or pick something ready-made up when I leave work. Yeah, I'll miss Bella when she finds her own place.

I noticed Kerry hardly ate at all, but my sister kicked my shin under the table the one and only time I commented on it. The angry glare she shot me when I was about to ask her what the heck she did that for shut me right up. I'm too tired to get into anything.

"If you don't mind," Kerry says softly from beside me. "I'm tired. I'm going to bed." She gets up and starts clearing away plates, when I take them from her.

"Go on. I've got these. I'll be up soon, too." With my free hand, I tag her behind the neck and pull her in for a kiss. With a little wave of her hand at Bella, she disappears up the stairs.

"You're staring."

I turn to my sister, who is grinning wide. "Better than looking at you, kid," I fire back, slipping past her to the kitchen, where I dump the dishes in the sink. Bella follows me in, carrying the rest of the stuff from the table.

"I like her for you, Damian." I turn on the tap to fill the sink, when I feel Bella's arms wrap around me from behind. "Don't fuck it up," she adds.

I snort loudly. "Seeing as I've never looked at

a woman I could see in my future before, I'd say chances are pretty solid I'll do just that. Fuck up."

"All you need to learn is three little words," my wiseass sister says.

"Don't rush me, Bella. It's too soon." I'm not sure I'm ready for declarations of love. She pinches my sides—hard.

"Not talking about *I love you*, dimwit. Might be early for that, but it's never too soon to learn to say *I am sorry.* It's kind of a mandatory addition to your vocabulary when you are of the male persuasion."

"Right. I'll keep that in mind." I don't bother telling her that I've already had an occasion or two where I've had to apologize to Kerry. Another first for me.

"I'll clean these up in the morning," Bella says, shoving me away from the sink. "Go see if she can find everything okay."

I hook my arm around her neck and kiss her on the head. "You're the best."

"Yeah, whatever. Get out of here." She rolls her eyes and turns back to the sink, but I can see the smile on her face.

I make it up the stairs and pause outside the bedroom door, lifting my hand to knock before I change my mind and push open the door. Knocking feels too much like taking a step back, and that's not what I want.

But the room is empty. The connecting door to the bathroom is open, but it's empty, as well. When I spot the door connecting to my bedroom at a crack, I perform an inner fist pump.

"There you are," I whisper when I see the outline of her body buried under my covers. Quietly, so I don't wake her up, I step back in the bathroom, going through my nightly routine of brushing my teeth and shedding my clothes. She's still in the same position when I sneak up on the bed. Her hair is spread out on the pillow, and her face is barely visible under the sheets she's pulled up around her ear. I carefully slip in behind her. The instant my hand finds her hip, she rolls toward me and opens her eyes.

"Do you mind? I just—"

"I'm glad," I tell her honestly, rolling on my back and pulling her on top. "Whatever you need, Gypsy."

"I need you," she says, her fingers trailing up my neck and into my hair, her soft mouth pressed to mine, a clear invitation.

My hands slide down to cup the cheeks of her ass as heat is fueling our kiss. She pulls her knees up to rest on either side of my hips and rocks herself on the length of my cock. My fingers look for the edge of her panties but all they find is the silky feel of skin.

"Fuck," I groan, slipping my fingers through her slick folds.

"Promise me you're clean," she pants against my lips, tilting her ass up to give me better access, while continuing to rub herself on me.

"Testing is part of my annual physical, and I never go without," I grunt as her hips pick up speed.

"Never?" she moans and I clasp her hips, stilling her movements. She lifts her head a little, and I can see the question in her eyes.

"Are you sure?"

"I'm on the pill."

She barely gets the last word from her lips before I've lined up my cock and surge my hips up, burying myself to the hilt.

"*Jesus...* " I hiss at the intense sensation. The last time I went bareback was my first time at fifteen, not old enough to be able to enjoy the feeling, I was too busy getting off. The period of sheer panic for two months after, when the girl told me she thought she might be pregnant, ensured I spent the rest of my life properly protected.

I bring my knees up, feet planted in the bed, and pull back slightly before I surge back up. Kerry throws her head back and grabs my legs with her hands behind her and finds her rhythm riding me as I fuck her from below. The soft grunts and open-mouthed moans as much a turn on as the feeling of her arousal coating my dick. It doesn't take long before she falls forward, changing her angle to look for completion. I power inside her more forcefully and grind my root against her clit at the end of each thrust. My leg muscles are burning, but I am beyond caring as my hips buck erratically in the chase of my own release. Just as I feel her pussy spasm around me and her teeth sink into my shoulder, I teeter over the edge. My mouth wide open and my head tilted back, I grunt as each stream of semen is forced from my body to hers. We don't move, we simply cling to each other, still very much connected, waiting for our heartbeats to calm and our breathing to slow down.

Just moments later, I can feel her body get heavier on mine as she falls back asleep. This is something I could easily get used to, skin-to-skin, her breath against my skin and my arms keeping her close—safe.

The faint ringing of a phone wakes me the next morning and has Kerry stirring in my arms. It's not my ringtone, but Kerry seems to recognize it, because all of a sudden she's scrambling to get out of bed. Before I can say anything, she's rushing toward the bathroom door, and I swing my legs out of bed and start following her.

She's standing beside the spare bed, rifling through her purse, when she finally pulls free her phone. Her eyes grow big when she checks the display and immediately looks for me as she accepts the call.

"Marya?"

CHAPTER 18

"MEET ME IN HALF an hour at Greenmount Cemetery, northwest corner, there's a trail just beyond the cemetery grounds."

He's not given a chance to respond as the line goes dead.

He knew he fucked up. Hopefully, he'd be able to do some damage control before the bottom fell out completely. The pressure had been building to show his efforts were paying off, but so far nothing has gone as planned. The shipment was still missing, and now his carefully placed surveillance had been compromised.

His mistake had been to think he could manipulate that little store clerk. She'd come in handy to get access to the shop and keep him updated on her boss's schedule. Heck, she'd been the one to spill that her *boss was picking up the box from Cortez. It had all gone south when he thought he could quickly check the camera feed off his laptop while she was sleeping in the next room. She'd caught him staring at a picture of the inside of her boss's house. She freaked and he panicked, needing to shut her up.*

She'd gone down instantly when he hit her, and he'd been able to load her in his new rental. He tried to wipe down the obvious things he'd touched in her place but couldn't be sure if he got them all. Grabbing her purse and her phone was a last ditch effort to perhaps make it look like she'd taken off for the day, before anyone would clue in.

The drive from her place to his hotel was easy, there were hardly any people or cars on the street in the middle of the night. Luckily, he'd had the foresight to get a room at the far corner of the hotel. He could park right by the back door that had stairs going straight up to his room. The only door he had to pass was a service door. Other than the night janitor in the lobby on the far side of the building, no one was up and about. A good thing, too, since the woman draped over his shoulder was as naked as the day she was born.

He'd been rattled, not sure what to do with her now he had her in his room, and when she came to, he may have been a little too forceful. He had to get her to stop her screaming. He tossed her bag on the bed, and with one hand had grabbed her throat, while with the other had twisted her arm up behind her back.

Now she's lying on the bathroom floor, looking nothing like the pretty brunette he'd had no trouble using for his purposes. In fact, it had been quite pleasurable, she'd turned out to be a bit of a wildcat. Unfortunately, however distasteful it would be, he couldn't let her blow the whistle on him and would have to take care of her in a more permanent way.

First he had to try and smooth over things with his partner, whose cold anger had been palpable, even through the phone. For just a second he wondered if he should be afraid, but then he reminded himself he was invaluable to this operation.

It would be his last mistake.

CHAPTER 19

KERRY

"I'M SO SORRY."

It takes my brain a little to register the faintly whispered words.

I hadn't planned on crawling into Damian's bed, but I needed to feel something familiar. Something safe. I'd brushed my teeth, donned an old nightshirt, and simply stood there in the door to his bedroom. Not like me to be needy, but tonight I wanted to feel safe. The moment I recognized his scent on the sheets, I was able to let my body relax. When I'd felt his touch, I let my instinctive needs take over before falling into a deep sleep in the protection of his body.

I could've slept for days if the sound of Marya's ringtone on my phone hadn't dragged me awake. I try to ignore the stickiness that clings to me as I rush through the bathroom to the other side.

"Marya? Where are you? Are you okay?" I'm shooting questions off as Damian sits down next to me on the bed.

"I've been so stupid," she says on a sob.

"Oh, honey, whatever it is, we'll fix it. I've been so worried." Tears of relief are running down my face.

Damian, who's trying to listen in, gently takes the phone from my hands and puts it on speaker.

"Marya? This is Damian Gomez. Are you alone?"

"I am now. I think I'm in a hotel room."

"Do you know which one? Which hotel? Are you still in Durango?"

"I don't know," she cries out. "I woke up on the bathroom floor, my phone was on the bed in the room. I have no clothes." The last is whispered so low I can barely make it out.

"Honey," Damian says patiently. "Here's what you do. Wrap yourself in a sheet from the bed. Can you do that right now?" We can hear some rustling in the back before she comes back on the phone.

"Good. Now put the night lock on the door. You know what I mean, right?" When Marya answers affirmative, Damian continues, "Are you able to look out the window? Describe what you see?"

Damian leans in and whispers in my ear. "Grab my phone from my jeans in the bathroom. Keith's number is speed dial seven. Call him." I hurry into the bathroom, hearing Damian calmly questioning her. My heart and mind are both racing. She sounds hurt. She's not okay. With fumbling fingers, I find

Damian's phone and hit seven.

"Son of a bitch, Gomez. I've been up all goddamn night. What do you want now?" Keith's angry voice blasts in my ear.

"It's Kerry," I tell him. "Marya's on the phone. Something is wrong. Damian has her on speaker and is trying to find out where she is. He asked me to call you."

"Christ, Kerry. Okay, this is good…take the phone to Damian. So I can listen in."

I pad over to the bed, where I hear Marya's weak voice describe a parking lot and the cars she sees. I hold Damian's cell close, so Keith can hear.

"…there are two motorcycles parked side by side. Oh, I see smoke. There's smoke coming up from behind a fence on the far side of the parking lot." A second later, we clearly hear a distinct train whistle.

"You did good. I think we have a good idea where you are. Have you met Detective Blackfoot, Marya? He'll be knocking on your door soon, and you're going to ask a question that I'll make sure only he can answer. He answers right, you can open the door. Does that sound okay? Hang in there, honey. I'm going to give you back to Kerry for a minute."

Damian starts barking into the phone, and I quickly take mine off speaker so Marya can't hear. "Did you hear that? The Durango-Silverton line. Yes. That's what I think, there are just a few near enough for her to see the smoke. Right." The next twenty minutes I spend listening to my friend say sorry, over and over again, as she quietly sobs. Every now and then I ask her if she's all right, but I don't ask her much else. I manage to glean she probably has a broken arm, she's sore all over, and there's blood covering her naked body. This information I pass on to Damian quietly and he relays to Keith via text. Until the police find her, I just want to keep her, and myself, as calm as I can, but I badly want to ask who did that to her.

"Someone's at the door," Marya's urgent whisper sounds in my ear.

"Okay, honey. Remember that question Damian gave you? Go ahead, ask it."

"I'm supposed to ask you what your favorite breakfast is," I hear her say, but I can't hear the answer.

"What did he say?" I ask her.

"Honey Nut Cheerios."

I put the phone back on speaker, and we listen to Keith's soft voice mumbling in the background. Suddenly, his voice comes over the phone. "I've got her. Durango Lodge room 212. I'm gonna call the EMTs up and will let you know the scoop as soon as I know more." He pauses a moment before he adds, "Kerry, honey? I promise I'll take good care of her." With that he hangs up the phone.

I jump up, pulling random clothes from my bag, ready to jump in the car and drive out there.

"You can't," Damian says, grabbing hold of my hands. "You can't rush into town before we even know what we're dealing with. Let Keith do his job. He'll make sure Marya is protected, and I promise he'll be careful with her. But if you run to her bedside, you're making yourself an easy target."

"She's my *friend*," I hiss in his face. "Whatever happened to her has something to do with me, or she wouldn't have apologized over and over again. I'm going." With that I yank my hands free, turn around, and hoist myself into a bra.

"Jesus, Kerry. You're not playing fair," Damian groans as he wraps his arms around me from behind, pinning my arms effectively to my sides. "Listen, I get it," he whispers against my neck. "I would react the same way, but it's not safe for you. And ultimately it might not be safe for Marya."

My body slumps in his arms. I hate that he uses her against me. I hate that he's right. I don't say anything, there's nothing much to say.

"I'm sorry," he says softly, dissolving the remainder of my anger and leaving only worry and sadness. He presses his lips behind my ear before loosening his grip. Silently, I pick up the yoga pants and oversized T-shirt I'd randomly pulled from my bag. With my clothing in hand, I walk into the bathroom and close the door. I feel like a fraud, given that I crawled in his bed last night, looking for his body to comfort me, but right now I just need a little time to myself. Luckily, he doesn't follow me.

Under the warm spray of the shower, I let go of my frustration, my anger, my uselessness, and my fear. With tears streaming down my face unchecked, I sit down in the bottom of the tub and pull up my knees.

DAMIAN

Son of a bitch.

I hear her crying through the door and I hate it. I want to rush in and wrap her up, but I recognized the determined set of her shoulders as she walked in the bathroom and closed the door behind her. The message was clear enough that she needed some time by herself. Knowing that she didn't hesitate to find my bed last night, when she needed to have me near, makes it a little easier to step back now. Kerry obviously knows her own needs, and if she wants to be alone right now, I have no business marching in.

No matter how much it goes against my instincts, I let Kerry be and head to my bedroom, quickly pulling on my discarded boxers and grabbing a change of clothes. I make my way to the second bathroom where I bump into Bella.

"Everything okay?" she wants to know, and I tell her about this morning's events.

"I'm just gonna have a quick shower in your bathroom while Kerry's using mine. Would you mind getting some coffee on? I'll do eggs when I get down."

"Yeah, no problem."

When I come down, only Bella is in the kitchen. Kerry must still be upstairs. I'm all for giving her what she needs, but if she's still up there when I'm done putting breakfast together, I'm getting her.

I get a start on bacon and eggs, while Bella sets out some plates and pops in toast. We work easily side by side without talking when I finally hear Kerry's footsteps coming down the stairs. I turn around and watch her coming straight for me, not a falter in her step, until she's plastered against me, her arms tight around my waist and her head against my shoulder. It takes me a minute to react and wrap her up.

"Thank you," she says. "I needed that."

"All right, you guys," Bella pipes up. "Thrilled you can't keep your hands off each other, but give this girl a break, will ya? No need to rub my nose in it." As she walks past, she snaps the tea towel in her hand.

"Dammit, Bella."

Kerry snickers when I rub my ass where the towel left a sharp sting. I like seeing the smile on her face, but it instantly evaporates when my phone loudly buzzes on the counter.

"Talk to me." The display shows Keith's number. With her eyes fixed on my face, Kerry sidles up to me and I pull her close, my arm draped over her shoulders.

"Just arrived at Mercy Regional. They're looking her over thoroughly, but the fucker knocked her around. EMT suspects they'll find her orbital bone fractured. It's the only thing aside from her left arm, which she can't use, that she'd let them have a look at. She kept that sheet wrapped tightly around her."

"Fuck. You think she...?" I feel Kerry go rigid beside me.

"Don't know, man. But she keeps asking for Kerry. I haven't been able to get a coherent word from her, and I'm thinking if you were to bring Kerry here, she might be able to get some information."

"Not sure if that's a good idea," I voice my concern. "She's safe where she is now."

"What? Are you talking about me?" Kerry pushes back so she can look at me. "Does she need me?"

"Babe…"

"Please, Damian. It's going to drive me insane being stuck here if there's something I can do to help. No offense," she says with an apologetic glance at Bella before turning her eyes back to me.

"No offense taken," Bella replies. "I totally get it."

"Gomez." Blackfoot's voice breaks through the stare down Kerry and I have going on.

"Give us an hour," I reluctantly give in. "Make sure you've got someone you trust save a parking spot close to an entrance. I'm getting Jas here to keep our six. He'll be able to spot any tails we might pick up and intervene." I didn't know gratitude could be seen in a facial expression, but I was reading it loud and clear on Kerry's face.

"Hit the employee parking lot on the west side of the building and call me when you're close," Keith says before he ends the call.

"I've got a few calls to make. You need to use that time to eat something," I order Kerry, who nods her agreement eagerly. She's not likely to argue when she's just gotten her way. Never mind that my stomach is churning at the thought of putting her out in the open again. The meaning of the strong, visceral reaction I have is something I don't have time to consider now. I have a safe transport to plan.

"Bella, can you find me a shawl or something to cover her hair?"

"She'd stand out like a sore thumb with a shawl on her head. It's eighty-five degrees out there already. I've got a baseball cap, that'll do the trick. I'll grab some stuff." With that, Bella rushes up the stairs and I dial Jasper.

I'm keeping an eye on my rearview mirror, where I catch glimpses of Jasper driving the Expedition and making sure to keep at least a couple of cars between. The tinted windows on the SUV make it difficult to see who's behind the wheel. With Jas driving, he can throw off anyone who locks in on my truck.

Kerry is in the passenger seat, her hair tucked away in the cap Bella handed her and her body covered with a thin hoodie over a pair of cropped yoga pants. All courtesy of Bella, as well, who astutely pointed out that Kerry's style of dress is as distinct as her hair. Kerry almost looks like a teenager in this get up.

I'm in the back seat of Bella's car, my head almost bumping the ceiling and my knees somewhere up around my ears. Bella is driving. I balked when she announced she was coming, let alone that she was driving, but she made a damn good point. Said that anyone would recognize me from a distance and that for all the effort we went through to cover Kerry's identity, the mere fact I was by her side would be enough to blow her cover. I hated admitting she was right.

The plan is for Bella, who has a legit reason to be at Mercy since she was supposed to go in to sign her contract this week anyway, to walk into the hospital with Kerry. No one would have reason to connect Bella to me or to Kerry. Keith said he'd be waiting by the elevator, right inside the entrance, and would take it from there. All I had to do was keep an eye on them from my vantage point in the back seat. Fucking hell.

The drive is uneventful, thank God. As agreed, the moment we pull into the west employee parking lot, a patrol car backs out of a spot right beside the entrance. Bella pulls in.

"Ready?" she asks Kerry, who hasn't said a word the entire trip but nods in response.

"Wait." I stop them, leaning forward as best I can given the limited space. With my hand in Kerry's neck, I whisper in her ear, "Be careful. Listen to Keith and I'll be right behind you."

"I will," she says, slightly turning her head so I can brush her lips with mine.

Sitting here, watching them walk away from me is a fuckload harder than I anticipated. Two women who have a firm hold on my heart. I catch a glimpse of Blackfoot inside the lobby and sigh a breath of relief when I see him hold the elevator door open and usher my girls inside.

As agreed, I stay in Bella's car for another few

minutes, just to see if anyone has more than a casual interest in those two. After a few minutes, I carefully unfold myself from the back seat and stretch my limbs when I get out of the car. A few blocks from the hospital, Jasper took off in a different direction and would be parking somewhere on the other side of the building by now.

"I'm looking for Detective Blackfoot," I tell the nurse manning the desk in the emergency room. She directs me to a small waiting room at the end of the hallway.

I don't see Bella, but Kerry is sitting in a chair with her back facing the door. A precaution suggested by Keith, I'm sure. He is standing with his shoulder leaning against the wall, seemingly casual but with his hand just a breath away from his hip holster. The moment he sees the door opening, he stands up straight—alert.

"Good," he says, relaxing visibly. "I've gotta run. Call just came in of a body found in the brush off one of the trails around the cemetery. A homeless woman camping out there flagged down one of the cemetery workers who called it in."

"Where's Bella?" I ask, taking the seat beside Kerry, automatically searching for her hand and lacing my fingers with hers.

"Gone to sign her papers, she shouldn't be too long. When we came in, the nurse informed us Marya's been wheeled into surgery for repairs on her arm and her eye socket. Bastard did some damage. She also has a lump the size of a goose egg on the back of her head. So likely a concussion. Looks like she was out for a good long while. Anyway, she mentioned it would likely be some time before she would be able to answer any questions."

"Dammit." Without Marya's account, we were dead in the water. "What about the hotel room?" I ask him.

"Browns has it under control. His team is going over every inch of it." He walks over and rests a hand on Kerry's shoulder. "If she comes out of surgery, and you're allowed in to see her before I get back, let her know I'll be there as soon as I can." With a final lift of his chin in my direction, he leaves, closing the door behind him.

When the doctor comes in two hours later, Bella and Jasper are on separate ends of the small room. They'd come in at about the same time, just after Blackfoot left, and the tension in the room was thick enough to cut with a knife. Not hard to see there is no love lost between these two.

"Family for Marya Berger?"

CHAPTER 20

KERRY

"SHH..."

I carefully stroke the hair back from Marya's face. Half of her head is bandaged up, and the part of her face that is visible is swollen and bruised. Her left arm is splinted up and strapped against her body. The spiral fracture in her forearm, which had broken both the radius and ulna bones, had required surgery to set and pin in place. Her arm had been pulled free from the shoulder socket, as well, which is why they had it immobilized against her torso. The doctor said it looked like the kind of combined injury you might sustain if someone twisted your arm behind you and forced it up too high.

On top of that, the bones around her eye had shifted out of place with the force of the blow she'd sustained and needed to be surgically repositioned. Several bumps and bruises, and a nasty cut on her scalp that needed stitches, rounded out her injuries. In all, she'd had a hell of a beating. When I asked if she'd been raped, the doctor responded that although he'd taken a rape kit, which is standard in violent assault cases like this one, she would have to answer that question herself when she woke up.

For the past half hour, I've been sitting here beside her bed with Damian holding sentry outside the door, watching her slowly wake up to the brutal reality of her broken body. Her soft sobs are breaking my fucking heart, and there's nothing I can do but wait until she's ready to talk.

"Hush, honey. It's gonna be okay," I mumble nonsense, trying to soothe her as best I can. When her uncovered eye finally opens a crack, I lean in and plaster a smile on my face.

"I messed up." Her voice is as cracked as her lips with the first words she utters.

"Whatever it is, we'll fix it," I assure her, but it only starts up the tears again. "Honey, you're going to make yourself sick with all the crying." Grabbing a tissue, conveniently left on the nightstand, I carefully wipe at her wet cheeks.

"It was him. I found him on the computer looking at your living room. You were sleeping on the couch with the FBI agent."

"What? Who was watching?"

"The guy I'd been…seeing." She barely gets the last word out. I grab for the Styrofoam cup with water and bend the straw to her mouth.

If she's going to talk, I should check to see if Keith has come back yet or at least get Damian in here. I don't want to make her tell it twice.

"Honey, did he…did he hurt you sexually?" I need to get that question out of the way before I suggest getting either one of the guys in.

She shakes her head. "No. I slept with him before… before I caught him." Relief rushes over me, but it is short-lived when I see the pained expression on her face.

"Do you think it's okay for me to see if Detective Blackfoot is outside? He's going to need to know some of this, and maybe we can avoid you having to go over it more than once." She winces but then takes in a deep breath and seems to lift her chin.

"He's the one who found me? I remember promising him I would talk with you here, if he held off calling my mother."

"Why? I mean, why didn't you want him to call her? She's worried about you."

"I know, but she'll rush back here and bring my boys. I don't want my boys to see me like this," she sniffles.

"I can understand that," I assure her. "Let me quickly check if Keith is here, okay?"

I pull open the door to find Damian sitting on a chair right outside. "How is she doing?" he asks.

"She said something about the guy watching us in my living room from his computer. I thought Keith or you should be in there.

"I just talked to him. He's held up at the cemetery."

"Then maybe if you would come in? I think she'll be okay with that."

"Sure," he says, getting up immediately.

"The detective was called away and is held up, but Damian is here," I say as we walk into the room, Damian right behind me.

"Hey, Marya," his deep voice sounds right behind me. "If you feel more comfortable waiting, or if I can call a female agent, just let me know."

"It's okay," she replies. "I want it over with."

I take my seat by the side of the bed again, and Damian stays standing by the foot. I take her hand and give it an encouraging squeeze.

"Remember the guy you told me to steer clear of?" she asks me. I do. I remember him well since he'd come back the next day and accosted me outside the store, repeating his invite to dinner, which I'd already turned down once. He hadn't liked it one bit from what I remember.

"Oh, Marya."

"Right," she says, a blush spreading over her cheeks. She shoots a quick glance in Damian's direction before focusing her eyes on me again. "So I may have kept that card he left. I didn't do anything with it, I swear," she rushes to add. "It's just when I happened to bump into him when I was at the library with the boys a few days later, I thought it maybe was a sign or something. I said hello and we got to talking.

He was really nice to the boys, and I thought I'd hit the jackpot." She looks at me pleadingly. "I know you said he gave you the creeps, but he was so nice to me. I thought maybe he'd had a bad day or something."

"That's why you didn't want to tell me who it was," I conclude. She doesn't have to answer; I see the truth in her eyes.

"What was his name?" Damian asks gently.

"Trevor Simms. He's from the UK. He said he was visiting but was thinking about finding a more permanent place here. He took me out to dinner and we talked about options. He said he didn't know anything about real estate but would want something temporary first. A rental. Asked a lot of questions."

I sense more than see Damian tense up at the foot of the bed, and the wiggling of Marya's fingers in my hand tells me he's not the only one. I release my hold on her and she carefully flexes her hand. "Anyway," she continues with a wry smile. "I'm the one who told him where you live. I said you'd found a great place with a one-year lease and that I could find out who your realtor was." She pauses for a moment. "That's the first time he made me feel a little uncomfortable. It was right after he said he hoped we could keep our connection quiet a little longer. Suggested that he'd prefer spending a little time really getting to know me, without other people crowding our space. But right after that, he suggested perhaps I could show him your place to get an idea of what is on the market. At the time, I remember it seemed a bit odd, but I liked him. I wanted him to like me. So I drove him out there." Marya's furiously licking her lips, and I try to hide my shaking hand as I grab the cup of water and bring the straw to her lips. "Thank you," she says, sending a quick, tentative look at Damian. "When we drove up, he asked if I ever looked after your place when you weren't there. If I had a spare key, he could maybe have a quick look around. I was a little shocked and told him I didn't have one. He easily waved it off, and we left right after. He never talked about it again. I honestly didn't think too much of it. Then he asked me about your schedule, where you were and how long you'd be. He started coming into the store while you were gone, and I thought it was because he wanted to see me but wasn't ready to be seen with me, you know?" I nod encouragingly, even though outright fear is running through my veins. Both for Marya and myself. "It wasn't until the night I walked in on him while he was on his computer, that I realized I'd been used. He hit me," she cries, disbelief in her eyes. "Next thing I know, I was in a different hotel room from his. He has a suite at the Hilton."

"Do you know if he's registered there as Trevor Simms?" Damian asks. His voice is gentle, but I can hear the steel underneath.

"The desk clerk called him by that name the one time he had to stop in the lobby to pick up some mail. I only knew him as Trevor. The other few times I was with him at the hotel, we went straight to the outside door to his suite. It was on the main level."

"Hold on one sec please, Marya. I have to give Detective Blackfoot a quick call." Damian rushes into the hallway, his phone already to his ear.

When the door closes, I turn back to look at my friend, whose face is riddled with guilt.

"I am so sorry, Kerry. The thought I may have…" I don't let her finish the thought.

"Listen," I say firmly. "That's enough with the apologies. You had no way to know." She barks out a harsh laugh.

"I should've known that a sophisticated man like that would have an ulterior motive for spending time with a single mother of three."

DAMIAN

"I have a name and a location," I inform Keith the moment he picks up his phone. "Trevor Simms, staying at the—"

"Hilton," Keith finishes, taking me completely by surprise. "His body is on the way to the morgue with a bullet lodged in his brain. Apparent suicide. Identification was in his pocket. Here's the kicker, though. The file Ella handed out at that first meeting? This guy's picture was in there."

"Let me guess." I take a wild shot this time. "Troy Sinclair?"

"Got it in one. I have a feeling things are coming to

a head. I'm on my way now, be there in ten. Coroner won't get to him until tomorrow morning, and I want to talk with you before we notify the rest of the task force."

"Gotcha."

I know why he wants to talk to me in person. Only a few know about Marya's hospitalization, and Keith apparently wants to keep it like that for now. There is something about this scenario that is too neat, and therefore it raises the hair on my neck. There's still the matter of the government-issued electronics we discovered. Not something that is easy to come by.

When I get back in the room, after checking in with Jasper and my sister for a minute, it looks like Marya is asleep. Kerry doesn't look too far off, as she's lain her head on the mattress and her eyes are at half-mast.

"Come on. Let's get something to eat or a coffee or something," I suggest. It's almost three in the afternoon, and we haven't had anything since breakfast.

"I don't want to leave her."

"You won't be far. I'll pick up something for all of us in the cafeteria, and we'll get Jasper to sit with her while we eat. Come on, Kerry." I reach my hand out to her, and after a brief pause, she grabs on.

I leave her with Bella in the waiting room while Jasper goes in to sit with Marya. I just piled a selection of food and drinks on a tray and am heading for the cash register when I spot Blackfoot heading my way.

"Let me grab a coffee and sit with me outside," he

suggests. The hospital cafeteria is on the lower level and has a few tables outside in a rock garden with a feature waterfall. By my guess, he picks that spot in hopes the sound of the falling water will wash out anything we say.

"Tell me," he says as he sits down across from me. "How likely is it that someone intent on killing themselves would fire a practice shot into a tree before drilling a bullet into his own brain?"

"Not very," I admit. "More likely scenario would be that someone wanted to make it look like a suicide and understands enough about forensics to know that one of the first things we'd check for is gunshot residue on the victim's hands."

"Those were my thoughts. Another inconsistency is that the victim had his iPhone tucked in his sleeve, clutching the cuff in his hand. The phone opened to a voice recorder app. Unfortunately, if it had been his intent to record, he wasn't successful. Other than a three second recording of footsteps crunching through underbrush, there's nothing else." Keith takes a sip of his coffee before he pins me with a look.

"So murder," I confirm.

"Murder," he echoes. "I made a quick stop at the Hilton to see if something would jump out at me in his suite, but it looked like housekeeping had been in already. Browns and his guys are going over it with a fine-tooth comb, but as you know, hotel rooms are teeming with fingerprints and DNA. It's not likely we'll be able to find anything useable, but we've got to try."

"You know this has to be shared with the task force."

"I know," he concedes easily, before he leans over the table. "But I want to keep one piece of evidence back."

"The phone."

"Bingo. I can't get over those high-tech electronics. All of this seems too convenient. For now, I want as few people as possible to have all the information, and the phone could be key to pinpointing who that might be. I want to have twenty-four hours to dig up any possible evidence it hides before I hand it over."

I take a minute to consider. "You know it could cost us our jobs," I point out.

"Me," he jumps in quickly. "It will cost me my job, because you'll be just as surprised as the rest of them. You'll be in a better position to gauge everyone's reaction, because one thing's for sure: the appearance of that piece of evidence is going to scare the fuck out of whoever might be involved."

"James will likely snatch it up and send it to the main lab in Quantico," I point out the most likely scenario.

"And I think James will clue in quickly on why I held it back when I hand over the bugs at the same time. He's a smart man. I'm guessing he'll want to keep a close eye on the evidence. He'll hand it to Boris to examine in his crime lab. And he'll be breathing down his neck the whole time."

"You don't think it's James." The relief I feel at that conclusion lifts a weight off my shoulders. James has not only been my boss since I joined the FBI but has become a friend, too.

"I don't. Mind you, I have a hard time considering anyone for this. It could still be someone lower on the totem pole, or we could be missing the boat completely, but something makes me highly doubt it."

I watch Keith run his hand through his hair and notice how tired he looks. I'm probably not much better off.

"I'm going to lay low for the next day or so. If you need me urgently, leave me a message, and I'll get back to you. I want some time to find out what I can before I'm pulled into a meeting."

"Fair enough. I'm going to bring this food up, and then I'm taking Kerry and Bella home. The longer we stay here, the higher the chance of someone clueing in," I say as I stand and grab the tray of food.

"I'll come up with you. I want to check on Marya." Keith gets up without looking at me. I don't say a thing, just lead the way up to her floor.

"I'm going to have to go back out," I tell Kerry when we get out of Bella's car.

We followed the same routine leaving the hospital as we did coming, with me in the back seat of Bella's car and Jasper driving my Expedition. We left Keith in charge of Marya, and the only way I managed to get Kerry out of there was with Keith's promise he would make sure she would be protected at all times.

Marya herself had urged Kerry to go, said she felt guilty enough for what happened, she couldn't handle the thought of Kerry taking any more risks because of her.

Still, it had been the promise of an armed guard that finally swayed the stubborn woman.

"Don't let me stop you," she snaps. I'm thinking maybe she's being lighthearted, but when I look over, she's displaying some serious attitude. Her head is tilted to the side, and there's a real challenge in her eyes.

Without a word, I firmly grab her upper arm and march her straight inside and up the stairs, ignoring her loud objections. I close the bedroom door behind us before I let her go.

"What the hell, Damian?" she protests, rubbing her arm. "Manhandling me under control? What an idiot I've been—"

"Shut up, Kerry. Let me enlighten you. I'm busting my balls here to do everything I can to keep you safe, and that means keeping you physically out of danger, while at the same time focusing on the investigation, so I can eliminate any threat. You were run off the road, your friend was assaulted so bad she needed surgery, and now we have a man dead." I hear Kerry's sharp intake of breath at that bit of news, but I forge ahead. "If I could be in two places at one time, believe me, that would make my life a fuck of a lot easier. But I don't have that option. Instead, I've broken rules and I've likely broken trusts these past few weeks, because for the first fucking time in my life, someone means more to me than my damn job. It's eating at me, but I'd do it again in a heartbeat, Kerry—for you." I close my eyes and take a deep breath and try to calm myself down. I continue with a little less volume. "What I don't need is you giving me attitude. I know you're scared. I know you're frustrated, and I know you feel you have no control. But what you don't seem to realize is that I'm doing whatever I need to do to make sure that situation is as temporary as I can make it."

I force myself to turn away from Kerry, who has slumped down on the edge of the bed under my tirade with her head bent low and her hair falling forward, hiding her face.

"I've gotta go," I say over my shoulder. "Don't wait up."

CHAPTER 21

KERRY

I FEEL SMALL.

I sit here and listen to his boots thumping down the stairs, without moving. I want to call him back, tell him I'm sorry, that I didn't mean to give him a hard time, but the truth is: I was a bitch.

He's right, I'm scared, tired, and mentally exhausted, and I fully took it out on him. Then to add insult to injury, I painted him with my ex's legacy. Accusing him of something I know in my heart is not him at all. If anything, he's done everything to leave me my self-worth. To keep me in the loop and not make me feel I was being managed—controlled.

I lie down and curl myself around the pillow. His pillow. My eyes burn with the tears that want to fall, but it's almost like I'm too tired to cry. Or maybe there's been enough crying already, I don't know. All

I know is I wish for them to fall, to relieve the pressure behind my eyes, and maybe wash away some of the guilt that's choking me. A man is dead. He didn't say who or what; I should've asked because now my mind is imagining who it might be. I can only hope Damian stays safe, because if something happens to him, and these are the last words we ever exchange...

I vaguely hear Bella come into the room, but I keep my eyes firmly closed, feigning sleep, until I hear the door gently close again. The soft click of the latch works like a trigger, and the tears slowly start rolling down my face.

I don't know what time it is. Sometime well after dark since moonlight appears to be streaming in through the uncovered windows. The mattress dips behind me and an arm snakes around my body, pulling me back against the broad expanse of a chest. Damian's familiar scent wards off any panic I might feel.

"I'm sorry." His low voice rumbles against the shell of my ear and settles deep in my chest. A new surge of tears washes the remnants of my earlier ones away, as I turn around and bury my face in his neck. His apology only serves to make me feel even more guilty than I did when I finally cried myself to sleep.

"I didn't m—mean it," I sniffle against his skin.

"I know that. I knew it then and still overreacted, which is why I'm the one to be sorry." He shifts his head back a little and looks at me. His dark eyes are soft and convey a slew of emotions. I don't even try to identify them, too afraid I won't be able to get my tears under control. "You've been crying," he says, following it up with a mumbled expletive.

Instead of trying to deny it, I place my hand against his face. "I'm done now. How are you?" He rolls onto his back, pulling my arm across him and covering my hand on his chest with his.

"Tired to the bone," he sighs. "I only have a few hours before I'm expected back at the office for a briefing."

"The dead man?" I inquire.

"Among other things. The identification in his pockets was a credit card and driver's license in the name of Trevor Simms, but in a side pocket of his wallet was a stack of bank cards, as well as a British driver's license in the name of Troy Sinclair."

A shiver runs down my spine. "It's not over, is it?"

"Not by a long shot," he says solemnly. "It was made to look like a suicide, but there were some things that didn't add up. Technically, this investigation should be handed over to the task force because of the man's identity, but Keith is keeping as close a rein on it as he can for now. That will all change in a few hours. We've not shared anything the past day or so, but we can't keep a lid on a murder or on the fact we found Marya. And once that comes out, so will the discovery of the camera and the listening devices."

"Why? Why keep that a secret?" I want to know, struggling to keep up with the sudden flow of information.

Damian turns back on his side, taking my face in his hands before he answers. "Because there is a possibility someone in law enforcement may have been involved, someone with access to top-of-the-line electronics, who might even be close to the investigation."

"That's why you said you'd broken rules and trust," I deduce, sounding much calmer than I feel. I'm terrified, even more so than I was before, and it dawns on me that I'm way out of my league here. Damian picks up on my rising panic, stroking his thumbs along my eyebrows.

"It'll be okay," he whispers with his lips against mine. "I'll make it okay."

I don't have time to respond before his tongue slips between my lips, slowly stroking mine to life. One of his hands leaves my face and slides down to pull my knee up over his hip. The rough calluses on my skin, as he brushes his hand along my thigh to my butt, stoke a fire. His long fingers knead my flesh, drawing a low moan from deep in my throat. My own hands move restlessly over his shoulders and down his back, registering every ridge and dip of his muscles.

"Stop me," he almost pleads when he pulls his mouth away, using teeth and tongue to caress along my jaw.

"Do you want me?" I utter breathlessly.

"I fucking need you, Gypsy, but I'll stop at your say-so."

"Not a chance in hell," I declare. I don't even

consider he has to be up for his meeting in a few hours. Not when his mouth latches on to my breast like a starving man. Not when the expression on his face as he slides inside my body reflects the utter bliss I'm sure is visible on mine.

DAMIAN

"You've got to leave?"

Kerry's sleepy voice greets me as I walk into the bedroom, a cup of coffee in my hand. She looks flushed with sleep and sex. A great combination on her.

It takes everything out of me not to strip off the clothes I just pulled on and climb back under the sheets with her, but the sooner we can get a handle on this investigation, the sooner I can start working on getting the stunning woman in my bed to stay there permanently. Instead, I sit down on the edge and set the coffee on the nightstand.

"I'll call as soon as I'm out of the meeting," I promise her.

She pushes herself into a sitting position, regrettably holding on tight to the sheet. "I'm going to have to do something about the store. I need to go in."

"Babe, I think you should keep the store closed until we get this sorted out. I'll have a better idea after the meeting this morning," I explain.

"I know, but it's going to hurt my business if people keep knocking on the door or calling and no one is there. At least let me scoot over quickly and put up a sign and forward my calls to my cell phone. I can even grab my laptop from home in a flash, so I can take care of my online store to some degree."

She's hard to resist, making sense while she's naked in my bed. *Fucking hell.*

"Let me check in with Luna. If she calls you from the store, can you walk her through forwarding to your cell?"

"Yes, it's not that hard. But what about—"

"She can run up to your place after. Just let her know where to find everything."

I'm glad she seems on board with that plan, at least I think she is since she wraps her hands around my neck and drags my mouth to hers.

"Be safe," she softly says against my lips.

"I will. I'll call."

With a last hard kiss, I force myself to get up and walk out.

"Where's Luna?" Jasper leans down and whispers in my ear.

I wave him to sit down next to me and bend toward him. "She's running an errand. She'll be here shortly."

I watch as Boris, Ella, and James take a seat around the table, and the last to walk into the boardroom are Blackfoot and Browns. My eyes skim over the others in the room, trying to pick up any kind of reaction. If someone had a hand in the murder of Sinclair, they would be sitting on hot coals right now. The only one who has a visible reaction, more than perhaps a general mild curiosity at Blackfoot bringing along his forensics guy, is Boris Parnak. Not all that surprising, since normally he and Keith work in tandem on major investigations, and I know for a fact, Keith's been avoiding him the last few days.

"Okay," James starts. "A brief recap then have updates first. There are a few loose ends I think need to be addressed. We have two boxes with valuable books shipped from The Gilded Feather. Right now, both boxes are missing. One of them held a shipment of stolen manuscripts that we suspect ended up at Kerry's Korner. Jasper, you were looking into Willoughs? I received confirmation from the IT team that the second box was shipped from The Gilded Feather warehouse to the post office box you discovered." He hands Jasper a sheet of paper. "That's the UPS tracking number."

"Matches what I have. The box was picked up a month ago by Willoughs himself," Jasper informs him.

"All right, so it's about time to bring Mr. Willoughs in and ask him some questions. Gomez?" He focuses on me.

"On it."

"Keith, any luck finding the box that disappeared from Ms. Emerson's car?"

"I had a team scouring the side of the mountain. They came up with nothing," he answers James.

"It can't just be gone," Boris pipes up. "Are we sure the store owner is telling the truth? She may have been lying."

I'm halfway out of my chair already when Jas grabs my waistband and sharply yanks me back down. A few eyebrows are raised, most obviously by James, who lightly shakes his head.

Keith saves my ass. "Unlikely, Boris. She didn't conjure up the pickup that almost knocked her off the side of the mountain since it was witnessed by the truck driver. That reminds me; did you find anything on the missing pickup truck yet?" He bounces the ball right back into Parnak's court, who's been assigned recovery of the hit-and-run truck.

"Nope. I have a few teams out on it, and it's like the damn thing's disappeared."

"Funny how that can happen, right?" Keith fires right back.

"All right, that's enough." James looks sternly between the two local lawmen. "Moving on. Any news on the woman that went missing?"

"Actually," I jump in. "She was found, Keith's got some info on that."

As agreed, Keith details the circumstances of Marya's discovery and those of her disappearance. He fills them in on the discovery of the tracker on Kerry's car, the listening devices and camera inside Kerry's house, and the ones found in the store. When he announces the equipment looked to be government-issue, I scan the room for reactions. James is staring right at me, his eyebrow slightly lifted. He knows we kept this close to our chest for a reason.

"Is she going to be okay?" James asks, deflecting the focus.

"She will be," Keith answers with conviction. "Especially since the man who did that to her was found dead in the cemetery, apparently with a self-inflicted gunshot wound. Trevor Simms...or Troy Sinclair, he apparently answered to both."

That bit of news gets a round of raised eyebrows and exclamations of disbelief.

"No shit?" James says questioningly.

"His body is with the coroner, which is where Browns and I are heading after," Keith fills him in. "There are some questions around the circumstances leading to his death."

"Interesting," Ella speaks up. "Especially now that we know Willoughs was likely the intended recipient of the stolen goods. It's reasonable to assume he would've been in contact with Sinclair. Would've wanted some restitution for the money I'm sure he had to fork out for those manuscripts. He may have been fed up."

"You might have a point," Keith says, his eyes sharp on Ella. "Browns just confirmed this morning that, despite the fact the cell phone that was found on Sinclair's body was a burner, it had one text message that seems to point a finger at the millionaire. It's the only one remaining on the phone, everything else was deleted. The message simply stated: *NW corner cemetery 1 hr. BW.*"

"Bruce Willoughs?" Parnak asks.

"Would seem so," Keith responds. "After the meeting, Browns will see if he can get anything else off the phone."

"I'm coming," Boris announces, and Keith's about to protest when James pipes up.

"Good idea. See what two sharp minds can come up with," he says, giving both men a meaningful glare.

After that, the meeting quickly breaks up. Boris tags along with Browns and Blackfoot to the lab, and Ella announces she's heading back to her hotel room to brief her superior. James stays behind.

Once Jasper leaves the boardroom, he turns to me. "Is she safe?" he asks, and I don't have to guess who he's talking about.

"Yes," I simply state.

"Good. Keep it that way." He picks up a pen from the table and starts twirling it between his fingers. I wait for what I know is coming. "I know you wouldn't normally drag your ass on reporting information important to an investigation. Given the nature of the information, I can understand why, in this case, you chose to do just that, but I have to tell you it doesn't sit right with me. I thought after the many years we've known each other, worked together, you'd be able to trust me with your suspicions."

Fuck.

"You thought right," I start. "All I can say is I've never been in love before." James' signature eyebrow lifts and a smile tugs at his mouth. "It appears to trump years of trust and loyalty. Especially when the woman I've fallen for is up to her eyeballs in the investigation. I just couldn't take the chance."

"I hear you. But if I'd known where your head was at, if I'd been kept in the loop, I might've conducted this meeting a little differently. With everything out in the open, we've given out all the cards. I might also have reminded you that with the kind of money Willoughs has, there is little in the world that can't be bought. Not even government-issue electronics."

"Blackfoot's guy checked with the manufacturer. These gadgets are made for government agencies exclusively and produced in exact quantities as per agency purchase orders," I point out.

James takes a minute before he repeats, "With the right kind of money, there's little that can't be bought."

Before I have a chance to respond, Jasper slams the door wide.

"It's Luna…"

"I'm fine!"

I just get out of the car when I hear Luna's angry voice. She's sitting on the porch steps of Kerry's house and is batting away Blackfoot's hands from her head. I'm not sure how he got here so fast.

"I was barely out," Luna snaps angrily when Keith persists examining her head. She's got some blood in her hair.

"The neighbor called 911 because she couldn't

wake you. There's blood on your head, Luna. Dammit." He parts her hair and a nice cut becomes visible. "Good thing I was around the corner, or you would've walked off without medical care. I know you."

I'm surprised at the familiarity between the two. "ER, Luna," I order. "Right after you tell us what happened."

"Fine," she grumbles.

"Why can't you be that agreeable with me?" Keith asks and is rewarded with a ball-shriveling glare. "Never mind." I hear him say under his breath.

"I stopped at the bookstore, like you asked," she says to me. "Forwarded the phone, picked up the mail and a few messages, and was just hanging up a sign on the door when the guy from the hardware store walked in the back. About gave me a heart attack, and probably vice versa, since he barely got a foot inside the door before he was staring down the barrel of my gun. Anyway, I explained Kerry had been called away on a family emergency, and I was making sure the shop was properly closed off. I could tell he wasn't buying it, but it helped when I showed him my badge. Still, he said he'd keep an eye on the place, make sure the mail doesn't pile up and stuff, just like he'd been doing. I told him sure and was about to lock up when the old man mentioned a large SUV he'd seen do a slow drive-by a few times in the past couple of days." She takes a deep breath before continuing. "I should've paid better attention, because when I pulled into Kerry's driveway, I noticed a dark brown Suburban parked in front of the house. It looked familiar, which is maybe why I wasn't as cautious as I should've been. Or maybe because I didn't want to be running errands when an important meeting was taking place." The last she directs at me. I just shrug it off. She can be irritated all she wants, but she fucked up when she let down her guard. "Next thing I know I'm on the ground, feeling like my head was just caved in. The last thing I remember was watching a pair of argyle socks in Ferragamos walking away and thinking that didn't look exactly like mountain attire."

Blackfoot is faster than me and is already barking instructions to send a few units to Willough's place into his phone. Apparently he'd come to the same conclusion I had.

Only one man in La Plata County who'd be vain enough to traipse through the mountains in those ugly-ass designer shoes.

CHAPTER 22

KERRY

"I'M HEADING OUT!"

Bella is hollering up from the bottom of the stairs. She has a full day of orientation at Mercy today before she starts her first shift on Monday.

"Have a great day!" I yell back.

Damian already left for work about an hour ago. I'd barely seen him in the last week. Since Luna got hit over the head and was ordered to take sick leave, he'd been shorthanded. According to Damian, she was knocked unconscious by Bruce Willoughs. I still can't believe the immaculate millionaire, with a penchant for pretty things, would risk getting his hands dirty like that. I'd like to know what the hell he was doing ransacking my house, but he's been in the wind ever since.

Frustrating—especially since I'd hoped with

Sinclair out of the way, I'd be safe to get back to my house and shop. Not that I don't love it here, because I do. It's gorgeous, and it doesn't hurt that despite his busy days, Damian always ends up curved around me at night. But I miss my stuff, my store, and my customers. Besides, without Marya to back me up, I was forced to keep the store closed. She had a long recovery ahead of her. Not just physically, but emotionally as well. I spoke to her a few times on the phone and know her mother and aunt brought her boys back to town and are looking after her. Last time we talked, she mentioned she was thinking about heading up to stay with her aunt in Silverton for a while. I told her that might be a good idea and that her job would still be there when she came back. How exactly, I don't know, since every day the store's doors stay closed, I lose income. I'm not sure how long I'll be able to tough it out.

So when it came to going back to work, I argued hard, but now that Willoughs was out there somewhere, Damian felt it better to hold off on returning to business as usual for a bit. He'd even contacted Malachi, my friend Kim's husband, to see if he could keep his ear to the ground on Willoughs' whereabouts. Of course, that resulted in Kim blowing up my phone until I finally caved and answered it. Needless to say, she was pissed the hell off that I'd been keeping some things from her and insisted she was packing up Asher and driving out here right away. Luckily Mal had been there and intervened, but it had gotten a little ugly.

Damian had brought back my laptop, and I kept myself busy updating my web store and managing emails and messages that were coming in from customers who were concerned when they found the store closed. A lot of work, but little to show for it in revenue.

The one financial highlight was the recovery of the box of first edition American classics I had dropped five grand on. It was found in Willoughs' home office. Even though it was being kept as evidence for now, chances were good I'll get them back, provided there were no stolen items in there. Keeping my fingers crossed.

It's pretty clear the box that disappeared from my car had held the missing stolen works. Hearing Damian tell it, the estimated total value is in excess of twenty-five or so million dollars. I couldn't help but chuckle when I heard that, to think I was toting around more money in the back of my ratty old wagon than I'd likely ever see in my lifetime.

I'm just on my way downstairs to refresh my coffee when my phone rings. Now that I'm basically camping out in Damian's bed every night, he suggested I use the spare room as an office. I left my phone on the small desk in there and rush back in before it stops ringing.

"Hello?" I answer a bit out of breath.

"Gypsy," Damian's familiar rumble comes over the line. "Did you reset the alarm when Bella left?"

Shit. Totally forgot his very specific instructions.

"Just about to do that," I lie through my teeth. "How did you know she just left anyway?" He just chuckles. "You made her promise to call, didn't you? Dammit, Damian. If I didn't like you a whole bunch, I'd be really—"

"I like you a whole bunch, too, honey." I can hear the smile in his voice when he interrupts me. Every time I get worked up about something, he finds a way to disarm me. Sometimes it's the things he says, and sometimes it's just the way he touches me or looks at me. Funny how I don't seem to question his integrity anymore. I'm not ready to admit it, it's too soon and things are too chaotic now, but I think I'm in love. And the kicker is I think he feels the same way about me.

"Kerry? I'll be home at around six. Be ready to go grab a bite in town. I've made reservations at the Mahogany Grill for seven thirty."

My inner teenager jumps up and down. Perhaps a case of putting the cart before the horse, but the prospect of dressing up and going out on a proper date with him is making me giddy.

"Isn't that at the Strater Hotel?"

"Sure is. It's their upscale restaurant. Why?"

"Well…" I hesitate, not wanting to insult him. "Do you think I could still dress up if we went to the Diamond Belle?" The sound of his laugh makes me smile.

"You want saloon fare over fine dining?" he teases.

"You know you're near perfect, right?"

"Near?" I sputter, mock insulted.

"Perfection is boring, but near perfection? There isn't a thing more intriguing, more tantalizing, more beautiful than that. See you at six, honey."

The phone has gone dead against my ear, but I barely notice since, once again, his words leave me mute and feeling all quivery inside.

The moment clarity hits me, I move like someone lit a fire under my feet. *I have nothing to wear.* It takes me all of two minutes to empty out the bags I've been living out of the last couple of days. All clothes selected for comfort, and therefore, none suitable for a date. I look at the pile of discarded items on the spare bed to see if anything salvageable jumps out at me. What I wouldn't give for my little black dress to have found its way into one of my bags. All I have to work with are two pairs of jeans, some leggings, yoga pants, a collection of oversized shirts, a few tunics, and my bright floral kimono. *Well, hell.*

Resigned to go on my first real date with Damian wearing my ratty old jeans, I grab my discarded coffee cup and head downstairs for that almost-forgotten refill. I remember to reset the alarm on the way to the kitchen. On the counter, by the coffee pot, is a note from Bella with her cell phone number and instructions to call her if there's anything I need from town.

A light bulb goes off and I rush back upstairs to grab my phone.

"Bella?"

"Kerry? Everything okay?" she answers with a worried edge to her voice.

"Fine, it's fine. Look, I'm sorry to bother you but I have a quick question."

"Shoot," she prompts me.

"Damian's taking me out to dinner tonight and I don't—"

"Have anything to wear," she finishes my sentence on a giggle.

"Bingo," I sigh.

"No worries. What size shoes?"

"Eight."

"Mmmm, I'm a seven-and-a-half, but feel free to go through my closet," she giggles again. "I bring my entire closet with me when I travel. Damian almost had a heart attack when he offered to bring in my bag and ended up hoisting a bag and two suitcases from the trunk of my little car." I smile at the visual. "Anything in my closet is yours, but I suggest the little black stretchy number. Best purchase I ever made. Almost a one-size-fits-all because of the material. Try it," she urges.

"You're a lifesaver."

Oh my God. The moment I pull the stretchy number over my body and check it out in the full-length mirror in Bella's closet, I'm the one about to have a heart attack. There is not one thing on my body hidden under this material. How Bella manages to pull off this dress with her voluptuous curves, I have no idea.

Nothing but a full body corset would be enough for it to look good on me. Like a second skin, the material clings to every damn lump and roll. Dejected, I plop down on her bed when my eye catches sight of a pair of multicolored sling-back wedges of manageable height in the bottom of the closet. It gives me an idea.

With the wedges in hand, still wearing the little black number, I rush to the pile on my bed.

DAMIAN

"You've got it bad."

I turn away from the view over Durango through my window to find James leaning against the doorpost. I shrug my shoulders in response. I'm not about to deny the obvious, I know I have it bad. James closes the door behind him, saunters in, and takes a seat on the other side of my desk.

"No progress on locating Willoughs?" he asks.

"Durango PD found his Suburban parked at the far end of the Mild to Wild parking lot." At his confused look, I clarify. "A rafting company on the north end of town. They have a couple of old school buses to haul people to and from the river, and he'd slipped the truck between them. The place is always packed this time of year, so they didn't notice until early this morning. Blackfoot is out there to see if anyone remembers when it was left there."

"So he switched rides. Not like we weren't expecting that. He's probably long gone," James concludes.

"I don't think so," I disagree. "I'll be the first to admit I never liked the guy—mainly because he thinks he can own everything he sets his mind to, treats people like belongings, too— but didn't make his fortune by running scared. As long as that damn box is out there, he's not going to go far."

James nods in understanding. He walks to the window and stares out. "Is it?" he asks cryptically.

"Is what?"

"Is it still out there? The stolen goods?" He doesn't turn to look at me, but I can feel the tension coming off his back.

"Not sure if I understand the implication." The hair on my neck stands on end as I burn holes in his back with my eyes. Finally, he turns around.

"Easy, my friend," he folds his arms in front of him and gives his head a little shake. "You can't blame me for asking. It's what I would try, if I thought someone close to the investigation might be involved, I'd be careful what I shared and didn't. I'd even hold back evidence to try and shake them loose."

"I thought we'd covered that already?" I point out, but my tense shoulders relax. I trust James. His calmly observant demeanor, keen deductive skills, and sharp intuition have always been attributes I've strived for. Even the parental way in which he calls me out when he has concerns is something I've tried to implement since I was handed this field office. An example and father figure.

He doesn't even blink.

"We don't have it. Blackfoot suggested at some point having Kerry pretend she had it—draw the players out—but..." I clarify.

"I'm sure you knocked that idea down fast," James chuckles. "Not a bad idea, though," he continues, holding his hands up defensively when I threaten to come out of my chair. "Relax. I think that ship has sailed. We've got Sinclair down and keeping a close eye out for Willoughs. We're left with two obvious problems. Who killed Sinclair? It's clear someone other than the man himself pulled the trigger, but are we comfortable with Bruce Willoughs in the role of cold-blooded killer? And where the hell is that damn shipment? We can safely assume Sinclair is the one who ran her car off the road. Doesn't make sense he went back to retrieve it from the wreck, or he would've been gone a long time ago."

"By the same reasoning, we know Willoughs obviously doesn't have it." I hesitate, uneasy about bringing up the elephant in the room again. "What if it was taken after it was towed? Blackfoot had it locked down in the forensics lab, which is under camera surveillance, but what if it was someone who has reason to be there? Someone they wouldn't look at twice? No one may have actually looked at those tapes, just taken the word of whomever was manning the cameras." I don't mention names out loud, but

James is keen enough to figure those out by himself. Both Boris Parnak and Doug Browns would be frequent visitors there.

"Call Blackfoot. See if they have surveillance tapes of that night. I have to meet with Ella, try and calm down some jurisdictional bullshit around Sinclair's body. She wants him put on ice and shipped back to the UK. Feels our local law enforcement is not equipped to deal with a high-profile case like this." James rubs a hand in the back of his neck. Looks like he's starting to feel the strain of this investigation, as well.

"Bet that went over well with our local PD," I say, with a heavy load of sarcasm. I know for a fact that that would not only piss off Parnak, but Blackfoot, as well.

"You're not lying. Bedside manner is definitely not one of Ms. Friesen's strengths. I've called in our own forensics investigative team to go over the findings to date. She'll have to learn I'm not the right guy to play hardball with; she'll lose every time." With a half-assed wave, he opens the door and walks out, before sticking his head back in. "By the way—how's Agent Roosberg doing? If you need an extra hand in the meantime, let me know. I can probably spare Dylan."

Dylan Barnes is technically one of my agents who was last to join the Durango field office. As youngest of our team, he'd had the least opportunity to get some field experience under his belt. When James mentioned he could use some help in Denver on several active cases, I'd offered it to Dylan. He jumped at it and had been there for almost a year now.

"Luna should be back in a day or so. She's impossible to keep away from the job, and I'm tempted just to give in and give her the green light so I don't have to deal with the constant phone calls. We'll manage until then, although, you know I'll want Dylan back at some point, right?" I shoot James a sharp look, which he shrugs off smilingly.

"Turning out to be a good agent, that boy."

"Hardly a boy anymore," I point out.

"Hmmm. I guess." He straightens away from the doorpost he's been hanging on to. "No worries. A few months more on the case he's been involved in and you can have him back." He raps his knuckles on the door. "Well, I'd best be off. I'll be in touch."

I get up and close the door behind him before pulling out my phone to call Blackfoot. When I tell him what I want from him, he bristles at first, just as I would've done had the loyalty of my colleagues been called into question.

"Goddammit, Gomez. You're killing me here."

Instead of responding, I just wait. I know he'll find his way there on his own. He doesn't keep me waiting long before he gives in.

"I'll get on it," he bites off before ending the call. I know he will.

The rest of my day is hectic.

Jas and I spend a couple of hours chasing down a lead on Willoughs that goes nowhere. One of the employees at Mild to Wild remembered seeing a man walking away from the Suburban and crossing the road to the Hampton Inn on the other side. She swore she saw the guy getting into a red Ford Ranger, with an upside down wheelbarrow in the back of the pickup. A patrol car spotted a truck matching the description heading south, and we caught up to it just past Aztec. The old, nearly toothless gardener we found behind the wheel looked nothing like Willoughs. He'd been at the Hampton to see if they needed a landscaper.

The entire time we were chasing the truck, Luna was blowing up my phone. She'd picked up that initial call over the scanner, and I barely managed to hold her off from coming. It ended up taking me to concede to her returning to the office tomorrow. The woman drives a hard bargain.

I haven't heard back from James yet but assume he is either still furiously negotiating or has already won the jurisdictional battle. Otherwise, someone would've informed me by now.

Blackfoot was undoubtedly busy with the home invasion that was discovered this morning, which left one person dead at the scene. A problem that was fast getting out of hand in Durango. A case, now that they've graduated into murder, I'm sure we will end up getting called in on sooner rather than later.

Jasper's already gone when I leave for the day at a little after five. He's been burning the candle at both ends, so I'm glad to see his desk empty. We all carry a set of keys, and as long as everyone spends some time in the office each day for briefing, we usually let the workload guide our hours. I turn the lights off and lock the door behind me.

As usual, when I turn off the highway toward my house, the view and the silence seems to melt away the stress of the day. So much so, that when I pull up in front of the house and get out, I don't really feel like going out. I'd much rather spend the evening with Kerry on my lap in the lounger on the back deck. Then I remember the excitement in her voice at the prospect of a *genuine date* and realize she's been cooped up inside the house for days.

The decision is easily made; I'll take her out for a nice meal, maybe drive her up to the overlook at Fort Lewis College to watch the lights. After that I'll take her home—to bed.

The moment I open the door and see her coming down the stairs, every thought I just had evaporates from my head, leaving only one—*to bed*. Her hair piled messily on her head, large silver hoops in her ears, her dress looking like something painted on and only made passably decent by the floral thing she is wearing over it. She looks like a fucking wet dream.

I don't even slow down but keep walking until I meet her at the bottom of the stairs. Standing on the last step, her eyes are level with mine. Her hands are tangled in my hair and her mouth is on mine before I even have a chance to wrap my arms around her. When we come up for air, her face has that gorgeous flush and her lips are wet and slightly swollen.

"Hi," she says breathily, a soft smile playing on her lips.

"I may have changed my mind about going out," I inform her, my voice hoarse with passion, but the look of disappointment ghosting over her face has me quickly change direction. "But we'll need some nourishment for what I have in mind for you."

The blinding smile she rewards me with is worth every second of discomfort my raging hard-on will cause me tonight.

CHAPTER 23

"THEY FOUND THE BOX."

He was surprised when the burner phone rang. As far as he knew, only Sinclair had that number and he hadn't used it since the last time he'd contacted the Brit. This voice was unfamiliar, yet he knew instinctively this was the Brit's, to this point, silent partner. A shiver of fear, or maybe anticipation, ran down his spine. Whoever this was, there was only one person they could've gotten this number off of and he is dead.

"Where was it?" he wanted to know, excitement starting to crowd out any fear.

"That's irrelevant. More important question is, where is it at now? I have reason to believe the woman had it all along."

"The bookstore owner? That doesn't make sense,"

he points out.

"No? She disappeared right after Sinclair so clumsily botched up yet another attempt at retrieval. Any and all attempts by law enforcement to find it have been fruitless. But perhaps I made an error in judgment in contacting you," the voice sounds derisive and slightly threatening.

"I know where she is," he blurted out before thinking. He'd been able to keep a low profile and at the same time keep an eye on the house. No one was looking much further than Durango at this point. Amateurs. He made looking like the typical, spoiled millionaire into an art. "Have had an eye on her this whole time," he boasted. "Have you heard of geo tracking software? It's something I used for years in my company. Very effective. It took me all of five minutes to install on Ms. Emerson's laptop."

"Ingenious, but isn't there a limit to the range?"

"On the old versions, but not on this one. It uses the same framework as any GPS. I had no trouble pinpointing her just north of Hermosa. Agent Gomez has kept her at his place this entire time."

A loose cannon, but one that would serve the purpose well. Pompous beyond belief at the careful strokes to his ego and therefore not as careful as he should be. The suspicion he might be used to advantage is nicely confirmed—he bites immediately when presented with the retrieval of his treasured manuscripts.

From here it would be simple.

"So Gomez has known the shipment was under his roof the entire time." This is said as a foregone conclusion, and the rich idiot swallows it down whole.

"Would seem that way, wouldn't it? To think it was under my nose the entire time." He's eager, as expected.

"I would suggest giving it a day or two, make sure you plan carefully, and—"

"What's in this for you?" he interrupts.

"I'd like to continue our business relationship, it's mutually profitable, so let's just call it customer service. If you give me an hour notice before you go in, I will make sure law enforcement is duly distracted. It's the least I can do."

"Of course," he swiftly agrees, not knowing that in doing so, he's signed his own downfall.

CHAPTER 24

KERRY

I CAN HEAR THE FAMILIAR piano melody as we walk into the Diamond Belle Saloon, and my eyes are immediately drawn to the old man behind the keys. His eyes are on the door and he smiles in recognition when he spots Damian. For me, he has an almost lascivious wink, and I can't hold back a chuckle when I hear Damian growl under his breath behind me.

"Dirty old coot," he mumbles, causing me to laugh out loud. One of the waitresses turns her head at the sound and moves in our direction, a smile on her face.

"Regular booth?" she asks Damian, who gives her a friendly nod.

"Bring all your dates here that you have a regular booth?" I tease him over my shoulder. The hand he rests on my hip as he guides me through the restaurant squeezes slightly. Once we're seated and left with menus and an order of drinks on the way, he grabs my hand over the table.

"I don't," he says with a serious face. "The only people I've ever brought here have been my sister, Gus once, and Jasper and Luna for lunch at Christmas. Mostly I come alone because no one seems to appreciate the music."

"Are you serious?" I blurt out, a tad skeptical.

"As a heart attack. Gus would rather have found a quiet spot to talk, Bella almost walked out until Clive started playing modern songs she recognized and Jasper…let's just say Jasper is more of a hardcore rocker. The manly music, as he so often likes to remind me." The look of horrified disbelief on his face is comical.

"Well, I love it. Mind you, I love all kinds of music. Don't have any one particular style preference over another," I admit with a shrug of my shoulders.

"I'm glad," he says, bending toward me. "I much prefer sitting here with you than anyone else."

It occurs to me that we have much left to learn about each other. The unconventional progress of our relationship is a lot like being thrown into a pressure cooker. Intense circumstances, high levels of chemistry, and close proximity have brought us to a point that would normally take months to grow.

This place really has a fabulous atmosphere and not just because of the music. I'm surprised how easy and effortless conversation flows over dinner, from favorite movies to first childhood memories and from fears to family dynamics. It seems we've covered it all.

I shove my plate away from the edge and put my hands over my stomach in the universal sign for *stuffed*. "I'm thinking I need to find a dress like this," I announce, loving the way the stretchy material simply stretches a little more to accommodate my food gut. I'm glad I threw my kimono on over top since it hides a lot of sins.

"Don't remind me," Damian groans across the table. "I've been working hard to try and ignore the fact, that thing leaves nothing to the imagination."

I catch some movement from the corner of my eye and turn toward it. *Fucking hell.* I don't know who this person is, but from the look on her face, she's bringing trouble. Her eyes are shooting daggers at me. Tall, busty, heavy on the makeup and with a mane of sleek, almost-black hair, the woman virtually charges at our booth. For some reason, the name Cora comes to mind.

"Darling," she purrs when Damian finally turns his head in her direction. His initial shock is quickly replaced by a narrowing of his eyes as she closes the distance. Once close enough, she has the gall to run her hand proprietarily through his hair. *Oh, this is going to be fun.* Damian grabs her firmly by the wrist, pulling on her hand and moving his head out of the way at the same time.

"What the fuck, Cora?"

Bingo. I give myself a little round of applause and

sit back to watch the fireworks. There was a time when a display like this would have me sick with insecurity but not anymore. And certainly not with Damian's anger at the intrusion permeating the air. Yeah, I'm good.

"I just popped in for a quick drink and noticed you sitting here. Thought you might like some company," she simpers. Sure, I bet she spotted him through the window and decided to try and stake a claim. Damian's eyes flick to mine, and I smile encouragingly.

"As you can see, I have company," he bites off.

"Ah, yes." A smile as fake as her massive tits accompanies the hateful glare she directs at me. I smile broadly, which immediately has her turn the charm back on Damian. She plants a hand on the table and leans forward, her assets almost piling out in front of us. In a voice that's dropped so low I have to strain to listen in, she says, "I'm afraid I was referring to the kind of company that has me on hands and knees and you trying to decide which end to fuck first, my ass or my mouth. Somehow she…" She throws me a pitying look. "…seems a little too *vanilla* to give you what we both know you need."

Alrighty, then. A little more information than I banked on.

I watch in fascination as Damian rises to his full height from the booth, causing Cora to stumble back a little. He's intimidating, to say the least, with barely contained rage rolling off him in thick waves.

"Enough," he barks.

I vaguely notice Clive's earlier ballad transition into a hefty ragtime, drawing the attention from some of the patrons whose ears and eyes had started pointing in our direction. Bless his heart.

Damian grabs a firm hold of Cora's arm and turns to me. "Excuse me while I take out the trash, Gypsy." His voice is angry, but the look he shoots me is soft and pleading.

"Of course," I automatically reply, waving a dismissive hand.

Instead of marching her through the entire length of the restaurant and out the door, he leads her to the back passage to the hotel lobby. A much shorter walk, but long enough to draw even more attention, especially with Cora voicing her displeasure rather loudly. I try to make myself as small as possible, in the far corner of the booth, to avoid the curious and pitying looks being fired in my direction. I focus on Clive, who throws me a wink and does his best to cover the collective hush that has fallen over the restaurant with some lively tunes.

The minutes crawl by as little, nagging doubts start eating away at my earlier confidence. A vivid imagination is my downfall, as I can't seem to stop visualizing the picture Cora painted with her words. It describes a side of Damian I haven't seen yet. Is he holding back? The thoughts start bouncing around my mind, and the comfortable fullness of my stomach just minutes ago starts churning with nausea.

Jealousy. Such an ugly and uncontrollable emotion.

By the time Damian slides into the booth across from me, my eyes have been focused on a spot on the wall while insecurity has gradually taken over. I even considered leaving, but the last vestiges of common sense had me stay right here, where I was relatively safe in the public eye.

"Gypsy?" I turn my eyes to him at the sound of his voice. I'm not sure what he sees in mine, but he's out of his seat again in a flash. Taking his wallet from his pocket, he tosses some bills on the table. "Let's go," he says, helping me out of the booth and pulling me tight to his body, his arm protectively over my shoulder. I keep my eyes focused on the floor in front of me until I feel fresh air hit my cheeks.

DAMIAN

The drive home is relatively quiet. Mostly because every time I start to apologize, she plasters on a smile and tells me she's fine. Deadly words, those—I'm fine. Especially since it doesn't take much to know she's anything but *fine*.

That was an ugly-ass scene back there, and I'm pissed as hell that what was a great night, and shaping up to become phenomenal, came crashing down around my ears when that bitch showed up.

Son-of-a-fucking-bitch. I've never come so close to clocking a woman, but more than once I had my hand already fisted during that encounter. The way she insulted and embarrassed Kerry had me furious, which is why I marched her out. She hadn't liked that, but just as quickly she turned back to her seduction when we hit the hotel lobby. Her hands slipping inside my jacket, her boobs pressing against me— it took every effort not to toss her on her ass. I am angry at myself because not that long ago, that whole scene might've had a much different outcome—and that's all on me. I took my time to make sure Cora understood exactly where I stood. Still, it took me telling her how deadly serious my involvement with Kerry was before she listened. And that ticked me off, too, that I was forced to take words I hadn't even spoken aloud to the woman who deserved them, to warn the bitch off.

I played fast and loose long enough, without much concern who I was playing with, and I probably deserved every bit of what happened.

But Kerry doesn't.

"Talk to me," I try again, my hand searching hers. "And don't tell me you're fine. Just tell me what's going through your head. I hate that she had an opportunity to spew her vindictive words before I got her out of there. I hate that she got her claws in—"

"She didn't," Kerry interrupts, turning toward me for the first time since we started driving. "I just…it threw me, that's all."

I can't focus my attention when I'm driving, so I pull off into the James Farm parking lot. Turning off the engine, I turn and face her. "Bullshit." I watch her flinch at that, but before she has a chance to turn her head away, I put my hands on her neck, keeping her jaw in place with my thumbs. "Babe, I can see the questions swimming in your eyes. Spit it out. Whatever it is, just get it out."

"It's not bullshit," she argues. "And I *was* fine… but then you took a while, and I started thinking: *What if he gets bored with me?* I don't know. I'm pretty sure you have a lot more adventurous experience to draw from than I do. I honestly don't even want to think about that, but her description of what you apparently like was pretty damn vivid. Truthfully? I could've done without that."

"Okay, a few things," I interrupt her almost-breathless flow of words. "My so-called experience is probably not half as adventurous as she made you think. Her view of things is generally self-serving and far from the truth." I rest my forehead against hers. Her beautiful, gray eyes blink furiously in an attempt to hold the tears at bay and still one or two escape. I wipe them away with the pads of my thumbs. "I'm sorry I left you alone," I continue in a softer voice. "I had to make it clear to her, once and for all, that the reality of her never was a match to the dream of you." A little hitch in her breathing, and her hands coming up to clutch at my wrists, gives me hope I'm getting through. "As for getting bored with you? The likelihood of that happening doesn't exist, so get that out of your head right now. There is so much of you still to discover, so much I'd like to discover with you."

Her eyes close and I press a soft kiss on her mouth.

"I'd like to get you home now and get started on that," I mumble as my lips skirt along her jaw and to her neck.

"Mmmmm," she hums. "I think I might like that."

A second later, tires spinning, we're back on the road, racing toward home.

The moment I turn off the engine, we are both scrambling to get out. Kerry is already halfway to the front door when I round the Expedition. I jog to catch up with her and scoop her up in my arms.

"Damian!" she scolds, but she's giggling as she does it. Wrapping her arms around my neck, she holds on tight as I carry her to the door, which opens just as I'm trying to figure out how to get to my keys with my hands full of woman.

"I thought I heard something," Bella smiles from the hallway.

Right. Not sure how it slipped my mind that Kerry was not my only guest, but ever since I saw her coming down the stairs in that little black body sleeve, she's all I've had on my mind.

At my sister's appearance at the door, Kerry starts wiggling to get down, but I'm determined not to let myself be distracted from my goal again.

"Close and lock behind us, Bella," I order over my shoulder as I walk past her into the house. "We're turning in."

"Damian!" This time Kerry angrily hisses my name, her fingers knotting painfully in the small hairs of my neck. The sound of heels follows me to the stairs.

"I should probably tell you…" Bella starts when I'm halfway upstairs.

"Tomorrow," I snap impatiently.

"But…"

"Tomorrow, Bella."

I'm not sure what it is she's muttering, my focus is on the bedroom door at the end of the hall. Once I maneuver Kerry safely through, without knocking her head on the doorpost, I kick it shut behind me. Only then do I carefully let go of her legs, keeping her steady until she's found her balance. The moment she does, her little hands shove me hard in the chest.

"You're an ass." Her mouth is set in an angry line, her eyes shoot fire, and all I can think is how to get inside her in the next two seconds. "That was incredibly rude and embarrassing," she bites off, turning her back to me, shrugging out of that floral jacket, or whatever it is, and tossing it on the chair. Then she bends over to take off her shoes.

She's probably right, I'm an ass and that was rude, but right now every working brain cell I have is focused on the deliciously round ass, encased in slinky black, sticking up in the air—calling to me. I don't even think about it, I simply drop on my knees behind her, put both hands on her hips and put my teeth in one of the juicy cheeks. I'm not sure what

I was thinking. I might've expected anger, maybe a slap, but that wasn't enough to stop me. Obviously. But the deep groan coming from her is a surprise. A pleasant one.

Encouraged, I nuzzle her backside while my hands carefully slide down to the hem of the dress, only to work their way back up, taking the material with them and uncovering only skin.

Fuck me sideways. She's as naked as a jaybird underneath. The ass I'm getting closely acquainted with, an absolute piece of art. The slight reddening of the pale skin where I nipped her is an invitation to match it with a similar mark on the other cheek. This time there is no fabric barrier, and I love the feel of her heated skin against my mouth. The moment my teeth press down, she groans again, this time with a slight gyration of her hips.

KERRY

Oh my.

I was about to tell Damian whatever moment we'd been building up to had passed, but then he bit me. A love bite. Strong enough to feel the sting but not hard enough to hurt. Just burn. The most erotic sensation I've experienced.

I don't even think about the fact he's behind me, at eye level with my less than perky backside, but the soft hum as he nuzzles me from behind, while pulling up my dress, has me toss any lingering insecurities out the window. This turns him on. And by God, it does me, too.

I stay where I am, bent over and slightly shivering, when I feel the air hitting the newly exposed skin. His open mouth brushes over the other side before I feel his teeth sink in. This time my knees buckle. I slowly straighten up, not too fast, I don't feel like doing a face-plant on the rug. Behind me, Damian licks the mark I'm sure he left, and I feel the electricity ripple over my skin all the way to the top of my head. It leaves goosebumps in its wake all over my body.

"Turn around," he whispers, his hands steady on my hips. I step out of my shoes and turn to him.

He's on his knees, still fully dressed in dark jeans and steel gray dress shirt, with his eyes nearly black as they travel slowly up my body to meet mine. Even with the dress pushed up around my waist, undoubtedly looking a little silly, he still makes me feel desired. It's a heady feeling. There are no words needed, I can see it reflected in his eyes, on his face. I can feel it in the reverence of his touch as he unapologetically runs his fingers over every blasted dimple and imperfection on my skin. It makes me feel powerful. This man could probably kill me with his bare hands, yet he is on his knees—worshipping.

I let my gaze roam over his features and use my hands to trace behind. My heart does a little skip when he closes his eyes and ever so slightly tilts his face into my palm. *Powerful.*

This is discovery.

No shields, no shame, no covers…completely naked, despite the remaining clothes covering us. Exposed and vulnerable, but without fear.

This is trust.

The need to share every flaw, every thought, every honest moment.

This is love.

CHAPTER 25

KERRY

"YOU CAN'T GO IN THERE!"

The sound of voices approaching the bedroom door brings me fully awake.

I woke up a while ago, still wrapped tight in Damian's arms, and I didn't want to open my eyes yet. Instead, I snuggled a little deeper and relived every moment of last night in minute detail. The air had been rich with arousal and emotions, even though we barely exchanged a word. The slow pace of exploration made it feel like we'd been suspended in a time void. The usual rush to completion before reality knocked simply not there last night.

With Damian still on his knees, I'd slipped off the dress before I pulled him up by his hands. It surprised me, how easily he allowed me to undress him—let me take control. The only time I could see him struggle for control over his body was when I slowly stripped down his jeans and boxers, sinking on my haunches in front of him this time. I'd pulled off his boots so he could step out.

I remember being mesmerized by his beautifully erect cock, only a breath away from my face and stroking my index finger along its length, tracing the engorged veins. The drop of moisture slowly sliding down its flushed crown begged to be licked. With my hands bracing the backs of his thighs, I leaned in and lapped with the flat of my tongue. His loud groan and the clench of his muscles under my palms had me press my core on the heel of my foot.

His taste was rich on my tongue—all Damian— but when I went back for seconds, he stopped me.

"I don't think I can stay standing," he whispered, stroking my hair. He took a few steps back and sank down in the wing chair, slid his butt to the edge so he could spread his legs. Wide. He groaned when I dropped to my hands and knees and crawled to him. His hands were digging into the muscles of his leg. I might've been the one on the ground, but I felt no less powerful than before. Reaching up, I placed my hands over his, holding them pinned as I dropped my eyes to his cock. Nestled in short, dark, graying curls, it was curved up against his stomach, darkly flooded with blood and in sharp contrast with the olive tone of his skin.

I'd barely slid my mouth down his length when my control ended. Or maybe I should say his. Muttering expletives, he lifted me up by my armpits, turned me around and pulled me onto his lap. With his hands underneath my legs, he pulled up my knees and spread them over the armrests. I remember shivering when I felt his crown, wet from my mouth, skim across the puckered skin of my ass as I was pulled into position. He'd just growled in response, with the promise there was always more left to explore.

He fucked me right there in the chair, my body completely spread open and at his mercy as he sharply powered his hips up, hitting every active nerve. We were so primed, it had not taken much for me to roll my head back on his shoulder and bite down on his hand that had come up to cover my cries. I was still pulsing around him when he clamped his mouth in the crook of my exposed neck as his body shook and bucked inside and around me.

He'd carried me to the bed where we continued our explorations, finally falling asleep exhausted, but completely sated.

Damian is still asleep, at least he was, but Bella's voice outside the door has him stirring behind me.

"What's going on?" he asks, his croaked voice still heavy with sleep. He pushes his upper body off the mattress and looks down on me before casting his eye on the door. "Who is it?"

"Not sure," I say, staying safely under the covers as another voice joins Bella's in a discussion outside our door.

"Damian—*Es su madre!*"

I don't speak much Spanish, but I clearly understand *that*.

"Fucking hell," Damian swears in a low voice.

"Watch your mouth, *mi hijo!*"

Clearly not low enough for his mother. I hide further under the covers to stifle my giggles. I don't know what seems so funny about this situation, which clearly spells disaster of massive proportions, but I seem to think it's hilarious.

"Stop it," Damian hisses, pulling the sheet off my head. It doesn't help. It only makes me laugh harder.

"Gypsy…" he threatens, but the slight tugging at the corner of his mouth proves he's having a hard time keeping a straight face, too. It is kind of a ridiculous situation. We're not kids, for crying out loud.

Outside the door, I hear Bella herd their mother back down the hall.

This may not have been planned, and I'm pretty sure meeting his mother is not high on Damian's list of priorities for me, but she's here and we may as well deal with it. Resolved, I get out of bed, slip on yoga pants and a tank top, and grab last night's kimono off the floor, tossing it on for extra coverage.

"Babe, seriously…" Damian scrambles to get out of bed and hops on one leg as he tries to get the other into his sweats. "Hold up."

"Damian, really—she's your mom. She's just a little old lady. It doesn't faze me." A puzzling smirk settles on his face as he finally shrugs his shoulders and with dramatic flourish, opens the door for me.

He follows closely behind as I make my way downstairs and into the kitchen where I can hear activity. When I round the corner, I stop in my tracks, Damian bumping into my back and chuckling. "What I was trying to tell you," he whispers, his mouth in my hair, "is that my mom never travels alone."

"Clearly," I choke out, taking in the kitchen full of women, all paused mid-motion and gawking at the picture I'm sure Damian and I make. Damian snickering over my shoulder as I stand with abject horror plastered on my face. Four heads turned our way. Bella seems moderately apologetic, but the other three are just blatantly curious. Two of the women are short and dark like Bella, maybe a bit older, but the third is different.

I had envisioned this sweet, gray-haired lady, wrinkled and stooped with age. Perhaps even smaller than her youngest daughter. But nothing prepared me for the tall, statuesque woman, whose gray-haired pixie cut only enhanced her youthful appearance. She has to be at least seventy-five, if not eighty, but you would never think it, looking at her straight shoulders and clear eyes.

Bella obviously doesn't get her penchant for pretty things from any stranger. Before I have a chance to escape and get changed into something a little more fitting of the fashion display in Damian's kitchen, he moves around me, grabs my hand, and tugs me toward his mother. To my surprise, she's almost as tall as he is.

"Mama," he says, as he leans in to kiss her cheek. "This is a surprise." The tone is slightly scolding as he throws his youngest sister a look. Bella just sticks out her chin. In all honesty, I vaguely recall her trying to tell him something last night. I'm guessing this surprise visit may have been it.

"Your sister knew. She said she needed the rest of her stuff. We're here to deliver her stuff. Left the house at six this morning and now we're here." The older woman's voice is strong and firm and surprisingly holds no sign of an accent, although she did throw in some easy Spanish earlier. The moment she stops talking, her eyes come to rest on me. I feel like a bug tacked to the wall.

"Mama," Damian says, putting his arm securely around my shoulders, probably still fearful I will run. "This is Kerry Emerson. Kerry, this is Carmella, my mother."

"Pleased to meet you," I mutter by rote, sticking my hand out, which makes her look but subsequently ignore completely, as she literally drags me toward her. Folded in some seriously strong arms, with my face buried in her ample bosom, I barely hear her speak well over the top of my head.

"Ahh, *mi hijo*. *Preciosa*. Obviously not Mexican, but lovely all the same."

I'm forcefully pulled from her arms and just catch Damian rolling his eyes at his mother. "Knock it off, Ma. You're about as Mexican as biscuits and gravy. What was it? Your great-great-grandmother? You are

Texan, born and raised. Probably didn't even speak Spanish until you met Papa."

His sisters snicker behind their mom, who casually shrugs her shoulders before turning back to me. "My girls take after their father. Obviously." She turns her head slightly to look at Bella. "You clearly know Isabella, she's our baby and may or may not be disowned, depending on her excuse for keeping important information from her mother and sisters." This time it's Bella rolling her eyes. It must be a family thing. "And this is Francessca, she was number four," she continues, casually pointing over her left shoulder. I wave at the woman who is smiling back broadly. I just now notice the little ring in her nose. Cool. "And next to her is Christina. She's two years older than Damian."

"Three," a voice sounds behind the older woman before the face comes in sight. Also smiling. A striking lock of almost white-gray hair amid the dark brown hangs over her forehead.

"Whatever," Carmella waves her hand in the air irreverently.

I feel like I've gotten stuck in a sitcom. A little disorienting, slightly overwhelming, but gradually becoming amusing comedy. Especially when I hear the sighs coming from Damian behind me.

"Damian, though? He's always been the perfect mix. He's got the best of both of us." I chuckle when I hear the sisters collectively groan at that declaration.

Five minutes later, I find myself donned in an apron

behind the stove. Since Bella thought it necessary to assure her mother I could cook, something she seemed dubious about, I was basically shoved in here. I'm throwing together stacks of banana-maple stuffed French toast with whipped, sweetened cream cheese at Damian's request.

"Mama has a sweet tooth," he whispers in my ear before heading upstairs to grab a quick shower. Leaving me to feed his family, their chatter a soothing sound in the background as my lips stretch into a smile.

DAMIAN

"How come you're working on a Saturday?" Mom asks me.

I just dropped my plate and cup in the sink. Breakfast was a major score for Kerry, although I never had any doubts she'd quickly win them over—with or without kitchen prowess. I managed to whisper a quick apology to Bella earlier for not giving her the two seconds it would've taken her to warn me of their coming. The apology was for her sake, not mine. My night with Kerry would not have been the same with the knowledge of my family descending, in only a few hours, hanging over our heads.

I wrap my arms around Kerry from behind, as she puts some dishes back in the cupboard, and turn with her in front of me to look at my mother.

"Because I have an active case I'd like to see cleared up sooner than later," I explain, giving Kerry a squeeze.

"You need to keep the weekends for your *familia—tu novia.*"

"Ma!" my sister Chrissy jumps in. "Don't try to guilt him. You already succeeded in making me feel bad enough to take an unscheduled day off today, don't make him do the same."

It doesn't surprise me, my mom is Catholic and a master at playing the guilt card. Not too subtly, either. Mama believes everything should be dropped for family—something I love about her—but isn't always possible. Chrissy has a family and also has her own psychology practice. She tries hard to schedule her work around her kids. Their father has them on alternate weekends, and I'm sure her secretary is cursing her right now for having to reschedule her Saturday appointments. It doesn't stop Ma.

"Still," she persists. "We're leaving again tomorrow." I try to hide my flinch at that bit of news and looking at Bella's shocked face, she had no idea, either. Giving Kerry another reassuring squeeze, secretly praying she doesn't run from the house screaming before the weekend is over, I decide to just go with it.

"Okay, so I'll make sure I'm home at a decent time. We'll have a nice barbecue on the deck, and I'll see if I can bring any work I have left home for tomorrow.

In the meantime, you have a chance to get to know Kerry a bit better. How's that?" Ma may be the master manipulator, but we kids have learned a thing or two from her over the years.

I feel a little guilty throwing Kerry under the bus like that, but if I thought my sisters wouldn't stand up for her, Bella for sure, I wouldn't leave her with Ma. My mother can be a little invasive, albeit loving. It's not random that I chose a career that afforded me a lot of travel initially. And that when I was able to settle down, I did it close enough so I could get to my family when I wanted, but far enough that my mother wouldn't come into my house and pick up my dirty socks every day.

I blame my dad. He is crazy for that woman and has allowed her to run roughshod over him their entire married life. Invited it, even. Personally, I grew out of enjoying being babied by the time I turned three. I had a doting mother and two older sisters, for fuck's sake.

"Fine," she reluctantly concedes—as if she had a choice. "We'll go into town and get some proper food."

"Ma," I start, wanting to explain it wouldn't be safe for Kerry, when Bella saves my butt. Explaining would've taken me another hour, if not more, and I'm already burning daylight here.

"Go," she points at the front door. "I've got it."

Blowing Bella a kiss, I pull Kerry with me to the porch out front.

"Holy shit," she mutters drily, and I crack up.

"I know," I snicker.

"That was intense. I feel like I've just been tossed around in a spin cycle. Is it always like this?" she asks, turning to me and putting her hand in the middle of my chest where I cover it with mine.

"No exceptions," I admit, watching her eyes get big. "Scared?" I tease her, and she squints her eyes at me.

"I don't scare that easily, but I can tell you this; I've always believed in small doses. Little bits at a time." I tuck her hair behind her ear as she smiles up at me. "All kidding aside, though, I like your family. Your sisters are great, your mom is kinda hilarious, if she's not being scary, and the dynamics between you all is a treat to watch. I'll be fine. I may decide to make you pay me back for abandoning me with them, but I promise I won't make it too painful."

"Hmmmm," I growl, pulling her close with a hand in her lower back and the other fisted in her hair. "Promises, promises." I slant my mouth over hers and kiss her deeply.

Three words are on the tip of my tongue—and they're not *I am sorry*.

"Be safe," I say instead, even though I know she'll be fine with my family. As long as she stays in the house. Papa would always say that the combination of my mother and my sisters could scare off the devil himself. He had a point.

"You, too," she says sweetly against my lips.

"I...I'll see you later." I catch myself at the last

minute. Not the time. Not when my family probably has their ears pressed up against the door on the other side and when I have this fucking case still open.

With a last press of my lips on hers, I reluctantly walk to my Expedition. I get in and wait until I see Kerry go safely inside before I start driving. I've barely left my drive when my phone rings.

"Yes, I set the alarm." I can hear the smile in her voice. "I just didn't want you to worry."

"Thanks, baby."

I'm feeling pretty damn good, driving into town. All the way to the office, until I see all the cars in the parking lot. *What now?*

Luna is waiting at the top of the stairs, the only reminder of her encounter with Willoughs a slight yellowish tint along the side of her forehead.

"Bullshit, boss," she says as I meet up with her. "We've got a tug-of-war going on over the damn evidence."

"What evidence?" I hold her back when she starts walking ahead of me.

"The gun found at the murder scene, Sinclair's phone, his body, the bugs, you name it—she wants it." I assume Luna is talking about Ella Friesen, who already made a play for Sinclair's body earlier.

"Is James here?" I want to know.

"Called in earlier on his way to the airport. He's been called back to Denver. Said he'd call you as soon as he finds out 'what the fuck is up.' His words, not mine," she clarifies with a raised eyebrow.

That's all we need. We have an unsolved murder, a possible suspect on the run. We have a missing shipment worth twenty-six million bucks. We have electronic evidence we've not been able to explain, and now we have an interagency war on our hands and James is on a plane to Denver. Fucking fabulous.

When I walk into the boardroom, I find Jasper parked against the wall inside the door, shaking his head. All three, Boris, Keith, and Ella are leaning over the table yelling at each other. I almost miss Browns, who is sitting quietly with his chin down on his chest, carefully studying his folded hands. This is a fucking mess.

"Quiet!" I bark, but the three whose attention I'm trying to get just continue their bickering.

"Enough!" I pound my fist on the table three times, and this time the din stills. "Jesus Christ! What the hell is going on?"

All three start talking at the same time. I raise my hands to stop a repeat of what I just walked into. "One at a fucking time. We're in pretty sad shape if we haven't learned the art of communication yet." I sit down heavily, a headache already forming. I notice that Keith follows suit first and the other two shortly after. "Since you can't seem to talk to each other, I'll talk first." I take a deep breath and motion both Jasper and Luna to take a seat before I continue. "Here's what I know. James is on his way to Denver as we speak, so he's not here to help sort out this mess. I know there's been discussion between you, Ella, and James about where the evidence belongs." I look at her and watch a small muscle twitch in her cheek. "After James told me, I made sure to check up on my facts. And as I already knew—I'm sure you do, too—Interpol itself has no jurisdiction in any country. Now—" I lift my hand when she threatens to interrupt. "I know you are stuck in the middle between whomever your contact is in the UK and us, but let me remind you, you are part of this task force as liaison between agencies and for your expertise in this field. That's where it ends. Even if we were to come to an agreement on the evidence between the agencies, which is unlikely since this is still very much an active case, it would be either accompanied by one of our agents to the UK or one of their agents would have to come and get it. There are protocols we need to follow. That said, if you feel you can contribute to any part of the investigation, if you think your expertise will be of use when we examine evidence that falls under your knowledge, you will be most welcome to do so. Just one last thing, though—I don't appreciate it when our local police, our FBI field office, and my agents are being played for fools. Don't underestimate us. That was a mistake."

With a screech of her chair, Ella pushes back from the table and stands, her face beet red. "I'm flying to the UK this afternoon and I will file a report with my superiors." Her jaw clenched tight, she tugs her briefcase under her arm and marches out of the office.

I bite my tongue on any retort I might want to

throw out there and grab a bottle of water from the table, taking a deep tug before I turn to Blackfoot and Parnak. That was not pleasant. I will, however, enjoy this one.

"As for you two. This isn't the first time, not even the first case, over which you guys have bumped horns. Worse than interagency politics are interdepartmental squabbles. You're both on the city's payroll, for fuck's sake. I don't care what beef you might think you have with each other, just get the fuck over it!"

This time, I push back my chair and get up. I turn back by the door. "I need to cool down. Give me five minutes, make sure you have cool heads and are focused, and let's get this goddamn case solved."

I close the door of my office behind me, pull my chair to the window, and look out at the Animas River. Almost instinctively, I reach for my phone and dial.

"Hey," I hear Kerry's voice on the other side. "Everything okay?"

"Better now," I sigh, leaning back in my chair, one hand behind my neck. "Are you looking out at the river?"

"I wasn't, but now I am. Why?"

"You know that the water that flows past you flows right to me."

"I guess it does," she says hesitantly. "Are you looking at the river, too?"

"I am. I like how it connects all the important parts of my life. My work, my house…and now you."

"I like the thought of that." I can hear the smile

in her voice. For a minute, I just watch the river and listen to her soft breathing.

"Honey? Are you sure you're okay?"

"Yeah, Gypsy. Having a tough meeting and just needed to hear your voice."

"Oh." She pauses for a second before she continues, "That's kind of sweet. I miss you, too."

I chuckle softy, her admission sitting warmly in my chest.

"Bye...*mi amór.*"

A little hitch in her breath and then a gentle, "Bye, honey..."

CHAPTER 26

KERRY

"I'M GUESSING THAT WAS my son?"

I'm still staring at the river with my phone pressed against my face and a ditzy smile when Carmella walks into the kitchen behind me.

"Yes, it was," I tell her as I turn around.

After seeing Damian off, I excused myself to go have a shower and get dressed. I left Bella in charge of the kitchen and her family, and I took my time getting ready. I'd just walked into the kitchen to get another coffee when he called.

"Did you want another coffee?" I pick up the pot and motion at the cup in her hand.

"No. Two is my limit, or I'll be bouncing off the walls. Trust me," she winks at me. "I'm told it's not a pretty sight." She rinses her cup and puts it in the dishwasher while I doctor up my coffee. "I could see it, you know?"

"Sorry?" I look at her, a bit confused.

"*Mi hijo*—I could tell it was him on the phone from the look on your face." She tilts her head to the side as she looks me up and down. "You love him."

Oh dear.

"I…well…we've only known each other for a little over a month…" I stammer, in full-fledged panic mode.

"Bella tells me you met years ago."

"Well, that's technically true…but we never really talked."

"Why? Did you not like my son?"

Jesus. The woman is like a terrier. A very tall, very stern-looking, angry terrier. This is one of those damned if you do, damned if you don't situations I try to avoid like the plague. Hoping for a last-minute rescue, I look in the direction of the living room, where the sisters seem deep in conversation. No help there.

"Mrs. Gomez…Carmella," I quickly correct when she gives her head a sharp shake. "I liked your son just fine." *That's a lie. I thought he was an asshole.* "I *really* like him now. I care for him. A lot." I watch for a reaction but her face stays stoic. "At the time I first met Damian, I was actually married. Not happily. My ex-husband…let's just say he wasn't a very nice or forward-thinking man." I forge ahead as I watch a range of different emotions expressed on her face. I just can't tell what they are exactly. "I've been divorced about two years."

"Good," she says after a long pause that had me sweating buckets. "Kids?"

Damn. Going straight for the jugular.

"No." My voice sounds a little funny with the lump stuck in my throat, but she doesn't seem to notice.

"What—you don't like kids?" Her eyes squint, and I feel the bottom fall out of my stomach. This is killing the euphoric mood Damian left me in.

"I couldn't have them. I mean," I jump in when I see shock on her face. "I thought I couldn't have them. We tried, Greg and I. That's my ex-husband's name," I quickly explain. "We never got pregnant. He didn't want fertility treatments and made me think there was something wrong with me. Except I found out in our divorce he'd had a vasectomy before we were even married. He just never told me."

"*Hijo de puta!*" Her voice is loud. So loud, it has the sisters come running.

"Ma! What the hell?" Bella comes storming into the kitchen, immediately spotting my face and turns to tear into her mother. "What did you say to her, Mama? Look—" she points at me. "You almost made her cry. Damian's gonna be pissed when I tell him." Without even stopping, she's got her phone in her hand.

"Wait!" I call out, grabbing the hand with the phone. "Bella, your mother was just asking some questions. She's concerned about her son. There's nothing wrong with that." I don't mention it felt more like the Spanish Inquisition. "I was telling her about Greg." Bella knows the story. In fact, Bella knows just about everything there is to know about me. As I do about her. We've spent enough time together. Her face softens and she gives me a little smile.

"Who's Greg?" Chrissy asks, looking from one to the other.

"Her husband," Carmella blurts out.

"Ex! Sorry," I apologize for yelling. "But I really don't want everyone to get the wrong idea. He is my ex."

For fear I will forever be explaining things, I decide to make a fresh pot of coffee and tell them what they need to know all at once. It takes me close to two hours with constant interruptions. Something the women in this family all seem to do. It's quite funny actually, now that I know to expect it. They throw out random thoughts or words assuming that's what you mean, right in the middle of what you're saying. Mostly they're wrong, and you end up spending more time correcting them than it would've taken them to let you finish your thought in the first place. It does get tiring after a while.

"So you can have babies?"

I burst out laughing. The woman is relentless. I ignore the sharp *Ma!* coming from all directions and turn to Carmella. "I guess I could if I wanted to. And although I might well be a bit too old, the equipment is all there. *But…*" I stop Carmella as she opens her mouth. "That is something to be discussed between a woman and a man—not a woman, a man, and his mother."

Hoots and whistles come from the Gomez girls, but Mama isn't laughing.

"My Damian wants babies."

"All right," Chrissy grabs her mother by the arm and starts dragging her out of the kitchen. "That's enough, Ma. It's none of your business and if Damian knew you were trying to interfere, he'd be all over you. Now let's go get some fucking food, already!"

She pulls her mother straight to the door, completely ignoring her barked, "*Language!*"

"Don't worry," Bella says, as she puts her arm around my waist. "I already told the girls a little about your situation. Enough for them to know that you and I are going to stay here and they'll get groceries without us."

"You don't have to stay," I try to assure her.

"Oh yes, I do," she says, turning to face me. "There's a reason I'm moving to Durango, aside from my job. More than an hour or two at a time and my mother has me reaching for the rat poison...*for me!*"

When the family comes back two hours later, it looks like they've not only bought enough supplies to feed an army battalion, but each comes carrying in bags from Target.

"Bella, help me get those damn boxes out of the van!" Fran yells from the front door. I follow behind Bella as we navigate through what has to be half the store inventory in the familiar white and red bags.

Carmella has already taken over the kitchen, barking orders at Chrissy, and I'm glad to escape before I get hit in the cross fire.

Fran is standing at the back of the van by the open gate, and I'm shocked at the number of boxes stacked in the back.

"Holy crap. Where are we gonna put all those?" I blurt out. "There's no room in the garage." The two-car garage has been converted into two spaces; one half serves as a home gym, a place I've learned is sacred to Damian, since he goes in there regularly to work off frustration of any kind. The other half is jam-packed with a table saw, building materials, camping gear, golf clubs, fishing poles, riding lawnmower, snowblower, and other assorted flotsam—you name it, it's there.

"Good question," Bella says, surveying her belongings. "Laundry room?"

With the three of us hauling, it doesn't take that long to transfer the boxes into the small room off the kitchen. Twelve good-sized boxes are now stacked on the appliances and covering the floor. Good thing I just did laundry the other day, because there's no way we can get to the damn washer like this. I quickly close the door.

"Are you getting a place of your own soon?" Bella's mother pins her with a sharp glare, her hands in a large metal bowl I'm sure wasn't here before, kneading what looks to be some kind of bread dough. "You know three's a crowd, right?"

"I'm looking, Ma." Bella does the eye roll thing as she shoves Fran to the side and helps unpack the vast collection of Target bags.

"Kerry, you know how to clean ribs?" I smile at the dramatic brow wipe Bella performs as Carmella's attention shifts to me.

"I do," I tell her with more confidence than I feel. The woman has me seriously doubt any skills I thought I had.

"Good. Get on it." She tilts her head to the four full racks of ribs stacked on the counter. "Those foil trays are for the ribs. Two racks per tray."

I grab a cutting board, a paring knife, and go to work, carefully slicing the tough membrane covering the back of the ribs and using my fingers to pull it off. Before long, Fran and Bella have the dining room stacked with kitchenware, bath towels, sheet sets, four new pillows, a box of dinner plates, twelve soap dispensers, and a stack of boxer shorts. I can't help it, I start laughing and once I start, I can't stop. Soon Bella and her sisters join in when they see me looking at the collection on the table.

"What?" Carmella looks from one to the other. "His shorts are almost threadbare." That has us laughing even harder.

"Mama, he's forty-four," Bella points out. "I'm sure he can buy his own underwear. And he has a linen closet stacked with towels."

Her mother huffs and shrugs her shoulders. "You can never have enough towels."

Carmella has us working like a well-oiled machine and in no time, we have bread dough rising, potatoes boiling for potato salad, vegetables cleaned and chopped, ready to go into the oven to roast last minute. The ribs are in there now on two racks, slow-cooking in a marinade she made that smells fabulous. Fran has pulled out a massive bottle of white wine and is pouring us all a generous serving in the new, unbreakable wineglasses. Too risky to use real glass on the deck, Carmella explains.

We take our glasses outside while we wait for the potatoes to cook. It's nice. Despite the hectic day, Carmella's inappropriately invasive ways, the family's constant bickering, and my complete lack of control over any of it—it was very nice. This is what family's supposed to be like. Warm, contentious, tolerant, dysfunctional and above all, loving. Not something I had growing up.

"You have a house of your own?" Carmella asks, drawing my eyes from the water I know flows right to Damian.

"I rent a place for now. I'm still looking for a house." I smile at her and she smiles back. It looks innocent, until…

"What's wrong with this house? Bella needs a place, she can rent your house. You just stay here. It's a beautiful house."

"Ma!"

DAMIAN

The moment I walk in the door, the familiar smells of my mother's cooking assault me. Automatically, my stomach starts growling. Other than breakfast, I've not had a thing to eat and I'm starving.

All the way home, I was mulling over the case, but the moment I hit the top of the hill, seeing the river valley below with my house nestled on the shore, it all drained away. Home—made all the more so because of who is there waiting for me.

No one is in the kitchen, but I can hear them outside. Walking up to the sliding door, I just catch Mama telling Kerry to move in with me, and I stop in my tracks as one of my sisters scolds Ma.

I know my mother loves me to distraction, as she does all her kids, but she loves with the finesse of a drill sergeant. Always convinced she knows best how to make her kids happy. She rarely does, but I can't deny the thought of Kerry here permanently *does* make me happy. And having Bella take over Kerry's lease would be a good solution all around. Seems like all this estrogen invading my life again is seriously debilitating the straight-lined, logical, cautious parts of my brain I'd painstakingly developed after leaving home.

I slide open the door and step on the deck, moving behind Kerry's chair. She has her head tilted back and a smile on her face. Relief at seeing her relaxed, and the clear invitation on her gorgeous mouth, has me bend down and kiss her with everything I feel. I don't give a damn my sisters or Mom are getting an eyeful.

This is my house—my woman.

Dinner is a rowdy affair.

After I get over the pile of unnecessary crap my mother bought me, and shake off the endless ribbing by my sisters over the fact my mother insists on buying me underwear at every opportunity, I really enjoy the evening. Better yet, so does Kerry, who seems to have found her place with my sisters and is starting to find her ground with my mom.

As for Mama, she may not express it in words, or even in action, but she really likes Kerry. It's in the little glances from under her eyelashes as she observes Kerry interact with the girls. The soft tilt to her lips when she catches Kerry watching me with warm eyes. She likes her—for me.

Good. I like her for me, too.

"Night, Ma," I tell her when she announces she's going to bed. She'll be sharing the room with Bella, while Fran and Chrissy are taking the spare bedroom. The girls actually worked it out that way, and I'm grateful. With a bathroom connecting the master and the spare, I don't even want to think about having my mom in there. "Thanks for dinner. It was very good." She smiles at me and simply nods.

"Breakfast tomorrow is yours, Kerry," she announces from the doorway. "I bought some more bananas and cream cheese. And I picked up some chocolate syrup."

I turn to Kerry, who is chuckling at my mother's retreating back before she turns her smiling eyes to me. "Your mother is something else. I think she just gave me a compliment and a way to improve my recipe at the same time."

"Our mother is demanding of the people she cares about but never more demanding than she is of herself," Bella points out, very astutely.

"And that's the truth," Fran confirms with a smile.

Ten minutes later, Kerry gets up and bends down, her hands bracing my neck. "I'm heading up."

"Right behind you," I mumble with her mouth pressed against mine. I watch her head inside before turning back to my sisters, who all wear smirks without exception.

"You know," Fran speaks up. "I never thought I'd see the day, but I'm happy for you, brother. She's smart, she's independent, and she seems to be getting a handle on Ma. I'm gonna kick your ass if you fuck this up," she finishes, folding her arms determinedly over her chest.

"I second that," Chrissy adds.

"Me three," comes from Bella.

"And on that note," I announce as I push out of my chair, wisely removing myself from the line of fire. "I'll take kitchen duty and hit the sack."

The ten minutes it takes me to clean the last of the dishes flies by as I listen to my sisters' quiet voices and occasional laughs coming from outside. As much as the lot of them, save perhaps Bella, get on my nerves after a while, it feels good to have them all here.

By the time I make it upstairs, Kerry is already in

bed. As many nights before, I strip in the bathroom, toss my clothes in the hamper and join her in bed, where her body instinctively snuggles against mine. My mind instantly goes to my earlier thoughts. I've come to terms with the fact I've fallen for this woman. Despite believing most of my adult life I was doing fine on my own, the thought of not being able to come home to her at night has already become something I dread. I know without a doubt she will think it too soon. She's protective of her independence.

"I can hear you, you know," her sleepy voice startles me. She pushes up off my chest and lifts her heavy-lidded eyes to me. "The wheels are loud in there." She taps my forehead with her fingers. "Everything okay at work? I didn't even ask you after this morning."

"Mostly everyone's frustration at the lack of progress. No tag on Willoughs yet. Other cases popping up, requiring attention, and leads drying up without other ones to investigate. Keith's hope of finding something on the video feed from the lab that might help us figure out what happened to the missing shipment came up empty, too. These things tend to wear on patience, and mine ran pretty short this morning, too. Talking to you helped."

I tuck her head under my chin and breathe in her scent. She presses her face in my chest, and her limbs curl around me in a full body hug.

"Good. I'm glad," she softly replies.

"I'm sorry I left you here to fend for yourself. My family, they—"

"Shhh," she hushes me. "Your family is great. You're very lucky. It just took me a minute to get used to the intensity, that's all. I don't have siblings, and my parents... Well, my mom is sweet, but she's never understood my need to venture out on my own. She's built her life about caring for her husband. And my dad? He works, comes home, reads his paper, and starts drinking until it's time to go to bed. The next day is just the same. I don't think they even noticed when I moved out. I don't even bother going home for holidays anymore. Just the occasional phone call."

"I'm sorry," I say again. Bella would be proud of me, as those words seem to be rolling almost effortlessly from my lips now. I am, though. I can't imagine growing up in a place where you're not noticed. Puts growing up in a house where everyone's in your business in a whole new perspective.

"Don't be," she says. "I'm just telling you how it was for me, to explain my momentary shell shock when confronted with your family. I adore them, though." She lifts her head again to look at me. "Your mom, too."

I chuckle at that, burying my nose in her neck. "I'm glad. I hope she didn't scare you with the underwear. I really do buy my own, you know. I just can't seem to break her of the habit."

I feel her body shake with suppressed laughter. "She brought home half of Target," she snickers.

"I know," I groan. "Worst part is, she does this every time."

I can feel her yawn against me. "Get some sleep, baby."

"Okay. You, too, honey. Don't think too much," she mumbles.

"I promise I'll just be thinking about how much I like you here."

"In your bed?"

"In my bed, in my house, on my river...In my life."

CHAPTER 27

KERRY

"I'M OFF!" BELLA YELLS from downstairs, on her way to her new job.

We finally said goodbye—with promises to visit soon—to Chrissy, Fran, and their mom late afternoon, after spending a much more relaxed day yesterday. A few times Carmella tried to push her idea of a perfect housing arrangement on us, but she didn't get far. As wonderful as the weekend had turned out, I was a bit relieved when we had the house back, and it was just the three of us again over dinner.

While Damian sat at the table going over some files and tapping away on his laptop, Bella and I watched a few episodes of *Chopped,* exchanging ideas on how we'd use the sometimes weird ingredients the contestants were saddled with.

Damian snuck behind me in bed, well after

midnight, and woke me with his mouth on my neck and his fingers playing between my legs. In the dark, I could see the shine of intensity in his eyes as he rolled me over. He slid inside me with his hands cupping my face, his eyes holding mine, and his heat covering every inch of my skin.

Our lovemaking was slow and sweet. My climax washed over me gently instead of hitting me like an explosion. It was a different experience. Peaceful.

"Would it be so bad?" he asked as his hips still slowly rocked his length in and out of me.

"Wha-at?" My breath hitched as his cock touched a sensitive place inside me. Little electric impulses skittered out from my core and over my skin.

His rocking stopped. "Living here. With me."

"No…" I hesitated, bringing up a hand to stroke along his set jaw. "I'd be lying if I said the thought hadn't crossed my mind. But Damian, it's early days yet. We haven't even been able to go on a normal date—Friday's attempt notwithstanding."

"It's fine," he said, ducking his head as he pulled out of me. I could feel his disappointment when he climbed off the bed.

"Damian…" I wait until his eyes meet mine. "I *love* it here…with you. I don't think I've ever lived in a place that's so peaceful—so glorious—or with someone who makes me feel so safe and cared for. I don't think that's going to change once life returns to normal for me, but I'd feel much more confident about such a decision if I could make it when I feel I have some control back over my life."

He put a knee on the mattress and covered my body again with his, resting his head between my breasts, his ear pressed against my skin. "You're right," he said simply, as he listened to my heart beating. After lying there quietly for a few minutes, I could just hear him say, "For me..."

I almost told him my feelings right then, but instead just stroked my fingers through his hair until we both fell asleep like that.

This morning, he'd woken me up with coffee and a quick snuggle in bed. I'd thrown on some easy clothes and had come down for a bit of breakfast before he had to go. We were standing on the front porch when he took my hand and pressed it palm down against his chest, right over his heart.

"For you..." he said, before kissing me and walking with long strides to his SUV. My brain didn't kick in until I had closed and locked the door behind me.

He kills me.

"Good luck today!" I yell back downstairs, as I boot up my computer to check emails and my brand new Facebook page. Bella's idea. As was the Twitter account. I put a halt on it there, because although I've had a private Facebook account for years, I hardly check it and a business page is a totally different animal. Twitter is entirely alien to me, so I've decided that until I can get back in my store, I'm going to use the time to climb the steep learning curve of social network marketing.

A ping on my phone alerts me of an incoming text.

Damian: *Reset the alarm?*

Shit.

I put down the phone, grab my now-empty coffee cup, and head downstairs to the kitchen. I have my focus on the alarm panel by the back door and curse myself for constantly forgetting. I'm in my head and not only do I not hear a thing, but when an arm wraps around my neck from behind, it takes me a minute to react. My coffee cup shatters on the floor, and immediately my hands start clawing at the arm. I can't get a sound out. I try to kick, but with my toes barely reaching the floor, I have no leverage. Struggling as hard as I can, I keep my eyes focused on the water—drawing strength from the knowledge that it will flow to Damian. Already darkness starts bleeding into my peripheral vision, until all that remains is a pinpoint of light.

Then even that turns dark.

DAMIAN

"Sorry I left you holding the ball Saturday."

James Aiken called right after I sent a text to Kerry, reminding her to put the alarm back on. Apparently he's back en route to Durango after clearing up what turns out to have been a miscommunication by his office.

"I may have dropped the ball," I confess, thinking about Ella storming out after I tore a strip off her in front of everyone. "She, Blackfoot, and Parnak were having it out by the time I got here. Ella was trying to steamroll them. I told her, in no uncertain terms, she was overstepping her responsibilities and reminded her exactly what they were. She announced she'd be filing a report with her superiors in the UK. She apparently checked out of the hotel Saturday afternoon. I called the front desk when she didn't answer her phone. I was hoping I could salvage something."

The silence that follows is a bit uncomfortable. "James?"

"I'm here," he says. "I don't think you need to worry about Ms. Friesen. What I could gather from the early morning call I had with her office in Birmingham, and what I hope you can keep confidential, she'd been assigned to a desk for the past two years because of similar issues on prior cases overseas. This was supposed to be a probationary assignment because she was familiar with the facts leading up to it. Her boss apologized profusely and is offering to fly out himself. I told him I'd communicate with him directly, and if it was necessary for him to attend, we would link him in on video conference."

I sit back in my chair and rake my fingers through my hair. "Phew. That's a relief. I was willing to take the lumps if anything came of it. We're all ready to be done with this case."

"I hear you," he chuckles. "I'll probably be there by around three. If I pop into the office, are you still gonna be around?"

"Should be."

"Good, 'cause I may have found the source for those electronics. One of the manufacturer's warehouse employees was caught almost a month ago selling discards on the Internet."

"Discards?"

"Apparently, the company works with very precise specifications per purchase order. Even items with just minimal flaws—cracks in the casing, uneven cuts, scratches on lenses, those kinds of things—are collected in bins to be destroyed."

"Let me guess," I jump in. "That was supposed to be the guy's job."

"In one," James says. "Money, Damian...for the right amount, everything is possible."

"Boss!" I swing my chair around to see Jasper come tearing into my office, his face worried. "Picked up noise over the scanner. sheriff's office got called out to investigate report of an illegal campsite spotted just north of Hermosa along the river. Patrol just radioed in their report; it looks like someone's been there for a while. They found an ATV, a small boat trailer, and a high-end telescope aimed towa—"

"Aiken!" I yell into the phone still at my ear. "A mile north of Hermosa. Exit just south of the James

Ranch parking lot. The road splits about three hundred yards in, hang right. Only house on that road…"

"Go," he says in a deceptively calm voice. "Take Jas and Luna, I've got it."

"Call Keith, tell him—" I know I'm panicking but I can't seem to stop it.

"Gomez. I've got it. Go."

I turn to Jasper while my fingers are already dialing. "Get Luna, grab tactical gear. You drive." I toss my truck keys at him and listen to Kerry's phone ring…and ring. Fuck no!

My feet start moving toward the door, and by the time I hit the hallway, I'm running full speed. Luna is at the top of the stairs, pulling whatever she can carry from the equipment locker. "Let's go!" I yell at her as I pass her and run down the stairs, two at a time. Jas is just tossing duffel bags with gear in the back and stops me with a hand on my arm.

"Boss, Jesus…what about Bella?"

"Started work today, she should be there already. She called me on her way out," I say, walking toward the passenger side door, as Luna stuffs Kevlar vests in the back and closes the hatch.

The phone still clutched in my hand starts ringing, just as we're speeding through Durango with full lights and sirens.

"We've got State Patrol closing off your road at the highway," Blackfoot jumps right in when I put him on speaker. "James is on the horn with the sheriff, making sure everyone keeps their distance. I've got two patrol cars ahead of me, and Boris is leaving his office now."

"Okay. James give you coordinates?" My training is finally kicking in, and I feel the blood in my veins freezing as my focus sharpens.

"South of James Ranch parking lot. Hang right at the split?"

"You've got it. Put a call out for everyone to hold up, right after a sharp right curving up a ridge. Once over that ridge, anyone at the house can see you coming."

"Gotcha. How're you going in?" he wants to know.

"Working on it." I click off and turn in my seat to Luna. "Got your laptop?" She shrugs a backpack off her shoulders and pulls out her Mac.

"What do you need?" she asks, her hands poised over the keyboard.

I think for a minute before answering. "Find me a boat launch," I tell her. "Pull up satellite and look for any open spots along the river with a farmer's lane, a dirt road, anything that looks like it could be tracks leading to the road."

"Jas—see if you can get through to the sheriff's office. They may know of any river access south of my place, north of town."

"You think he's got wheels waiting downriver," Luna states from the back seat.

"I do."

I stare out the side window, barely noticing Jasper talking on the phone as he tears through a red light.

I'm too busy trying to catch sight of the river.

"Got something," Luna leans forward, twisting the screen so I can see. "See that trail along the water that starts in the bend, just south of you? It runs all the way south into town. Hooks up with Animosa Drive and right to the 550. A lot of the shore is flat there, so it wouldn't be too hard to pull a small boat or raft right into shore."

"In Hermosa, take Animosa Drive to the end," I tell Jas, who thanks whoever was on the phone and hangs up.

"Check. I know where it is."

I turn back to the screen and follow the barely visible path all the way back up. "If you had to hide a car, where would you leave it?" I ask Luna, who doesn't hesitate to point out a spot not too far south of where she initially picked up the footprints.

"Right there. The prints end right in the bend, where the river curves toward the highway, just south of the house. Follow the line of the river and you see it meander sharply south again. That's where most of the vegetation ends until you hit town. I'd tuck it into the trees right where it makes that sharp turn."

"That can't be more than three or four hundred yards from my house. Closer than the ridge," I observe.

"Walking distance," Luna points out. She's right.

"Then we approach from there."

With that decision made, I call Keith, who answers immediately.

"Where are you?" he asks right off the bat.

"Coming up on Hermosa. Change of plans. I'm coming in from the south. There's a trail running all the way from Hermosa, north along the river, and comes to an end just south of my place. We think that's how he's planning to get away. We're gonna follow that trail to the end and go in on foot. Get a car down Animosa Drive behind us to close off the access to the river, just in case we somehow miss him on the trail. It probably wouldn't hurt to get some coverage along the river to the south, if for some reason he heads further downriver."

"All access and exit points have been covered on the highway and on the river. Except that one," he says. "I missed it."

"Luna picked it up." The silence on the other side is deafening until I hear a deep sigh.

"Good catch," he mumbles, clearly with a great deal of reluctance.

"I'll call you when we get there. Before we go in from behind, I need you guys to create a very careful distraction on the road in front of the house. Start getting your head around that." I slide my thumb across the screen to end the call and look up. As Jasper flies down Animosa Drive, I catch glimpses of the river as it gets closer by the second.

KERRY

I gasp awake at a wave of ice-cold water in my face. I try to reach up to wipe the water from my eyes but find I can't move my hands.

Slowly, realization comes back. Someone is in the house. My eyes fly wide-open, and I blink furiously at the water blurring my vision. I'm on the floor, with my back leaning against the side of the couch, and my hands tied behind me. The man standing over me is very familiar, but the rage distorting his face is new.

"Where are they?" he hisses out between his teeth, and I almost gag when the rancid smell hits my nostrils.

"Where are...what?" I don't move fast enough when I see his fist hauling at my face. The impact knocks me right over, and I hit the ground with a loud smack.

The pain is blinding, but I have little time to react because the next thing I know, I'm pulled upright by my hair. He bends his face closer and this time when he speaks, I feel spittle hitting my cheeks. "Birds. My box with the birds—where is it?" he blasts me directly in my face. It's inevitable, the combination of the excruciating pain and his vile breath has the contents of my stomach come surging up. For a moment, I feel a little tinge of vindication when he violently pulls my head back to try and avoid the stream of vomit shooting out, and as a result gets most of it on him. The feeling is short-lived because he jumps up and kicks me hard in the ribs when I'm shoved to the ground.

"Fuck you!" he yells. "You're disgusting!"

Good. The thought pops in my head as he stomps off to the kitchen and starts wiping himself with a wad of wet paper towels. If he had any thoughts about getting close to me, I'm sure he's rethinking them now.

With a frustrated growl, he tosses the towels in the sink and walks past me, disappearing out of view.

"It's gotta be here somewhere," he mutters under his breath as I hear the sound of tearing, banging, crashing—glass breaking. "I was assured it was here. Where the fuck is it?"

I try to stay as still as possible, hearing the mania in his voice as he rants and raves through the house. Not that I can move or speak if I wanted to. The thought of dying teases at the edge of my fear, but I push it away. I feel helpless, completely out of control. Even if there's not a doubt in my mind Damian will come for me, I can't just wait to be rescued. I have to do something—I have to move.

While the bangs and crashes continue from upstairs, I start moving my hands against whatever he tied them up with. Tape? My legs are free and I move them a little, trying not to make any noise. I gingerly lift my head, ignoring the stabbing pain behind my eyes. From where I'm lying, I can see into the kitchen. The floor is covered with the contents of the cupboards and drawers. Broken glass spreads well into the hallway. This is not the result of a coherent search—this looks more like a mad rampage.

Turning my head slightly, I see the door to the laundry room propped open. Piling out are Bella's boxes, ripped and torn, with the innocent contents spilling out. A loud crash, sounding like a large piece of furniture falling over, comes from upstairs and spurs me into action.

I never realized how hard it is to get up off the floor without the use of your hands. Using the couch as leverage, I manage to get to my knees but no further.

Sharp. I need something sharp. My eyes are automatically drawn back to the kitchen, scanning what I can see from the counter and the floor. I'm already shuffling on my knees in that direction when I spot the knife block on its side on the edge of the counter. I automatically drop my gaze to the floor immediately below and see the grip of one of the steak knives sticking out from under a pile of kitchen towels. My eyes stay focused there as I move as fast as I can in that direction. I don't even notice the shards of glass breaking my skin as I crawl on my knees toward it.

Upstairs, I hear him moving from room to room. Every time I hear the tread of his footsteps on the wood floor of the hallway, I hold my breath, waiting until they get muffled again by the carpet of another bedroom.

When I reach the knife, I slide on my ass and turn, feeling around with my hands. Once again, I hear his heavy treads coming out of a room, but this time they don't stop. The heavy thump of feet on the stairs sends me into a panic, and I almost miss the handle as my fingers frantically skim over it.

There's no time. I barely manage to get a grip on the knife, slump down on the floor and pretend to be passed out as his footsteps hit the tiles at the bottom of the stairs. It's hard to try and play dead when your heart is beating its way out of your chest and your breath wheezes through your teeth from pain and terror.

"The fuck?" His footsteps rush closer, and I struggle not to wince when they stop just inches from my face. A hand grabs me hard by the hair, and this time I feel chunks being torn from my scalp as I'm brutally yanked up. I'm obviously not cut out to be an actor because his voice hisses in my ear, "Up, you bitch! You can't fool me." He shakes my head violently, and I have to fight to stay on my feet.

"I…I don't know what you want. I don't know wh…where your books are," I pant through clenched teeth at the pain in my body and struggle to keep a tight grip on the knife behind my back.

"Twenty-six million dollars. You think I will hesitate, even for a second, to take you apart bit by bit in order to get back what's mine? Where did you hide it?"

When I feel cold steel pressed hard against the soft tissue under my chin, my eyes finally snap open. The knife clatters uselessly from my hand to the floor, yet he doesn't even blink. There's madness in the eyes glaring back at me.

Calculated madness.

"Please, Bruce…" I beg in futile hope that I can somehow reach a single fiber of humanity inside this lunatic. "I don't know where they are."

The last words have barely left my lips when I'm swung around in front of his body and his arm hooks around my neck.

"Kerry—Down!"

I don't know whether it is from sheer relief at hearing Damian's voice or from paralyzing fear that my knees seem to buckle underneath me. He's unprepared for my sudden collapse, so my head easily slips through his arm, just as the front door slams open behind us and shots ring out.

CHAPTER 28

DAMIAN

"42563192," I WHISPER in my head set.

"Jesus, boss," Jasper groans back. "You couldn't stick to an easy four-number combo like a normal person?"

I hear Luna's soft chuckle behind me. "The first three digits ensure it's disarmed silently, smartass," I send back.

We found a raft pulled up on the rocks along the river, just out of sight of the house. If we had any doubts before, we have none now. Keith is monitoring our movements on the radio and is currently holding off. Luna and I have a visual of the house and are waiting in the tree line for Jasper to move around to the side door into the garage. I can't know if Kerry ever had the chance to put the alarm back on and sent Jas around to make sure it's off before we attempt to barge in.

The element of surprise is our only option, since we have no decent visual except through the sliding door in the kitchen, and in order to use that to our advantage, we'd have to make ourselves visible.

"Putting in code now, and...off." Jasper's voice is barely audible but the highly sensitive earpieces allow us to hear a pin drop.

"Hold position. We're going to approach from the deck."

The shortest open route is at the corner of the deck that runs the width of the house. The deck is about two feet off the grass, with two steps coming down. I keep my weapon trained on the sliding door as I wave Luna ahead. She sprints past me toward the edge of the deck with her body crouched low. There's no movement from inside. The moment she ducks down out of sight, using a corner post to give her cover as she takes over aim on the door, I follow behind in similar fashion.

Peeking over the edge, I have a much better view of the kitchen, just as the large shape of a man walks in and bends down before I get a decent look.

"Visual on the suspect." Luna sees him, too.

"On 'go'," I alert my team, knowing that Keith and Jasper both will be at the ready.

In the next moment, my heart literally stops in my chest and all cool, collected focus flies right out the window. I can clearly see Willoughs suddenly straightening up, pulling a barely recognizable Kerry up by the hair. I watch as he shakes her, sticks the barrel of a gun under her chin, and yells in her face.

I don't realize I'm moving until I hear Luna say, "Go. Go. Go," in my ear. I have my hand on the sliding door when he hears me. Already made, I don't bother hiding the sound of the door sliding open as he wraps his arm around Kerry's neck, turning her as a shield.

"Kerry—Down!" My voice booms through the house.

I don't think, I let muscle memory take over as I watch Kerry slip through his hold, revealing just enough of his head to pull the trigger on the weapon in my hands. More shots are fired, but all I need to see is the instant, brief look of surprise on that cocksucker's face as the bullets hit. I'm already running, barely hearing the calls for cease fire around me. At first I can't see her, just the large shape of a very dead man bleeding out on the floor. I grab him by the collar and without a single care, toss him to the side to find Kerry's much smaller body, covered in blood and brain matter, crumpled underneath.

I vaguely register someone dragging the dead body into the hallway as I slide down to the floor, my back against a cupboard, and carefully pull a catatonic Kerry in my arms.

"Is it over?"

Her voice sounds raw. I tap her lips with the straw and wince when she tries to crack her eyelids. Her eyes are almost swollen shut. Some of it is from the beating she endured and some of it happened when that bastard's blood got in her eyes and caused an irritation. Part of me wishes he were still alive so I could kill him with my bare hands this time.

Despite the thorough flushing they did of both her eyes when we first got here, it'll likely take some time before the swelling subsides. Just like it will take a while for her throat to heal, as well as the two cracked ribs she sustained from his boot.

"It's over, *mi amór*," I say, gently stroking her hair from her face as her bloodshot, gray eyes squint up at me.

"You know that's the second time you've called me that," she observes quietly.

"It is," I admit. "It's also the truth."

"I know," she says, with a valiant attempt at a smile.

"Because I came for you?" I'm curious to know, but she carefully shakes her head.

"No." Even with her voice hoarse, she sounds confident. "I know, because I never doubted you would."

The difference is subtle—but the message is loud.

I don't really have a chance to react before the door to the room flies open, and Bella comes flying in, tears already running down her face.

"Are you okay?" She squeezes between me and the bed, completely ignoring my presence. There's nothing I can do, shy of wrestling her for position, so I reluctantly make room. Jasper is chuckling from the doorway, and Bella whips around at the sound. "You can go now. Thank you," she says, with one of the most insincere smiles I've ever witnessed. Now it's my turn to suppress a laugh, as Jasper, duly chastised, starts backing out of the room. It's a new experience for him to be so callously treated by the opposite sex.

"Bella!" Kerry croaks, shooting my sister a scolding look before turning to Jasper. "Stay, Jas—seriously—I wanted to thank you. Damian told me if it hadn't been for you monitoring the scanner and putting two and two together, you guys wouldn't have been there so fast. Or at all," she adds, her body doing a top to toe shiver.

Jasper looks a mite uncomfortable with the compliment, but the smile jerking at the corner of his mouth is a lot better than the beaten dog expression he was wearing earlier. I'd moved to the other side of the bed when Bella muscled me out of the way. This time it's Jasper bumping into me to get to Kerry.

"Careful," I growl as he bends down to give her a hug. Well, mostly it's Kerry hugging him because he knows damn well that if I so much as hear a peep out of her mouth because he wasn't careful, I'll kill him. I'm still carrying too much adrenaline. When he straightens up, I'm surprised when he faces Bella, who looks a little sheepish.

"And that," he says, pointing a finger in her face, "is how grown-ups show gratitude." Without another word, he stalks out of the room. Kerry's mouth falls open before she snaps it shut and shoots a pitying look at my sister, whose head is still turned to the door as if she can't believe what just happened. Myself, I have to literally bite my lip to keep from laughing. They both carry around giant chips on their shoulders, but I've gotta admit, this round goes to Jasper. This could get interesting.

Jasper has barely cleared the room when my once-enemy, now-good-friend Malachi sticks his head around the door.

"She's here," he says over his shoulder. The door is promptly pulled from his grip as Mal's wife, Kimeo, also Kerry's best friend, storms in and stops right at the foot end.

"This is the absolute last time," she warns Kerry, barely containing her emotions as her pleasantly-rounded body almost vibrates. "If I have to find out from anyone, other than you, next time something happens, I will officially divorce you as my best fr... friend." Just like that, the spectacular head of steam she had worked up deflates like a days-old balloon. Mal steps in behind her and puts his arm around her front, while giving me a chin lift and a wink.

And it's not just Kim dissolving in tears. Bella's mouth is trembling, and Kerry is fighting hard, chewing the skin off her bottom lip. I lean over her and pull it free with my thumb. "No tears, Gypsy," I caution her. "Your eyes will never return to normal."

Well, that did the trick, judging from the ball-pulverizing glower thrown in my direction. In that strange, unspoken pact of female solidarity, all three women instantly huddle together, completely ignoring the men in the room. I look at Mal who just shrugs, nudges his chin to the door, and leads the way out.

KERRY

"Are you done with this?"

The friendly volunteer who was in earlier, bringing the tray with limp chicken noodle soup and Jell-O for my dinner, is back to pick it up.

"All done," I smile at her, even though I haven't touched a thing. One look was enough.

I haven't seen Damian since he left with Mal earlier, but I'm assuming there is business to be discussed. Luckily, Bella and Kim kept me distracted and my mind off just what that business might entail.

The two hit it off, like I expected they would. And when, right after my dinner was delivered, a doctor came in with a nurse in tow to examine me, I sent the two of them off to the hospital cafeteria to get something to eat. The doctor announced that I would likely be released around eight, right after the shift change. A nurse would be in to tape my ribs, since nothing is broken, and aside from some pain pills he would prescribe, no treatment other than rest was recommended, he felt it was safe to send me home. Thank God.

It's been very quiet since. Only the volunteer who just walked out of the door with my untouched tray. My thoughts get loud when there's no noise to distract me, and it's difficult to keep the flashes of this morning's events at bay. The smell of blood is still in my nose and my gut churns at the memory of...

I barely manage to roll over and hang my head over the side as a fresh wave of nausea has me spitting up the water and limp tea that had been swirling in my stomach. Of course, that's when the door opens and Damian walks in, closely followed by Keith Blackfoot and a man I don't know. Wonderful.

"Give us a minute." Damian immediately dismisses the two men and dives into the small, attached washroom. Before I can straighten myself out, he's by my side with a wet towel and a roll of toilet paper. He doesn't say a word as he wipes my face with the warm towel and crouches down to clean up the mess on the floor, and I stay silent as well. I'm too embarrassed.

When he's dumped everything in the trash can in the corner of the room, he disappears in the washroom again. I hear the tap run as he obviously washes his hands. When he comes back in, he has another wet towel. This one cold. He folds it carefully lengthwise and lifts my head to place it in the back of my neck. He still hasn't spoken.

Not sure whether it's the cold compress, this morning's memories, or my tight control cracking, but my body starts to shake violently.

"I was waiting for this," he gently says, as he carefully climbs in bed on my good side and rolls me carefully in his arms. It hurts when I move, but I don't care. I burrow myself into him and let myself fall apart in his hold, knowing he will keep me together.

I'm unsure how much time has passed, but the firm press of his lips on my forehead and the soft stroking of his fingers through my hair finally quiet my shakes. My breath does that weird hiccupy thing babies get when they've cried a long time. But my tears have dried up, although I'm not sure the relief has done the condition of my eyes much good.

"I'm glad I don't have a mirror," I randomly say, and his chest starts to move with silent laughter.

"You don't need a mirror," he says, a smile evident in his voice. "You've got me to tell you how incredibly breathtaking you are."

I lift my face, but instead of kissing him on the mouth—vomit breath and all that—I press my mouth to the hollow of his throat where I can feel his heartbeat steady against my lips.

"For me..." I whisper against his skin.

"For you," he confirms back to me.

"I love you," I say, tilting my head back to look him in the eyes.

"I know."

If all I had to go by was the look on his face when his eyes are on mine, I still would never be able to question his feelings for me.

A cautious knock on the door interrupts the moment, but both of us are still smiling as we turn in that direction.

"Sorry to interrupt," Keith apologizes, as he sticks

his head around the door. "I understand if this is a bad time, but it would help us move forward if we could ask a few questions now."

"Come in." I take the initiative and wave him in. "Might as well get it over with," I mumble under my breath. Damian swings his legs over the side and sits up, but doesn't leave my side. The man following in behind the detective is a bit older, maybe mid-fifties, and has a distinguished head of salt-and-pepper hair. Still, something tells me the hair, the pleasantly smiling face, and the designer suit are only a cover. This is not a man to mess with. He walks up to the bed and holds out his hand. "Sorry about earlier," I hasten to say as I shake it.

"Not at all," he says in a clipped but friendly manner. "James Aiken, I'm—"

"Damian's boss. Yes, he mentioned you."

"Good. In that case, call me James." He turns his eyes to Damian, with the barest lift of his eyebrow, before stepping back and leaning his hands on the windowsill.

"Kerry, I know you'd rather forget all about this morning, but the sooner we have all the information we need, the faster we can wrap this thing up, once and for all," Keith suggests.

"Are you sure?" I challenge him. "The man seemed to think those damn books—or manuscripts or whatever—were in the house. That makes it obvious he didn't have them. I sure as hell don't have them. And unless you have them, I don't see how anything

I say could help you wrap this up 'once and for all,' because what you were looking for in the first place is no more found than it was before." I'm not sure where that came from, I just know I don't particularly like being placated, and he is catching me on a very bad day.

"I like her," James says to Damian with a chuckle, and that right there is the straw.

"Look," I turn on him and ignore the little squeeze of Damian's hand on mine. "I'm pleased as punch you like me, but I'm right fucking here. This was not a good day, this was not a particularly good week, and this certainly has not been a bloody good month! So spare me the pats on the head, because as you were able to see firsthand earlier, I'm this close to coming apart at the seams, and I'm not adverse to puking on someone to get my point across. You may have seen evidence of that this morning, as well." I put my head back, close my eyes, and take a deep breath before opening them again. Without waiting for any prompting, I launch into my statement, starting with Damian's text reminding me to reset the alarm.

It takes me a while, but with occasional encouraging nods and squeezes from Damian, and the odd clarifying question, I manage to get through.

"One last question," James concludes. "From your account, it sounds like Willoughs was...erratic? Cold and calculating one moment and mumbling incoherently the next?" he clarifies.

"Mostly crazy as a loon, it seemed to me," I answer

honestly. "I got the impression he was hearing voices, I remember him muttering to himself a lot, throwing things around, and talking about being sure it was there. Most of what he said made little sense to me. At some point, he was yelling about birds. A box with his birds or my box with the birds. Something like that."

"*The Birds of America*, by John James Audubon," James explains. "At last auction, it sold for twelve million."

I'm sure my mouth fell open. "Twelve million? For a book? Rich people are crazy."

James chuckles. "I won't disagree with you on that. For the most part," he slightly amends.

The moment the door opens and a nurse walks in, both James and Keith jump up. "We'd best be off," Keith says. He bends over the bed and gives me a kiss on the cheek. "Take care of yourself, sweetheart. I'll be in touch in a day or two." Before I can say anything in return, James takes his place by the bed and takes my free hand in his and pats the top of it. "Kerry—a pleasure. I hope you'll forgive me the somewhat rocky start we had earlier, because I'm sure we'll be seeing a lot more of each other."

With a final pat, he follows Keith out of the room and I turn to Damian, only partly noticing the nurse setting some paperwork on the foot of the bed. "He turned out to be nicer than I thought." Damian laughs as he hops of the bed.

"Probably because I'd warned him that if he upset you, I'd rip his arms off."

Our heads simultaneously turn toward a sound at the foot of the bed to see the nurse with her hand covering her mouth.

"It was a joke," I tell her, before turning to Damian. "It was a joke, right?"

His smile is big when he answers. "Sure."

CHAPTER 29

DAMIAN

"*MI HIJO*, HOW IS Kerry doing?"

With my house a crime scene, we'd all piled into Kerry's bungalow. A bit cramped since there's only one bedroom, which meant either Bella or I had to take the couch. Kerry didn't want to stay at a hotel. She said she missed her things. I didn't really say anything to that. Although, it had been on my tongue to tell her we should just pack her shit up; bring it home with us when we could head back. I think Bella read my mind because she gave her head a sharp shake before I could say anything. She offered to go to a hotel for a few days, pointing out there was one just the other side of Highway 160, but Kerry said she'd feel better if Bella stayed close by.

So my sister ended up taking the couch, and I found out just why Kerry wanted us all close when I crawled into bed with her. Her teeth were chattering and her entire body shook. She said she couldn't stop it, and she was afraid to close her eyes. That first night it took three hours before she managed to fall asleep. By the time she finally did, I was afraid to. I didn't want to let her out of my sight. Literally. Guess it'll take us both a while to get over that.

Last night was better for both of us when Kerry found a position that made her feel safe and didn't cause any discomfort. She had rolled up a winter quilt, used it like a body pillow with her body curved around it, and had me snuggle up behind her. It made her feel safer.

Kim and Mal had decided to stay the night in town. They'd left Asher safely with Mal's brother and sister-in-law. They headed out after a brief visit yesterday morning and assurances from both Bella and me that we'd look after Kerry.

Then there'd been Mama. Bella had held off calling until yesterday morning. She didn't want to wait any longer. She said she was still in the doghouse for not telling Ma I was involved with someone. I love my mom, but she can be a bit much to take. I could hear Bella try and deter her from driving straight here. Finally, when it had gone on long enough, I took the phone from my sister and told Ma, in no uncertain terms, that it would definitely not be helpful to Kerry's recovery to have my crazy family hovering. It had taken promising a visit to Farmington in the near future, as well as the concession she could call at any time to check up on Kerry.

That was yesterday morning, about twenty-four hours ago, and this is the seventh time she's called.

"Mama—Kerry is fine, but if you keep calling and waking her up, she'll never get any rest."

I left Kerry in bed this morning with the promise I'd bring her some breakfast. Jasper and Luna are popping in at some point to go over some stuff, and I want to avoid bringing up the investigation in front of her.

"Oh, is she awake?" Ma wants to know.

"I hope not," I firmly say. "It's going to take some time for her to heal and she'll get restless soon enough, so I want her to get as much sleep as possible now."

"Are you sure you don't want me to come? Don't you have to work? Who will look after her then?"

"Thanks, Ma, but for now I'm gonna try working from home. At least for the next couple of days, until we can get back into my place."

She reluctantly gives up and spends the next few minutes questioning me about Bella's new job, until I inform her that I have to get some breakfast going.

"At least let me know when you can head back to your house, Damian. From the sounds of it, it's going to need to be put in order and that's something your sisters and I can do."

"I can hire a crew—" I try, but Mama cuts me off.

"You will not," she snaps. "Why would you spend money on something your sisters and I are perfectly capable of doing? We'll make sure the place is ready for you." Knowing my mother, she won't rest until she feels she's done something useful.

"Thanks, Ma. That sounds good," I give in without argument. She and the girls will make sure there are no visible reminders of what happened.

I'm just sliding the last blueberry pancake out of the pan when there's a knock at the front door. Jasper and Luna are on the doorstep, and I indicate for them to keep it down as they follow me into the house. Both of them move straight to the dining room table, where they immediately pull out their laptops, while I pile a few pancakes on a plate and pour Kerry some coffee.

"Be right back. Pancakes on the stove, coffee in the pot," I mention to them as I make my way down the hallway to the bedroom. Kerry is still wrapped around her makeshift body pillow, and I make a mental note to ask Bella to pick up a proper one in town today.

"Morning, Gypsy," I mumble in Kerry's hair, after I place her breakfast on the side table.

"Mmmm," she moans as she slowly pulls the sheet down. I try not to react when I see the ugly bruising on her beautiful skin and instead focus on her drowsy, gray bedroom eyes. "Morning. Was that your mom on the phone?"

I lean in to kiss her before answering. "Yup. She's relentless. Brought you some breakfast, do you need any help?" She winces as she tries to sit up. I quickly stuff a pile of pillows behind her back and give her a hand.

"Looks good," she says, smiling when she's taken

a look at the plate. "Not sure if I can eat them all, but it won't be for lack of trying. Thank you, honey." She tags me behind the neck and pulls me to her mouth. Her kiss is sweet at first, but then I feel her fingers tangling in my hair and her mouth open, inviting my tongue. Not like me to turn down an invitation like that, especially since I can't touch or taste her without craving more.

"Jas and Luna just got here," I explain, dragging myself away from her wet, warm lips. "I'd love to have you for breakfast, but I probably shouldn't keep them waiting. Besides, you're hurt."

"I'm not that hurt," she says, sounding a little breathless herself, slightly scratching her nails over my scalp. It makes me want to curl up in her lap and never leave.

"Hmmm…maybe after they leave, when you've finished breakfast, I can help you bathe."

"Deal." She lets go of me, and I put her plate on her lap before I make my way back to my team, dragging my feet.

"Hope you left me some," I comment when I see both of them diving into breakfast.

"Three left," Luna mumbles with her mouth full.

When I sit down, my own plate in front of me, she shoves a file at me. "I wrote out your report for you, since I was right behind you coming in, but you'll need to check it and sign it."

I read through it, make a few minor adjustments, and sign it. I know both Jasper and Luna will have had to file a report, too. It's required each time one of us discharges a weapon, let alone kills someone. I know at some point Kerry will have to go over her written statement, as well, but it would just have to wait until she feels up to it.

"Anything else on the docket?"

"Just clean up. I think James has the toughest job," Jasper says. "He has to deal with his counterparts in the UK. They're making noise, upset all the players are dead and we still haven't been able to recover the goods."

"Do we have anything on that? Any leads?"

"Blackfoot and Parnak have everything that was found at Willoughs camp at the lab and are going through with a fine-tooth comb," Luna fills me in. "It's just not that high on the priority list, with another house invasion last night. They've got more urgent things on their minds."

"Another victim?" I ask.

"Not dead this time but pretty badly beaten, apparently. They haven't been able to get a statement. The woman hasn't regained consciousness yet."

Jasper speaks up. "Blackfoot mentioned something about wanting a sit-down as soon as possible with you. Pick your brain before he puts in an official request for assistance."

"Figured that was coming. Tell him to drop off copies of the case files and I'll go over them," I suggest. "Now, is there any news on my house?"

"Nice digs by the way, boss," Luna mentions.

"Gonna have to keep my eyes open for something like that."

Luna has been hopping from one temporary rental to the next since she moved to Durango. She's always had plans to buy but just never got around to it.

"Just don't move into my backyard," I tease. "I see enough of you as it is."

She dramatically grabs for her chest. "You wound me." Earning her a shove in the shoulder from Jas.

"Bullshit," he says. "Nothing wounds you. You've got a Teflon hide."

At the very least she puts on a good show, because every so often I see something shift in her eyes, which makes me think there is much to Luna under the surface.

Kerry

"Hi, Mom."

I managed to finish my pancakes and have been lying back, listening to the low hum of voices coming from down the hall. I know they're keeping it down for my sake, but part of me wants to be able to hear whether they've found out anything more.

A bit bored, I pull my bag onto the bed and fish around for my phone. Someone must've put it on silent at some point, because three voicemail messages are blinking. I'd been adamant about not calling my parents, so when I see all three are from my mother, I feel a little guilty. I don't even bother listening to them, I just call her.

"Kerry! Where have you been? I've been trying to get a hold of you for a few days. Jim—It's Kerry!" she calls out to my father without moving the phone away from her face. The only result is an almost-blown eardrum on my part, because I know for a fact my father could care less. My mother likes to pretend ours is a normal family, when it's anything but.

"I've just been under the weather a bit and let my phone die on me. I just noticed it now," I stretch the truth a little.

"You know, I saw Greg last week at the grocery store." She launches right into the reason she was probably wanting to talk to me, totally ignoring what I just said. I know I should know better, but the lack of care stings, especially when on the other side I have Damian's mother itching to nurture. And I'm not even her daughter.

"Oh yeah?" I try for a normal reaction. Greg moved back to Grand Junction right after our divorce, and I haven't kept tabs on him. I know my mother was heartbroken when we split. She simply couldn't understand why I would leave a man who could provide me with all my worldly needs. Her words, not mine. I didn't bother trying to explain a life of servitude was not my idea of wedded bliss—it would've been a complete waste of breath.

"Yes. At the deli counter in Safeway. He looked a

little lost, a little disheveled. I think he really misses a woman's touch, dear." I can hear the suggestion and the eager hope in her voice and roll my eyes.

"Not happening, Mom," I immediately try to avoid getting pulled into that vortex. "I'm happy now. I have a business to run, friends I enjoy. I have a good life, Mom."

"Yes, but you have no one to look after. No one looking after you."

I slow down my breathing, in an attempt to calm down. She always does this, and although I know she means well, it drives me up the wall nonetheless. "I have lots of people to look after and lots of people who look after me."

"It's not the same," she hisses, losing patience with me now that she recognizes the topic for the dead-end street it is. "What is a woman without a man?"

"I have a man, Mom…" The moment the words come from my mouth, I realize the mistake I made.

"You do? What does he do? Can he provide for you?" The excitement in her voice is unmistakable, and I drop my head back on the pillow, my eyes staring unfocused at the ceiling. Big fucking mistake.

"I can provide for myself. Have done so successfully for quite a while." I squeeze my eyes shut, knowing I have to stop letting remarks like that push my buttons. My mom will never change, but I can change how I choose to react to what she says. So I continue in a softer voice, "He's nice, Mom. He's in law enforcement and is good to me. He's good for me."

I feel the mattress dip and my eyes shoot open to find the subject of conversation sitting on the edge of the bed, his dark eyes smiling on me.

"Law enforcement? Oh, sweetheart, that's wonderful! I hear they have fabulous family benefits. Of course, you'd have to be married. Are there any plans? After all, at your age, finding an eligible man only becomes more and more difficult."

"I'm not marrying someone for his benefits," I groan, exasperated with my mother's one-track mind.

Damian leans close and whispers in my ear, "I wouldn't object."

"I have to go, Mom. Something's come up. I will give you call soon, okay?" I say quickly, trying to ignore Damian.

"Of course, sweetheart. Say hello to…what's his name?"

"Love you, Mom. I really have to run," I cut her off, not even giving her a chance to respond.

"I'm guessing you told her about me?" Damian smirks as I toss the phone on the mattress, not even caring as it bounces off and lands on the floor. I may change my number altogether.

"It was a mistake," I whine, dramatically throwing my arm over my eyes. "She has this way of making me say shit I know I'm better off keeping to myself."

"So I'm your dirty little secret?" I know he's teasing me as he pushes up my nightshirt, pressing an open-mouthed kiss to the swell of my stomach.

"I could get used to that," he mumbles. "Especially if that means I can help you get rid of the guilt and the tension after." His lips never break contact with my skin as he talks his way down my body, carefully taking my underwear down with his hands. "All you have to do is lie back." Once he relieves me of my panties, he pushes my legs up and open, settling himself in between.

"Wait," I cry out. "What about...?"

"They left," he cuts in, not slowing down for a second.

There's something highly erotic about a fully dressed man going down on a very naked you. The slight scrape where the material touches bare skin has my nipples peaking to firm points, and I feel myself get wetter as he pushes me wide to expose me. I force my eyes to stay open as I look down at his dark head, with the occasional hint of silver, between my legs. I watch him purse his lips and blow softly over my exposed flesh. With his thumbs, he spreads me open to his eyes, and for an instant I have to resist squeezing my legs together. He lazily rubs the pad of his thumb over my slick lips and already my hips move for better friction.

The almost feral smile as he lifts his eyes, dark with hunger, right before he deliberately lowers his mouth, has my toes curling. The moment his tongue strokes over me, I am caught on a wave of sensation. The low rolls when he softly rubs and licks, only to drive me up on a crest with deep explorations and hard flicks to my clit. His arm comes to rest on my hips to keep me in place, as he renders me mindless with the addition of two fingers, playing in the crease between my legs.

After he makes me come quite spectacularly, he helps me to my feet and leads me to the bathroom, where he spends the next twenty minutes bathing me as promised. By the time he is drying my hair, I'm so relaxed, I can barely stay seated.

"You're amazing, you know that?"

He lifts my head with a finger under my chin so he can look me in the eye. "Only in your eyes," he says with intensity before he carefully pulls me up. "Okay, let's get some clothes on you before I forget myself."

I feel bad, but I tried twice to give him some relief while in the tub, but both times he stopped me. "This is not about me," he said. I promise myself to devote the same type of attention on him once I'm a little more healed.

By the time he has me installed on the couch with the remote, I'm ready for a nap again.

CHAPTER 30

DAMIAN

CHRIST, WHAT A WEEK.

I finally got access back to my house four days after a man came in and terrorized my Gypsy—*In. My. Fucking. House!* As promised, Ma came in with Fran and Gabby and had even dragged my father along. For heavy lifting, she'd said. I almost laughed out loud since my father is almost a foot shorter than my mom, at five foot six or seven, plus he has trouble lifting the coffee pot in the morning. Not exactly the *muscle* she makes him out to be.

But I left it in her hands. She was thrilled to finally be able to do something, and I was thankful to scratch one thing off my list. I didn't think she'd take the job of cleaning so seriously.

After three fucking days, Ma calls me to let me know it'll be ready tonight. I'm not sure what the hell took them so long, and part of me dreads to find out.

Now there's Kerry, who claims to be good enough to just stay *home*. God save me from stubborn women.

"You still have trouble getting dressed with your ribs messed up. How in the hell are you gonna manage on your own?" I ask her, fighting off the urge to just toss her over my shoulder and haul her off. She's sitting on the couch, dressed in leggings and an old T-shirt ending just below her knees. She can't even wear a bra yet because it hurts too much, let alone raise her arms to wash her hair.

"I'll be fine. Besides, I'm going to have to open the store in the next few days. Marya is still in Silverton with the kids, and I'm guessing she'll be out for another five or six weeks with that arm of hers. As it is, it's going to be a while before I get my business back up to where it was. On top of that, I have to find a new car since my old one is scrapped. It's just easier from here."

I take a deep breath and try a different angle. "I know you don't need my help, but would you like me to come with you to find a car? We can go this afternoon so you'll at least have some wheels." Initially she looks at me suspiciously, not quite buying that I'm really giving in. I show her my best *sincere* face.

"I know you've got something up your sleeve, but regardless," she says with a little smile, "I would love to get the car thing out of the way, and I would love your help."

I let out a relieved breath, when she pins me with a wagging finger. "But don't think I won't have my eye on you."

It is not going well.

Kerry is dead set on getting another Subaru, no matter how much I try to explain that a real Durangoan would not be caught dead driving one of those Kerry doesn't seem to care, and knowing the car is only part of the struggles ahead, I decide—with pain in my heart—to let this one go. I'm picking my battles, but instead of making her happy, she seems even more suspicious when I turn the Expedition south to the dealership.

A long and painful hour later, Kerry signs the contract on a brand new Forester. They don't have the color she wants in stock, something called *Quartz Blue Pearl,* and so she'll have to wait for them to order it in. I try to suggest a navy one, to me blue is blue, but that earns me a stink eye.

I have my eye on the slick salesman when he tries to sell her the undercoating, for an exorbitant price, he's hiding in the monthly installments she'll be paying. I have a little chat with him, and in the end he throws in the undercoating, plus one or two other add-ons for free. That time Kerry's gray eyes sparkle and I suddenly can't care less about the car or the color, as long as I can see that sparkle in her eyes.

Kerry's monthly expenses are going to put a serious dent in her income and—opportunist that I am—I'm going to add that to my arsenal of reasons she should just move in with me. Working as a field agent for many years, before I set down roots here, allowed me to live from a duffel bag and stockpile my money. It means when I bought my place, I was able to do it without the need of a mortgage. Taxes, utilities, and groceries are all I have to pay, and my SUV comes with the job.

"Don't you love that color?" She smiles big as we drive away from the dealership, a brochure with her new car in the exact color she picked clutched in her lap. "I wish I could show Kim."

"If you love it, that's all that matters," I say, prying one of her hands away from her lap and entwining our fingers. "But if you want, we can head up for dinner at my place, see what my crazy family has been up to. And at the same time, you'll have four women to show your new *Quartz Blue Pearl* car off to." I ignore the hard stare I feel coming from her.

"Low, Gomez," she scolds me. "Also, very effective. Fine, I'll come home with you, but just for dinner with your family."

I hide my smile behind our laced fingers when I bring her hand up for a kiss. "That's all I want," I lie bold-faced.

The moment we turn off the highway, I feel Kerry stiffen beside me, and I realize what an idiot I've been. First chance I get, I pull off to the side in the grass and turn the engine off.

"Why are we stopping?"

I turn, take her face in my hands, and kiss her

gently. "Because for someone who is generally pretty observant, I've been stupidly blind. I know it'll take you some time to properly process what happened to you. Hell, I'm pretty sure it's gonna take me some time. I just never clued in that you might be scared to come back here. Do you want me to turn around?"

She doesn't say anything but stares out through the windshield. When I follow her line of vision, I notice we are parked right on the crest of the hill, overlooking the river and my house.

"It's beautiful," she finally expresses. "I was afraid I wouldn't be able to see it anymore, but I still do."

I shove my seat back, fumble with the damn seat belt and finally manage to pull her across the console and on my lap. "It *is* beautiful," I agree. "Don't give him that kind of power." I wrap my arms tight around her waist and rest my head against hers.

"I'm sorry," she says, as she climbs back over the console into her own seat. "I don't want to turn around. There's an armada of vehicles in your driveway. I wouldn't let you face such an onslaught alone. Besides," she adds, a little grin tugging at her lips. "Who else would I show my pretty new car to?"

I start the car and pull back onto the road. "I love you," I say, without turning my head, eyes fixed on the view below.

"I know," she softly answers, but when I quickly look over, she has the widest grin on her face.

"Have some more," Carmella urges, as she shoves the pan in my direction. "I swear, you've lost weight."

I chuckle because I doubt that missing a couple of meals, the first two days after I sustained my injuries, has hardly put a dent in my surplus thirty or so pounds. I've learned to like my surplus, though, and I have no doubt Damian likes it, too.

The moment we got out of the Expedition, the front door flew open and the entire family, minus Chrissy, who apparently stayed home with a sick child, came filing out of the house. Damian managed to round the front of the car and slip a protective arm around me before leading me through the hellos and well-wishes. Carmella was standing with her arm around a much shorter man with an impressive shock of silver hair, a strong nose, and deep set, warm brown eyes. His entire face was deeply lined, but despite his age and rather short stature, he made a striking figure. He was introduced as Ignacio, and completely disregarded the friendly hand I held out. The older man placed his hands on either side of my face, kissed both my cheeks, and then my forehead before letting me go.

"*Preciosa,*" he rumbled in a surprisingly deep voice.

Before I even realized what was happening, I'd been herded through the house and was sitting on the back deck with a drink in my hand. The lively noise of chatter and the smell of rich, fragrant foods instantly washed out any hesitation I might have felt walking in. If not for the new, deep sunflower-yellow color I noticed on the kitchen walls, I wouldn't have known anything had happened here.

It wasn't until a little later, when Bella announced dinner was on the table and we all filed in, that I realized this *homecoming* had been very carefully orchestrated. I could feel every eye on me as I sat down, watching for any signs of a breakdown. Instead, I smiled at Carmella and said, "I'm starving!" Immediately, the rather loaded silence lifted and the boisterous sounds of a large family dinner filled the room.

I sit back and put my hands on my food-filled belly. "I don't think I'd survive another bite, Carmella. That was out-of-this-world delicious. The way this family cooks, I'll need to invest in a new wardrobe soon."

"You're no slouch yourself, Kerry," Bella points out. "You could give Papa a run for his money with your desserts."

I turn to Ignacio with big eyes. "You cook, too?"

"I can do the sweet stuff. I can cook but not like my wife. We split tasks so we don't fight each other in the kitchen," he explains, chuckling softly.

"We'll do dessert with coffee," Carmella says, getting up from the table. "*Mi hijo,* why don't you take Kerry upstairs while I put on a pot? You haven't had a chance to inspect it up there."

Damian squints his eyes at his mother before getting up, pulling my chair out, and holding out his hand. "I can tell my family's been up to something," he says, bending down to me when I stand. "Best get this over with."

With my hand tucked in his, I follow him quietly up the stairs. He heads straight for the master bedroom. Right away I notice the subtle changes in decor. A dove gray is painted on the walls, and there are new sheets on the bed, a lighter gray with a chocolate-brown border. Throw pillows in the same colors but embroidered with subtle olive green stitching are piled on the bed, and matching curtains have replaced the utilitarian blinds to cover the large windows on either side. A proper dressing table, with a stool, has replaced the simple dresser against the wall, and when I look closer, I see a few familiar items I would have sworn were still in my house when we left this afternoon.

"Son of a bitch," Damian mutters from behind me. "I swear, I had no idea," he says. as I turn around and watch him step into the walk-in closet where my clothes are neatly stored, right across from Damian's.

"How…" I start as I walk in past him and run my fingers along my entire wardrobe that somehow miraculously made its way here.

"Bella," he says by way of explanation.

"Actually," Bella's voice pipes up behind us. She's leaning against the closet door, a half-guilty smile on her face. "Fran and Gabby helped. It was Mama's idea all along. I guess she felt you needed a nudge. I would have put a stop to it if I didn't think it was a foregone conclusion things would end up like this anyway." She turns her big, brown eyes on me. "Are you mad?" I think about it. I probably should be, but oddly enough, I'm relieved any decision-making was taken from my hands in this case. If I'm honest with myself, I knew I'd end up here eventually anyway, I would've just agonized over the move a little longer.

"No—surprisingly," I admit, a little giggle escaping me.

"Phew," she wipes the back of her hand over her forehead in dramatic fashion. "In that case, look what else we've done."

I hear Damian growl as his sister grabs my wrist and pulls me along to the room on the other side of the bathroom. The walls in here are painted the same soothing, gray color and the double bed, which had been centered against the far wall, is now fitted in the corner and made up like a daybed. A thick, bolstered pillow runs along the back and some loose throw pillows turn it into a huge, comfy couch. The reclaimed wood desk under the window is new, as is the leather high-back chair behind it. Also new are the matching bookshelves, running from the edge of the desk to the far corner, giving the room a library feel.

"We didn't want to presume and take out the bed," Bella explains, which elicits a derisive snort from Damian. "Although Ma had a couch picked out, as well."

"This desk...these shelves... they're beautiful." I run my fingers over the dips and divots of the old wood.

"Papa made them." Damian steps into my view and examines the shelves.

"He had the desk already done at home, but he built the shelves right here," Bella explains. "Anyway, I just wanted to make sure our highly inappropriate family isn't completely scaring you off. I promise they'll be heading back home tonight."

"Are you okay?" Damian asks, holding me back at the top of the stairs. I take a minute to really consider the question. I think even as little as a few weeks ago, I would've bristled at the not-so-subtle manipulation, but strangely enough I feel rather laid-back about it now. Not that I was really given a choice, but the family's meddling is growing on me. It actually makes me feel cared for.

I press my cheek against his chest and wrap my arms around his waist. "I think it's sweet," I simply tell him.

The *churros* Ignacio has made are delicious. Light and crispy, not overly greasy, and with the cinnamon and sugar dusted on top, it's difficult to stop after just one. That's why I barely manage to get out of my chair when Carmella announces they should get going.

It's getting dark outside, and the bugs have come out in full force when we wave after the four sets of departing taillights. Bella's included. She's going to stay the night at my place, suggesting we take the night to make sure this is what we want before she actually moves all her stuff from the spare room.

I won't need the night to decide.

DAMIAN

"You haven't said much," she stops me inside the house.

I carefully close and lock the door behind me and walk her backwards into the living room.

"I don't usually talk much around my family," I explain, as I sit her on the couch before dropping down on the coffee table in front of her. "I tried enough of that as a teenager, and I was never able to make myself heard over my sisters. I just try to take them in stride, like my father does."

It's true, my dad spent all night engaged and enjoying himself, yet he barely strung two words together. It's the way it's been since I can remember. The irony is that with his silence, he manages to get more accomplished than if he'd duked it out in a verbal war.

"Okay," Kerry says carefully. "But they're not here anymore, and I really want to know how you feel about this."

I give up my seat on the table for a spot next to her on the couch, carefully tucking her against my side.

"I couldn't care less about colors and decor as long as stuff isn't pink, but I do care about turning this into *our* home instead of just mine. Obviously, my family couldn't resist leaving their own stamp on our house, but they did it for you—so you would feel at home. That's all I want, too."

"We'll have to sort out the finances, though. I expect to pay half of everything." She's not quite pulling off the stern look she is trying for, and I have a hard time not chuckling at her scrunched up face.

"Okay," I answer cautiously, knowing full well I'm heading into a potential minefield. "I actually thought about it." This clearly surprises her. "I figured there are a few ways we can do this. I'd feel better just paying for any expenses, but knowing you, that probably wouldn't fly."

"You've got that right," she mumbles under her breath.

"You'd probably prefer something like contributions at income ratio." This time I don't hold back when I see her nod her head enthusiastically. I burst out laughing. "You know you're predictable, right?" I tease. "But I don't like the idea of obligation from one to the other. So here's the deal; we split bills. Utilities, maintenance, and taxes I take care of, and you can take on groceries."

"Okay, that's hardly a fair division," she inserts sharply.

"It actually is." I give her a quick breakdown of the monthly average expenses and my income, and then I hit her with my one condition. "Once we're married, though, I don't want any of this nonsense. We build a life together—we share it all. The house is transferred into both our names, and we never talk about *mine* and *yours* again." I expect resistance but not the utter shock I see on her face.

"Married?" she squeaks. "I was barely muscled into moving in with you—how did marriage get into this?" She's cute when she panics. Her eyes dart around like she is looking for an escape route, but I'm not about to let her get away.

With care for her ribs, I pull her on my lap and with my hand to the side of her face, force her to look at me. "Where did you think this was leading, Gypsy? Not this week, maybe not this year, but at some point I'll want a chance to call you my wife."

"I vowed I'd never get married again," she says pensively.

"Never get married, because of marriage, or because of your ex? Because if you're going to stick by that vow as a result of him, you're not being fair to yourself or to me. Married or not, I hope you know I will always, always be keeping your six."

The hand she places over my heart is Kerry's only response, but it's more than enough.

I wake up in the middle of the night to Kerry's lips sliding down over my cock. In the dark, I only see the shimmer of her eyes peeking up at me through her lashes. Her fist is tightly wrapped around the root, and I feel more than see her cheeks hollow as she sucks the length against the roof of her mouth. *Fucking bliss.* Instinctively, my hands burrow in her hair and my hips surge deeper.

"Gypsy…" I groan, as I threaten to lose myself in the wet, stroking heat of her mouth. "I need to feel you come around me." With a sharp plop, she releases me and her eyes never waver from mine as she makes her way up my body, stopping only when her soaking wet core finds my dick. With her hands braced on my chest, she starts moving with rhythmic tilts of her hips, rubbing herself on my cock.

Frustrated I can't see her, my hand automatically reaches for the light on the nightstand, but she stops me. "Don't," she whispers. "Just watch my eyes and feel me."

I fucking feel her all right. Slick and hot with these little gasps and moans that drive me so wild, I almost come like this. I watch her, though. It's too dark to see color, but I don't need it to see the need in her eyes. I want inside her and grab her hips to lift her up. When she catches on, she stills her movements and obliges by bracing herself on my tip, sinking down slowly until I'm buried to the root. Then she slowly rides me, the slap of skin on skin where our slippery bodies meet, the only sound other than our breathing.

It could've been minutes or hours, but when I feel Kerry's body give in to the slow buildup of tension, and she starts bucking on my cock, I can do little but hang on for the ride. My hips pump up in tandem until, with a loud groan, Kerry grinds herself down, pinning me to the mattress. Swiveling her hips, she rolls her clit hard on my root, fighting for her release. Barely able to hold off my own orgasm, I slip my fingers through her wet crease and press the tip of my middle finger firmly against her ass. The moment I penetrate the tight ring of muscle, she finds it, her body pulsing around mine, dragging me over the edge right behind her.

CHAPTER 31

KERRY

"HOW MANY MORE BOXES?"

Jasper just showed up this morning, driving a large
pickup truck. Apparently, Damian had mentioned we
were moving me out and Bella in, and he offered to
lend a hand. Very kind of him, but I have a suspicion
his motivation may run a bit deeper than just kindness.

"I think just three from the bedroom," I yell back
at him.

Damian went ahead with a load, and Bella was
quick to hop into his truck. She claimed that way
she'd have her stuff packed up and ready to go when
we got there with the last load, but I know she's trying
to get as much distance between her and Jas. Those
two have some interesting chemistry going on.

Jasper, who is loading the back of his truck, plods
past me into the house, where I am trying to decide

which of my kitchen gadgets I need—given that there's a fully equipped kitchen at home—and which ones I should probably leave behind for Bella. I finally decide to just bring my KitchenAid Pro, my baking pans, my measuring cups, and my favorite Santoku knife. If I find I am missing something, I can always buy it.

After seeing what Damian's family had done a few days ago and the subsequent conversation he and I had after, I think I've finally wrapped my head around moving. Our financial arrangement will even allow me to pay down the car loan faster for my new Forester, which, by the way, is ready for pick up this afternoon.

I've tossed what I need from the kitchen into my last box and hand it, plus my KitchenAid, to Jasper when he's finished loading the three other boxes.

The drive to Hermosa is only slightly uncomfortable; just because Jasper is asking some pretty detailed questions about Bella.

"You know, Jas," I try gently. "Bella's story is not mine to tell. I'm sure that when she decides to open up to you, you'll have a better understanding of why she's perhaps a bit distant in her approach." He laughs out loud at that and the sound is warm and comfortable.

"I'm sorry, Kerry. You're right, of course, if a bit distant is your euphemism for blatantly hostile." I have to grin at that. She has been pretty asocial around Jasper in particular. "I just can't quite get my head around that woman," he muses out loud.

Jasper helps unload, and with Bella firmly locked in her bedroom, supposedly putting the last hand at packing her stuff, he leaves shortly after.

"Am I dropping you off at the dealership or do you want to unpack first?" Damian asks when he closes the front door. "I have to go into work for a bit this afternoon, but we can maybe do it tomorrow?"

"Hell, no. I want my wheels now." I feel like a kid at Christmas. Besides, I want to pop into the store and see what needs to be done. I'm sure there are some things that I'll have to pick up at the grocery store for the coffee shop, but I can probably do that tomorrow when I get some baking supplies.

Damian pulls me in his arms and puts his chin on top of my head. "I was just gonna welcome you home, but your mind is already gone again, isn't it?"

I smile against his shirt. "I was just going over my mental checklist of things I'll need for Monday. I might stop by the store just to check on things."

"Just don't lift anything heavy," he cautions. "I'd better let Bella know we're off."

"I'll go let her know," I offer, lifting on my toes to give him a kiss.

Bella's door is open a crack and I can see her sitting cross-legged on the floor, sifting through what looks like a box of pictures. Instead of barging in, I knock and her head swings around as she wipes her hand over her face. Yeah, she's so not ready for anything. Too much is going on under the surface she isn't sharing with anyone.

"Do you want to come along to pick up my new car?" I ask, pretending I don't see her red-rimmed eyes.

"I'm actually almost done," she says, closing the lid on the box. "I don't have that much left, and it should all fit in my car easily, so I'll probably head out myself, once I have it packed up."

"I'd offer to help, but Damian would probably frown if I did any lifting. I can ask him, though?"

"I'll be okay," she smiles, "I'm actually excited about moving in there. It's a great place. Good thing this house is also pretty awesome or else I can't imagine you ever wanting to leave."

"True," I agree. "I had some decent incentive, though."

"This decent incentive needs to get going," Damian growls behind me as he climbs up the last few steps, coming to a stop right behind me. "How about I grab a few boxes on my way down, sis?" he says, already stepping into the room and hoisting two in his arms without waiting for an answer. Bella rolls her eyes, but a smile tugs at her mouth.

An hour later, I am the proud owner of a beautiful, shiny, Quartz Blue Pearl Subaru Forester. Damian, in true Gomez family fashion, rolls his eyes as I roll down the window, blast the radio, and zip out of the car lot. I throw a last glance at my rearview mirror, where I see him standing next to his dull Expedition, his hands in his pockets, watching me drive off with a smile on his face.

I'm almost disappointed when I pull into the parking lot behind the store. My new wheels drive like a dream and I want to keep going. I barely get out of the car when Bill Franklin steps out of his back door.

"About bloody time," he half-yells across the parking lot, and I walk up to him with a smile on my face.

"I'm just popping in today, Bill. Monday things are back to usual. Thank God."

"You can say that again," he tries to sound stern, but the twinkle in his eyes spoils the effect. "I'm getting sick and tired of people running down my door, only to find out when you're gonna be back. None of them even have the decency to walk out with some screws or a tape measure." When I get close enough, he pulls me into a careful hug. "Missed your coffee, girl," he grunts.

"Missed you too, Bill," I answer with a smile before turning toward my door.

"Hey, wait," he calls after me. "A woman's stopped by three times already to drop something off for you. I offered to hold it for her, but she insisted she wanted to hand it over in person. Left you her number, I'll quickly grab it. Hang on." Two minutes later, Bill is back with a slip of paper. "Give her a call, will ya? Otherwise, I might have to start charging you for secretarial duties." He turns away with a wink, but before I have a chance to stick my key in the lock, he calls out again. "Nine o'clock on the dot on Monday, girl. I'll have a large latte with skim milk. Don't want the wife to catch me cheating."

I'm still chuckling as I push open the door and walk into the storage room. I love the smell of books. There's something comforting about it. Only a few places carry the smell: libraries and well-stocked bookstores. Flicking lights on as I go, I'm surprised at how dusty it's gotten. My office still needs a new computer, something I'll maybe ask Jasper about. Good thing I got my laptop back a few days ago, after Keith Blackfoot had his forensics guy have a look at it. They discovered an electronic tracer on my hard drive that I assured them I had never installed. It had taken Jasper about two minutes to get it off, but the rest of the day to make sure there weren't any other surprises hidden on there. Damian said he figured Willoughs must've installed it when Luna caught him at my house. That's how he managed to locate me.

A shiver crawls up my spine, and determinedly, I refocus my thoughts. I sit down at my desk and pick up the phone, dialing the number scribbled on the slip of paper Bill handed me.

"Hello?" A vaguely familiar woman's voice answers after only two rings.

"Hi, this is Kerry from—"

"Kerry, yes." The woman cuts me off before she rushes on to introduce herself, "It's Jeannie? Jeannie Brooks?"

No wonder her name sounded familiar. She's one

of my best customers. "Oh, hi, Jeannie. I'm so sorry you found the door locked a few times. I apologize for the inconvenience. It's a bit of a long story I'll be happy to tell you over coffee when things settle down. I'll be open again at regular hours starting Monday."

"Actually," she says hesitantly. "If you'll be there for another ten minutes or so, I'd like to quickly drop in. I'm just at Walmart and can be there shortly."

"Should be," I tell her. "I planned to do a little tidying, so I should be here for a bit, you can just come to the back door. My neighbor mentioned you had something to give me?" I can't hold back the curiosity.

"It's actually the weirdest thing," she explains. "My husband and son were working near the creek, along the far side of our property, when our boy spotted a box in the brush. It was my husband who spotted your name. Anyway," she continues, oblivious to the shocked silence on my side. "I've had it in my car for over a week and want to get rid of it."

"O...okay," is all my brain allows me to say. It's too busy trying to connect the dots. I'm afraid to even think of the possibility.

Five minutes later, I'm still sitting at my desk, staring blindly at the piece of paper with Jeannie's number in my hand. What are the odds? Before I recognize what I'm doing, I've dug my cell phone out of my purse and hit the preset for Damian's number.

"Gypsy," his familiar voice comes over the phone, instantly calming the chaos in my head. I can hear people talking in the background but focus on his sound alone.

"I think I know where the books are," I say, stating what I was afraid to give voice to just seconds ago. It's too bizarre a coincidence.

"What?" he blurts, sounding like he is covering the phone with his hand to block out the sound. "Say again?"

"I know where the box is," I repeat, this time a little more confidently.

"Talk to me," he orders, and I do.

I tell him about Bill and the phone number, and then I tell him about Jeannie and what she had to say. "She's on her way here now. She's had the box in her trunk all this time," I giggle nervously.

"Kerry." His stern tone pulls me back from the brink of hysteria. "I'm at a crime scene in the mountains just north of the city. My whole team is, Keith called us in. I'll try to get to you as soon as I can, but in the meantime, don't open the box in front of Jeannie. Just take the box, thank her, and lock the door behind her. Sit tight, babe. I'm heading out."

As soon as he hangs up, I get the shivers. I know it's just a box of books, but all I can think of is twenty-six million dollars and the people who've gotten hurt and even died over it.

I jump up at the sound of a knock at the back door and race to open it. Jeannie is standing on the other side, a bruised and dented box in her hands. As instructed, I don't invite her in but awkwardly accept the box she holds out.

"Thanks so much for dropping it off, Jeannie. And I apologize again for any inconvenience. Coffee is on the house from now on." I smile at her, but all I can feel is a muscle twitching in my cheek.

"No problem, Kerry, it was on my way. I'd better head home and get dinner on the table. I'll be in on Monday or Tuesday, I've run out of reading material."

Somehow I manage to thank her again and tell her I'll see her next week. I wait for her to close the door behind her before I turn around, walk over to the packing table, and dump the heavy box on top, immediately taking a step back. It's tempting to open that box and have a look, but I'm terrified I'll mess something up. Instead, I head back to the door to lock it.

My hands are shaking so hard, I can't even manage to get the lock turned. Next thing I know, I'm flying back as the door is shoved open suddenly and slam my back into the shelving unit. The knock to my already-injured ribs takes my breath away. It takes me a second to catch my bearings.

DAMIAN

I only take a second to explain the situation in shorthand version to Luna, who is closest by. Trusting that she'll find Blackfoot and inform him, I jog to my car and rush down the mountain. The thought of Kerry with that blasted box makes me inexplicably nervous. As far as we know, aside from the missing books, the case was tied up neatly with only some of the staff at The Gilded Feather facing trial and jail time. The other players are dead. There is no reason to worry, is there?

I see Kerry's new car parked in the back parking among a handful or so of other cars, including Bill's cargo van. There is no sign of anything out of order, but still I approach the back door carefully, my sidearm in hand and slowly turn the knob.

It takes me a minute to register what it is I'm looking at. Kerry is sitting on the floor beside the packing table, glaring furiously at the woman holding a gun against her head. I want to yell but am afraid that doing so might startle her, and that's the last fucking thing I want to do when she has her finger on the trigger.

"Come in, Agent Gomez, and I suggest you drop your gun," she coaxes, having clearly picked up on my presence. "I'd know your nauseating scent anywhere."

"It's called shower gel, Ella," I shoot back at the Interpol operative I thought had long returned home to the UK. "Couldn't quite give up on the money, could you?" I taunt her, hoping to lure her gun away from Kerry's head, but instead she presses the barrel right at the top of Kerry's shoulder. At this angle, the shot would not kill her but certainly destroy her shoulder joint and part, if not all, of her arm.

"Drop the weapon and carefully kick it over here, or I will happily dismember Ms. Emerson limb by limb," she grinds out. I have no reason to disbelieve her. After all, she's got nothing to lose at this point. Grudgingly, I drop my weapon and kick it over, watching her as she carefully bends down to grab it, her gun hand barely shifting position.

"I'm surprised you got here that fast, you must've been camping out in the dumpster out back," I poke at her again, as she places my gun on a shelf above her head, and finally I get a reaction.

"And you never spotted me, you self-righteous prick," Ella spits out as she swings around to face me, the gun now pointing at me. It doesn't feel good, but at least it is better than having it pointed at Kerry. I try not to think of the Kevlar vest I left in the truck as Ella continues on her rant. I only partially listen, I'm too focused on the familiar gray eyes full of trust now turned to me, as I try to keep an ear on any sounds from outside.

"Like a true hero, you were so busy protecting your girl, you never even noticed I've been camped outside this entire time, watching and waiting. Of course, I was smart enough to switch rentals every few days to avoid garnering suspicion, but a decent investigator would have noticed." She smirks when she sees me unable to hold in a wince. "You didn't think every effort would be made to retrieve something so valuable, did you? It was days and days of dedicated surveillance that finally paid off when that woman arrived; carrying a box suspiciously similar to the one your stupid girlfriend here lost." I shift when I think she's going to turn back to Kerry, and just that easily, her eyes find their focus on me again. "So many utterly stupid moves. I barely had the patience to sit through those bumbling task force meetings. The incompetence was painful to witness," she haughtily spouts. "It's unfortunate that Troy became more of a liability than he was an asset when he took that woman. I knew what had to happen the moment I discovered he obviously botched up with the store clerk. At that point, he simply became collateral damage." I see Kerry wince at the callous way she describes her friend and the cold-blooded murder of Sinclair.

"It was actually quite amusing how predictable your reactions were to the breadcrumbs I left behind," she jabs again, gloating in the knowledge she bested us. "Which brings us to Mr. Willoughs." She sighs as if disappointed. "As much as I would've preferred to keep that particular customer happy, he became more valuable as an easy target. A useful distraction, if you will. Not hard to manipulate and quite mad, actually." I can't help but think the man was clearly not alone, but the pale blue eyes of the woman staring back at me are anything but deranged. They are ice-cold and calculating.

"Why would you risk coming back, though?" I interject, hoping to keep her talking to buy time, while simultaneously finding out as much as I can. "We've all but closed the case, leaving responsibility square on the shoulders of your dead compatriots. Why would you chance it?" I watch as a small, triumphant smile ghosts over her face. Fucking megalomaniac.

"Do you know what's better than twenty-six million, Agent Gomez?" she asks with a raised eyebrow, before going on to answer the question herself. "Fifty-two million—that's what," she declares without apology. "There is a private collector very interested in the wares, it'll be an easy sale, doubling the money poor Mr. Willoughs already handed over. That kind of money makes it possible to disappear to places you can't be found, unless you want to."

I try not to let my eyes flick to Kerry, who Ella seems to have forgotten all about. I'm not about to draw attention to her again. The woman is so incredibly narcissistic, she seems to revel in the captive audience I provide and continues her self-serving bluster.

"I was never far away, Agent Gomez. Simply waiting for the heat to die down and opportunity to knock. A chance to ensure my future—" She motions to the opened box on the packing table. "And here I am, provided with an opportunity to settle an unresolved personal matter." At this, she points the gun directly at the center of my chest, and her voice lowers threateningly. "It's never a good idea to dress down a woman in public, Agent Gomez. That's something a woman never forgets—or forgives. You humiliated me, cost me my job, and took away my ability to build on this lucrative sideline I spent years developing."

I've been slowly moving, while letting Ella rant uninterrupted. So wrapped up in her little fist pump performance, she doesn't notice that her body is now almost between Kerry and me. My intent was simply to get Kerry out of the line of fire, but Kerry appears to have different plans.

I try to keep a straight face as I spot her in my peripheral vision, reaching over and carefully picking up a book from the table. Everything in me wants to shake my head to warn her off, but with Ella's eyes intently focused on my every move, there's no way I can risk it.

I faintly hear movement outside of the door and keep a close eye on the former task force member, but she doesn't seem to hear it and instead carelessly shrugs her shoulders. "Pity—but I'm sure the sweet memory of putting a bullet through your heart will make my loss a lot more bearable."

Time seems to slow down as I watch her finger tighten around the trigger. I'm so focused on Ella's hand, I don't notice Kerry move until a book comes flying up, hitting Ella's wrist. The sound of a gunshot in such a small space is loud. Loud enough to momentarily stun your senses. Perhaps that's why I don't feel the impact until I hear Kerry scream.

CHAPTER 32

KERRY

I DON'T THINK I'VE EVER felt such rage.

She shot Damian.

I can't hold back. The moment Keith storms through the door, Luna right behind him, and the two of them tackle that woman to the floor, I pull myself up on my feet and haul out as hard as I can, landing a solid kick to her ribs.

"Whoa, tiger," Jasper's familiar voice sounds in my ear, as he wraps an arm around my midsection and swings me around. The anger instantly transforms to fear when I see Damian sitting on the floor, blood covering the left side of his shirt. I struggle to get free and drop to my knees in front of him, my hands flying over his torso, looking for holes.

"Gypsy…"

I hear his voice but it doesn't stop me. Strong

hands wrap around my wrists to still them.

"*Mi amór*...I'm okay."

I hear the words but I don't believe them—my eyes are glued to the blood running down his arm.

He lightly shakes me once, and then again, until I finally lift my eyes to his. "The bullet grazed my shoulder. I promise I'm okay." This time the message gets through, but I don't look away from his eyes once, not even when EMTs rush in and start cutting away his shirt. Damian answers questions when they're asked, but he doesn't glance away, keeping me grounded and safe in the hold of his eyes as the paramedics patch up his shoulder.

"Miss, are you hurt?"

"I'm fine," I manage.

"Are you sure?" Damian asks softly.

"I'm fine," I repeat, "I just want to go home."

Luna ends up driving us in the Expedition. She doesn't even question the fact that Damian crawls into the back seat with me. Our hands are clasped together, sticky with his blood, and his head is resting on mine. I can feel every breath he takes. We ride home in silence, the only thing on my mind: the man in the seat beside me. For a moment there, I thought I'd lost him—reacted too late. I don't think that would have been something I could ever have recovered from. But he's right here, breathing the same air I'm breathing and traveling the same road I'm traveling. Something I will never take for granted again.

"Is it over?" I say as we pull up to our house,

knowing I've asked this before but asking anyway.

"Yes, Gypsy—It's finally over."

Luna stays downstairs to wait for Jasper and Blackfoot, who said they would follow us here, while I head upstairs, pulling Damian along. I move us into the bathroom and draw a bath, while I remove the remains of Damian's tattered shirt. He lets me without argument, instinctively recognizing this is something I need to do. I wince at the blood still staining his skin. The EMTs wiped off the worst, but I need it all gone. He automatically stands up when I start unbuckling his belt, easily kicks off his shoes, and steps out of his jeans when I pull them down to his ankles, taking his socks right along.

Seated in the tub with his arm resting on the edge to stay dry, Damian watches me as I completely strip down and slip in the tub across from him. I take my time washing him, and when I'm done, every hint of blood is gone from his skin. Then I start scrubbing at my own hide, but Damian soon stops me, taking the washcloth from my hand. With slow, firm strokes, he cleans my skin and when he's done, he urges me to turn and lay back against his chest, his right arm crossing over my shoulder, between my breasts with his hand resting on my stomach.

"Does this happen often?" I ask, both hands holding his arm firmly in place, afraid of the answer but needing to know anyway.

"This wasn't the first time," he says calmly. "I suspect it might not be the last."

It's not a surprise, but I still have to swallow hard before I can react. "Okay."

"Does it help?" he asks me, and I don't have to think before I answer.

"Yes. It helps."

"Good," he acknowledges. "Then this will be how we deal."

By the time we get downstairs, Luna is in the kitchen working on some grilled cheese sandwiches, one of which is rapidly disappearing behind Jasper's chomping jaw. Keith is leaning against the counter, appearing relaxed at first view, but the tick of a muscle in his jaw reveals he's anything but.

"You okay, boss?" Jas is the first to notice our arrival.

"Just a scratch," Damian says from behind me. I can't hold back the derisive snort. His arm snakes around me from behind. "In our line of work, that's what it is, Gypsy," he rumbles in my ear before addressing his team. "What have we got?"

"An international mess," Keith volunteers. "Jas called James, who is on his way and has instructed us to hold off on interviewing Ella. So for now, she's sitting in a holding cell." He pulls out a stool and sits down heavily. "How did we miss this?" His question is mostly directed to Damian.

"She was clever. Kept her finger to the pulse, and whenever she got uncomfortable with the direction of the investigation, she made sure to tie off any exposed leads with viable explanations. Not really hard to manipulate a case when you're playing both sides simultaneously." Damian pulls out a stool for me to sit when Luna slides a plate in front of me. "Eat," he orders. Normally I would've probably given him hell, but I'm still a little numb, and besides, that grilled cheese sandwich looks really good.

While Damian gives a detailed account of his part in this afternoon's events, I manage to clean my plate. Then it's my turn to describe what I remember. Feels like I'm becoming an old hand at this statement business. I've sure given enough over the past little while.

The low hum of conversation slowly fades into the background as fatigue suddenly overwhelms me, and I rest my head on Damian's shoulder. Next thing I know, I wake up with him peppering kisses over my face. "I'd carry you upstairs, babe, but my shoulder is a bit messed up. Jasper offered, but I threatened to tear off any limb that came near you. Looks like you're going to have to walk, Gypsy." I lift my head off his shoulder and notice everyone is gone.

"I didn't even thank Luna for the sandwich," I mumble.

"That's okay. You can thank her later," he says as he shuffles me up the stairs and into the bedroom. Once there, I barely manage to shrug off my yoga pants and fall face-first into bed.

I feel the mattress shift as Damian slips in beside me, and like a homing beacon, my body immediately seeks out his heat, snuggling against his side. My hand automatically comes to rest in the middle of his chest, where the edge of the bandage under my fingers is a sobering reminder of how much my life has changed.

DAMIAN

"Are you up for this?"

Kerry's fingers absently rub along the tape stuck on my chest. They stop moving at my question.

"This?"

"Life with me," I answer, letting my own fingers trail along the soft skin of her arm.

I've never questioned my career choices. I've never even considered the impact my job has on those around me—I'm ashamed to admit—but I sure as hell am thinking about it now. I freely admit it has me worried. What woman, in her right mind, would want to share her life with someone who willingly puts himself in danger on many occasions—who could come home hurt, or worse, not come home at all?

"Here's the thing," she sleepily answers. "Stability, predictability, control, and independence—those have always been my goals. I thought if I could build my life on those four cornerstones, I'd be riding high." She chuckles, her breath tickling the hair on my chest. "I ended up finally having all those when you first walked into the shop. I had them and I was satisfied, but I wasn't happy or whole. In the past however long it's been since that day, I've lost every single one of them at some point, and yet oddly enough, I don't feel the sense of loss I would've expected." She pushes up and leans her chin on my chest, her beautiful, gray eyes clear on mine. "Instead, I'm more cared for than I think I ever have been in my life. I feel safe and protected every second of every day with you keeping my six." I smile at her law enforcement slang as she continues. "I'm made to feel equal and valued, and I am grounded in my love for you. So if you are wondering if your job and all it comes with scares me? Then the answer is fuck yes, but I've never been happier." I have a hard time keeping my face impassive because her words cut right to the heart of me. She slightly tilts her head to one side. "Is that a good enough answer?"

"More than good enough," I say, my voice thick and my lungs full with emotion as she lays her head back down on my chest.

Every word from her mouth could have come from mine had she asked me the same. Stability, predictability, control, and independence for years have been at the root of my own life. Ironically, those were all reasons why I never even considered linking my life to someone else's—until her. We're more alike than I thought, and I'm positive that will be cause for some head-butting in our future. But for some reason, it doesn't worry me. This love is too mired in reality to get damaged by an occasional scuffle.

I place Kerry's hand palm down on my heart, and

I hear her sigh. "For you," I whisper.

"I know," is her soft response. "I love you."

I'm not sure if I even deserve to be this lucky.

THE END

ACKNOWLEDGMENTS:

As always I need to thank some amazing ladies.... My Barks & Bites group of friends who always, always have my back. They pimp, they tag, they promote—all for the love of my books. I don't know how I got so lucky with this incredible group of women.

My beta-readers who never fail me. I message them to let them know another book is ready (often with little or no warning and on a pretty tight timeline) and they do everything in their power to make sure the manuscript I need to get into the hands of my editor, is as clean as can be. They can be brutal, but they are always brilliant and are indispensable.

These ladies have probably forgotten this story already, as they worked on it well over a year ago.

Catherine, Lena, Deb, Kerry-Ann, Sam, Pam, Debbie, Nancy and Chris—Love you! Don't EVER leave me.....

My fabulous friend and editor, Karen Hrdlicka, whose dry humor is right in line with mine and who seems to understand my characters as well as I do. It is an absolute pleasure to work with you and I'm just thrilled I manage to make you blink away the odd tear. I adore you, woman!

Joanne Thompson, friend, colleague, cheerleader, critic, and also a brilliant proofreader, who has made it her mission to make me look better than I really am. Her knowledge of the English language is scary!

Thank you for always, always having my back. MUAH!

I need to include my wonderful, awesome and delightfully politically incorrect friend, Dana Hook in my acknowledgments. She was my Alpha reader on this book and always forces me to be better than I believe I can be. If not for her ongoing encouragement and faith in me, I might have thrown in the towel a time or two. You have my heart, babe!

Linda Funk, my twin, my cheerleader. This woman is why I create flawed but indestructible heroines. She is one. She is also that special friend—the one you can have silent conversations with and who will stand by you no matter what. I'm so incredibly blessed to have you in my life.

I'm always grateful to my family who quietly support, and are quietly proud. I'm the loud one of the bunch and I know it. But they give me the time , the space, and the courage to pursue this 'wild hair' of mine into a writing career. I love you and am eternally grateful for you.

Finally my readers, my reviewers and my critics: With every book I write, you push me further, demand more of me and make me a better writer than I ever thought I could be. Thank you from the bottom of my heart, for your kindness, your wisdom and your friendship. I hope we have an opportunity to meet face to face one of these days. Love you all.

ABOUT THE AUTHOR

Freya Barker inspires with her stories about 'real' people, perhaps less than perfect, each struggling to find their own slice of happy, but just as deserving of romance, thrills and chills, and some hot, sizzling sex in their lives.

Recipient of the RomCon "Reader's Choice" Award for best first book, "Slim To None," Freya has hit the ground running. She loves nothing more than to meet and mingle with her readers, whether it be online or in person at one of the signings she attends.

Freya spins story after story with an endless supply of bruised and dented characters, vying for attention!

CONTACT FREYA @
freyabarker.writes@gmail.com

Made in the USA
Middletown, DE
14 June 2019